JANET CHAPMAN

From Kiss to Queen

*She saved his life
with a kiss...*

J
JOVE

$7.99 U.S.
$10.99 CAN

S ▷ EAN

ISBN 978-0-515-15519-8

5 0 7 9 9

Jove titles by Janet Chapman

HIGHLANDER FOR THE HOLIDAYS
SPELLBOUND FALLS
CHARMED BY HIS LOVE
COURTING CAROLINA
THE HEART OF A HERO
FOR THE LOVE OF MAGIC
THE HIGHLANDER NEXT DOOR
IT'S A WONDERFUL WIFE
FROM KISS TO QUEEN

From Kiss
to Queen

✦ ·· ✦

JANET CHAPMAN

JOVE BOOKS, NEW YORK

JOVE

An imprint of Penguin Random House LLC
375 Hudson Street, New York, New York 10014

FROM KISS TO QUEEN

A Jove Book / published by arrangement with the author

ISBN: 9780515155198

PUBLISHING HISTORY
Jove mass-market edition / July 2016

PRINTED IN THE UNITED STATES OF AMERICA

10 9 8 7 6 5 4 3 2 1

Cover art by Jim Griffin.
Cover handlettering by Ron Zinn.
Cover design by Emily Osborne.
Text design by Kristin del Rosario.

Penguin
Random
House

Chapter One

✦—··—✦

The sharp, roaring shrill of a powerful engine shattered the slumberous quiet of the deep Maine woods. Birds scattered, chipmunks scurried for cover, and Jane Abbot instinctively ducked when a fast-moving aircraft shot overhead just above the treetops. Deciding someone was doing a bit of *illegal* scouting for next week's moose hunt, Jane frowned when she noticed the wing flaps on the floatplane were set for landing. Except that didn't make sense, since the closest lake big enough to land a plane that size on was at least twenty miles away.

Surely the pilot wasn't eyeing the pond she'd just passed.

Jane actually screamed when another plane roared overhead, this one smooth-bellied instead of rigged with floats. Her shotgun hanging forgotten at her side, she stood in the center of the old tote road and watched the sleek, twin-engine Cessna sharply bank after the first plane like a metallic hawk trying to drive its prey to ground.

What in holy heaven was going on?

The floatplane roared past again, this time low enough for Jane to see the male pilot was attempting to line up with the pond. A sudden burst of gunfire drew her attention to the second plane, where she saw a man kneeling in the open rear door holding a machine gun, his entire body jerking as spent shell casings rained down on the forest below. A small explosion pulled her attention back to the floatplane in time to see smoke coming from the nose of the aircraft as its floats brushed the tops of several towering pines. The plane was landing whether it was possible or not. No more chances for the desperate pilot to circle around and get it right. He was going down—now.

Jane finally came out of her stupor and started running at the sound of breaking branches and the sputter of a dying engine. A tree snapped with enough force to vibrate the air just seconds before the unmistakable thud of the plane hitting water echoed through the forest over the retreating drone of the deadly, victorious plane.

And then complete silence; no sounds from the pond, no birds chirping . . . nothing. Jane realized she'd stopped running and was holding her breath—listening. Waiting. Hoping.

Aw, heck. Give her a sound. Something! A whirl of water. A splash. Something to tell her the pilot of the downed plane was making his way free of the wreckage.

But still no sound, except for the sudden intake of her

own breath as she awkwardly started running again. He couldn't be dead. She didn't want to witness a man's valiant attempt to save himself and lose. Jane dropped her shotgun and backpack when she reached the pond and quickly shed her jacket. Not bothering to take off her boots, she frantically splashed into the water while keeping her eyes trained on the mangled remains of the upside-down floats a hundred yards from shore. She dove into the cold Maine water fueled by a combination of adrenaline, determination, and a lifetime of braving more than one cold swim in similar waters.

She arrived at the plane, gathered her breath, and used the float strut to pull herself down under the water—the rising bubbles making the journey difficult and her vision foggy. Finding the door handle of the upside-down plane and giving several unsuccessful tugs, Jane sank lower and looked in the window to see the pilot struggling with his seat belt, his movements jerky and clumsy. She grabbed the door handle again, braced her feet on the fuselage, and pulled with all her might—only to shoot away when it suddenly opened. She quickly righted herself and reached inside and touched the pilot.

He jerked, his head snapping toward her as he grabbed her wrist and hauled her through the opening. Jane thought about panicking, but realized almost at once that his grip was loosening. She moved closer, bringing her other hand up and touching his lips. He flinched, then stilled. She freed her wrist from his grip and brought a second hand to his face, clasping his head as she touched her lips to his and sealed them. Quickly realizing her intention, the man pulled some of the air she'd been holding into his mouth.

Jane broke free and reached for his seat belt buckle at the same time he did, only to find her own strength waning. She backed out and kicked to the surface, took several deep breaths as she groped for the knife on her belt, then gathered one last supply of air and dove back down to the open door to see the man fumbling with his seat belt again. Jane touched him, he jerked, and in a repeat of before, grabbed her. Not fighting him this time, she reentered the plane and sealed her lips to his again. He relaxed slightly and pulled in more of her life-sustaining air, then went back to fumbling with his belt.

Jane simply cut through the restraint and backed out of the plane while guiding him with her. They broke the surface together beside one of the floats, and Jane found herself having to hold his head above the water as he coughed and spit and gasped, his eyes closed and his face racked with spasms of pain.

He said a word. A curse, it sounded like, in a language she didn't recognize.

"Come on," she croaked on a shiver as she started dragging him toward shore. Hearing the other plane approaching, Jane stopped swimming when it roared overhead and sharply started banking again.

"Dammit! They're back," the man ground out. "Where are we?"

Jane looked at him. He'd spoken English. "We're in the middle of the pond. Where do you think we are?"

"I can't see. Are we exposed? How far to shore?"

Jane gaped at him, realizing the skin on his face was red, as if sunburned. His eyes were running with tears and repeatedly blinking as he stared at the sky. There was a gash on his forehead, and he was keeping one hand tucked close to his side under the water.

He was blind?

"How far to shore?" he repeated, giving her arm a shake.

"Fifty yards," Jane said as she watched the plane begin another low approach.

"If they start shooting, dive under the water."

Neither had time to say anything else as the man in the plane diving toward the pond did, indeed, start shooting. She was suddenly pulled below the surface just as the water around them became a frothing web of streaking bullets. Feeling a searing sting on her upper arm, Jane silently screamed and frantically tried to surface. Surprisingly strong hands held her down until the frothing stopped and she was suddenly pushed upward.

"Where are you hit?"

"In the arm," she said, remembering he couldn't see. "I'm okay. It just grazed me."

He cocked his head, listening. "We need to get to shore," he said, shoving her in the wrong direction.

Jane shoved him in the right direction, which seemed to startle the man. She gave a small, hysterical laugh, which seemed to startle him even more.

"Don't panic on me now," he ordered harshly.

Afraid he might blindly try to slap her, Jane decided to bring him to account for his high-handedness once they were safely on shore. The plane of death flew over the lake once more, and the gunman unleashed his weapon again just as Jane and her half-drowned pilot touched shore, forcing them to run and stumble as she dragged him to a large stand of pines.

Never, ever, had she felt anything like the terror of being shot at so relentlessly. The machine gun sprayed the trees, the bullets kicking up the surrounding dirt as broken branches rained down on them. All Jane could do was crouch against the trunk of a thick pine, her knees locked to her chest and her eyes shut tight, not even able to manage a respectable scream. The pilot of the sunken plane was pressed against her, actually protecting her from flying debris and oncoming death. Jane instantly forgave him for sounding like a bossy jerk in the water. He was blind, in pain, and trying to protect her.

Well, he should! He was the one they were obviously trying to kill. She was just an innocent bystander. Heck, she was even a hero. She'd saved him, hadn't she? He deserved to take a bullet for her.

No, then she'd have to deal with a blind, *bleeding* jerk.

Jane wiggled out from between the man and the tree the moment the deafening gunfire stopped, barely escaping his blindly grasping hands. "Oh, put a sock in it!" she snapped. "I'm starting to get a little angry here. I'm cold and wet, you're bossy, and someone is actually *shooting* at me. Well, Ace, I intend to shoot back!"

With that off her chest, Jane limped over to where she'd thrown her backpack and gun. She rummaged around in the pack until she came up with a box of shotgun shells, then unloaded the bird shot from her gun and replaced it with the new ammunition.

"Come back here!" the man ordered in a guttural hiss. "Now, before they return."

She looked over and felt a moment of chagrin. If it wasn't bad enough the guy was blind, he was also in the middle of nowhere with a stranger who was semi-hysterical and very angry. His plane was wrecked and somebody was trying to kill him. And somebody he couldn't see was ignoring him.

Jane took pity. "It's okay," she assured him. "I have a gun. I can shoot back."

"What kind of gun?" he asked cautiously, apparently not knowing if he should be alarmed or thankful.

"It's a shotgun."

He snorted.

"I have slugs for it. Sabots can go through anything short of armored steel. And their range is impressive."

"What were you hunting? Elephants?" he asked dryly.

Jane took back her pity. "I was hunting partridge."

He snorted again.

"I was planning to find a gravel pit later and do some target practicing," she said defensively.

"Are you out here alone?" he asked, apparently dismissing the issue of the gun.

"Yes."

He dropped his head and muttered that single foreign word again as he rubbed his face in his hands, then sighed and looked in her direction. "How far are we from civilization?"

Jane didn't get a chance to answer. The plane was back. She ignored his second command to come to him—also ignoring the fact that he sounded rather angry himself—and stepped onto the small beach and shouldered her shotgun. She knew she'd only get off one or two surprise shots before they flew out of range, but she intended to give them something to think about before they left.

The plane swooped low over the lake again, the man with the machine gun straining out the door trying to spot his prey. Jane fired off a shot at the approaching plane, then slid the action on her gun and fired again, causing the Cessna to sharply bank away when her slug connected with metal. She quickly jacked another shell into the chamber and fired one last time at the turning plane, satisfied to see the man in the door throw himself back when the slug tore through the fuselage over his head.

She shouted in triumph at the retreating plane, then danced her way over to the wounded pilot, setting down her gun and going to her knees in front of him as she boldly stated she'd just scared those monsters silly. She never noticed he wasn't exactly celebrating with her until he reached out with unbelievable swiftness and blindly grabbed her. He hauled her toward him with surprising force, repositioned his grip on her shoulders, and shook her.

Jane squeaked in alarm and tried to break free. "You're hurting me!"

"I'm going to throttle you, you little idiot! You could have been killed!"

"Well, I wasn't. And neither were you, thanks to me," she shot back, forgetting her precarious position. "And you're welcome, you Neanderthal!"

He shook her again.

"If you don't quit manhandling me, you're going to find yourself back in the lake," Jane said, her voice a whisper of warning as she tugged on his wrists.

Although she did register the fact that she was gripping what felt like solid steel, she didn't back down from her threat, not caring if he could see her glare or not. She broke free and immediately stood up, then backed a safe distance away and simply stared at the scowling pilot.

He was a huge, wet, battered mess if she ever saw one, his face scorched and his eyes watering and blinking frantically. But even sitting on the ground in an undignified heap, the guy still looked lethal—his wet leather jacket clinging to a trim torso and his large hands clenched in either anger or pain or both.

Jane quietly stepped to the side and watched his blinking gaze follow her movement. "Just how blind are you?" she asked suspiciously.

"I can see you," he confirmed. "But you're blurry," he added, rubbing his eyes.

"Don't do that." Jane rushed back to him and gripped his head between her hands, then leaned down and studied his injuries. "You'll make it worse. Your face is red, but I can't see any real damage to your eyes. It's possible they're only badly irritated."

He leaned away from her grasp. "A fire broke out just before I hit the water."

"Well, it was a lovely landing, Ace."

He snorted again. "If you don't count the fact that my plane is upside-down in a lake."

"You walked away."

"Just barely. Ah . . . thank you," he said, trying to focus on her.

"You're welcome."

"We have to get out of here. They will be back."

Jane looked in the direction the Cessna had disappeared. "They're going to eventually run out of fuel."

"Is there a place near here where they could land?"

Jane shrugged, then remembered he couldn't see her. "The closest airport is thirty miles to the south, but some of the tote roads might be wide and straight enough in places. Do you think they'd risk landing and come after you—us—on foot?"

"I think it likely. Do you have a vehicle nearby?"

Jane nodded, then sighed, again forgetting he was blind. "It's a couple of miles away."

The man cocked his head. "Is it parked out in the open? Could the plane spot it?"

"Ah . . . yes."

"Thanks to your shooting at them, they know I'm no longer alone. Your car is not a safe destination. How far to the nearest town?"

"About twenty miles in any direction."

He stopped mid-sigh and suddenly perked up. "Do you have a cell phone?"

Jane finished sighing for him. "It's in my car. And even if I had it with me, it would take me several hours to climb a mountain to get a signal."

The man said that nasty word again. And even though she was tempted to ask what it meant and what language it was in, Jane decided the less she knew about him, the better. She was already more involved than she cared to be, and figured that once she got him to safety, the authorities could deal with him.

"What do you have for ammunition?" he asked as he slowly stood up. He staggered, then steadied himself by leaning against the giant pine and looked at her through still blinking eyes.

"I have a shotgun with maybe ten rounds of bird shot

and now seven slugs. And I have a handgun with a box of twenty bullets."

"How big a handgun?" he asked, taking a step toward her.

"A .357 Magnum."

He stopped, one side of his mouth lifting slightly. "Loaded for bear, aren't you?"

Jane bristled, taking her own step toward him. "Only an idiot would come out here alone without being prepared."

He detected her movement and held his hands up in supplication. "I'm not complaining." He cocked his head again. "You seem to be able to take care of yourself just fine. Where did you learn that trick of feeding me air while I was trapped in the plane?"

"I didn't learn it anyplace. I just thought it might help."

"Well, you are most resourceful. And your lips were most welcome. You tasted of butterscotch," he added with a grin as he ran his tongue over his teeth.

Jane was glad the man was nearly blind when she felt her face heat up. "Come on. You said we've got to get out of here."

He bowed. "I am in your care, madam."

"The name's Jane Abbot."

"And my name is Mark."

"Mark what?"

"So which way, Jane?" he asked instead of answering.

Jane frowned in the direction of her vehicle. "My car is still the quickest way out of here. You need to see a doctor. Are you hurt anyplace else?"

He shrugged, then winced. "Everyplace. But your vehicle is not a safe destination."

"You think you can walk twenty miles?" she asked, thinking the hike to her car would be a stretch for him.

"If I have to. And you? Are you hurt anyplace? You said a bullet grazed you."

Jane lifted her left arm. "It's only scratched. It's not even bleeding now." She looked at the man named *just Mark*, and then she looked at the floats out in the center of the pond. "Is there anything in your plane you might need? Medicine or anything?"

Rubbing his eyes again and looking at the pond himself, Mark seemed to think about that. Finally he sighed. "I have some things I would like to retrieve, but it's too cold to get them."

"I could get them," she offered, repressing a shiver.

Mark looked in her direction again. "It's too cold," he repeated.

"What's in the plane?" She gasped when he hesitated. "It's not full of drugs, is it? I'm not standing in the middle of a drug war, am I?"

Mark stilled, then barked out in laughter—only to quickly cradle his ribs. "I'm not a drug runner. Leave the plane. I will find a way to retrieve my belongings later."

For some reason, probably stupidity, Jane believed him. "Well, come on, then. We've got a two-mile hike ahead of us, because *driving* is our only viable option of getting out of—"

A long burst of distant gunfire suddenly shattered the air, immediately followed by a muted explosion forceful enough to scatter the already disgruntled birds from the nearby trees. Mark moved with surprising speed and gathered Jane into his arms, pressing her head to his chest as he looked in the direction of the blast.

"What was that?" she whispered, closing her eyes as

she wondered if the plane had crashed trying to land—not that that explained the gunfire.

"I would guess your car."

She snapped her head up to look at him. "They blew up my car?"

He stepped back. "We are like sitting ducks. Do you know these woods, Jane Abbot? Can you lead us to safety without leaving a conspicuous trail?"

"Oh, yes. I've spent nearly my whole life in these woods."

He suddenly shot her a warm, genuine smile. "I have the damnedest luck. I've crashed into the arms of a guardian angel, have I not?"

"And don't I just have the darnedest luck," Jane shot back. "I was minding my own business one minute and dodging bullets the next." She picked up her jacket and backpack and shotgun. "Come on, Ace, the sooner we start walking, the sooner I can get rid of you," she muttered, grabbing his hand and heading in the opposite direction from her destroyed car.

They'd blown up her car!

"Would you happen to have any more butterscotch, Jane?"

Chapter Two

✦ ⋯ ✦

Mark blindly followed his little heroine, even as he wondered what else she had in her backpack besides a rather lethal handgun, plenty of ammunition, a Band-Aid (which she'd gently put on his forehead), a spare hat (which she'd motheringly put on his head), and butterscotch candy (which she'd plopped into his mouth with a sigh). He also wondered who Jane Abbot was, what she was doing out in the wilderness all alone, and where she got her bravado.

He didn't know many women who would have remained as calm through such a ruthless attack, only to jump up and start shooting back like an avenging angel. Hell, he didn't know *any*. And all after braving the cold waters of a lake to rescue a complete stranger.

She definitely was courageous. She was also quite

resourceful, as he'd likely be dead if not for the slightly used but welcome air she'd given him. And now the woman was leading him to safety as calmly as a mother taking her child on a woodland adventure, seemingly determined to continue rescuing him. All of which didn't exactly sit well, as he was afraid Jane would endanger her own life again to save his, should the men in the plane catch up with them.

Not a hundred yards into the trees, Mark suddenly came out of his musings and planted his feet. "You lied about being hurt. You're limping."

She didn't say anything for the longest time. But he could see well enough to know she was staring up at him. He could also see a telltale blush creep into her cheeks.

"I didn't lie," she whispered, her gaze dropping to his chest. "I have a permanent limp."

Mark stared down in silence, waiting for her to elaborate.

"It's nothing," she added, shrugging.

"You can walk twenty miles through the woods with this limp?" he asked gently.

She looked up. "As well as you can, Ace."

Mark wished he could see her features more clearly. She was a short guardian angel, not coming up to his chin, and he could make out that she had long, dark wet hair that was trying to curl. The hand holding his was small, but her grip was strong and sure. She was as soaked as he was and had put on her jacket for warmth, but she looked more like a drowned puppy in need of care than the brave little terrier she was trying to portray.

"We have to get our clothes dried," he felt compelled

to point out, despite this being her rescue mission. "But first we must put some distance between us and the lake. Are we leaving a blaring trail?"

"Not really. And if we move east for a while, we'll come to some hard ground and can turn north to throw them off. Do you really think they'll follow us?"

"We must assume so," he answered honestly, straining to see her expression. His eyes stung like hell, but his vision was slowly getting better. He reached up and carefully feathered a finger down her cheek. "You're remarkably calm. And I'm sorry for inadvertently bringing you into this mess. But please don't worry. I won't let anything happen to you."

Mark didn't need to see her expression, as he could feel her frown against his finger. "You should be sorry," she softly scolded with a sudden smile. "I was just minding my own business when you fell out of the sky practically in my lap."

"And I'll buy you a new car," he promised, dropping his hand.

She went back to frowning, then suddenly gasped. "Everything I own was in that car!"

"Everything? Why?"

"I was headed for the coast. I was hunting one last time before moving to Bar Harbor."

"Are there people in Bar Harbor expecting you tonight?"

"No."

She'd answered him rather bluntly, without hesitation or emotion. "No family? Parents? Husband? Boyfriend?" he persisted.

"No."

Mark sighed. Now was not the time to be finding out about Jane Abbot. Tonight would be soon enough. "Let's go, then. I'm freezing."

"Zip up your coat," she ordered—only to do it herself, as if he were a five-year-old. She then patted his chest in a motherly fashion. "Even wet, the leather will hold in your heat. I know a place about an hour from here where we can stop and build a small fire that won't be seen from the air. We should have just enough time to dry our clothes before the sun sets." She smiled up at him. "Be thankful it's Indian summer."

Mark let her take his hand again as she started off through the dense trees, even as he hoped she had matches in her backpack—which she'd refused to let him carry. It might have been Indian summer, but he would bet the nights were frosty nonetheless.

For the next hour Mark walked, tripped, cursed, and shivered. His angel, he knew, was also shivering and sometimes cursing. But her expletives were rather civil. No damns or hells or taking God's name in vain; she cursed like a nun, with holy this and holy that, and darns, shoots, and hecks. And even those mutterings were quiet, as if she didn't want him to hear.

She led him up over gullies that could be classified as small gorges, around boulders the size of cars, and across a couple of streams. She never hesitated, always seeming to know where she wanted to go, and Mark uncharacteristically resigned himself to her care while being curiously charmed and utterly enchanted.

She had literally saved his life. Hell, she was still saving it.

Jane Abbot was an enigma; he'd seen her scared, courageous, calm, angry, and blushing. He'd felt her worry, her compassion, and her confidence. Even despite her limping gait, she was holding her own on the rugged terrain, often helping him over some of the rougher spots. But for all of her abilities and bravado, she was still a feminine little thing. The hand he was gripping was contrastingly smooth against his, her bones fine, her body petite. When he'd been so angry at her for shooting at the plane that he'd shaken her, Mark had felt a delicate neck he could have easily snapped with a mere flick of his wrist.

Only she hadn't seemed to notice that fact. She'd gotten angry and threatened to throw him back in the lake, even though he outweighed her by nearly a hundred pounds.

She hadn't seemed to notice that fact, either.

"We're here," she said on a sigh of relief, suddenly stopping.

"Where is here?" Mark asked, looking around the dark, dense forest.

"Here is about three miles from the pond. The trees are tall and thick enough to disperse any smoke a fire will create, and we definitely can't be seen from the air. This is . . . um, it's probably a good place to spend the night," she hesitantly offered.

The first hesitation Mark had heard from Jane today. He squinted down at her and grinned. "It sounds as if you've chosen well. And we can both use the warmth and rest. We should be able to make it to safety tomorrow, do you think?"

"Yes." She shrugged out of her pack and leaned her

gun against a tree. "There's a small settlement about twenty miles from here that has a phone."

"Twenty more?" Mark asked, gingerly lowering himself to the forest floor.

"I kind of led us out of our way to cover our tracks," she admitted. "But I know where there's a canoe stashed not far from here," she rushed to explain. "We can do most of those miles by water."

"A canoe? Stashed?"

"Sporting camps leave canoes on various lakes every spring so they can fly clients in for a day of fishing and then pick them up that night."

"And you know where one of these canoes is stashed?"

"One of the camps I used to work for always kept one on a large pond not far from here."

"You work for a sporting camp?"

"Used to. Actually, over the years, I've worked for several."

"Doing what?"

"Cook. Chambermaid. Fishing guide. General gofer and bottle-washer."

Mark just stared at her. That certainly explained her being comfortable in these woods. But it only brought more questions to mind. "What would you like me to do?" he asked when he saw her start gathering wood. He went to rise, but her words stopped him.

"You can take off your clothes."

"Excuse me?"

She straightened with a stick in her hand and looked at him. "I mean you could . . . you should probably get out of your wet clothes."

Mark would bet she was blushing again. "Got any fig leaves handy?" he asked dryly.

She chuckled nervously and all but ran to her pack. "No. But I've got a Mylar blanket you can wrap around yourself while your clothes dry," she said, rummaging around in the pack and then tossing a small packet toward him.

"I'll get out of my wet clothes when you do," he said, fingering the packet and watching her face. He wished he could see well enough to see her blush, but his eyes were still blurry and the trees had darkened the day to a cave-like dimness.

"I will just as soon as I get a fire going."

"I'm not helpless," Mark shot back, tired of being treated like an invalid.

She set her hands on her hips and looked at him, her head cocked to the side. "I know that," she said, her tone placating—which angered him even more. "But this will only take me a minute. You can . . . you can brush the spruce needles away in a circle for the fire," she offered— as if he were a child in need of busywork.

Mark threw down the blanket and got on his knees and started brushing the ground clean of flammable debris, *his* soft muttering more heated and in Shelkovan.

True to her word, the little wonder woman had a small but lively fire going within minutes. Then, with the blurry eyes of an amazed man, Mark watched her run a rope between two nearby trees and drape another blanket— which she'd pulled from her magical pack—across it with the reflective side toward the fire. After that she snapped off several pine and spruce boughs and placed them on the ground in front of the hanging blanket, then pulled out *another* blanket and spread it over the boughs.

Then she waved him over. "You'll be warm in no time. Get out of those clothes and I'll hang them near the fire. It won't take them long to dry. Then we can eat."

Mark could only stare, dumbfounded, at the woman.

Until she put her hands on her hips again and scowled at him. "Is your brain addled from the crash? You have to do as I say or you're going to catch pneumonia. Strip off, Ace."

Mark felt a twitch come into his cheek just below his left eye. He slowly reached down and unlaced his boots, pulled them off, and carefully set them on the ground near the fire. Next he worked off his damp socks, then raised his hands and slowly unbuttoned his shirt, never once taking his narrowed, blurry gaze off Jane Abbot.

She suddenly became very busy rummaging through the contents of her pack.

He would get undressed, and then he would undress her if she didn't soon do it herself. She was as wet and cold as he was, and she didn't have his body mass to fight the chill. Nor did she have his stamina—although she seemed to think she did.

But he could tell she was tiring; not just from their walk, which had been hard with her limp, but from the entire day's events. The woman had taken a swim in frigid waters, been shot at and forced into running for her life, and was now taking care of him as if he were a helpless kitten. Well, this particular kitten was going to become a tiger the next time she tried to order him around.

Mark gave orders. He did not take them well. He'd been giving orders all of his adult life and didn't intend to stop now—which Miss Abbot would learn the very next time she opened her bossy, angelic mouth.

"I have some granola bars and powdered soup," she offered, her head nearly buried in her pack again. "And some hot chocolate. Ah, here it is," she said, pulling out a square of tinfoil.

"Jane."

"I can mold this into a pot to heat water." She looked around and found a small canteen that she'd pulled from the amazing pack from Oz. "I need to find a spring before dark."

"Jane."

"And I've got some salve I can put around your eyes," she went on, pulling out a small, square container that must be a first-aid kit.

"*Jane.*"

Mark didn't shout; he merely made sure his quiet voice reached her this time. He'd moved over to the bed of boughs and sat with the blanket wrapped around his hips, leaving his chest bared to the warmth of the fire. Jane Abbot stilled at the third sound of her name.

He smiled. She was getting the picture. More than the picture, if the way she was looking at his chest was any indication. "Jane, come here."

Her mouth opened but nothing came out, and she suddenly buried her nose in her pack again.

"I've got some dry socks in here someplace," she whispered into the bag.

"If I have to come get you, you won't like it."

Her head popped up and she blinked at him. "Wh-what?"

Mark sighed. "Do you happen to have another brain in that pack, Miss Abbot? I suggest you come over here and warm up," he softly . . . suggested.

She blinked again.

"The food can wait until you're dry and warm."

"But—"

"I am not a man noted for my patience," he warned her. "Nor am I used to having my orders ignored."

"Orders?"

He started to rise and Jane Abbot hastily scrambled to her feet, dropping the pack on the ground. "Are you threatening me?"

Mark nodded.

Able to see more clearly with the light of the fire, he watched her start to bristle, then saw the moment she suddenly thought better of it—likely because he was standing now, completely naked except for the blanket anchored around his waist. Mark knew he was a formidable sight, especially to women the size of Jane. She couldn't seem to keep her eyes off his chest. Finally, after thirty silent seconds, she reached down and grabbed her pack, then carefully approached the bed of boughs. Mark stepped aside and sat down, leaving her plenty of room to sit beside him.

"I don't think you should be giving me orders," she whispered while staring at the fire, her pack cradled to her chest. "Is your ego bruised or something?" she asked, turning her head to look at him. "And you suddenly feel the need to assert yourself?"

What he felt was the twitch return to his cheek. "I am

going to kiss that insolence out of you," he very softly threatened.

With much satisfaction, Mark saw her tense. Then she laughed nervously and turned back to the fire, which pleased him even more. The woman was wary, and well she should be.

What she didn't need to know was that he intended to kiss her whether she was insolent or not—he vividly remembered the feel of her life-giving lips earlier when she'd come to him out of nowhere, literally saving him with her breath. And he wanted to kiss her for it, long and slow and passionately; to share with her his joy of just being alive, to taste and savor the bravado and strength of will she possessed.

"You really must be blind," she said, still looking at the fire. "Even when I'm cleaned up, I'm not a woman men want to kiss," she told him somewhat self-consciously. "And tonight . . . well, I look like a drowned rat."

Mark turned to her in surprise, trying to focus on her face. She was serious!

She believed she wasn't kissable? Hell, he wanted to sink himself into her very soul. "Who in the hell said you weren't kissable?"

The woman blinked in surprise, then suddenly rolled her eyes and started laughing. Not nervously, but with deep-bellied mirth. "What a conversation we're having. We're both freezing and hiding in the forest like frightened rabbits, and you're threatening to kiss me." She snorted. "One or both of us is crazy."

This time Mark had to forcibly pry his jaw loose before he cracked a tooth. One of them was crazy, all right. He may be the one with the bump on his head, but she was daring to pull a tiger's tail. "Hand me your soup and canteen and foil, and while you're undressing I'll start supper," he offered, forcing himself not to pounce.

Jane sobered and started rummaging through her pack again.

Mark looked around the makeshift camp she'd thrown together in a few short minutes, then looked at that amazing backpack. "Lady, I'm expecting you to pull out the kitchen sink next. Is there anything you *don't* have in there?"

She smiled up at him, laughter still lingering in her large eyes. Lord, she was pretty. And quite kissable.

"I don't have any M&M's. I ate the last of them this morning."

"Peanut or plain?"

Her smile intensified. "Plain."

Mark shook his head, dispelling the last of his anger.

"Will you settle for"—she dug through the pack again and pulled out a small tin—"some more butterscotch?"

"I've grown partial to butterscotch," he whispered, taking the tin.

She blushed again. "I'll go find some water."

Mark caught her jacket sleeve. "Undress," he said, softening his order with a grin.

She grabbed still *another* blanket, raised her nose in the air as she stood up, and went around behind the blanket she'd suspended on the rope. To hide, Mark guessed. Well, once the woman got her clothes off, she wouldn't be so sassy.

As soon as she disappeared, he popped the butterscotch into his mouth, then grabbed her pack and dumped its entire contents onto the blanket. Then he just stared, still a little blurry-eyed, in amazement.

Then he snorted.

"What are you doing?" she asked two minutes later as she limped past the makeshift reflector with the regal air of a queen, her blanket draped around her like a royal mantle.

"I'm just checking to see if you have any land-to-air missiles," he drawled, poking his finger through the eclectic mess he'd made. "Lady, you give new meaning to the idea of always being prepared."

"I grew up in these woods," she said haughtily, coming over and sitting down beside the mess. "I like to be ready for anything. I've seen some strange things happen in these woods."

"Like?"

"Like people suddenly falling out of the sky," she drawled, trying to mimic his accent.

Mark waved a hand to encompass their camp. "Who taught you all this?"

"I'm a Yankee," she said, as if that explained everything.

"Yankee?"

"Never heard of Yankee ingenuity, Ace?"

"No."

She cocked her head on a mischievous smile. "Well, with a little common sense and plenty of imagination, a good Yankee can turn anything available into whatever he needs."

"Which means you can survive in the wilderness with just the contents of a day pack," Mark speculated.

"And survive comfortably."

"Like I said, I am fortunate for falling in your vicinity."

"Yes, you are," she shot back, lifting her chin on a smirk.

Mark silently sighed. Being naked, with only a thin slip of material to cover her, hadn't made her any less sassy—only more enchanting. He grabbed the foil and began fashioning a pot, filled it with water from the canteen, and set it beside the fire.

Jane spread both his and her clothes over the rope behind them, then began repacking her pack. "What nationality is your accent?" she asked, her attention on her task.

"Shelkovan."

She looked up. "Excuse me?"

"Shelkova is a small country just across the Bering Sea from Alaska."

"I thought Russia was across from Alaska."

"Nearly the size of the whole of your New England states, Shelkova only reemerged when the former USSR broke up. Our climate is cold, but the forests are beautiful and productive. We export lumber mostly, although we are also fishermen and farmers—and thankful to be under our own rule again." Mark grinned at her frown. "You would love my country, Jane. The forests are similar to Maine's, only with older growth. And our ocean is beautiful and stormy, our coast rugged."

"Heavens, you sound like a travel bureau. And yes, I think I would like your country. I like wildness and nature and storms."

"I was going home when I . . . fell on you."

"You were?" she asked, sounding startled. "But that's

halfway around the world. You were going to fly a float-plane to Shelkova?"

"No. My destination was Bangor International Airport. I was going to fly in a slightly larger, faster aircraft for the rest of the journey."

"Oh. Yes. That makes sense," she agreed with a cough. "Why were you going home?"

"Word came to me this morning that my father is ill. I must return as quickly as I can."

"I'm sorry. We'll start out at first light tomorrow and should reach a phone by noon."

"Noon? You said twenty miles."

"Most of it by water. With both of us paddling, we'll make good time."

"Then we should eat and rest. We've both had a rather trying day." Mark grinned when her eyebrow suddenly arched at his orders.

Lord, he could almost see her clearly now. She had an expressive face and an impertinent little nose she was fond of raising, her light brown hair curled in tangles around her cheeks and down her back, and her eyes appeared to be a stormy gray in the waning daylight as the small fire reflected their luster. Her face, when it wasn't scowling or frowning, was oval, set over a long, delicate neck that beckoned a man to feel her life-pulse when he kissed her.

Which he intended to do . . . eventually. Certainly before noon tomorrow. And maybe more than once. Oh, yes. Jane Abbot was most kissable. Either the men of Maine were idiots or the woman wouldn't recognize male interest if it hit her on the head.

Mark was beginning to suspect it was the latter. Except for staring at his chest, Jane treated him no differently than she would a child or a man of ninety, almost as though she thought *herself* sexless.

So was she naive? Or just shy?

She'd hung her clothes over the rope, but he'd noticed her wrapping something in her jacket as she'd limped around the blanket. When she'd gone to answer a call of nature later, her limp noticeably more pronounced, Mark had peeked. What he'd found was a leg brace that appeared to fit over her right foot, inside her boot, that would come up to just below her knee. It was light and inflexible, with an innovative hinge at the ankle that would stop all lateral movement but still allow her to walk almost unimpeded.

A permanent limp, she'd stated simply. But she'd blushed, which was telling. Jane Abbot was self-conscious about her limp, thought she was un-kissable—even when she was cleaned up—and treated him like a brother.

Actually, she treated him like a gelding.

So instead of shy, maybe she was merely . . . inexperienced.

No, that couldn't be it. She appeared to be close to thirty years old, so even if she had spent most of her life in the wilderness, she couldn't have lived like a nun.

"Our clothes are dry enough, I think," she said, pulling his shirt and pants down from the rope. "The sun's gone and it's going to get chilly really fast."

"Using that blanket as a reflector works wonders," he said, taking his offered clothes. "Both my front and back are warm."

She took her own clothes behind the reflector, but Mark

noticed she left her brace under her jacket. "How far did you say it was to the canoe?" he asked through the barrier.

"Two or three miles. But it's on a lake with a navigable stream that will take us almost directly to Twelve Mile Camp. It's just a store and some rental cabins, but there's a phone," she added, limping around the blanket and sitting down, then tucking her socked feet beneath her.

Mark's eyesight was sharp enough to see that her right foot curled inward slightly, her ankle appearing skinnier than normal.

"We can call the police from there and report what happened," she continued. "And also notify the FAA and Inland Fisheries about your crash. I think Inland Fisheries gives you a week or something to get the plane out of the pond."

Mark looked at the dying fire. "I don't wish to notify anyone of what happened."

"What?"

"It would be better if the incident is forgotten. I will quietly have the plane removed."

"You can't mean that. Someone tried to kill you."

He turned to settle himself facing her, ducking his head to look her level in the eyes. "It would accomplish nothing. Like me, the men in the other plane are not Americans. Reporting what happened would only delay my returning home to my father."

"But—"

He reached out and took hold of her hands. "Try to understand my reasoning, Jane. If I report this, I will be held for questioning, the police will never find a trace of the other plane or the men who were in it, and I will be delayed for days. I must return home immediately."

"But—"

"I would ask that you trust me on this. I know what is best."

"Are you in this country illegally? Were you telling the truth about not carrying drugs?"

Mark shook his head. "I'm not a criminal. Today's attack was against my family." He squeezed her hands. "It's important you believe me, Jane. You saved my life, and I don't want you regretting it."

She silently looked at him, apparently wondering if it was wise to question him further, considering she was in the middle of nowhere with a complete stranger, then hesitantly nodded.

Using his grip on her hands, Mark slowly leaned forward and lowered his mouth to hers.

She didn't move. And she stopped breathing. Her lips were soft and pliable but unresponsive—likely surprised he was kissing such an un-kissable woman.

Mark applied more pressure, using his tongue to tease her lips. She sighed and finally opened her mouth, letting Mark delve deeper into her sweetness before he pulled back to find her eyes looking more confused than wary.

"Thank you, Jane Abbot," he whispered, leaning close enough to give her another kiss, this one fleeting and chaste. "For saving my life today and for believing me now. Thank you."

"You . . . you're welcome," she whispered in return, staring at his mouth.

Mark leaned back, stretching out on the makeshift bed and wiggling into a comfortable position before he drew Jane down next to him, ignoring her startled squeak. "For warmth," he murmured as he wrapped an arm around her waist to anchor her while placing his other arm beneath her head. "Sleep," he softly commanded as he closed his own eyes on what had to have been the strangest day of his life. He'd nearly been killed by assassins, had crashed his plane, and had been rescued by a guardian angel he was tempted to keep.

Not completely understanding the sentiment, Mark only knew he had powerful feelings for Jane Abbot. Not only was he in awe of the woman—he found himself wanting to possess her with such an overwhelming passion that he was in awe of himself.

Which might seem strange to some, but not to the men in his family, who had a history of stumbling onto their life-mates—usually at the damnedest times and in the damnedest places. And whenever they gave in to the tug on their hearts, they were blessed with happiness, love, and lots of male children. Always males. If the Lakelands wanted a female, they basically had to import one into the family through marriage.

Mark had always scoffed at the notion of the men in his family so abruptly falling prey to passion's magic, but there was no denying his attraction to this volatile, independent, bossy woman in his arms. No, Jane would not join the past women of his life as a fleeting passion. In fact, fate had likely taken that choice away from him this afternoon.

Jane Abbot wasn't going to like it, but she had sealed

her own fate when she'd sealed her lips to his and saved his life. She was now in as much danger from the men in the second plane as he was. Mark knew they would have noted her license plate before they'd blown up her car, and by morning they would know Jane's identity. And he didn't doubt they'd retaliate against her for her role in depriving them of their goal today.

So Mark fell asleep without questioning his feelings for Jane. His only thought was how he was going to hold on to the dynamic little wood-sprite long enough to keep her safe.

He'd have to hold her tightly, of course, and very, very carefully.

Chapter Three

❖⋯❖

Jane stirred to the oddest sensation. Her chest felt warm and tingling and her heart was racing, her back was pressed against a blast furnace, and her nose felt so cold it was numb. Every muscle in her body ached, and she had an overwhelming urge to sneeze.

Which she did, bringing her completely awake.

Which made her remember.

Which made her gasp at the realization that a good amount of her discomfort was being caused by the large, rather possessive *male* hand covering her left breast. During the night, Mark-with-no-last-name had somehow managed to sneak his hand under her shirt.

Jane's racing heart skipped several beats. Was he awake? Was he aware of where his hand was? Was that her nipple she felt pushing through her bra against his palm? And why did she want to wiggle her backside more firmly into his lap?

No, the real question was would Katy believe her when Jane told her best friend—okay, her only *real* friend—that she had spent an entire night sleeping in the arms of a man? And that instead of giving the guy a black eye for copping a feel, she'd just lain there like some sex-starved hussy hoping he didn't wake up anytime soon so she could savor it?

Naw; she'd never even get to that part, because Katy would be too busy laughing her head off after Jane told her the guy had actually kissed her, and that she'd just gotten up the nerve to kiss him back when he'd suddenly stopped. Darn. If she had her cell phone, she could have taken a picture of Mark when he was in the front of the canoe today to prove she wasn't lying. It would only be of his back, but at least Katy couldn't say she'd made him up.

Oh, wait; maybe she could sneak a picture of him using Silas' cell phone when they got to Twelve Mile Camp. Yeah, and Silas could back up her story. Well, not the part about them sleeping together, because she sure as heck wasn't telling that gossiping old rooster she'd—

Jane sneezed again.

The hand on her breast gently tightened and started to knead.

Jane closed her eyes as she felt the heat of a thousand suns rush to her cheeks. Holy heaven, was the man even aware of what he was doing?

"Good morning," Mark gruffly whispered.

Darn, he was awake. And his hand was still moving, still making her heart race.

"Ah . . . good morning," she whispered back. Afraid her heart might actually explode, Jane slapped a hand to her chest to still his actions—then sneezed again.

Mark sat up slightly behind her. He did move his hand, though, but only to slide it between her breasts and pull her tighter against him. "Are you sick?" he asked with soft concern.

"Could . . . um, could you move your hand please?"

He chuckled, his chest vibrating her back as his searing palm pressed against her belly and pulled her even closer. "Sorry," he apologized, an unrepentant lilt in his voice. "Instinct, I guess."

"Instinct, or . . . habit?"

He patted her belly then withdrew his hand altogether. "I don't make a habit of sleeping curled around beautiful women with frost on their noses," he offered by way of answer.

Picturing him curled around beautiful women, Jane suddenly gasped. "Are you married?"

"No. Are you sick?" he repeated.

"No," she said on a sniffle and rubbed her nose—which her blush had apparently thawed to the point that it had started running. "I'm not sick," she continued as she nonchalantly rolled away and sat up, then made herself busy by folding the thin Mylar blanket they'd used for cover.

She squeaked again when Mark pulled her back, facing him, and pressed her nose against his throat. *He* gasped then, and Jane sneezed again—although this time she was pretty sure it was because his chest hair was tickling her nose.

"You are sick."

"It's probably just an allergy," she lied, not about to admit she'd been too shy the day before to get out of her wet clothes quickly enough.

"What are you allergic to?"

Your soft, nice-smelling chest hair, Jane wanted to shout. "The woods," she said instead, tugging against his hold. He let her go, but then stopped her from scrambling away by trapping her with his eyes.

They looked better this morning. Clearer. Brighter. Actually, they looked positively gorgeous; a stark, molten gold, keen and intelligent and . . . narrowed in suspicion.

"Your face is red. You've caught a cold."

I'm blushing, you oaf. But Jane decided being sick was less embarrassing than admitting her hormones were on the verge of rioting. Heaven help her, the man she'd pulled from the lake was beautiful.

Okay, she may have noticed that fact yesterday, but she'd been determined to ignore it. She couldn't now. He was sitting right in front of her, and she couldn't help but notice his hair was sticking out in a tangle of mahogany waves, brushing the collar of his unbuttoned shirt and falling over his forehead just short of his gorgeous eyes. His jaw was slightly shaded with whiskers, which only accentuated his sculpted features. And his mouth? The one that had kissed her last night? It was wide and sensual and . . . appeared set with determination.

"You're a stubborn woman, Jane Abbot."

"It's how I survive. And it's my business if I want to be stubborn."

"You'll probably die of pneumonia before I get you back to civilization," he muttered, standing up.

He got *her* to civilization? This was her rescue operation, not his. *She* was saving *him*.

Apparently now that he had his sight back, the man intended to take charge. Well, she'd see how close he got them to civilization without her help. He might be big and strong, but he didn't have a clue where they were going.

And she'd let him in on that little secret just as soon as she stopped gawking.

"I would like a few minutes to myself," she finally managed to say. "And since you seem so capable all of a sudden, why don't you go find us some water." Jane tilted her head, intrigued by the little twitch that came into his cheek.

"I'll find us water," he whispered, sounding more threatening than agreeable. "Have the fire built back up by the time I return."

"Yes, sir," Jane snapped, her cheeks red again for a completely different reason. *Oh! Ordering her around like he was king of the forest or something.*

With his cheek still twitching, Mark grabbed the canteen and stormed out of the camp. Jane scrambled to find her brace and put it on over her sock inside her dry but stiff boot, pulled down her pant leg, then checked to make sure the comfortable old brace was hidden. She'd been wearing one since before she'd learned to walk, and considered it a welcome old friend that allowed her mobility and a degree of confidence.

She hadn't been born with a bad ankle, but the nuns at Saint Xavier's had told her she'd come to them with the injury. Since then she'd had several operations and many fittings of braces. No one knew how her ankle had become crushed; only that she'd had the injury when they'd found her—not three days old, it had been determined—on the steps of the hospital in Abbot, Maine. No one knew who her parents were, either. And twenty-seven years later, the sources of her injury and parentage were still unknown.

Jane no longer cared. She was contented with her life and making the best of what she *did* have. The only thing she craved was a family. And until a month ago, it was the one thing she was afraid she might never get. That is, until she'd suddenly realized she could have a family of her own—an actual blood tie—if she were to have a baby. She could be a mother.

And finally be *somebody*.

By the age of twenty-three Jane had figured out she probably wouldn't ever be a wife, only to have that lesson drilled home again last month by a groping, drunken lout who'd offered to set her up in a cabin of her own in the woods as his mistress. That's when, despite Sister Roberta's adamant cautions about what happens to immoral women, Jane had seriously started thinking about having a baby out of wedlock. Because honestly? She'd willingly spend *eternity* in purgatory in exchange for having a family of her own right here on Earth.

And she didn't really need a husband for that to happen— just some sperm.

But how was she supposed to get the ingredients for motherhood when *sober* men were turned off by her limp and lack of sensuous beauty? Like Mr.-No-Last-Name Mark; sharing a bed and waking up to find himself holding her breast hadn't done a thing for his libido, apparently.

He'd just calmly pulled his hand out of her shirt like it was a common, everyday mistake and focused on her illness instead. And when he'd kissed her last night, his hormones hadn't even sparked, much less run away with him. Heck, he'd told her to go to sleep.

Okay, maybe she wouldn't tell Katy about their sleeping together, because she really didn't want her friend—who happened to be a tall goddess with shining gray eyes and the body of a swimsuit model—to give her *another* lecture about getting over the silly notion that she was nobody.

"You didn't start the fire back up," Mr. Dead Libido said from behind her. "You really are sick, aren't you? Your face is flushed and you haven't even finished dressing. You only have one boot on," he added, giving her that intense, golden look again. He set down the canteen and stirred the dying embers of their fire. "Just sit still and I'll fix us something to eat. Do you have any aspirin in your pack?"

"Yes," she croaked, reaching for her other boot just as she sneezed again—making her finally admit she was sick. Okay; maybe her melancholy was from having a cold and not from having shared a bed with a gorgeous man who, like most sober men, didn't see her as a woman.

And with that quiet capitulation, Jane lost complete control of her rescue operation. As soon as she dug out the aspirin, Mark procured her backpack and its contents, cooked soup and hot chocolate, then dismantled their camp right before her disbelieving eyes. He let out the straps on her pack to fit his wide shoulders, hefted her shotgun in one hand and held out his other hand for her to take—their roles of yesterday unquestionably reversed.

"Which way?" he asked once she was standing, albeit bewildered and stuffy-headed.

"Ah . . . north," she whispered, fighting back another sneeze. Jane thought she should tell him everything now, since she didn't know what condition she might be in later. Heck, she was liable to lead them in circles. "Follow this ridge until you see a good-sized stream on the left. Then follow it downstream to the lake. The canoe should be where the stream enters the lake."

With a smug grin that said he was fully in charge, Mark started along the ridge, his hand securely holding hers. Now that the man could see well enough, he had no trouble covering the rough terrain with his long, powerful legs, but he matched his pace to hers, and even helped her over steep places by simply grabbing her around the waist and lifting her up.

And every time she sneezed he turned and frowned at her, and every time she stopped to blow her nose, his eyes silently scolded.

When they reached the lake and found the canoe, Mark tossed her in the front and took over the stern. "If you don't feel well enough to paddle, just rest," he offered with obvious concern and another frown. "Tell me which way to the outlet, and I'll take it from here."

Beginning to really simmer now, whether from fever or building anger, Jane pointed to the other end of the lake, then closed her eyes and decided to let him do all the work, if that's what the bossy man wanted. She was sick, he was arrogant, and maybe paddling a canoe for seventeen miles would take some of that cockiness out of him.

Within minutes she was fast asleep.

* * *

Mark watched the flushed, sick, angry woman sleeping in the bow. She hadn't liked relinquishing control this morning, and he guessed that if she hadn't been feeling poorly they'd still be back at camp slugging it out over their respective roles in this odyssey.

Jane Abbot was a capable, independent creature who appeared too stubborn for her own good. He wondered where her family was. He also wondered why some intelligent man hadn't put a ring on her finger and bound her to a home.

But then, for all he knew some man had. Maybe she hadn't liked the situation and had left. Then again, maybe she was simply too independent for marriage. Mark certainly couldn't picture Jane as a complaisant wife to some domineering husband.

But she'd been totally flustered this morning to find his hand on her breast. And a nice, plump breast it was, he remembered warmly. He'd given her an excuse for her red face by blaming it on her illness, and she'd jumped at the offer. Jane had been disconcerted by his touch, which led him to believe she'd never been anyone's wife.

After many hours of paddling in the surprisingly warm late October sun, and hoping he hadn't passed the settlement, Mark shored the canoe and gently shook Jane awake. "Jane. Come on, honey. Wake up and tell me if we're close."

She groggily sat up and promptly sneezed again. Her nose was bright red and had been running most of the morning, her sleep had been restless and her breathing labored. She was working her way into a terrible cold, and he wanted to get her comfortable and some medicine down her throat as soon as possible.

"It's a little farther," she said hoarsely, looking around. "There's a beaten path from the stream that leads up to Twelve Mile Camp," she explained. "You can't miss it."

Then she closed her eyes and fell back to sleep.

Mark scowled at her and then at the river. Then he scowled at his watch. It was already afternoon. He was hungry, and they were down to three granola bars. He shoved off and headed downstream again, glad they were at least going with the current. He found the path twenty minutes later, and he banked the canoe and pulled it all the way onto shore. He unloaded the pack, the gun, and Jane, setting her on her feet and not letting go until she quit swaying. Mark held the canteen for her to take a drink, popped the last butterscotch candy in her mouth, hoping it would ease the sore throat he suspected she had, then took her hand and headed for the settlement.

Which was a generous description of Twelve Mile Camp, Mark decided half an hour later when he spotted the store and five disreputable cabins. There was another beautiful lake backing the cabins, but not a soul in sight.

"Jane, we're here," he told the quiet woman beside him, giving her a worried look. "You're sure they have a phone?" he asked, looking for and not seeing any telephone lines.

"Cellular," she explained, her voice raspy. "He's on the fringe of reception."

Mark hated like hell to see the energetic, scrappy woman so listless. He touched her forehead and drew back his hand as if it had been scorched. Jane Abbot had a raging fever.

"Come on, sweetheart," he said, wrapping his free arm around her shoulders and leading her forward. "Maybe they have more aspirin in that . . . store."

"I just want an ice-cold Pepsi."

"I'll get you one," he promised. "Just hang in there."

The screen door was so old the meshing was rusted. The proprietor obviously didn't need a bell to tell him when a customer arrived, as the creaking hinges served nicely. It was definitely a Maine woods store, Mark decided upon entering. In the middle of the expansive room was a large, rusted potbellied stove that stood taller than he did. He guided his ailing angel over to one of the chairs positioned near the cold stove, then steadied her descent as she collapsed in a boneless heap with a sigh of relief.

Mark turned and faced the gaunt, aging man walking out of a back room. "I need a cold soda and the use of a phone."

"Sure thing," the man replied with a grin as he sized up his latest customer, his eyes darting to and dismissing the woman sitting with her back to them. "Soda's in the cooler and the phone's right here," he added as he reached under the counter and pulled out an ancient cellular bag phone. "The call will cost you ten bucks."

Mark pulled an American twenty-dollar bill out of his wallet and tossed it on the counter. If the call cost ten, he didn't even want to ask the price of the soda. "Keep the change," he said as he strode to the antiquated cooler and slid back the cover, which had a limited choice of beverages all standing in cold water. He pulled out an unfamiliar brand, having discerned there was no Pepsi, and twisted open the cap as he returned to Jane.

"Here, honey. Drink this. It will help."

He had to hold the bottle at first, but the cold drink seemed to revive her enough that she finally grabbed hold and served herself. Mark then returned to the counter.

"Reception's better if you take it outside," the man said, grinning again.

"I'll do that. You have any aspirin?" Mark asked, mentally reminding himself to check the expiration date before he gave any to Jane.

"Sure thing. Aspirin's five bucks," the man responded, going over to the wall and pulling down a small envelope containing two aspirin.

Mark raised a brow as he accepted the medicine, noticing the twenty had already disappeared. After checking the expiration date and deciding six months wasn't that long ago, he pulled out another twenty and set it on the counter. "Give me three more packets," he said, already ripping open the one in his hand. He stuffed the extra packets in his pocket, grabbed the phone, and returned to Jane. "Here, take these," he softly ordered. "If they don't kill you, they'll make you feel better."

He had to put the tablets on her tongue, but she swallowed them with the last of her soda. Mark got her another one out of the cooler—tossing another twenty on the counter before walking out to the porch to make his call. By the time he returned, Jane had finished her second soda. She suddenly sneezed again, dislodging a rather unladylike burp, which made her gasp weakly.

"Do you have a cabin available?" Mark asked the proprietor, even as he shuddered to guess what that would cost him.

"Well, now. I think maybe number six is free," the man said, rubbing his chin. "I'm pretty sure old Matilda finally moved out with her young'uns."

"Matilda?" Mark asked, wondering if the guy knew he only had five cabins and hoping cabin six wasn't actually a bear's den.

"Matilda's a raccoon that took a liking to my number six cabin," he explained in all seriousness. "I'm pretty sure she moved on last week, though."

"Give my appreciation to Matilda," Mark drawled. "Do you know how the lady and I can get to the nearest town?"

"Well," the man huffed more than said, rubbing his chin again. "Seeing it's Thursday, Lester's headed to Milo tonight. He could probably take you there."

"Lester?"

"He comes through here about midnight most weeknights with a load of saw logs."

"We're talking about a tractor-trailer, right?" Mark clarified.

"Yup. Lester's got himself a right nice rig."

"Is there any way I can contact Lester?" Mark patiently asked. Lord, this was like pulling teeth.

The man apparently had to think again. "Well, you could call him on my phone. Lester's got hisself a phone in his truck."

Mark pulled out his wallet, opened it, then stopped and looked across the counter. "How much for the cabin until Lester comes through?"

"I take Visa," the man said, leaning forward to surreptitiously peer down at the wallet. That was when Mark knew he was dealing with one of Jane's Yankees, realizing

the guy had sized him up as an out-of-stater before he'd
even opened his accented mouth. Then again, it might
have been his battered but expensive clothes that had given
him away. Hell, his leather jacket alone probably cost more
than the whole settlement. Or maybe it was the fact that
he'd walked in and demanded a phone while blithely
throwing twenty-dollar bills across the counter.

The only thing that seemed to be troubling the proprietor was Jane. Looking at her quizzically, the man obviously noticed she was homegrown. She was dressed like
a Mainer who knew these woods; she wore wool and
sensible boots, and the shotgun leaning against the stove
was practical and well-used, not fancy.

Jane suddenly stood up and turned to face them. His
wallet still open in his hands, Mark looked from her lop-
sided smile to the man behind the counter.

The change was instantaneous and quite telling.

"Jane Abbot! Is that you, girl?" the proprietor shouted,
forgetting all about his plump victim and scurrying
around the counter. "Now don't you look a mess for my
sore eyes! What's the matter with you?"

"Hi, Silas," she croaked, her smile warm. "I have a
little cold, is all. You got a cabin for us?" she quietly
asked, letting Silas enfold her inside an awkward embrace.

"Sure do, girl. Number two is all clean and ready. You
just go on over and lay down before you fall down. I'll
run upstairs and get you a kettle of tea and some medicine." He stepped away and frowned at Mark. "This guy
with you?" he asked, sounding suspicious.

Jane patted his arm. "He is, Si. So you be nice to him."

Silas, it seemed, was duly chastised, hiding his chagrin

behind his hand as he cleared his throat. "You . . . ah, you gotta get to Milo, Jane?"

"I think that's the wrong direction," she said, turning questioning eyes to Mark. "Aren't you trying to get to Bangor?"

Mark shook his head. "There's been a change of plans. I need to get to a town on the coast called Stonington."

"Stonington? But I thought you wanted to go to the airport."

"The friend I just called asked me to meet him in Stonington."

Giving him a quizzical look, then snuffing and rubbing her nose, Jane nodded. "Okay," she said, turning to Silas. "My car broke down, so can you help me find a way to get him to Stonington? I think it's on Deere Isle, on the east side of Penobscot Bay."

"You . . . ah, I could let you take Manly."

"Your truck? Silas, that's so sweet of you." Jane rested her hand on his arm. "I can get it back to you tomorrow or the day after. Will you trust me with your baby for two whole days?"

"You know I'd trust you with Manly seven days a week. Hell, girl, I owe you my life."

"Thanks, Si. And you don't owe me anything," she answered wearily.

Mark saw her eyelids drooping and hurried over to her, putting his wallet away as he went. He placed a hand behind her knees and swept her up in his arms, ignoring her squeak of alarm, which promptly turned into another sneeze.

"Lead the way, Silas, to number two," Mark told the gawking man.

Silas worriedly eyed Jane. "Maybe you should carry her to my place upstairs."

"The cabin will do fine for us," Mark answered, using his don't-argue-with-me voice.

Silas obviously thought about arguing, though, but only for a second before he spun on his heel, grabbed up Jane's pack and gun, and led the way out of the store.

"You settle her on the bed and I'll go get some lemon tea and honey," Silas said in a rush, pushing open the door to the cabin. "And I've got some cold medicine she should take," he added, busying himself with lighting a match to the waiting kindling in the stove.

"That's fine," Mark agreed, straightening from laying Jane on the bed. "Do you have a map of Maine? I need to see how long it will take us to get to Stonington."

"I know it's two hours to Bangor," Silas offered, rubbing his chin again. "But I don't know how far it is from there to Deere Isle. I got a map I'll bring back with the tea."

As soon as Silas was gone, Mark began unbuttoning Jane's jacket. She protested at first and then tried to help, but he brushed her hands away and told her to be quiet. She tried glaring at that command, but finally conceded and went as limp as a rag doll.

Mark was starting to worry. Her forehead was burning, her cheeks were bright red, and she was becoming even more listless, the hike up from the stream probably doing her in. But it was the fact that she was obeying him that was most frightening. And she remained docile until he tried to take off her boots. Jane bolted upright and slapped his hand away from the laces on her right boot. Mark tried undoing them again, so she hit him on the shoulder. It was a weak protest, but enough for him to remember the brace.

"Go away and leave me alone," she said in a winded croak. "Maine woods-women prefer to die with our boots on."

Mark thought about kissing her—until he remembered her cold. Then he thought about ignoring her protests and making her comfortable—until he remembered her hiding the brace from him last night. So, not wanting to upset or embarrass her, he left her boots on and went to add some wood to the stove.

Silas came back with the tea and medicine, and the map. They managed to get the first two down Jane's throat, then spread the map out on the scarred, wobbly table.

"Here's Stonington," Silas said, pointing to the southern tip of an island connected to the east coast of Penobscot Bay by a bridge and causeway. "It looks to be a good hour and a half, maybe two, past Bangor," he guessed.

Mark looked at his watch. "We should leave no later than seven, then. That will give me an extra hour."

"You're meeting your friend at midnight?" Silas asked, his eyes going to Jane on the bed.

"Yes," Mark responded. He softened at the sight of the man's genuine worry. "Don't worry, I promise to take good care of her."

Silas straightened to his full height as he pulled his pants up by the belt and stuck out his chest. "Just what is she to you?"

"She's my guardian angel."

Apparently not knowing how to respond to that, the aged Yankee let his chest fall back to his buckle. "Well, she seems to trust you," he muttered, going over and pulling the blankets up to her chin. He turned and looked at Mark. "You just make sure she stays safe," he warned. "There's plenty of folks in these parts that'll come find you if anything happens to her," he added, his eyes gleaming with the bravado of all the folks in these parts.

"I understand," Mark said with a nod, which the old man returned before walking out of the cabin with all the dignity of a prizefight winner.

Mark woke to the sound of a large, over-powered truck pulling up outside and checked his watch to see it was seven p.m. He carefully untangled himself from Jane and padded over to the door and opened it just as Silas climbed out of the truck from hell, notoriously known as Manly, if the lettering on the bug-shield was any indication. The engine, which didn't seem to have a muffler attached, was definitely idling with the noise of fifty demons under the hood.

Grinning like an expectant father, Silas sauntered over to the cabin with his thumbs in his suspenders. "Now this here is Manly," he said, waving behind him. "And seeing how Jane ain't in no shape to drive, I want to tell you, young fellah, that you better be easy on my boy."

Mark could only nod.

"And you tell Jane not to try driving back until she's well," he instructed. "By the way, where'd her car break down?"

"It's back in the woods thirty miles. She hit a rock and

split open the oil pan," Mark said, still staring at the large red monster. It looked like he was going to need a ladder to get in the thing. "Am I going to have to stop every fifty miles for gas?" he asked, getting his wits back. But not his eyes. He couldn't seem to stop staring at that incredible, indescribable truck.

"Maybe, young fellah," Silas shot back just as dryly. "But most stations take Visa."

Mark forced himself to look at Silas as he took out his wallet, then held out his Visa card. "Run this through your machine and I'll sign the slip."

Silas shook his head. "Not for Jane. I owe that girl my life."

"How so?" Mark asked, respectfully putting the card back in his wallet.

"I wouldn't have all this," Silas said, gesturing at the store, "if'n it weren't for Jane. I was working at a set of sporting camps she was managing when she all of a sudden up and told me I was wasting my time working for someone else when I could be running my own camps." Silas shook his head on a humorless chuckle. "She came storming in my room one night and found every damn one of my bottles of whiskey. Broke every one of them, she did. Then she dragged me outside and pushed me in the lake. Hellfire, she was in a blazing temper. She babysat me for two weeks, then brought me here and told me this place was for sale. She even went to the bank with me." Silas shook his head again. "She weren't no more than a slip of a girl of twenty-two."

Mark pictured his guardian angel rousting the old man out of his drunkenness and pushing him in the lake, even as he remembered her threatening to do the same to him just yesterday. *Hellfire* was an accurate sentiment, he supposed, when a person was speaking of Jane Abbot. And right then Mark hoped he'd get to witness her blazing temper.

He held out his hand. "Thank you. I'll see that your truck is back within a few days."

"Good enough. You tell Jane to take care. If'n you can tell me where her car is, I can have it fetched, fixed, and waiting for her when she gets back."

"It's already being taken care of."

"Good enough," Silas repeated with a nod, giving Manly a fatherly pat on the fender as he sauntered back to his store.

Picking up his sick angel—and sending a prayer to his sick father in Shelkova—Mark carried Jane to the truck, made another trip carrying her backpack and shotgun, then drove through the star-laced night to his rendezvous.

J ane woke up stretching and yawning just as they were reaching Bangor.

"Need anything?" Mark asked the red-nosed, blinking woman beside him. "A Pepsi? More medicine?" he offered as he pulled into a gas station. It was his second stop since leaving Twelve Mile Camp, as Manly apparently got one tank an hour for gas mileage—which explained Silas charging five dollars for two aspirin.

"A . . . I need to use the bathroom."

"They have one here. You go in and I'll get you a soda. Wait!" Mark rushed on. "Let me help you out. You'll break your neck if you try it alone." He walked around to her door and helped her down. "Is this truck legal for the road?"

"I have no idea. Silas usually only goes to Greenville or Millinocket." She shrugged. "Nobody bothers him."

Once he was sure Jane was steady on her walk inside, Mark filled the truck with gas and then rushed through the store gathering up a few essentials. He came out carrying a large bag, which he was stuffing under his seat when Jane returned. The poor woman still looked like a rag doll; Mark remembered reaching over every ten minutes on the drive down to feel her forehead and growing more concerned.

"It won't be long now," Jane said in a rasped whisper once they were through Bangor. She was greedily sipping a whole liter of Pepsi and looking out at the Penobscot River on their right. "You'll meet your friend and soon be on your way to your father. I hope he's all right. Um, would you be willing to give me your address? So I can write and see how your father is?" she added. "I don't know where in Bar Harbor I'll be staying yet. I have to find a job first."

Mark looked over at her. "You're moving without having a job?"

She dropped her gaze to her soda. "I have enough money to tide me over until I find one. And I haven't decided what kind of job I want yet," she added, lifting her chin defensively.

"You're running from something."

That chin lifted higher. "A woman can go looking for a new adventure if she wants to."

"What are you running from?" he softly persisted.

"A husband and eight kids," she shot back.

Mark turned to hide his first smile of the day. Her face was still flushed, her eyes were still bloodshot, and her nose was still running, but she was back to being sassy. "I have something to discuss with you, Jane," he said quietly.

"What?" she asked, still defensive.

"About what happens in Stonington."

"I'll drop you off at your friend's and find a motel for the night, then head back to Silas in the morning."

"I want you to come with me."

"Where? To meet your friend? It's awfully late, Mark. I'm sure he doesn't want to be entertaining a stranger."

"To Shelkova."

"Excuse me?"

"I want you to come with me to Shelkova," he softly repeated.

There was a full minute of dead silence, then, "Thank you, but no."

"Why not? You're unemployed right now. You don't even have a car. And Jane," Mark went on, lowering his voice, "the men who shot me down will know who you are from your car's license plate. Staying here is not safe for you right now."

She looked incredulous. "Why would they come after me? And how could they find me, anyway? I no longer live at my old address. That's all they could learn from my license plate."

"Maybe through your family?"

"I don't have one."

He watched the road, not knowing what to say at that quietly given declaration. This wasn't at all going well, and Mark decided he preferred her listless and complaisant. "Then why not come see my country? You just admitted you're looking for an adventure."

"But you live on the other side of the world. I've never even been out of Maine."

"Really?" Mark looked over at her. "Never?"

She shook her head before he had to look back at the road.

"But wouldn't you like to? This is your chance."

"No. I'm doing just fine right here."

"Jane, I can't merely walk away and leave you behind. I'll worry about you."

He looked over again in time to see her smile sadly down at the soda bottle. "I've been taking care of myself almost my whole life. Go home and see your father, Mark. Give me your address and I'll write and let you know I'm fine."

Well, dammit, he had tried. She couldn't say he hadn't tried.

Reaching Deere Isle a full hour of stark silence later, Mark pulled off the main road onto an overgrown path marked with a milk crate a couple of miles shy of Stonington. He cringed when he heard branches scraping Manly and hoped they were soft enough not to scratch the paint. He came to a halt at the beach, and from the reflection of the stingy moonlight, could just make out the dock and waiting boat. As soon as he turned out the lights and shut off the noisy engine, a man emerged from the boat and came toward them.

Mark looked over at Jane to see her coming awake. "Feel like stretching your legs?"

"You're leaving by boat? That boat?" she asked in confusion.

"I am obviously not even safe in my own plane. But I can trust my friend to take me to a connection that will get me out of the country safely. Come with me, Jane."

She blinked at him as if just hearing his offer for the first time before apparently remembering their conversation. She shook her head. "I told you I can't. The only place I belong is here."

Mark sighed and closed his eyes, listening to Jane blow her nose. *The only place she belongs.* Damnation, the woman belonged in a palace surrounded by servants.

She belonged with him.

"At least come stretch your legs and meet my friend."

She finally nodded, and Mark rushed around the truck and helped her out, then slipped an arm around her as they walked toward the dock and his waiting friend. Nodding to him over Jane's head, Mark turned to her and gathered both of her hands in his. "I'm sorry, Jane," he whispered, tightening his grip as a cloth settled over her mouth, effectively stifling her scream. "I'm sorry," he repeated, holding her firmly while her hands were bound in front of her.

Mark then lifted her onto his shoulder while his friend subdued and bound her flailing feet, then carried her down the dock and onto the boat. "I am sincerely sorry we had to do this the hard way," he told his struggling angel as he laid her on a narrow bed in the cabin, watching with regret as her expression changed from anger to fear.

Chapter Four

❖ ⸺ ❖

S he was going to die.

Jane wanted to close her eyes and weep. And she would, just as soon as her stomach stopped twisting in terror. Her Judas laid her down in the cabin on some poor excuse for a bed, only to pull back and tell her how sorry he was again.

Sorry to be taking her out in the ocean to dump her off? She could see the regret in his eyes as he stood over her. He had to kill her, since she knew right where to find his plane, which probably *was* loaded to its tail with drugs.

She was so stupid!

When the boat dipped with the weight of his cohort-in-crime coming aboard, Mark muttered that nasty word again and left. As soon as he cleared the doorway, Jane went to work on her gag, dislodging it enough to sneeze.

She brought her bound hands up to her mouth and started working on the knots of the cloth tying them together. She had to stop and wipe her nose on her sleeve several times, but when she heard the engines start, she panicked, nearly shredding her hands in an attempt to escape. Finally the cloth came free and she sat up and quickly freed her feet.

Mark reentered the cabin carrying her pack and shotgun and another large paper sack. Jane rushed him with a shout of outrage, knocking him back against the steps, and tried to gouge out his eyes while repeatedly kicking him. He grabbed her shoulders and held her away, giving her a clear shot at his groin—his own angry shout ending abruptly when he doubled over on a pained grunt.

Jane lunged for her shotgun.

Mark lunged for her, but suddenly stopped at the business end of the shotgun barrel.

"You Judas! I'm not letting you kill me."

"What!" he shouted, his face going from red to purple. "What are you talking about?"

"You're not dumping me in the ocean," she hissed, poking his chest with the gun barrel for emphasis.

"Dump you in the—" He took a deep breath. "Jane."

"You're a criminal. You used me to get away, and now you've got to get rid of me."

His jaw snapped shut and his cheek started twitching.

She stepped away and raised the gun to her shoulder when he reached out. "I . . . I trusted you," she whispered, her eyes stinging as she blinked back tears.

And then she sneezed again.

Jane was jerked forward, there was a shotgun blast, and

she was flat on her back on the bed with a very angry giant glaring down at her. One of his large hands reached for her throat, and Jane closed her eyes, letting her tears escape.

Only the hand settled under her chin and lifted her face. "Jane," he said hoarsely, using his other hand to gently brush the hair from her face. "I'm not going to hurt you, angel. And you *can* trust me. I'm trying to keep you safe."

He slowly pulled away when she said nothing, then stood up and turned to the man standing on the cabin step holding a handgun. Mark said something to him in Shelkovan, and they both looked at the damage to the boat. Jane swiped at her eyes to also look, and saw a hole the size of a softball in the hull just above the water line. The man smiled crookedly at Mark, then picked up the shotgun and left. Mark turned and picked up Jane's backpack and the paper bag just as the boat lurched away from the dock.

Jane bolted for the steps.

Mark dropped his load with a snarled curse and grabbed her around the waist, tossed her back on the bed, and came down on top of her again. They glared at each other in silence, then Mark gathered her hands, clasped them in front of her, and bound them back up with the length of cloth she'd worked so frantically to untie. Only this time he took off his belt and slipped it through her bound hands and then around her waist, buckling it at her back. His jaw tight and his eyes hard, he bound her feet in silence.

She also remained silent, her glare accusing. That is, until she suddenly sneezed and her eyes started watering again.

Mark grabbed the paper bag that had ripped in their

scuffle, held it up for her to see, and dumped its contents on top of her. "If I intended to kill you, would I have bought you all of these?" he said ever so softly, gesturing at the bags and bags of candy strewn over and around her. Some were opened, spilling M&M's on her, the bed, and the floor.

Jane watched the man she'd pulled from the lake turn and walk out of the cabin, then further spilled the candy when she rolled over, buried her face in the bed, and burst into tears.

It was a good hour before he returned. The powerful boat they were in was speeding through the waves of the Gulf of Maine, headed for only the devil knew where. Her stomach rebelling at the sometimes rolling, sometimes jarring ride, Jane didn't even look up when she felt his weight come to rest beside her hip. And she didn't open her eyes, which were swollen shut from crying and a raging fever, when he cradled her head with one large, gentle hand.

All she did was moan.

"You must drink something. You're still burning up," he softly petitioned, brushing her tangled hair away from her flushed face. "Come on, sweetheart. I've got cold Pepsi. Don't go stubborn on me," he said gruffly when she tried to roll away. "You need liquids."

He wasn't going to leave until she drank. And she *was* parched. So Jane finally opened her eyes and tried to sit up. Mark helped, then had to hold her, since she couldn't seem to stop shaking. Heaven help her, right now she wished he *would* throw her in the sea so she could die quickly instead of slowly burning to death—even as she wondered if this wasn't what Sister Roberta's purgatory would feel like.

The boat lurched into a wave, spilling Pepsi over her face and chest and bed.

"It's okay, I've got you. Drink what's left."

It might have been easier if her hands were free, but she refused to ask the jerk for that concession. She didn't trust him, and she didn't believe his tender act now.

But he bought you M&M's, her befuddled mind whispered.

He likes them, too. It's an act. He's a criminal. You're in trouble, Jane Abbot. Big, gonna-die trouble.

I don't care. I'm dying anyway.

Jane tried to wipe her nose on her sleeve, but had to use her shoulder instead because her hands were bound.

"Christ, I'll be glad when I can get you to a doctor. If I untie you, will you behave?"

She shook her head. If he untied her, she was throwing herself off the boat and taking him with her just on principle.

Mark swore again, in English, for her benefit, she guessed. "I'll cure your stubbornness someday, witch." He cradled her head again, making her look at him. "Not long now. We're almost there, Jane. Just try to hold on a little longer," he added, gently lowering her down.

Jane closed her eyes in exhaustion.

B asically, the submarine she was looking at blew her drug-runner theory to smithereens. Criminals didn't have subs, did they? A person couldn't just go out and buy one, could they? So how had Mark-with-no-last-name gotten hold of such a large, deadly boat?

Jane watched the underwater craft break the surface of the night-shrouded ocean like a giant, lumbering beast rising from the bowels of the deep. If it weren't for the frothing waves lapping against the hull, she wouldn't have been able to discern it from the ocean, it blended in so well. The engine of the boat they were on had stopped ten minutes ago, and the sudden silence had awakened her. Now she was sitting on the deck in an undignified heap, watching a sight she was pretty sure few civilians ever witnessed.

Which made her ask her still-befuddled mind—again—who Mark was. A spy or secret agent? Russia had those. Did Shelkova? Or was he just a very wealthy, successful criminal? Maybe Russia had sold off some of their subs to raise a little capital after the breakup. Jane was sure she remembered seeing ads of Russian military surplus for sale; boots, binoculars, jeeps, even field rations. She'd never seen any subs advertised, though. And wouldn't Uncle Sam have something to say about foreign countries selling private citizens submarines?

Probably. Which brought her back to her spy theory.

She preferred Mark-the-drug-runner, because spies were . . . well, they definitely were below criminals on the bad-guy scale.

The devil himself broke into her thoughts, bending down to pick her up. "Come on, sweetheart. It's time to go."

Jane recoiled and tried to scurry away, even though her hands and feet were still bound.

Mark hesitated in mid-reach and frowned at her. "We need to move quickly. They can't stay on the surface for long, as we're still in American waters." It was pitch-black out, but she could see the flash of his grin. "And I doubt your government would appreciate finding a foreign submarine not fifty miles from shore."

Oh, heavens. He was a spy.

M ark finished picking up his wide-eyed, wilted angel, ignoring her struggles even as he wondered where she got the strength to continue fighting him. He lifted her to the railing and carefully lowered her to the waiting arms of two crewmen from the *Previa*, and, as careful as they all were, Mark, Jane, and the two men in the launch nearly ended up in the sea.

"Enough!" he snapped. "Sick or not, I'm going to put you over my knee if you don't settle down. This is hard enough without you fighting me every step of the way. Now cease!"

Apparently undeterred by the edge in his voice, Mark had to scramble over the rail and save the crewmen from her kicking feet by wrapping his arms around her and giving her a good squeeze.

"I'm not getting in that . . . that boat!" she screeched, nearly deafening him. "I'm not!"

Well, hell. She was in a near panic. Mark was suddenly glad for her weakened state. If Jane were feeling any better, she'd have them all visiting Davy Jones despite her petite size. He ended up having to wrap his legs around hers so the crewmen could start the launch, and even then she struggled the entire way to the *Previa*, her hysteria seeming to grow the closer they got.

She exploded completely when he carried her to the sail tower. Several other crewmen were standing aside as he hefted her—bucking and now hoarsely screaming—up onto the tower, then had to tell one of the men to untie her feet so he could stand her on the ladder. The man hesitated, clearly not wanting to get near her.

His own temper finally exploding, Mark barked the order again in Shelkovan, causing several men to flinch and causing Jane to lurch violently. Two crewmen finally grabbed her feet and unfastened the restraint, then helped him lower her onto the ladder.

"Stand up, Jane," Mark ordered harshly.

"No! I'm not getting in this death machine!" she screamed. "P-please," she suddenly pleaded on a broken sob. "Please don't put me in this hole."

Mark captured her head in his hands, bringing his mouth close to her ear. "There are no other choices, Jane. It'll be okay. I'll be right with you."

"You don't understand! I can't stand . . . I won't be . . ."

She was crying in earnest now, trembling all over while straining against his hold. Had she gone from believing he intended to kill her to thinking she might instead end up suffering a fate worse than death? Mark slid his hand to the back of her neck with a muttered curse, and softly pressed his finger to a nerve until she went completely limp.

He barked another order, making several men scramble to help lower her to outstretched hands below, where she was carefully held until he could climb down and take her again. The men parted at his order, one of them leading Mark along a narrow, low corridor to a cabin that had a wide, single bunk. He gently laid Jane down and quickly freed her hands, brushed the hair from her face, then pressed his palms to her cheeks.

Lord, she looked dead but for the flush of her fever. Because of her illness, he hadn't wanted to take away her consciousness, but hadn't had a choice. Sitting beside her waiting for the ship's doctor to come and hearing the signal that they were diving, Mark began to pray for her health and forgiveness for what he was putting her through. She'd saved his life and he was slowly killing her in return. If she would only get better, he would gladly stand unmoving before her and take any abuse she wished to give him. He deserved it.

Because angels deserved better.

Many women had come and gone in his life, all of them actively vying for his attention, and Jane Abbot had firmly captured his heart without even trying.

The doctor pointed out that the damp clothes were adding to her shivers as Mark helped him undress the fragile, vulnerable woman. The small, healing scratch on her arm—which he knew was from a bullet—made him wince. It was red, but the doctor assured him it was not the cause of her fever. Fatigue, a raging head cold, and possibly pneumonia were responsible for Jane's fever, which was likely responsible for her being listless one minute and hysterical the next.

The doctor gave her a shot, further assuring Mark she would eventually be fine. Rest, warmth, liquids, and more rest were prescribed after the doctor heard about Jane's last few days. Mark had to hand it to the man for not hiding his disapproval of how she'd been treated thus far, although the doctor did respectfully bow his leave.

Mark respectfully dismissed him, then pushed a button on the communications panel and ordered the captain to have Jane's clothes laundered and her boots dried. He set everything in the corridor and locked the door, then picked up her brace and studied it again, remembering the scars on her right ankle, which the doctor had said were evidence of several operations. He set the brace on the desk and headed for the adjoining shower.

She was awake when he came out. Maybe. Mark's gut tightened when he got a closer look at her. Jane was sitting up in bed with her knees pulled to her chest, staring at nothing, her skin ashen instead of flushed. Actually, she looked catatonic.

Frozen hysterics. He'd seen it before. Jane Abbot was claustrophobic.

Mark nearly roared in anguish. No wonder she'd fought him tooth and nail. Her rage hadn't been from fever; she'd been petrified of the submarine. He'd literally forced the woman into the bowels of her own private hell.

Mark hit the panel hard enough to break the switch. "Surface, Captain! Now!"

He was answered, frantically, in Shelkovan.

"I don't care if we're sitting in the middle of the Potomac River—surface!" Mark didn't wait for a response. He quickly dressed, putting on layers of clothes he pulled from the cabin's closet. They were too tight, but would have to do. He then wrapped all the sheets and blankets on the bed around Jane and lifted her into his arms, having to steady himself against the sudden upward shift of the ship, and stepped into the corridor and headed for the control room.

The captain opened the hatch himself, then held Jane while Mark climbed the ladder. He turned and lifted her into the fresh air, sat down inside the sail tower with her in his lap, and immediately started talking while pulling the blankets away to let the salt-laced air touch her face. "Come on, sweetheart. It's okay now. See, you're outdoors. The sun is coming up, Jane. Watch it rise. Look around, angel. You can breathe now, you're outside," he crooned on and on until she finally stirred.

And still he continued to talk, asking her questions, getting answering nods as she slowly came out of her stupor, her eyes blinking against the strengthening sunrise. It wasn't until she finally spoke that Mark began to breathe properly himself.

"I . . . I'm sorry," she whispered, her face turned to the breeze.

"Not as sorry as I am," he murmured against her hair, undecided if she was finally resigned to her fate or simply too exhausted to fight him anymore. "I should have realized. I should have listened to you."

She looked up. "You would have let me go back to shore?"

He closed his eyes on her pleading expression. "No. But I would have kept this ship above water, and I would have kept you out in the air, had I realized."

He opened his eyes to see her looking at him. "Who are you?"

"The man whose life you saved—despite not deserving it, for what I've put you through."

"How long will we be on this submarine?"

"I'll have another connection by this afternoon. Then we'll fly home in the morning."

She dropped her gaze from his. "You must know some pretty powerful people in Shelkova to be able to call up a submarine. Does . . . Are there nuclear missiles on board?"

Mark wasn't sure if she was awed or worried. "No. We disarmed and unloaded them the moment we acquired the *Previa*. Too much responsibility comes with such weapons. Sleep, Jane," he softly ordered, cuddling her closer. "Doctor's orders."

"What doctor?" she asked, only to look down and gasp. "Where are my clothes?" Then she moved her legs until her naked toes peeked out of the blanket and her cheeks turned crimson. "Who . . . who undressed me?"

"The doctor," Mark lied without compunction. "I was taking a shower."

He watched her face return to its fevered pink, but also noticed that she surreptitiously tucked her right foot deeper into the blankets just as the captain came up on deck and spoke to Mark in Shelkovan. Smiling at Jane's disgruntled frown, he answered the captain in Shelkovan and then dismissed him.

"You sound like a general most of the time, you know that?" she said, still frowning. "And in Shelkovan, you sound even more arrogant."

Mark felt rather disgruntled himself. "What do you mean, *arrogant*?"

"You spit out orders," she explained, lifting her impertinent little nose. "And expect to instantly be obeyed. That nice man came up to see how I was, and you dismissed him."

"That nice man," Mark drawled, "came up here to complain that you're making us stay exposed in American waters. He suggested I throw you overboard and be done with the problem before we're spotted and shot at."

"He did not!"

Thank you, God. Mark was thankful and relieved Jane was back to her scolding, arguing self. *I'll take care of her from here,* he promised. *Forever.* "And I did dismiss him."

"See what I mean!" she cried, getting huffy. "You're arrogant and bossy and . . . and . . ."

"And sorely tired," he finished for her. "Go to sleep, Jane."

He covered her head with the blankets, holding her tightly until she sneezed again and finally settled down. Within minutes both of them were snoring—Jane with ladylike grace and Mark with relieved fatigue.

Well, the next boat she saw blew her spy theory to smithereens. Countries didn't call out aircraft carriers for mere spies trying to get home to Daddy, did they?

Jane was running out of theories. If Mark wasn't a criminal or a spy, then he must be . . . well, the president or prime minister's nephew. But if their next rendezvous turned out to be a Sputnik space rocket, she'd have to guess *Mark* was the president.

"You connect with the most amazing boats," she said

to the man standing beside her as they approached the largest ship she'd ever seen. "And they just keep getting bigger and bigger. I can't wait to see what's next," she drawled—the effect she was going for ruined when it came out as a croak.

"They don't get any bigger than that, angel," Mark perfectly drawled back, even as he zipped her jacket up to her chin.

He'd gotten her back inside the submarine, but only after promising it would stay on the surface and the hatch would stay open. Hating the boat almost as much as she hated her fear of it, Jane had stopped in the control room and tried to apologize to the captain for exposing all of them for her sake. Mark had gruffly said she needn't apologize for anything, then swept her up in his arms—right in front of the captain and the entire crew—and carried her back to their room after a loud, English command to leave the hatch open. That last had been for her benefit. Heck, she wasn't even sure the captain or crew spoke a word of English.

Mark had left her alone to dress, telling her he needed to check on some details, after showing her where the communications panel was and making her promise not to lock the door against him. A man would be right outside—for her convenience, he'd quickly added, not to keep her from leaving. And no one would come in until she allowed it.

Jane had found her clothes all cleaned and folded on the stripped bed, and then she'd found her brace. It had been sitting right out in the open on the desk, and she could only hope Mark hadn't noticed. She didn't like the fact that all men saw was her limp, and she sure as heck didn't want this particular man seeing her brace.

Sister Roberta would tell her she was vain.

But Jane was just plain embarrassed. She especially never wanted Mark to see her skinny, scar-marked ankle and curled foot. It would disgust him, and remind him that she was just a crippled nobody from the backwoods of Maine. She liked that he thought of her as a heroine. Heroines were somebody—at least to the person they'd saved.

Mark had knocked on the door ten minutes later and led her back to what he explained was the sail tower. But instead of climbing the ladder, she'd stopped and thanked the captain and the crew again for being so patient and understanding. Everyone in the control room had smiled at her, their heads bobbing in unison.

And then Jane had really looked around.

And then she'd gasped hard enough to stumble backward. It was like being on the set of *The Hunt for Red October*. Sophisticated equipment busily blinked and beeped and pinged, men were scattered about looking just as busy, and there was a real live periscope!

Seeing her line of vision, Mark had grabbed her hand, telling her they had to be *underwater* for the periscope to be effective. Shuddering, Jane had let him help her up the ladder and back into the fresh air. Now they were watching the aircraft carrier—which Mark had told her was named the *Katrina*—grow larger and larger as they came closer and closer.

"The *Katrina*'s not in American waters, is she?" Jane asked.

Mark looked at her, his left eyebrow raised. "She'd be

kind of hard to hide. That's why the submarine ride to open waters."

"What would have happened if we'd been spotted?"

"I think it's referred to as 'an international incident.'"

"Oh. What would the captain have done?"

Mark chuckled. "Tossed you in a life raft and dived."

"Oh."

"You're feeling better?"

"Yes. Sort of. The air helps. But it also makes my nose run," she added with a small laugh as she turned away to wipe her sore nose on the gob of toilet paper she'd filched from the bathroom.

"You'll get a good night's sleep tonight," he promised, pulling her snugly against him.

Jane suddenly had a thought. "What about Manly? How is Silas going to get him back?"

"Manly," Mark said, leaning down and kissing her forehead, "is being returned to Silas by the man whose boat you shot a hole in. I gave him two hundred dollars for gas and a map." Mark chuckled. "I also gave him a quick lesson on Yankees."

"Who was the man in Stonington?"

Mark shrugged, shrugging Jane with him. "A fellow countryman who married an American and decided the Maine coast was as close to being home as he could get."

"Who are you?" she softly asked again.

"Mark. The man you pulled from a lake."

Jane sighed. He was never going to tell her. Maybe he was just a smart criminal who the country of Shelkova thought was a spy, who also happened to be related to the president.

More likely he was the devil in disguise.

Jane suddenly squealed. "Are we going to fly off that thing tomorrow?"

Mark eyed her warily. "Please tell me you aren't afraid of flying."

"Oh no! I even have my pilot's license. I've been flying floatplanes since I was sixteen. Are we going to take one of those really fast jets?" she asked, gripping the front of his jacket and tugging. "A really, really fast one? Something that will do Mach two?"

Mark laughed, hugging her to him. "I'll get us the fastest jet on the ship."

"Oh, boy. Oh, heavens. I've always wondered what it would feel like to fly in one of those F-something-or-others. I've always thought if I could just feel the power of one of those jets, I would die a happy woman. Oh, Mark, I can't wait!"

"I'm glad I finally got something right," he offered dryly, squeezing her again. "But we call them MiG-something-or-others."

"Close enough. I forgive you all your sins."

Mark couldn't help it. With the skill of a pouncing tiger he set his lips over hers—only to taste chocolate. She'd found the M&M's, he realized, not caring if he caught her cold. Using one hand to pull her closer when he felt her shudder, Mark used his other hand to shift her head and deepen his kiss—barely stifling a groan when her tongue shyly touched his.

Hearing a cough behind him, Mark reluctantly pulled away, but not before using a finger to close her slackened chin, then winking at her startled expression as he straightened.

"Oh, heavens," she whispered, hiding her face in his jacket.

Not knowing if she was invoking the heavens because of his kiss or because the captain had caught her starting to kiss him back, Mark frowned at him. The captain, a score of years older, instantly sobered and gave his information.

"Speak English," Mark ordered, "out of respect for our guest."

Jane straightened with a gasp.

"The launch is ready, Sire," the captain repeated in English, adding a slight bow.

Jane gasped again, her gaze darting between the captain and Mark, then shook her head, deciding the wind had made her hear incorrectly.

Mark held out his hand. "Thank you, Captain, for your timely and stealthy voyage. I will see that your superiors hear of your valor."

The captain bowed again after shaking his hand, and then Mark pulled Jane over to the ladder that led down to the launch. The seas were relatively calm for open water, but he still ended up lifting her over the rail to waiting hands on the *Katrina*'s launch boat. He climbed in after her and they were soon speeding through the swells.

Chapter Five

✦ ┄ ✦

With the wind in her face and the gigantic aircraft carrier looming ahead, Jane looked back at the submarine and, without thinking, waved. But she was too late. The *Previa* was already being swallowed by the Atlantic Ocean, and she'd just bet the captain was right now sighing in relief to be invisible again and finally free of his bothersome, hysterical . . . guest.

Suppressing a shudder as the submarine sank from sight, Jane tried to shake off the one word the captain had said that bothered her. Sire. *The launch is ready, Sire.* Or had he said *sir*? Yeah, that made more sense. Shelkova must have a president or prime minister or something. And a captain would call the nephew of the president *sir*, wouldn't he? Then again, Mark somehow seemed to command respect from people whether he'd earned it or not, his arrogant air compelling people to *sir* him.

And besides, a *sire* didn't go around flying his own plane and getting shot at; he traveled with an entourage, bodyguards, and pilots to do the flying. So the captain must have said *sir*, and Mark was just taking advantage of his relationship to the prime minister.

Or maybe instead of an uncle, his ailing *father* was the president or whatever. Yeah, that made more sense. Mark's father would certainly have the clout to mobilize an entire navy to get his son home.

Okay, then; Mark was the son of the president of Shelkova.

Jane was jolted out of her musings when the launch smacked into the back end of the aircraft carrier, and she barely stifled a scream when they suddenly started rising into the air before she realized they were on a ramp that was lifting out of the water like an elevator. The large inflatable raft was soon high and dry, and Mark helped her out and stood her on the gridiron ramp beside him, the ocean now frothing several yards beneath their feet.

Several important-looking officers were there to greet them, all appearing elegant in their crisp uniforms. Trying not to gawk as each man gave a slight bow while introducing himself to Mark, Jane felt better about all the attention now that she'd figured out *who* he was. The officers were speaking in Shelkovan, but she could see they respected Mark—or at least his father.

Heck, they even bowed to her, too!

She tried to bow back, but Mark kept a firm hand on

her arm and tugged her upright each time. So Jane tried
giving him a frown, only to get hauled against his side.
Yeah, well, he could be an arrogant jerk, but she continued smiling and nodding at every last one of the officers
who were going out of their way to get Mark home. Her
smile faltered, however, when she turned on the ramp
and saw what had to be a thousand men standing at attention inside what had to be the largest airplane hangar on
the planet.

And she had to limp past every one of them?

Mark turned her to face him. "Are you feeling steady
enough to walk, Jane?"

Walk or be carried? Which was more embarrassing?
"I'm fine," she assured him, smiling brightly at his suspicious look. "Really. I'm fine."

With her head held high and her arm tucked in Mark's
as he led her off the ramp, Jane concentrated on not limping. It was bad enough her nose was running and her
cheeks were probably blistering red and she was dressed
like a backcountry hick; she didn't want word to get back
to Mark's father that his son was dragging home a
pathetic-looking *invalid* from America.

"How about one of these, Jane?" Mark asked as they
walked along a row of jets whose wings were folded like
wounded birds. He stopped in front of a sleek fighter jet
that was more engine than aircraft. "Would you like to
take this one tomorrow? She looks fast."

"She looks like she only has two seats. Where's the
pilot going to sit?"

"I'll let you sit in the front and you can fly. Once I get
us airborne," he clarified.

"You know how to fly a fighter jet?" she asked, pinching the inside of his elbow.

Mark chuckled—causing eyebrows on the officers beside them to lift, she noticed. "Of course," he drawled. "I, too, like to go fast in a plane."

"No offense, Ace, but I've seen your flying, remember? So I think I'll ride with one of the *Katrina*'s stick jockeys," she drawled back, trying to mimic his accent.

That sobered him.

Several officers coughed. One actually choked.

Jane simply added a few watts to her smile.

Mark started off again past the crewmen of the *Katrina*, all still standing at attention, only their eyes following the progress of the small entourage. "I'll show you to your room and you can have a shower. Then you will sleep."

"Heavens, you don't take teasing very well, do you, Ace?" she asked, still smiling.

Mark stopped, causing the whole parade of officers to stop again. He looked down at her, then turned to the watching crewmen. "I want everyone to speak English in the lady's presence," he said loudly enough to be heard clear across the cavernous hangar. "She is my guest," he finished, looking pointedly at the officers, who all suddenly saluted—the entire crew saluting with them.

Jane pinched him again. "Stop that!" she quietly hissed.

"Stop what?"

"Being so bossy. You're taking advantage of your father's position," she whispered tightly, ignoring the indrawn breaths of several nearby officers and crewmen. "You can't expect everyone on this ship to do whatever you say. That's the captain's job."

Mark stared at her for a full minute. "And just who is my father," he asked softly, "that I am taking advantage of?"

"He's the president of Shelkova. And his being nice enough to help get you home doesn't give you license to go around acting so . . . so pompous."

Every single officer took a step back.

"*Pompous*," Mark repeated.

She nodded.

"Jane, Shelkova doesn't have a president," he quietly snapped before taking her arm and leading her out of the utterly soundless hangar.

Well, shoot. That blew that theory to smithereens. What was left? Maybe Shelkova had a prime minister. Or maybe Mark's father was a general or admiral or . . . whatever.

Yeah, an admiral would explain Mark knowing how to fly jets off aircraft carriers, if he was following in his father's footsteps. And who better to call up half the naval fleet to get his son home. It would also explain why everyone on the *Previa* and *Katrina* was being so nice; they wanted Mark to tell his father how efficient they were.

Now that she really thought about it, *this* theory made perfect sense.

Mark led her through what was turning out to be a seemingly endless maze of corridors until Jane thought about asking him to carry her. Heck, the ship was bigger than her hometown of Pine Creek! And she was getting short of breath and her right ankle was starting to hurt from *not* limping.

Jane sighed in relief when they finally stopped in front of a door just as she was working up the nerve to ask. "The captain has been gracious enough to give you his cabin," Mark said, his hand on the knob.

"What? No. I don't want him to— Oomph."

Mark covered her mouth with a hand. "You will take it if you don't wish to insult an entire ship of men. Shower and sleep, in that order," he commanded, turning her around and nudging her into the room.

Spinning toward him, Jane lifted a hand to her forehead. "Yes, sir!" she snapped—only to sneeze three times in succession.

Mark walked away laughing as the five officers who'd accompanied them spun on their heels and followed—some of their faces pale, some red, all incredulous.

He wouldn't wake her. He just wanted to make sure she was fine. And maybe just lie down with her awhile, so he could listen to her breathe. That way he wouldn't worry her illness was worse, and he could finally get some rest.

Mark took off his shoes and quietly slid into bed beside her.

He wouldn't disturb her. He knew Jane had taken the doctor's pills, so she should sleep deeply. No problem. She'd never even know she had a visitor.

But what did he discover? Little Miss Can't-Curse-Worth-a-Damn, Little Miss Prim and Proper, was buck naked.

Every noble intention, every promise Mark had made to himself concerning his soul, fled at the discovery he was lying in bed with the woman who had captured his heart.

He was going to make love to her. He was going to concede to the Lakeland legend and claim the woman who had sealed their fate by sealing her lips to his.

And damn if he wasn't going to enjoy this.

Mark sat up and pulled his shirt off over his head without unbuttoning it, then lay down and slowly rolled Jane onto her back and brushed the hair away from her face. He gently feathered kisses over the warm skin just below her ear, then slowly worked his way to her cheek, her chin, her nose, and finally her lips.

Jane gave a disgruntled murmur and tried to brush him away.

He moved on to her neck, her collarbone, and then her shoulder.

She swatted at the air again, this time muttering something about mosquitoes.

Mark began to use his tongue, stirring her enough to make her suddenly gasp.

"Hello, angel," he whispered, continuing his exploration.

"Wh-what are you doing?"

"Succumbing to temptation," he murmured, moving his mouth lower and gaining another gasp. "Sealing our fate," he added, lavishing the soft, tender skin.

"Oh. Ooohh. Oh, heavens. I-I don't think you . . . You probably shouldn't . . . Ah, Mark?"

"Shhh. It's all right, sweetheart. I want to touch you."

"Y-you do?" she whispered on an indrawn breath when he reached the soft tender skin of her breast. "Wait, have you been drinking?"

He stilled, then slowly lifted his head. "Excuse me?"

He sighed hard enough to move her hair. "No," he said, lowering his head again. "But I am seriously thinking of starting. Let me touch you, Jane. Let me make love to you."

"You really want to make love to me? Are . . . are you *sure* you're sober?"

"I'm sure. Are you?" he asked, working his way back toward her neck.

Her answer was a snort. "I . . . I guess so."

"That's good, angel. You can touch me, Jane. I'd like that."

"Oh. Yeah. Sure," she said absently, apparently more focused on arching her back into his touch as she slid her hands to his shoulders, only to gasp again when she felt bare skin.

Mark shuddered at her simple, unsettling touch and wrapped his arms around her as he rained kisses over her face and neck and lips. "That's it, Jane. Hold me. Touch me. Let me feel your life-giving lips on mine."

Growing bolder by the minute, his saving grace began kissing his jaw and then his neck, then blazed a searing trail down to his chest. Her touch was sometimes hesitant, sometimes bold, obviously unschooled—and telling. Jane Abbot had been no man's wife. Her awkward advances completely endeared her to him in the way only an angel could bestow her gift of innocence on a man who wanted to claim her for his very own.

Beginning to shake with overwhelming need, Mark quickly unbuckled his pants, lifted his hips to slide them off, and kicked them away, then rolled over to cradle himself between Jane's thighs, only to hesitate as he looked down on her wondering, mesmerized expression.

"I'm not going to be able to wait, angel," he whispered thickly, wrestling his raging passion for at least enough control to not scare her. "I need to be in you. Now. Let me in, Jane," he entreated, shifting his hips and urging her to open her legs, knowing that if he could just feel her heat surrounding him, he might have a chance of slowing down and fulfilling them both.

Her response was immediate and without hesitation as she eagerly accommodated him, wetting his manhood with her own passion. Lifting his chest and anchoring her hands beside her head, he watched her face as he shifted to slowly and steadily ease inside her until he tore through the expected barrier, making her give a hoarse shout and buck against his intrusion.

He waited until he felt her soften before he moved by kissing her face and crooning soothing words, then began an easy rhythm as he felt her slowly begin to move with him, once more arching her body to his. Her legs came around his waist, holding tightly against his increasing tempo, and even as he had the fleeting thought that he was forgetting something important, Mark barely remembered to breathe as he suddenly and gloriously gave himself up to an angel with a shout of wonder.

Mark rested his forehead on Jane's with a silent curse. She really was a virgin—or rather, had been. And he'd hurt her. She wasn't moving.

He didn't move, either, not wanting to see her tears. He'd taken her gift of innocence—that she'd trustingly given him—and in the process had probably killed her.

Finally getting his pounding heartbeat under control, and not being able to put it off any longer without adding emotional hurt as well, Mark lifted his head to find her looking up at him with wide, wary eyes.

"You didn't like it!" she blurted out. "Oh, I knew this would happen. I'm sorry. I just thought that because you don't know me all that well, it would be okay. You couldn't really see me, and you don't know my whole name, either, so it would be okay to just—ummpphh."

He kissed her to shut her up. "Jane," he said, lifting his mouth away. "I'm sorry."

"Oh! I am, too. I'm sorry you didn't like it."

"What?"

"You suddenly shouted and just stopped."

Mark dropped his forehead to hers again. "I liked it," he whispered. "And so will you—next time."

"Next time? You want to do it again?" she asked, the alarm in her voice making him rise up to see her eyes widened to saucers.

"Not this minute," he drawled. "But someday soon."

"Oh. Oh, heavens."

He cradled her face in both hands, his thumbs rubbing her flushed cheeks, and finally smiled. "We must have a little talk," he said gently, "about what happens now."

She nodded within his hands. "You should probably go back to your room."

"Excuse me?"

"Before someone finds you in here. It could be . . . embarrassing."

"I will not allow anyone to embarrass you," he growled, squeezing her cheeks.

"Not me," she said, sounding exasperated. "Your *father*."

"My father," he repeated.

She nodded again. "An admiral's son can't just bring his chippy onto one of his aircraft carriers like it's a cruise ship. Your father would lose the respect of his men."

Admiral? Chippy? Mark moved his hands from her face to her throat.

"Your cheek's twitching again," she warned him. "And you're scowling."

"So now my father is no longer a president, but an admiral?" he asked very softly, his hands touching the column of her throat but not squeezing—yet.

She nodded *again*, her jaw snapping shut when it ran into his unyielding hands.

"Let me see . . . First you thought I was a criminal. Right?" he asked calmly.

She nodded.

"Then you thought I was the son of a president."

She shook her head. "At first I thought you were his nephew."

"And now you think I am the son of an admiral. Is that correct?"

Jane nodded again. "Pretty good, huh, Mr. Just Mark?"

"Have I been anyone else?" he asked, his hands still not squeezing—yet.

"I . . . ah, I thought you were a spy," she confessed. "But only for a little while."

He gave her a good glare for that one. "But now I'm the son of an admiral, and you are my . . . chippy? Have I got it right?"

The suicidal woman nodded again. Hell, she even had the audacity to smile. "And you shouldn't carry on like this and embarrass your father," she apparently felt compelled to add. "Not after all the trouble he's gone through to get you home."

Mark finally squeezed, but only enough to get her attention. "If I ever again hear you refer to yourself as my *chippy*, whom I am *carrying on* with, you're going to find yourself wishing you never fished me out of that lake. Do you understand?"

Jane Abbot nodded again, rather vigorously.

Mark smiled. "Now," he continued. "You are going to close your eyes and go to sleep, and I am going to sleep right here beside you." He had to squeeze her again when she started to protest. "And tomorrow we are going to see my father *together*. I will introduce you to him, and then you and I are going to have a little talk. Understand?"

She didn't nod this time; she simply snapped her eyes shut.

Hearing her breathing eventually even out and figuring she had fallen asleep thinking about the fact that she was no longer a virgin, Mark started drifting off, wondering if the surprise she was in for tomorrow might not make the earthly little angel curse for real—only to snap open his eyes when he suddenly remembered something she'd said.

What in hell had she meant that he didn't know her whole name, either?

Chapter Six

❖ ⋯ ❖

Waking up cocooned between a warm—okay, hot—masculine chest and unquestionably strong masculine arms wasn't nearly as disconcerting as the realization that instead of being worried about spending a thousand years in purgatory for having sex without being married, Jane couldn't quit smiling.

Heaven help her, it had finally *happened*.

Despite her ordinary old everyday plainness, her crippled foot, and the fact that she was nobody special, a mysterious, handsome man had held her and kissed her and touched her in ways—and in places—she'd never been kissed or touched before.

He'd even seemed to be enjoying it, too, right up until he'd suddenly stopped.

Jane silently sighed, deciding it had been rather disappointing for her, too—although not certainly to the point of regret. She'd enjoyed parts of it. Okay, most of it. And she wasn't so naive to think the first time would be all romantic and mushy and passionate, but in fact a little painful and probably a lot uncomfortable.

The nuns at Saint Xavier's, God bless their big pious hearts, had tried to explain marriage and sex and men to her. On the first one they'd been adamant it was a must, but on the last two they'd been complete failures. They couldn't teach what they didn't really know, and definitely not when they were stammering and skirting the more important parts.

Which was why almost everything she did know about sex she'd learned from Katy. Well, and from all the teen magazines they used to read in their secret clubhouse in the woods at the back of Katy's parents' Christmas tree farm.

Her friend had lost her virginity three years after graduating high school, Jane knew, because Katy had told her it had finally happened when she'd moved to Bangor to live with her sister and taken a course at community college to become a paramedic. She'd also made Jane promise to never, ever get drunk if there were horny, handsome men around. Because, Katy had explained, liquor apparently made a girl's hormones overrule her good sense—especially the first time she didn't have overprotective brothers and male cousins scaring off every guy she even smiled at.

And even though Katy had been a font of sexual information—garnered over the next few years and a couple of relationships—it had been the men of the woods of

Maine who had given Jane her insights into the male mind. Because while Katy had eventually chosen a profession other than selling real estate in and around Pine Creek, Jane had started working full-time at her foster parents' sporting camps right out of high school, until her foster dad had died in an auto accident and her foster mom had sold the camps and gone to live with her sister in Georgia. Jane had worked at various camps after that, and what she'd learned was that some men were jerks, some were nice, and all of them were braggarts. While catering to a lodge full of sports or spending the day in a boat as their fishing guide, she'd heard enough one-upmanship and macho bragging to wish her ears had lids like her eyes.

She'd been taught from the age of twelve to hunt and fish and camp out just like one of the guys. It was her foster parents' way of giving her a place with them, as well as skills that would serve her well into adulthood. So she'd guided hunters and fishermen, and cooked and cleaned and flown parties in and out of camp. In Maine, in her woods, she was plain old ordinary, invisible Jane Abbot.

But now this handsome, arrogant, awesome man had seen her as a woman; as somebody to make love to. So despite the fleeting pain and abrupt ending, she was overjoyed it had finally happened. Jane smiled into the golden eyes silently watching her. "Do you think I got pregnant last night?" she asked.

"Pregnant!" he shouted, bolting upright and looking incredulous.

"Yeah," she said, hugging the blankets around her. "I could be, you know. I hope so."

"You *hope so*?"

She nodded. "More than anything in the world, I want a baby." Smiling dreamily, she elaborated. "I'm going to buy a nice little house on a lake. Near a town, of course, so my child can go to school. I hope it's a boy. I'd like to have a boy." She canted her head. "He could have your eyes. You have beautiful eyes."

"Jane."

"And someday I'd get him a brother or sister. He shouldn't be alone. Then we'd be a real family. Every kid should have a brother or sister."

"Jane."

"You may have saved me a lot of trouble, if I got pregnant last night. Thank you."

"Jane."

Hearing his growl, she looked up to see his cheek was twitching again—which she was coming to realize only happened when he was . . . agitated. About her maybe being pregnant? "Why is your cheek twitching this time?"

He sighed hard enough to nearly part her hair, and ran a hand through his own. "Jane, I . . ." He sighed again. "Well, hell."

"You shouldn't cuss. And I know you cuss in Shelkovan as well. You're going to spend a long time in purgatory if you don't quit."

His eyes grew incredulous again. "Who in hell brought you up, a bunch of nuns?"

She nodded.

His eyes widened even more. Then he said something suspicious in Shelkovan. "Jane, if you're pregnant, which I doubt," he said through gritted teeth, "you're not going to buy a 'nice little house' on a lake—near a town, of course. Do you think I'd let some woman having my child go off and live by herself?"

Jane lifted her chin at that *some woman* label. But then she sighed and pulled the blankets over her shoulders. That's all she was to Mark, certainly. Just *some woman*. "I wouldn't expect marriage or anything."

"Why the hell not!" he shouted, jumping up from the bed to stand over her with his hands on his hips—apparently not realizing he was utterly and gloriously naked.

"Well, because I just wouldn't," she whispered, fighting to keep her chin from quivering and her eyes on his feet. "All I want is a baby. That's all," she muttered. Jane looked him in the eyes, attempting to get her gumption back. "If I'm not pregnant now, I will be soon."

"What?"

He'd roared that time. And he took an ominous step closer to the bed.

"You are not going to make love with another man. Ever!"

"I don't have to go to bed with *any* man to have a baby. I'm going to see a doctor about getting one."

"Lady, your education is sorely lacking. You need a man to get pregnant."

"No, I don't. I can be artificially inseminated," she shot back, rising to her knees on the bed while holding the blankets to her chest like a shield. "That's what I've planned on doing all along. But maybe last night you simply saved me the trouble!"

She landed on her back, a red-faced, cheek-twitching,

angry male on top of her. Maybe, just maybe, she shouldn't have brought up the subject of pregnancy. Or last night, for that matter. Mark probably didn't like being reminded of how disappointing it had been. Well, or else how crazy he must have been to sneak into her room in the first place, now that he was seeing her in the light of day.

"You will not be artificially inseminated, either. Is that clear?"

"But I want a baby."

"I'll give you one!"

Oh yeah, she was sorry she'd mentioned anything this morning. Hoping to placate him, as well as get him off her chest, she frantically nodded agreement—not really knowing or caring what she was agreeing to.

Mark closed his eyes. After several deep breaths, he looked at her again. The fire was banked in those gorgeous golden eyes, and she could feel the tension leaving his body inch by gloriously naked inch. "This is a crazy conversation," he whispered. "One we will have later," he added with a sigh. He gave her a rather chaste kiss then got off the bed and walked to the panel of buttons by the door—apparently still oblivious to the fact that he was still naked.

Jane propped her head on the pillow and watched. If he wanted to parade around like that, who was she to complain? Until he bent down and picked up her brace from beneath the side of the bed. "Give me that!" she squeaked, lunging for it.

He pulled back, holding it out of her reach. "Why do you hide it?"

"I don't hide it," she lied, lifting her chin. "It's just nobody's business but mine."

He seemed to think about that as he studied the well-worn brace. Jane had had this one for nearly six years, and she was dreading the day she'd have to break in a new one. Heck, there was even duct tape on it. She blushed when she noticed Mark fingering the tape.

"Can you not afford a new one?" he asked, his voice suddenly tender. "This one is falling apart."

"I don't want a new one. That one's comfortable."

He looked at her, then back at the brace, then carefully set it down on the bed. "Will you tell me how you injured yourself?"

"I can't," she told his toes. It was either look at his toes or at his face, and she wasn't up to seeing the pity in his eyes. "I don't know how my ankle got crushed."

"How can you not know something like that?" he asked, genuine amazement in his voice. "If you were a child, then your parents would know."

"I have to go to the bathroom. Now," she added when his feet didn't move.

He sighed, then bent down and picked up his clothes. "We will also leave this discussion for later," he murmured as he slipped into his clothes. "Get dressed, Jane, and meet me in the galley. We'll have some breakfast before we leave."

"That's the cafeteria, right? How do I find it?" she asked, thankful he was leaving.

"Ask any crewman you meet. They all speak passable English. It's required."

"Really? Why?"

"They must know French, Spanish, Japanese, and Chinese, also. This carrier travels the world, and everyone aboard must be capable to some extent."

"Wow. Was that your father's idea?"

He straightened from tying his boots and eyed her for several seconds, then suddenly smiled. "Yes, it was my father's idea."

"I can't wait to meet him. I hope he's okay."

"I can't wait until you meet him, either," he agreed dryly. "And yes, he's going to be fine. I've already spoken with him. He is resting at home after having a minor stroke, apparently, and must now take it easy."

"He's home so soon?"

"Very minor. He is also looking forward to meeting you."

"You told him about me?"

"But of course. He wouldn't be seeing me if not for you."

"Oh. Yeah. That's right. Ah . . . Are you going to leave anytime soon?"

Mark strode back to the bed, leaned down, and kissed her on the lips. "Take a hot shower if you're sore this morning," he whispered. "And don't feel compelled to rush to breakfast. I have things to see to before I can meet you there. And don't be afraid of any of the crewmen. They will take good care of you."

Blushing at his suggestion she take a long hot shower, and why, Jane nodded and gave him a push to get him moving. He straightened with a chuckle and finally made it out the door.

And Jane finally made it to the bathroom.

Mark walked back into the cabin as soon as he knew Jane was in the shower. He went to the bed and stripped off the bottom sheet, which carried the telltale sign of her lost innocence. He folded the sheet, remade the bed so Jane wouldn't realize it was missing, then took it with him when he re-exited the room.

Jane had spent the last fifteen years of her life in a mostly male environment—the first twelve years at Saint Xavier's having been exclusively female—but the journey to the galley had proved a trying affair. All the men she met had kept bowing to her, treating her like some sort of celebrity. They'd stuttered and stammered trying to give her directions, and Jane had stammered and blushed and actually sneezed on two of them. Finally, one daring, frustrated soul had simply given up and led her to the galley—puffing up his chest like a drumming partridge whenever they met other crewmen in the corridors.

Jane had been embarrassed. Now she was perturbed. She was sitting alone off to the side at a table large enough for thirty people, being stared at by at least a hundred men. The cook had come out of the kitchen bearing a monstrous tray laden with every conceivable breakfast food, followed by another man carrying fancy china, polished silver, linens, and crystal glassware—into which he'd poured what she suspected was fresh squeezed orange juice. Looking at the tables full of crewmen, Jane had seen they were eating off metal trays.

So here she was smiling at the cook smiling back at her . . . expectantly. She ate something and shot him a beaming smile, which got him to finally leave, but not before telling her in broken English that he would be back with more food.

Not really shy by nature, and especially comfortable around groups of men she could be one of the guys with, Jane finally stood up, picked up her plate, and casually limped to one of the occupied tables. "Would you gentlemen mind if I sat with you? The other table is lonely."

Every man in the entire room quickly scrambled to his feet and every head quickly nodded agreement. Men pushed men aside and made her a place, and the moment she sat down, so did everyone else.

"Are all of you from Shelkova?" she asked, sweeping her smile over the nearby sailors.

Every man at the table nodded.

"Have you all been at sea long on this voyage?"

Everyone nodded again.

Jane sighed. She was going to have to ask questions that needed more than a yes or no answer. "What's Shelkova like?"

Nobody said anything.

"Have any of you met Mark's father?"

They all frantically shook their heads.

Well, heck. This was like pulling teeth. She finally singled out one sailor and smiled at him, causing his Adam's apple to bob. "Mark told me Shelkova is a lot like Maine. That's where I'm from, by the way. Is your coast rugged and rocky?"

"Y-yes, ma'am," the nervous man answered.

She was on a roll here. "Is the water too cold for swimming? It's right frigid in Maine."

"Y-yes, ma'am."

Maybe she should find an older sailor to talk to. This one looked barely old enough to shave. Eyeing each of the fidgeting men at her table, Jane homed in on one with touches of gray in his hair. "What do you do on this ship?" she asked.

"I run catapult."

Well, he was steadier than his shipmate, but looked just as uncomfortable. "And the catapult is . . . What?"

"That is what shoot jets off deck."

Jane sighed again. She noticed they'd all stopped eating, and took a bite of her own eggs, then motioned for them to do the same. Heavens, they were acting as if she were an alien from outer space or something. "What do you guys do for fun?" she asked, trying again.

Every fork in every hand silently returned to their trays.

"Oh, for Pete's sakes!" she sputtered on a laugh. "Mark isn't here. You don't have to be so formal. Eat your food. Old Ace can't have you keelhauled for *talking* to me."

Every face at the table paled.

"His . . . His Highness give order you receive much respect from us," one daring sailor stammered.

"His Highness? As in a king or something?"

Everyone nodded.

"Shelkova has a king?"

"We call him czar," another sailor offered, puffing up proudly.

"But there are no more czars."

"Yes, now. People bring back old family to rule," the same sailor informed her.

"Really? And His Highness said you have to be nice to me? But how does he even know I'm on this ship?"

"He bring you."

"What?"

"Czarevitch Markov bring you aboard last day," the now-sweating sailor told her.

"Markov? You mean Mark? What's a czarevitch?"

"You say . . . heir apparent, I think. Or prince."

"No. No," another sailor added. "Czar Reynard decide he is too ill to rule. Markov Lakeland soon be our czar."

Jane knew her mouth was hanging open, but couldn't help it. Mark was a prince? He was a darned prince! Oh, heavens. Oh, shoot. She'd had sex with a prince!

"Well dammit to hell!" Jane slapped a hand over her mouth. "I'm sorry," she cried through her fingers. "I didn't mean to say that."

All the men at the table, and the next table, and the next, were staring at her. She jumped up, causing every man in the room to jump up with her. Staring at them, Jane didn't know whether to burst into laughter or tears.

Both, probably—right after she catapulted Markov Lakeland off the deck *without* a jet.

"Oh, sit down!" she shouted.

Every man in the room instantly sat.

Holy heavens, this being the guest of a prince was dangerous stuff. Jane didn't doubt if she asked them all to jump off the boat, they would—if only to be in Mark's good graces.

Well, he sure as heck wasn't in *her* good graces. Oh, she'd heard of Markov Lakeland. She simply hadn't connected the dots. No wonder he was *just Mark*; the man was a prince from some country (which she now knew was Shelkova) who had come to America a month ago looking for an American bride. Heck, it had even made the *Pine Lake Weekly Gazette*, it was such titillating news. Some rich, playboy prince was supposedly romancing American women in hopes of furthering his country's ties to almighty America.

And she'd made love to that prince last night? Her? Jane Abbot?

The man was a rat. He'd taken the pathetic cripple from Maine to bed to thank her for saving his life. She'd given her virginity to a womanizing, *royal* rat who had just been . . . what? Toying with her? Or amusing himself on his latest odyssey?

No wonder he'd shouted when she'd told him she hoped she'd gotten pregnant. What soon-to-be king wanted an un-pedigreed, crippled orphan from nowhere to be the mother of his child? *Queens* had king's children, not plain Janes. The lying, deceiving rat was probably laughing his socks off with the captain right now.

Realizing the room had gone deathly silent, Jane turned to see Mark leaning against the head table, his arms folded over his chest. "How long have you been standing there, you rat?!"

"Not long. Mingling with the men, Jane?"

"Getting civic lessons!" she snapped.

"Learn anything interesting?"

"You're a damned *prince*."

"Tsk-tsk. Such language from an angel."

That was it. He'd made her swear again. Jane grabbed

a mug off the table and hurled it at Mark's insolent face. He straightened and ducked, letting the metal mug bounce off the wall behind him. The cook came running out of the kitchen, his eyes bugged out, just as Jane picked up another mug and hurled it. Having killed more than one partridge with a rock, she'd anticipated Mark's move and hit him square on the chest. "You lying, low-life pond scum!" she shouted, reaching for another mug.

The men at her table scrambled to their feet. One of them grabbed her, but Jane rounded on him. "Don't you dare try to protect that pompous goat!" she shouted at the sailor, poking him in the stomach when he tried to pull her back.

"He's trying to protect *you*," Mark said from right behind her.

Jane whirled and came nose to coffee-soaked chest with him. "From who?!"

"From me."

"Oh yeah? You and whose army, Ace? I might be small, but I fight dirty!"

"My own army, angel."

She kicked him. He was so close, and she was wearing boots, so she kicked him.

And then she wisely ran.

—right into an officer who was blocking the door and wouldn't let her pass. She thought about kicking him, too, but he was basically innocent. It was only Mark she wanted to pummel. Jane took a calming breath and walked back to the table—going around Mark—and faced the man she'd poked in the stomach. "I'm sorry I hit you," she whispered. "You're innocent. And it was nice of you to try to protect me."

His face blistering red, the man mutely nodded.

"Our plane is ready, Jane. Come. I've already gathered your things," Mark said from near the door.

"I'm not going anywhere, *Your Highness*. I'm staying right here."

"Here is in the middle of the ocean, witch."

She lifted her chin. "Then they're going to have to drop me off at the next port, because I'm not getting on a plane with you."

"It's a fast plane."

She lifted her chin higher.

Mark sighed. "Your stubbornness always makes things difficult," he muttered, walking toward her. "And always makes me the villain."

With that ominous declaration, he picked her up and hefted her over his shoulder like a sack of grain. Ignoring her growl of outrage and her pinching him on the back, he grabbed her pack and shotgun off the table on his way to the door, then stopped and turned. In a loud voice, Mark addressed the dining hall of stunned sailors in Shelkovan, then carried her away to the boisterous roar of cheering.

He stood her on her feet once they were topside, and all Jane could do was glare at him as he dragged her toward a waiting plane. It wasn't a fighter; it was a transport jet, with a pilot and copilot waiting in the cockpit. Frantic now, desperate, confused, angry, Jane broke away while swiping her shotgun in the process, then whirled and pointed it at him. "I'm not going with you! You're a prince!"

His face drained of color. "For the love of God, Jane, drop the gun. Now."

"No. Just leave me here."

"Dammit, you don't understand," he said hoarsely. He suddenly raised his arms and looked up past her head, then frantically shouted something in Shelkovan at the top of his lungs. Even though her back was to the men, Jane didn't dare turn around, and instead raised the shotgun to her shoulder.

"Jane. Drop the gun."

"D-don't you tell them to jump me. Just get in your plane and go away. I never want to see you again," she whispered, fighting the urge to wipe her blurring eyes on her sleeve. "I-I just want to go back to Maine, where . . . where I belong."

"Please set down the gun, Jane," he rasped thickly, his own eyes misting.

Jane remembered pointing her gun at him on the first boat, and he hadn't paled, hadn't backed away, and hadn't pleaded with her. She was suddenly scared. "Mark?" she whispered, watching him look behind her and hold up his hands again. "P-please, just let me go home."

"Walk toward me, Jane," he said calmly. "Keep your gun raised and slowly walk to me. Understand? Don't turn your head. Don't take your eyes off me. Just walk into my embrace."

She lowered the barrel of her gun, her eyes now running sightless with tears. "M-Mark?"

"NO!"

She felt the impact before she heard the accompanying crack of a rifle. Jane was slammed onto the deck, the force of the blow taking her breath, the sharp, searing pain in her back nearly rendering her unconscious. Strong arms lifted her on an anguished roar. Booted feet rushed forward, and her shotgun was kicked aside as forceful hands pulled at her, trying to tug her away from Mark. He roared again, the sound echoing through every cell of her body, and Jane flinched on a gasp and let her head fall back.

G oddammit! He couldn't believe she'd pulled a gun on him in front of an entire warship of sailors. It was a fatal mistake that Mark knew Jane never realized she was making.

She was just mad. And Lord knew when Jane Abbot got mad, things happened. Hell, she'd fired at his assassins. And she'd pulled that damn gun on him once before. But Mark knew she never would have pulled the trigger.

Only the sailors didn't know that.

They'd shot her—protecting him.

And now she was bleeding to death in his arms. Oh Christ, what a mess. He wouldn't lose her. He'd just found this amazing creature. He'd fallen into her lap and she'd kissed the breath of life into him.

"Sire."

"Don't talk. Save her, dammit!"

"You must let her go, Sire. We have to take her to the infirmary. Let go."

"No! I'll carry her."

"Sire . . . Markov, let me tend her," the white-haired man softly beseeched. "Let me stop the bleeding. Then you may carry her down."

Carefully handing her into the doctor's care, Mark

looked at Jane's ashen face, her eyes closed and flinching as the life drained out of her. "Speak English!" he snapped to the attending men. "She may be able to hear you. Speak English so she won't be frightened."

"We will, Sire. Please. Let us work."

Mark had to walk away. The crowd parted for him, and he walked over to the shotgun someone had kicked under the waiting jet. He picked it up with bloodied hands and stared at it, wishing he could fling it into the sea.

But it was Jane's; a serviceable weapon, the old etching on the stock worn smooth from being carried many miles on many hunts.

In Maine.

Where she belonged, she'd said. She felt she only belonged in the woods, where she could limp without eyes following her. Where she could love a drunken old Yankee who would loan her his truck without question. Where she had no family but the one she intended to build by any means possible, be it through her one time making love to a rat-prince or artificial insemination.

But she could just as easily belong to Shelkova. His people would fall in love with her on sight. Her limp would not disgust them or garner their pity; it would endear Jane in their hearts. And her spirit, her goodness, and her lectures on manners would complement an emerging nation that had so much to give the world by way of people and resources and courage.

Jane Abbot could match the courage of Shelkova. Hell, she could enhance it.

And she would.

Mark worked the action on the shotgun, opening the breach and confirming it was empty. It had been empty since before he'd taken it aboard the *Previa*. Which he was sure Jane had known when she'd pointed it at him this morning. Even in Stonington, Mark had known she wouldn't have pulled the trigger—even when she'd thought him a criminal who'd betrayed her.

Well, hadn't he? She was lying in a pool of that evidence right now.

"Sire. Do you wish to carry her?"

"In English!"

"I'm sorry, Your Highness."

Mark handed the gun to a sailor with orders to see it was returned to Jane's cabin. He had to shove it into the obviously shaken man's hands, then he walked over to Jane, whose shirt had been ripped away, her upper torso wrapped with pressure bandages.

"The bullet is still inside," the doctor quietly told him in English. "I will have to take it out, but need blood to give her."

"She will have it," Mark said, reaching under her and carefully lifting Jane to his chest. "Good Shelkovan blood. Screen her type, then screen every one of the men."

He needn't have bothered giving the order. By the time Mark had carried Jane down to the infirmary the corridors were lined with crewmen waiting to offer their blood. And at the head were the men she'd shared a breakfast table with not an hour ago. Men who had witnessed her spirit, her temper, and her good manners, which made her apologize to an awed sailor for hitting him in anger. Men who knew she never would have pulled the trigger.

Angels spit and hissed and shouted, but it was all bluster.

Mark left her in the care of the doctor, then went out to the corridor and told the crew how pleased he was with their concern. And then he asked for the man who had shot Jane to be brought to him.

Chapter Seven

◆—··—◆

This was the tenth time she'd opened her eyes in the last two days, but it was the first time Mark knew Jane was coherent. He watched her face register the fact that she was in pain, then watched her trying to remember why. He also watched her slowly turn and look at him, and saw sadness and betrayal written in every anguished line of her pale face.

Mark shook his head. "I did not give the order to shoot. I yelled for them not to. That's what I said in Shelkovan."

"I . . . I wouldn't have shot you," she whispered hoarsely, her voice as pained as her eyes. "The gun wasn't loaded, Mark. I was . . . I was just . . ."

"Mad," he finished. "And confused. And scared. I understand, Jane. And I'm sorry."

"Why didn't you tell me?"

He gave her a thoughtful smile and cocked his head. "I liked being just Mark to you. I liked that you treated me as just a man and not a prince or king. I liked our time together as . . . equals. I was selfish and didn't want it to end so soon."

"But we're not equals, are we?" she said flatly, looking away.

Mark gently clasped her chin and made her look at him. "No, we are not equals. You're the angel who pulled me from a cold, deadly situation, then saved my life again by leading me away from my assassins. You're the woman who spent the next two days enchanting me and the last two days scaring me to death. You are somebody very special, Jane. Somebody I can never hope to equal."

She closed her eyes, spilling her tears down her cheeks as she pulled free of his touch and tried to roll away, only to still on a whimper when the shifting caused her pain.

She turned just her head toward the wall. "How long have I been lying here?"

"Two days," he said sadly at her withdrawal.

She looked back to him, her eyes wide. "Why haven't you gone to your father?"

He shook his head again. "My father wasn't the one I thought was dying."

"You stayed because you thought I was dying?" she asked, clearly surprised.

But when he saw her eyes darken, he caught her chin when she tried to turn away. "Not from guilt. Not like you think. I am guilty of your being hurt, but I'm still here because I care."

Her face went blank beneath his stare, and she tried closing her eyes against him.

Mark gently squeezed her chin. "You have got to be the most stubborn woman I've ever met. What is it going to take for you to believe me?"

"Absolutely nothing," she said, pulling away and turning to the wall, only to flinch.

"I will get the doctor. He will want to see you, now that you're finally awake."

He went to find the doctor, then followed him back to Jane's room, but stood off to the side, out of her line of vision.

"Now, Miss . . . Abbot, is it?" the doctor asked, his expression tender. "How do you feel?"

Mark listened as Jane politely said she was just fine. Until she sneezed. Then she cried out in pain. Mark flinched but didn't move. The doctor immediately repositioned the bed until she was in a semi-sitting position.

"There, that will take a little pressure off your shoulder and hopefully help that head of yours," the doctor continued. "Your cold is much better, but you may have to cough or sneeze some, and that will be painful."

"What did the bullet do to me?" she asked, obviously thinking they were alone.

"I removed it from your shoulder," he answered truthfully. "You're going to be immobile in that arm for a while. And very tender. But you should heal quickly and will have full use of it eventually."

"Eventually?"

"Many months for complete muscle recovery," he explained. "But within a week or two, you will be able to use your left hand for small tasks, just not raise your arm very high."

Mark watched Jane think about that.

"Thank you. Ah . . . may I ask you a question?" she whispered to the man's chest.

"Certainly, Miss Abbot," the doctor replied, smiling at her blush.

"First, call me Jane. Or can you?" She looked up, wrinkling her nose. "Or has *His Highness* forbidden it?"

The doctor coughed, looking in Mark's direction. Mark smiled and nodded.

"Okay, Jane, what did you want to know?"

"Can I . . . If I were to have . . . Well, if I might be . . . pregnant," she stammered. "I mean, if I were just *barely* pregnant from, say, the night before, could my being shot have harmed the baby?" she finished in a blazing blush, her eyes back on the doctor's chest.

The man coughed again, his own cheeks darkening slightly. "Well," he stalled, this time looking everywhere *but* at Mark, who was feeling a little flushed himself.

Jane Abbot's mind worked in a most incomprehensible way. She was obviously quite serious in her quest for a baby, and quite hopeful her one time in a man's bed had gotten her with child—probably because she never wanted to have to go through that debacle again.

"Well," the doctor tried again, his chin resting in his palm as he tried to find an answer to her question. "If conception were possible, the trauma of your injury would probably prevent it. Your body has had quite a shock, what with the injury itself and then the operation."

"Oh."

"But," the doctor added, touching her hand at her obvious disappointment, "stranger things have happened. If a child is promised to be born, it will be. It's still possible, Jane, that you could have conceived, as the fertile egg is floating freely for the first week or two. It may not even know you've been shot," he finished, smiling at the hope in her eyes.

"Thank you."

"Is it a possibility? This pregnancy?" he asked.

Mark could only see the tip of her nose now, but it was bright red, and not from a lingering cold, either.

"Ah . . . yes. Yes, it is," she said more firmly.

"Then we will treat you as such," the doctor told her, petting her hand. "I will see that you are given nothing to harm your baby, Jane, how about that? And no more X-rays."

"Yes. Yes, I think that would be good. If I'm pregnant," she said, smiling through her blush, "then I want to do everything right. I really want a baby. It will be my family," she added. "And I'm sure the sisters of Saint Xavier's will understand why I didn't wait until I had a husband first, don't you?"

Clearly confused, the doctor could only nod. "I am sure they would."

Mark knew the poor man had absolutely no idea who the sisters of Saint Xavier's were. To that, neither did he. But he suspected. And he finally, slowly began to understand.

"You will sleep now," the doctor told her.

"But how long do I have to stay here? Mark—I mean His Highness—has to get home to his father. And it looks like the man won't go until I can go with him," she ended on a mutter.

Eyebrows raised, the doctor glanced in Mark's direction, then looked back at Jane. "I would like you to stay in that bed for two weeks," he said, smiling at her unlady-like snort. "But we can comfortably transport you in a day or two. The departure from this carrier pulls a lot of g-forces, and I would like you to be further healed first."

"You speak English well. Do you have a name?" Jane asked, the smile in her voice giving Mark hope his mischievous angel was back.

"Daveed."

"Oh, that's lovely."

"And now you will sleep?"

"Yes. I am tired."

"Do you hurt very much? I would like to keep the medicine at a minimum, in case there is a baby, but you needn't be in pain. I have safe drugs that will help," Daveed quickly added, noticing at once his mistake.

Jane would put the probably nonexistent baby before her pain.

"I . . . My shoulder does hurt some," she hedged. "But aspirin will probably work."

Like hell, Mark thought. If it hurt enough for her to mention, then it hurt like hell. Mark firmly shook his head, giving the doctor a speaking look.

"I will give you something intravenously," Daveed told her, quickly injecting the waiting medicine he'd anticipated she would need upon awakening. "It's safe, Jane."

"O-okay. And thank you, Dr. Daveed," she whispered, yawning and then flinching at the movement. "Tell Mark—I mean, tell His Highness to get some sleep himself, if he comes back here. He looked like he did when I pulled him out of the lake," she finished on a sigh, finally closing her eyes.

The good doctor nodded agreement despite the fact that Jane didn't see him, clearly not knowing what she was talking about. Well, he would soon, along with everyone on this ship. Mark wanted all of them to know she'd saved his life four days ago. And when he got her home, all of Shelkova was going to hear about it, too.

Mark rubbed his hands over his tired eyes, nodded his thanks to Daveed, and quietly walked from the room. He looked like hell because he hadn't left her for two days, not even to shower. He'd held her hand and prayed, and cursed the events that had brought Jane to the infirmary in the first place.

He'd talked to the man who'd shot her, intending to have him drawn and quartered, then flogged, then thrown over the side of the ship. But after ten minutes with the clearly distraught and nearly suicidal sailor, Mark had simply walked away.

He'd had more important things to think about. Like one stubborn angel who wouldn't die because he would not allow it. He headed for the captain's quarters that had been Jane's but were now his. He just wanted to sleep in the same bed he'd made love to her in; to close his eyes and thank God she'd be all right—eventually—even if she did hate him. He could live with that. And he would cure her little "I'm nobody" problem once he got her home.

She was halfway into her second day (not counting the two she'd slept through), and Mark was still coming to visit her even though she was actively—okay, nastily—trying to discourage him. But he would come anyway, and always leave with a clenched jaw and a small, persistent twitch in his cheek.

Jane knew she was being spiteful, snotty, and petty, not to mention disrespectful to an almost-king. But heck, the guy was letting her. Because he felt guilty and pitied her, he was taking her abuse. Yeah, well, he should; not only for kidnapping her with every intention of dragging her halfway around the world, but for making her feel special by making love to her and then crushing her newfound confidence. But his worse sin was lying by continually insisting she *was* special. So her only defense was sarcasm and sometimes indifference, or anything else that induced that little twitch in his cheek.

She'd had another persistent visitor for the last day and a half, but he stayed in the hall. In his hand he always had his seaman's cap, which was now a mangled blob of wool, and he would stand just outside her door and peek in her room when he thought she was asleep, the lines of his face distraught and his eyes usually tearful.

Jane had a pretty good idea who he was.

The guy was fifty years old if he was a day. He was tall, strong, and capable-looking, with shoulders that had once stood broad with pride but were now stooped with . . . shame, maybe. And Jane had noticed (through her half-closed lashes) that his eyes, when they weren't misted, were bright and clear and sharp. Sometimes he'd just stand there for over an hour before he heard someone coming and would quietly disappear.

This time, he was caught.

Two crewmen came upon him and pushed the startled man up against the far wall in Jane's line of sight, got their noses real close to his, and said something nasty-sounding in Shelkovan.

With her good but uncoordinated right hand, Jane picked up the carafe of water on the table by the bed and flung it with all her might at the men. She missed by a mile, but the clatter and splattering water was enough to gain their attention. "You better let him go, guys, or I'm gonna come over there and teach you some manners," she threatened, trying to sound forceful.

All three men stared in shock, their jaws falling nearly to their chests.

"I'm a guest of Prince Markov, so you better do as I say," she reminded them.

The two men immediately released their victim, who nearly slumped to the floor before he caught himself.

"So now you find my being a prince useful?" Mark drawled from right behind the men.

Jane shrugged her good shoulder, smiling sweetly. "Whatever works, Ace. I want to talk to that man," she rushed on, trying to sit up as she pointed at the deathly pale sailor frantically shaking his head.

Mark clapped him on the shoulder and drew him into the room, skirting around the fallen water jug, then lifting a brow at her. She just smiled again. Mark turned and dismissed the two sheepish assailants.

"Could you please come here?" she asked the man, waving him over.

Mark had to give him a push to start him on his way. The sailor's poor hat was now being twisted into oblivion, and his eyes were looking at the floor.

"What's your name?" she asked.

"D-Dorjan," he whispered to the floor.

"Well, Dorjan, could you come closer, please, and give me your hand?"

He gave her his hat. He quickly stuffed it in his pocket, then reached toward her again, holding out his shaking hand for her to take.

She squeezed it. "Thank you," she told him simply.

His head snapped up, and Jane gasped when she saw the bruise on his cheek. She turned and glared at Mark. "Did you hit him?"

"No," Mark replied, shaking his head and grinning.

She looked back at Dorjan, who was giving her an incredulous look. "Wh-why you thank me, lady? I . . . I am one who shoot you," he finally got out in broken, heavily accented English.

"I'm thanking you for not killing me," she said, squeezing his hand again. "I would bet you're an excellent shot, aren't you?"

He nodded stiffly, his face reddening.

"And you wished to save your prince, but you didn't wish to shoot me, did you?"

He nodded again.

"And so you placed your shot accordingly. Thank you. I appreciate your . . . aim."

The poor man dropped to his knees by the bed and kissed her hand, which was still holding his. "I am sorry, lady, for hurting you. I was told by first officer to protect Czarevitch. I am best shot. But I not want to shoot you."

"Well, it was a good compromise, Dorjan. I'm glad it

was you they asked, and I'm glad you hit what you're aiming at. You were aiming for my shoulder, weren't you?" she asked with a small laugh.

"Yes, lady," he confirmed, nodding frantically.

"Well, a small wound is better than dead. Now tell me how you got that bruise."

He lowered his eyes again.

Jane squeezed his hand. "It's okay, I've got a fair notion where it came from."

She turned and glared at Mark again, who was looking at her with gleaming eyes, then looked back to Dorjan.

"When I go to the plane this afternoon, I won't be able to walk very well, because my ankle . . . well, it seems I twisted it as I was falling when you shot— Yes, well, I can't imagine what an ordeal it will be to maneuver a wheelchair over all those hatch-like doors in all the hallways, and I was wondering if you would maybe carry me up to the flight deck. If it's not too much trouble for you," she quickly tacked on.

Dorjan's mouth fell open again as he looked up at her and then darted a frantic look at Mark, who slowly nodded.

"I would appreciate it," she told Dorjan, squeezing his hand again.

Those broad shoulders suddenly straightened, and Dorjan finally found a smile. "I will be honored, lady."

"Good." She let go of his hand and tugged on his sleeve. "Will you get up now? You make me feel like some queen at court or something." She rolled her eyes. "You understand, right? I want you to realize that I appreciate your position, and what you had to do. But mostly

I appreciate you were thoughtful enough to put my shoulder in your sights and not my head."

Dorjan nodded, flushing again, only to flinch when Mark clapped him on the shoulder and then talked to him for several minutes—in Shelkovan. At first Jane was disgruntled, but when she noticed Dorjan's shoulders going back even more and his eyes filling with pride, she forgave Mark his rudeness. With a final clap on his shoulder, Mark sent Dorjan away. The man turned and bowed at Jane, smiled shyly, then finally left.

Mark walked over, bent down, and firmly planted his lips on her startled mouth. And he left them there for the longest time—nearly making her eyes cross.

"Wh-what did you do that for?" she squeaked once she got her mouth back. "And don't do it again," she snapped once she got her wits back.

"I did it because I am in awe of you. Of your perception of your sniper, your insight into his bruise, and your solution to a very delicate problem," he said, spoiling his speech by bending down and kissing her again.

"I don't know what you're talking about," she muttered.

Mark cocked his head. "Maybe you don't. You're not a calculating woman; just natural."

She didn't know what that meant, either. "When are we leaving for your imperial home?"

"One hour. Do you feel well enough to travel?"

"And if I say no?"

"Then we will wait."

"Really? Why can't I just follow you later?"

"Because," he whispered, getting close to her face again, "the minute I left, you would have every man on this ship under your spell, and would end up getting someone to fly you back to Maine."

Well, it had been worth trying. "I don't want to go home with you."

"Why?" Mark asked with an exasperated growl, straightening and running a hand through his hair. "What is so terrifying about coming home with me?"

"I bet you live in a grand house, don't you? Or a castle or palace or something. I'd stand out like a sore thumb. I don't belong there."

"You belong wherever you happen to be. You hide in your woods."

"It's my home. Living where I was brought up doesn't mean I'm hiding."

"Why haven't you married?" he asked. "Why were you still a virgin at your age?"

"Because I didn't want to be a mistress!" she all but shouted, only to clamp a hand over her mouth.

"Whose mistress? What man asked you to be his mistress?"

"None of your darn business."

They stared at each other, both refusing to back down. Dr. Daveed walked in and practically had to pry them apart. Shaking his head, he spoke to Mark in Shelkovan.

"In English," Jane snapped, only to cover her mouth again. "I'm sorry. I didn't mean to sound like . . . like . . . I didn't mean to sound bossy," she finished on a contrite whisper.

"It is I who should ask forgiveness, Jane. I was being rude. I was just saying that I wished to get you ready for your journey."

"How long will that be? Shelkova is on the other side of the world and we're still in the Atlantic, aren't we?"

"It's a short distance if we fly over the North Pole," Mark answered for him. "Not many hours. We will be in a transport, but it will be fast. Although not Mach two," he told her with a smile. "Next time, okay?"

Jane snorted. "I'm not traveling with you again, Ace. Not even to walk to the store."

Mark pivoted on his heel and walked out muttering something. Jane couldn't tell if it was in English or Shelkovan, only that it had sounded . . . ominous.

M ark stood out of the way like a spare wheel. Jane, it seemed, was going to run this show. She had the doctor, the captain of the *Katrina*, several stupidly smiling officers, and Dorjan in the infirmary, all tripping over themselves to help her.

She was oblivious to it all.

The only thing Jane appeared worried about was that she would be too heavy for Dorjan to carry. Trying not to insult the man—apparently understanding male egos better than the men themselves did—she wanted a wheelchair brought for her to use until they made the flight deck.

And poor Dorjan, not wanting to lose the honor bestowed on him, kept trying to pick her up. But that was a difficult thing for a shy, nervous man to do to an angel. Dorjan kept leaning forward, hesitantly positioning his hands this way and that as he tried to work up the nerve just to touch her. Mark wasn't worried. Dorjan looked rugged enough to carry a tank up to the flight deck. He also knew that once the poor man finally managed to get Jane in his arms, dynamite would be needed to pry her free.

"I'm not fat, Dorjan," Jane told him for the third time. "And I know you're strong and everything. I just didn't mean you had to carry me through the entire ship."

"My pleasure, lady," Dorjan told her for the third time. "My . . . gift," he added with a beaming grin, trying to find the right word to show his honor.

Jane sighed in defeat, and Dorjan again began the trying task of deciding where to position his hands. She finally wrapped her good arm over his stooped shoulders and wiggled to the side of the bed, all the time working frantically to keep her legs covered by the blanket. Daveed came to the rescue and pulled the blanket free and tucked it around her legs, encasing her like a mummy. Jane smiled at him and guided Dorjan's free arm to her knees, and everyone sighed in relief when he finally straightened with her in his arms.

The parade that followed gave pomp and circumstance a whole new meaning. Mark realized Jane was in awe, if not downright bewildered. Every blessed crewman was turned out in dress uniform and lining the corridors that led to the flight deck, each one falling into step behind the entourage of Jane and Dorjan, Mark, the captain, the doctor, and the officers. And when they reached the flight deck?

There were two rows, three sailors deep, forming an aisle to the waiting jet. Mark saw Jane bury her face in Dorjan's puffed-out chest—right after she patted down her hair with the hand that was supposed to be wrapped around Dorjan's neck. She did lift her eyes long enough to glance at Mark, who was right behind her, carrying her pack and shotgun despite several officers offering to take his burden. But if he couldn't carry Jane, he would carry her things. She gave him an embarrassed look, which he answered with a reassuring smile, then she buried her face in Dorjan's neck again.

Mark was pleased.

Especially when she asked Dorjan to stop right in the middle of the aisle of sailors and pretended she had to adjust her blanket—which was just fine.

"Dorjan," she said loud enough to deafen the man, "I'm so glad you're such a good sharpshooter. I did a very foolish thing, and you saved my life with your quick thinking and compassion. Thank you," she practically yelled. And then Jane Abbot, understander of men and angel of God, leaned up and kissed the man's flushed cheek.

"Okay, I'm ready now," she told him, readjusting her perfectly adjusted blanket.

"Th-that fine, lady," Dorjan stammered, walking again.

"Jane. You must call me *Jane*, Dorjan. After all, you saved my foolish life."

Mark hid his smile. Dorjan would definitely be deaf after that shouted endorsement.

"And I'm going to write to you and make sure you're getting along *just fine*," she added meaningfully, glaring at the line of sailors watching in astonishment.

Mark felt invisible, since all eyes were on Jane.

And she called *him* pompous. Hell, she could give a show fit for a queen—or a lowly crewman out of grace with his shipmates. Dorjan was now the envy of everyone on board.

For the first time in more days than he could remember, Mark was happy. Contented. Hopeful. And quite anxious to get on with the rest of his life, no matter that it was going to be the taxing life of a king.

Jane, he knew, would keep him sane, if also humble and polite and forever looking over his shoulder—and around corners and under desks—to see what trouble she might be getting into. Imagine, a shotgun-toting queen who liked Pepsi and M&M's.

Maybe, just maybe, he would eventually get to see that blazing temper poor old drunken Silas had seen, for he suspected Jane's little gun-waving threats had just been the tip of what had the potential to be one hell of an iceberg.

His father would be pleased with his quest to find an American bride.

Jane Abbot didn't know it yet, but she was being imported into the Lakeland clan.

Chapter Eight

S he nearly died, Dad," Mark whispered to the man sitting up against the headboard of the massive, ornate bed. "The woman saves my life and nearly gets killed for her efforts."

Reynard Lakeland shrugged a set of shoulders as broad as his son's and only slightly stooped with age. "You were right to bring her here, as I don't doubt our enemies would have gone after her for no other reason than to prove they're willing to draw innocents into this war in hopes we'll back down. And what did Jane Abbot expect would happen if she pointed a gun at a prince in front of an entire ship of his warriors?"

Having paced to the window, Mark turned with a frown. "Jane doesn't think of me as a prince. To her I'm merely a man whose life she saved and who has given her nothing but trouble since. And she couldn't have realized what she was doing. She was just . . . angry."

"What kind of woman pulls a gun on any man?"

"An avenging angel." Mark shook his head, remembering. "I wish you could have seen her. She knew the gun wasn't loaded. She was just mad that she had no control over her fate."

Reynard raised an imperial gray eyebrow. "A tantrum, you mean."

Mark shrugged. "She was entitled. I basically kidnapped her after nearly killing her with pneumonia, then nearly killed her again by forcing her into a submarine. And then I took her virginity," he continued, watching both of Reynard's eyebrows rise into his hairline. Lord, his old man was a rock. "And then I got her shot and nearly finished her off again today with the plane ride here. She drank three liters of Pepsi and ate a pound of M&M's on the way home. Mostly, I think, to keep her mind off her pain." He suddenly grinned. "She did enjoy being catapulted off the *Katrina*, even though it had to have hurt her shoulder." But then he turned sad. "She looked at me with wondrous eyes and said all was forgiven for that simple experience."

"And when will I meet this angel?"

"She's sleeping. She's exhausted and in pain, and she told me not to wake her for a week."

"I suspect that's where my private nurse has gone?" Reynard asked in amusement.

"I'm sure you'll survive, even in such a weakened state," Mark returned dryly, watching the gleam in his father's eye intensify.

"I could die," Reynard whispered as he smoothed out his blankets. "Any minute now I could be knocking on heaven's gate. You dare to make light of my illness?"

"Heaven, father? And yes, I dare to question your doctor."

"You leave that poor man out of this."

"Why didn't you simply ask me to come home?"

Up went that brow again. "Without the American bride you're so convinced we need to establish Shelkova as a player in the world economy?"

Mark crossed his arms over his chest and planted his feet, giving his father a lazy grin. "Did I not come home with an American woman?"

Reynard's gleam was back, his own grin that of a man who knew his son had fallen prey to the Lakeland legend. Reynard's wife, Katrina, had captured him on their very first meeting, which had taken place during a fierce storm that had literally blown her into his arms. Mark knew the story. And though he had loved his mother with all his heart, he didn't like that his father was expecting him to perpetuate the legend.

Which he was, apparently. A king should be married, his father kept reminding him. And he should have babies—which very well might happen sooner than the old man would like.

Reynard had an open relationship with all of his sons, but Mark was his firstborn and heir apparent. Although Shelkova was slowly emerging as a sovereign nation, the Lakelands had been here for centuries as royalty but for the last several generations, during which time their reign had existed only in the hearts of the people.

Having been given the crown—and the power that came with it—within a week of Shelkova declaring its independence, four months ago Reynard had started insisting Mark take over. He didn't want to be king, or *czar* as the people fondly liked to call him; he wanted to advise but not lead. Their people needed a man with intelligence, charisma, and the energy of youth to drag them—kicking and screaming, if need be—into the twenty-first century.

Mark had been visiting with his father since he'd gotten home three hours ago. He'd chased everyone out of the room, then simply stared until Reynard's innocent look had turned disgruntled. And then they had hugged, long and silently and powerfully.

Then Mark had begun to talk.

Not about the two months he'd been away, but about the last six days. About the touch of an angel's lips that had saved him from a cold, watery grave. About a man named Silas and a truck named Manly. About a woman who limped and sneezed and threw tantrums, and an amazing pack he had then brought over and dumped on the bed.

His father had been duly impressed. "Take me to her," Reynard suddenly said, pushing back the covers and standing up.

"What?"

"Take me to meet my future daughter," Reynard repeated, rubbing his hands together. "She sounds like she'll make a fine queen."

Mark snorted. "A queen who thinks she's nobody. Besides, I didn't say anything about marrying her," he said just to goad him. "She's here for her own protection."

Reynard raised a brow. "You apparently couldn't even

protect the woman's virginity—which is why I will be making sure it doesn't happen again until *after* the wedding."

"She will give you a real stroke, old man, within a week."

Donning his robe, Reynard looked for his slippers and then started for the door without them. "I handled your mother just fine; I believe I can handle a mere slip of an angel."

"Dad, it's after midnight and that angel's asleep, drugged to her eyeballs," Mark reminded him, only to follow him from the room with a loud, audible sigh.

"I just want to peek."

And peek they did, as they stood at her bedside smiling like fools. Mark pulled the blankets up to Jane's chin and Reynard adjusted her pillow, using the excuse to brush her wildly curling hair from her face. The woman murmured something unintelligible and swatted at the air, making them both jump back.

Mark smiled. "They have plenty of mosquitoes in Maine, I believe. Any disturbance makes her swat at them instinctively," he whispered.

"She's beautiful," Reynard said softly, sounding pleased.

"Then tell her that. Often. She doesn't know it, apparently, and refuses to believe me when I tell her."

"I certainly will," Reynard said thickly. He took hold of Mark's arm and pulled him into the hall. "Well, what do we do with her now?" he asked as he quietly closed the door.

"Let her heal. Teach her to love our country too much to leave. Give her . . . importance."

"But no babies," Reynard ordered. "Your firstborn will be timely."

"Jane hopes she's already pregnant."

"Well, Markov, you had better hope she's not. Your people would likely accept your not marrying a virgin, but I doubt they're modern-minded enough for your bride to be pregnant when she says her vows." Reynard headed down the hall with a decided spring in his step. "Now go to bed. You look like hell."

Having spent five full days holed up in a monstrous bedroom with an attached bathroom bigger than her last manager's cabin, being catered to by a nurse and various . . . staff, Jane finally had to admit she was hiding. Heck, she'd figured that out three days ago. Mark probably had, too, although he was smart enough not to come right out and say it. The sharp, jabbing pain in her shoulder had grown to a persistent dull ache and her cold was completely gone, but Jane kept telling anyone within earshot she was still too weak to venture out of the room, torturing herself and probably not fooling a soul.

Mark visited her at least twice a day, but never stayed long; she assumed because he had a lot of . . . prince stuff to do.

She missed him. And she didn't like that, because she really didn't want to like *him*.

She couldn't know yet if she was pregnant, but that didn't stop her from hoping. And with nothing else to do for five boring days than imagine herself holding her very own baby, Jane had decided if she wasn't already pregnant she was going to find a doctor who could find her some sperm just as soon as she got home. Oh yeah, she wanted a baby more than anything now; a child she could love and cherish and would never, *ever* abandon like unwanted trash.

It hadn't been until she'd started kindergarten that Jane had realized most kids lived with their parents, and she'd asked the sisters at Saint Xavier's how come she lived with them and not her own mom and dad. Obviously prepared for the question—Jane was one of six girls at the orphanage at the time—Sister Roberta had explained that the social worker thought her dad must have died and her mom hadn't been able to raise an infant by herself, but had loved her baby so much that she'd given her up to their care. But having lived with the idea of being pregnant for almost a week now, Jane knew the only way she'd ever give up her child was if someone pried it out of her cold dead hands.

Even though she'd blurted out her hope to Mark that morning on the aircraft carrier, she wasn't so naive as to think she'd really get pregnant the very first time she had sex—Sister Roberta's dire warnings notwithstanding. And despite her friend Katy swearing that several of her MacKeage cousins had gotten pregnant the first time they'd made love to their future husbands, Jane was pretty sure her best bet was artificial insemination. But for that to happen she had to get out of here; first out of this room before she went stir-crazy, then out of Shelkova. Which might be easier said than done, since her checkbook and credit cards had blown up with her car, and she only had about seventy-five dollars in her backpack—wherever the heck that was.

Was there an American embassy in Shelkova?

Well, she guessed the only way to find out was to *ask*, which meant she had to venture into the mainstream of Mark's home. She had to meet his father, too, but she'd been avoiding that little duty as well. It had been one thing to meet *just Mark*'s father, but another to be meeting a real live *king*. And so she'd been telling Mark every day when he asked that she was in no shape to meet anyone yet.

Okay, then; the door was right there. And she knew it wasn't locked, because she'd tried it the first time she'd gotten out of bed four days ago. She'd done a little snooping after and found her brace and some clothes in the wardrobe. The clothes were elegant and they fit, but wearing them made her self-conscious. She wasn't sure, but thought the blouse was silk. She'd never touched silk that she could remember, being more of a fleece and flannel person.

So all dressed up in borrowed clothes, her hair combed but not braided, and with the sling Dr. Daveed had given her cradling her tender left arm (the one she needed for *everything*), all she had to do was walk out of her self-imposed prison. Jane walked to the small desk between two tall windows instead, pulled out the chair and sat down, then stared at the ornate telephone just like she had at least five times a day for the last four days. She knew it worked, because she'd forced herself to pick up the receiver three days ago and had heard a dial tone. Heck, she'd actually dialed Katy's cell phone yesterday, but had quickly hung up when she heard it ring and realized the call had gone through.

She hadn't had any idea what to say then, and still didn't.

Hi, Katy, it's me, your in-really-big-trouble, really dumb friend. What's that? No, I'm pretty sure you're going to agree with me this time. You see, I fished this really handsome guy out of a pond when his plane crashed, then tried to help him get home to his sick father. Only I got myself kidnapped, dragged onto a lobster boat, then a submarine, then an aircraft carrier—which I was catapulted off of—then flown over the North Pole to a fairly new country on the other side of the world called Shelkova. Oh, and that home the guy was trying to get to is a PALACE, and his sick father is a KING.

Jane figured she'd be shouting that last part, what with Katy laughing so hard.

Wait, it gets even better. Did I mention I made love to my kidnapper, who just happens to be a PRINCE, when we were on the aircraft carrier? Yeah, that should sober her friend. *After which,* she would rush on into the sudden silence, *I got shot in the shoulder for pointing my shotgun at him in front of an entire ship of sailors sworn to protect him.*

Jane picked up the receiver, dialed Katy's cell phone and listened to a series of clicks and beeps, then took a deep breath and forced herself not to hang up when she heard it ringing.

"Hello?" Katy said hesitantly on the third ring, apparently not recognizing the number.

"It's me, Jane."

Silence. Then a squeal. "Jane! Ohmigod, you're alive! Where in hell are you?"

Darn, it felt good to hear a familiar voice. "I'm in Shelkova."

"Shel-what? Is that near Stonington? Because I hope you know I've been going crazy trying to reach you ever since Silas called to tell me a stranger brought back his truck a couple of days after he lent it to *you*. I thought he'd started drinking again when he said you showed up out of the blue with some foreign guy you were helping get to Deere Isle."

"Shelkova is a country across the Bering Sea from Alaska."

Silence again, and then a whispered, "Please tell me *you're* drunk."

"Sorry," Jane said on a sigh. "Remember that article in the *Pine Lake Weekly Gazette* last month about a prince who was in America looking for a bride? Well, the foreign man Silas said I was with is Prince Markov Lakeland of Shelkova . . . Hello? Katy, are you still there?" Jane asked, afraid they'd been cut off when she couldn't even hear any breathing.

"So help me God," Katy said softly, "if you tell me you ran off with some guy claiming to be a prince from a two-bit country that isn't even on the map yet, I swear I'm getting on the next plane and—"

"No! That's not—"

"AND," Katy shouted, cutting her off, "I am kicking your stupid ass all the way home. I thought you were dead! A hunter found the burned-out remains of your car in the woods, and Silas said the last time he saw you was when you drove off with some guy to Stonington *eleven freaking days ago*. I keep calling the game wardens, the sheriff, and the state police. Hell, I even have Robbie and Jack looking for you."

Katy had asked her brother to search? Jane knew Robbie used to be in the military, in special ops or something, and she'd always been a little afraid and a lot in awe of the quiet giant. And Jack Stone, Pine Creek's police chief and some relation to Katy, was legendary for finding people, whether they were lost in the woods or hiding in some city halfway around the world.

"I'm sorry for scaring you," Jane cut in when Katy stopped her little tirade to take a deep breath. "Did anyone happen to find a floatplane sitting upside down in a pond two or three miles east of where my car was found?"

"A plane? No, I haven't heard anything about anyone finding a plane. So what happened to your car, anyway?"

"The men in the second plane who shot down the floatplane blew it up."

"Huh? Dammit, you *are* drunk. Just tell me where you are and I'll come get you."

"I'm on the other side of the world," Jane snapped. She took a calming breath. "If you will kindly listen without interrupting, I'll explain everything. And then you can help me figure out how to get home."

"Oh, I'll help you, all right," Katy said, the growl in her voice making Jane smile. "Even if it means having to kick your dumb ass across an entire continent and freaking ocean. I thought you were *dead*."

"I'm sorry," Jane repeated, her smile vanishing when that last part came out in an anguished whisper. "I should have called you five days ago."

"*Eleven* days ago," Katy said, trying but failing to put the growl back in her voice.

"I . . . I wasn't exactly in a position to call you then." Jane took another deep breath, then began her tale with her minding her own business out partridge hunting one last time before moving—which Katy had been sad about but resigned to—and continued right through to picking up the phone this afternoon. She left nothing out; not the part about her waking up in the woods to find Mark's hand on her breast, or about having sex with him and foolishly hoping she was pregnant, or stupidly pointing her shotgun at him in front of a ship full of sailors.

Heck, she even confessed to losing her temper when she'd found out Mark was a prince, and that she'd cussed for real and punched some poor innocent sailor in the belly.

Katy never interrupted once during the long-winded tale, even though hearing herself relating one outrageous detail after another made Jane realize she *did* sound drunk. She finally ended by explaining she was healed enough to go home now, only she wasn't sure how one went about reentering the country without a passport. "And I'd rather not create an international incident by walking into the American embassy—assuming they have one here—and saying Mark kidnapped me."

"Then I guess that means you're gonna have to stay put," Katy said, not even the hint of a growl in her voice.

Jane went momentarily silent. "Did you get the part about my being kidnapped? And being dragged from boat to boat against my will? And about getting *shot*?"

"I think we both agree your getting shot was your

fault," Katy said dryly. "As for being kidnapped, did you really expect the guy to leave a woman who had just saved his life to the mercy of his assassins?"

"You're taking *his* side?"

"I'm sorry, have we met? I'm Katherine MacBain, but you can call me Katy. Oh, and all these towering males constantly popping up around me? They're my overprotective brothers and cousins who are always acting like asses for my own good." A very unladylike snort came over the line. "Brody's home on leave, and I kid you not—last week he tossed me over his shoulder right in the middle of Pete's Bar and Grill when he overheard some idiot ask if I wanted to take a moonlight drive to go look for moose." And then a sigh. "Your prince may have taken the *I'm doing this for your own good* thing to the extreme, but . . . I'm sorry, I'm glad he did. Because Silas also told me," she rushed on when Jane tried to interrupt, "that the day after you left, three guys showed up looking for a tall man who spoke with a Russian accent who might be traveling with a local woman. Si said they also had heavy accents, only different, and that they were hard-looking bastards that he wouldn't trust any farther than he could spit. So he told them a man and woman had come through the day before and hitched a ride to Milo with some trucker."

"Are you serious?" Jane whispered.

"If they were the men in the plane who shot down Mark and blew up your car," Katy continued softly, "you truly were in danger. And if he hadn't forced you to go with him, you could have . . . We might not be having this . . ." A shuddering sigh came over the line. "Damn,

Jane, there's a good chance I might never have seen your beautiful face again."

Holy heck, Mark hadn't been exaggerating. "Even so, I can't just stay here."

"Sure you can. You saved the man's life, so now let him save yours."

"But what if I am pregnant?"

"All the more reason to stay put—at least until the Lakelands have dealt with their enemies. Why endanger your child when you're probably in the safest place on the planet right now? And from what you told me, it sounds like your prince has a bad case of the guilts, so why not take advantage of his hospitality?"

"Maybe because I don't belong here? I feel like I landed on another planet. The clothes in my closet are made of *silk*. My food is served on bone china, and I have a private nurse and three *maids*. And all the sailors kept *bowing* to me."

A heavy groan came over the line. "You belong wherever you are. I don't care if you're in a sporting lodge or a city or a freaking palace—you *belong*. And if you do come home," Katy continued, the growl in her voice again, "I am personally kicking your ass *back* to Shelkova."

"You're gonna need a bigger boot," Jane snapped, unable to believe her friend was taking Mark's side.

All that got her was another snort. "I'm pretty sure we established back in third grade, when we decided Jason Biggs needed to stop calling Cindy Pace *Creepy Four-eyes*, that you fight about as well as you cuss."

"I still have the scar from where he *bit* me," Jane shot back. "And are you forgetting I gave him a bloody nose?"

"The *tree* he ran into gave him that bloody nose when

he saw Sister Roberta headed toward us decked out in her full uniform of God."

"I had to say two novenas," Jane reminded her. "One for fighting and one for saying it was my idea to ambush Jason on his way home from school. That's eighteen days of my life I'll never get back, and to thank me for not ratting you out you tell me to *stay put*?"

"Oh, no, you don't. You're not playing that guilt card again. We agreed the statute of limitations is once every five years, and this is your second time in six months."

"Eighteen days," Jane said softly, fighting to keep the smile out of her voice. Oh, yeah; they didn't make friends like Katy MacBain anymore. "On my knees. In a dark, musty chapel."

"Then we're even, because I just spent eleven days *thinking you were dead*."

She might not be able to whoop Katy physically, but Jane won more of their battles of will than she lost. "During the warmest spring in years. I missed the town Easter egg hunt."

Silence again, and then what sounded like a sigh of surrender. "I tell you what; give me your phone number and let me talk to Robbie and Jack about what you should do."

"Thank you," Jane whispered, her sigh one of relief.

"But you need to understand," Katy quickly added, "that if they decide Mark Lakeland is one of the good guys, there's a good chance they're also going to tell you to stay put. Especially if it turns out you are pregnant. Because," she rushed on over Jane's gasp, "men don't like sticking their noses in other men's business unless they suspect there's abuse."

"You can't tell them I might be pregnant! They'll know I had sex. With a virtual stranger, no less. I'll never be able to show my face in Pine Creek again."

"I won't have to tell them," Katy said with a chuckle. "They'll assume if Mark wasn't . . . oh, let's go with *interested* in you that way, then he would have dropped you off at the nearest police station, thanked you for saving his life, and gone on his merry way."

"Bound and gagged," Jane persisted. "Dragged down into a submarine. Shot."

"Did he rape you?"

"No!"

"Did your poor repressed hormones finally explode and you raped him?"

"No! It was . . . Neither one of us . . . It just happened!"

"Then congratulations, Miss Abbot," Katy drawled. "You may officially call yourself a woman now. Oh, and welcome to the twenty-first century."

"So you're going to church and lighting candles for me to shorten my time in purgatory for having sex with a man I wasn't married to?"

"Hell, no. I'm going to buy you a case of condoms. Come on, Jane," Katy said, lowering her voice to a sultry whisper, "now that you know what you've been missing, aren't you anxious to do it again?"

Jane toyed with the phone cord. "Not particularly."

Silence, and then, "First times for anything are always awkward. I promise the next time will be better."

"I doubt it was Mark's first time. And judging by his reaction, there isn't going to be a next time—at least not with him. He's been coming to visit me every day and . . .

and he hasn't even tried to kiss me again. He just sits in a chair beside my bed and tells me stories about how his father met his mother—she died five years ago—and how his grandfather met his grandmother, and how other Lakeland men met their wives. And then he asks about *my* family."

"And what have you told him?" Katy asked softly.

"What I tell everyone; that I grew up in a big old drafty house with a bunch of sisters."

"You do know that little prevarication is going to catch up with you one of these days, don't you?"

"But not today. And definitely not with Mark. I need to get out of here, Katy. Now. I wasn't putting myself down earlier; I truly don't belong here. And if I can leave while Mark still thinks of me as the angel who saved his life, I will always be somebody special to him. And to his father and brothers. Heck, probably even to the people of Shelkova."

"Time isn't going to change that fact, Jane. Do you really think the guy would care if it was an angel or an orphan who pulled him out of that plane?"

"I'm pretty sure he'll care about making a baby with a woman who has no business being the mother of a future king or queen."

"Another fact that won't change," Katy growled in obvious frustration. "Not if you're already pregnant." And then she sighed. "You're not winning this one, Jane. Because as much as it pains me, I have to side with Robbie and Jack if they feel you're better off staying put. Give me your number and I'll call you after I talk to them."

"I don't have a number," Jane snapped. "I just picked up the phone in my room and dialed. I'll have to call you."

"Okay. But give me a couple of days. And while my guys are checking out your guy," she added brightly, "I'll see if I can't overnight you some condoms. I should be able to send them to Jane Abbot, care of The Palace in Shelkova, don't you think?"

"I think you're insane," Jane whispered, fighting a smile. Geesh, if she'd called the moment she'd spotted the phone, she could have saved herself five days of wondering how to tell her best friend what really big—and possibly pregnant—trouble she was in.

Oh yeah; no one could turn a mountain into a molehill like Miss Silver Lining MacBain.

"And while you're waiting for them," Katy persisted, "you get your beautiful angel ass out of that room and scope out the palace—specifically where Prince Charming sleeps. And you sneak into his bed just like he did yours. But not until *after* the condoms arrive."

"Oh, I'll scope out the palace, all right, looking for a chapel," Jane drawled back, letting her smile break free. "And then I'm lighting every candle in there to shorten *your* stay in purgatory. You do know encouraging someone to sin is a sin, don't you?"

"We'll keep each other company," Katy said with a chuckle, only to go silent. "Be your smart, courageous self, Jane," she said, suddenly serious. "Keep that temper in check and don't point any weapons at anyone. And please, for me, could you at least try to enjoy yourself?"

"I . . . I'll try."

"I love you. And I'm so very glad you're alive."

"Yeah, me, too. Except I love you *more*," Jane added

loudly, hearing her friend's snort as she gently set the receiver down on the ornate cradle.

Jane then walked to the window and stood staring out at the ocean as she tried to decide how she felt about Katy's revelation that three men had showed up at Twelve Mile Camp the day after they'd left. Okay, then; it would appear Mark really had been saving her life.

But why make love to her? It's not like she was some raving beauty who turned men to lustful idiots with just a smile. Well, not *sober* men, anyway. Really; she didn't even own lipstick. And she dressed like a guy. She could out-shoot and outfish them, too. She couldn't dance, but she could run a fully loaded canoe down class IV rapids without cracking an egg. She'd never eaten at a restaurant that had more than one fork and knife and spoon at a setting, but she could fry up a mean dish of trout and fiddleheads over an open fire. And last she knew, eau de fish guts wasn't exactly a come-hither scent, any more than wet wool was.

Jane leaned her forehead on the window. Geesh, she had to have looked like something the cat dragged home the night Mark had made love to her, considering her nose had been running like a river, she'd been so hot with fever she hadn't even bothered to sleep in her shirt, and she was pretty sure croaking bullfrogs sounded sexier.

So why would a prince looking for an American bride crawl into bed with a backcountry nobody? Because really; even orphans knew better than to believe in *family legends.*

Chapter Nine

＊ ⋯ ＊

She was in a palace. She knew that. She'd surmised that fact from what she could see from her bedroom window. Oh, but what a grand place this must have been generations ago; although the furnishings appeared of high quality and everything was spotless, it was obvious the Lakelands hadn't gone crazy spending their emerging country's money on frivolous restorations. Heck, just the hallway was a study in architecture, history, and old wealth. The walls were stenciled in slightly faded but still rich colors, lined with paintings and artifacts and . . . and a note, if she wasn't mistaken—addressed to her!

Jane walked across the hall and carefully pulled the beige envelope with a green border off the wall. On closer inspection, the border was a small forest of fir and pine trees. On the back was what appeared to be a royal crest, made up of more trees and gold lettering that said *Lakeland*. She carefully pulled out the card inside.

If you are well enough to leave the palace grounds, I will consider you well enough to—
    Well, don't make me have to come after you, angel.

                                                    Love,
                                                    Mark

Seriously? Jane came within an inch of tearing the thing to shreds, but stopped and pressed the card to her chest instead. As love notes went, it lacked a little something, but it was from Mark *to her*. And he'd signed it with the one word she'd given up hope of ever seeing addressed to her. Although he'd only used her name on the envelope and not the note itself, Jane decided to keep it. No matter that he hadn't meant it that way, she would show it to their child someday, if they'd made one.

Spinning back toward her room to put the note away, Jane got another surprise. On a table beside her door was a small bouquet of flowers and another beige envelope bordered by green trees. Pulling out the card and reading it, Jane smiled, then sighed, then giggled. This note was from Reynard Lakeland, and said these flowers were for a pretty little angel who knew how to breathe life into a man.

Jane decided Mark's father could say she was pretty because he'd never seen her, and she was keeping this card as well. Picking up the flowers and giving them an appreciative sniff, she reentered her room and set both notes and the vase on a bureau. And on a whim, she pulled a flower free and tucked it in her hair like Sister Patricia used to do whenever Jane was feeling sad with herself.

So with a silly smile on her face, she ventured into the big, scary world of Markov Lakeland. Holding her head high, Jane limped down the hall as if she belonged there while silently appreciating the beautiful surroundings. She'd gleaned from the maids and nurse who had paraded through her room, all of them speaking broken but adequate English, that this palace had once been the Lakeland seat of power generations ago. Several tall doors lined the hall, all of them closed to the contents they housed. Jane ignored them all, wanting to get outside to the fresh air and the sea that had been beckoning her for the last five days. But it was a trying task; the rabbit warren of halls was seemingly endless.

It was a frustrating ten minutes before she found the stairs, which appeared wide enough to hold an entire orchestra; long and carpeted and impressive in that they opened up to a gigantic foyer that made the White House look like a log cabin. But across the foyer was the door to freedom, and Jane took the steps at a rushing pace despite her weak ankle, having developed a rhythm for stairs at an early age in order to keep up with the other children of Saint Xavier's.

She would have made it, too, if the three men hadn't crossed her path just as she reached the bottom step. She ran headlong with a grunt into the first man, knocking him into the second and forcing him to grab her shoulders to steady her.

Jane yelped as his hand wrapped over her wound. He

immediately let her go, only to grab her waist when she started to fall. He saved her by smashing her nose to his chest, pinning her sling-covered arm between them and wrapping his arms around her.

"Ho, what is this I've caught?" he chuckled, giving her a squeeze. "Could it be an angel that's flown into our midst?" he asked over the top of her head.

"This angel is going to bite you if you don't let me go," she said into his shirt.

That got her a chuckle. "Ah, Sergei, an angel with teeth."

Deciding the bite threat was a little risky, Jane instead pinched him right on the fat of his side, only to feel solid flesh—she was suddenly glad she hadn't bit him. He did release her, though. She took a step back and looked up into Mark's eyes but not Mark's face. This face was younger, far less serious, and *almost* as handsome.

The man wrapped his hands around his waist and bowed deeply. "My apologies, angel, for bumping into you," he said, still bowed.

"Th-that's okay." Jane looked at the two men accompanying him, and *they* smiled and bowed. But not until she'd seen their eyes, which were also exact duplicates of Mark's.

"Please," the first man entreated as he straightened. "Let me introduce myself. I am Alexi, youngest brother to Markov. And this smiling fool is my brother Dmitri, the next youngest. And Sergei here has the privileged distinction of being Reynard's second son."

Jane could only stare at the three obvious devils acting like civilized men. And they were all Lakelands!

Dmitri picked up the flower that had fallen from her hair, and, smiling like the devil himself, carefully tucked it back in her hair. "And you must be Mark's beautiful angel, Jane Abbot of Maine, giver of life and owner of that wondrous pack we have heard about," he said, giving her a mischievous wink.

Still stupidly staring, Jane blushed to the roots of her unbraided hair.

"I am sorry I hurt you," Alexi apologized. "I did not stop to think."

"That's okay," Jane repeated to his chest. His physically fit chest. She could see now that there was no fat anyplace—on any of them.

"Where is it that you were going in such a hurry?" Sergei asked.

"Just outside."

"May we escort you someplace?"

Not in this lifetime. Not you three devils. "I think I'll . . . ah . . . I was looking for a bathroom first."

"I will show you," Sergei offered, gesturing in the direction *away* from freedom.

Just wanting to get any door between herself and these gorgeous specimens of manhood, Jane rushed ahead, nearly tripping when her ankle faltered. Sergei quickly took her right arm and tucked it in his, then led her down another hall as the others followed.

Jane was mortified. Three men were escorting her to the *bathroom* as if they were taking her to high tea. And she was facing another stupid, endless hall. But at least this one was on the ground floor. Heck, she could jump to freedom.

Which is exactly what she did just as soon as she closed the door on their smiling faces. Jane ran over and threw open the window. It was only a five-foot drop, no worse than most boulders she scaled in the course of a hike. Not feeling the least bit guilty, and wishing she could be a fly on the wall when the men realized she wasn't coming back out, Jane slid a leg over the ledge and, with one-armed awkwardness, jumped to freedom.

Jane spent a good hour walking the cliffs and watching the sea churn up foam against the rocks below. Seagulls, birds of the world, soared on the wind and gave her a spectacular aerial show, their soothing caws slowly un-frazzling the tension of the last eleven days.

But the horizon finally darkened with the encroaching night, forcing Jane to return to her gilded sanctuary. She reentered by way of a door set into the side of the house. No, *palace*. But it did seem to be a home, with a father and at least four sons. Jane was pretty sure the Lakelands could live in a shack and still be a strong, close family, and she envied them that gift.

Her first mistake was not looking to see what room she was entering. Her second was not checking to see if it was occupied. It was; by an older man with white hair, broad shoulders, and the eyes of his sons.

"Oh, I'm sorry. I didn't realize this was . . . That you were . . . I'm sorry. I'll just go out and try again."

"Please don't run away, Miss Abbot," Reynard Lakeland said. He set down the book he'd been reading and stood, extending his hand. "Come sit and talk to this old man." His eyes took on a shine. "Or are you anxious to face my four disgruntled sons?"

"You're not old. Your Highness," she tacked on. "And your disgruntled sons don't scare me." She frowned. "Four?"

Reynard Lakeland laughed. "Once those poor, unsuspecting boys decided you weren't coming out, they ran to Mark with tales of an angel who had flown away on ungrateful wings."

Jane could picture the three princes running and complaining like pouting children.

"So come sit with me, child, that I may thank you for letting me keep my eldest son," Reynard entreated, motioning to two chairs facing each other beside a large, marbled hearth.

Jane felt herself turning red. "I didn't really do anything," she said, conceding to the slight plea in his voice and taking a seat across from him. As soon as she sat, so did he. Jane had been around a lot of men, but none with manners like the Lakelands. They had a way of making a woman feel . . . special. And her uncomfortable.

"According to my son, you dove into the cold water of a pond and pulled him free of his wrecked plane. Is this a frequent habit of yours?"

"No. I mean no, Your Highness."

"I am no longer a 'Highness,'" the man told her. "In two weeks, I will be just Reynard."

"You don't even get an honorary title? After being a king?"

"Well, maybe," he admitted. "But I have been king for

only three years. I'm more used to *Reynard*. Will you accommodate me on this, Miss Abbot?"

She gave him a smile, letting him know she knew what he was doing. "Okay, Reynard. If you call me Jane."

"I've been told you're a perceptive woman." He suddenly scowled. "You are chilled. Shall I call for a fire to be set? We have a couple of hours before dinner."

"Oh, I can do it." Jane jumped up, glad for something to do. "I love building fires," she explained by way of apology at his surprised look.

He leaned back on a sigh. "I suppose you do. Will you tell me about yourself, Jane?"

Kneeling in front of the large hearth, she turned and gave him a wary look, Reynard noticed. She was shy and perceptive and compassionate, just as Mark had told him. And she was beautiful, her cheeks rosy from her walk and maybe a little blushing. Her hair was a mess of windblown knots, and she was self-conscious, running her fingers through the tangles while trying to be discreet about it. The clothes fit, although they were outdated by several years. They had been Katrina's, and Jane was just her size. And just as beautiful, and as alive with a zest and innocence that rendered a man helpless to her charm. Lord, he wished Katrina could be here to see how well her son had chosen. She would approve.

Reynard watched with amusement and no little amazement as Jane awkwardly but confidently assembled a log tower of kindling over paper, lit a match to it, then leaned several logs against it. With only one hand available, the woman was still able to make the task a simple undertaking. Her face awash with the glow of the flames, she dusted her hand on her pants and leaned back, putting her weight on her good leg.

As Mark had said—repeatedly—she was a capable woman, comfortable with what she knew. But she was not comfortable with him or with praise or with her position here. It was obvious in the way she surreptitiously looked around the room, her eyes filling with awe whenever she spied something strange or opulent.

"You have a beautiful home," she said, looking back over her shoulder.

"It belongs to Shelkova, not to us. They have kept it intact and beautiful, hoping for the day it would be lived in again as it should be."

"Your family has been a part of Shelkova's history for centuries?"

"Yes. And now we will be again."

"It's an awesome undertaking, isn't it, being responsible for an entire nation?"

"It can be. But it is also rewarding. The people take care of themselves for the most part. We have a parliament and the people all have a voice. It was their voice that put us back in this house. Shelkova is a sotto-democracy in many ways, but unlike in England, there is a need for a figurehead who can have the recognition and clout to establish our country as an economic part of the world. As king I was able to make trade agreements and pacts, using only my word for collateral. And soon, Markov will be making those decisions."

"Heavens! I've been sitting here like a dead stump. I haven't asked how you're feeling. Mark said you had a small stroke," she finished on a shy whisper.

"Yes, minor," Reynard agreed with a chuckle. "Enough to make me give up my throne."

"And you're better now?"

"Yes. I am better."

"I'm glad. Mark was worried and in a hurry to get home to you."

"He is a most dutiful son. And a very special man."

Reynard wasn't sure, but he thought she gave a little snort under her breath. She set more logs on the crackling fire, then finally got up and came back to her seat.

"Now, I believe you were going to tell me about yourself," he reminded her, smiling at her frown.

"I believe you would be bored, Your—Reynard. I grew up in the woods of Maine, which isn't all that exciting, and worked for sporting camps most of my adult life. And then one day while I was out hunting partridge, your son fell out of the sky and into a pond I happened to be passing. That's it."

In a nutshell, Reynard decided; a very guarded nutshell that would take a great deal of effort to crack. And patience and cunning and trust. "How is your shoulder healing?"

"Fine," she said, blushing again through a sheepish smile. "I did a very foolish thing."

"And then you did a wondrous thing by forgiving the man who shot you, making him a hero in the eyes of his shipmates. That was a very noble thing to do."

"Noble? Dorjan was just following orders to protect your son. I'm fortunate the man is good with a gun."

"And you, Jane? Are you good with a gun?"

Her blush deepened. "I usually hit what I'm aiming at."

"And you know when a gun is loaded or not?" he prodded.

"I've carried that particular shotgun over many miles in the last twelve years. It was a gift to me from my foster parents. I can tell if it is loaded just by the weight of it."

Reynard noted the mention of the people who had raised her. Not her blood parents. He also noted her little chin rising defensively as she obviously wondered where this conversation was leading. And he noted she was tiring from her first journey from her bed. "You were never taught not to threaten what you can't back up?" he asked. "That pointing an empty gun is a dangerous bluff?"

That chin rose higher. "I was angry and wanted to make a point. Your son was dragging me from one ship to the next and halfway across the world."

"Mark just snatched you away without explaining why?" Reynard persisted. "Without explaining the danger to you if you stayed in Maine?"

Her chin lowered slightly. "He said something about not wanting to leave me, that he felt . . . guilty." She raised her chin again. "I can take care of myself. I don't need his guilt or pity."

"Pity! You think Markov pities you?" Reynard choked out, only to laugh at her scowl. "My daughter, the last thing my son feels for you is pity. In fact, I believe he'd like to throttle you most of the time." He cocked his head at her startled look. "What surprises you more—that Markov would like to throttle you, or that I called you daughter?"

She snorted. "I know what your son would like to do to me, since he threatens it enough." She suddenly smiled. "Not that he ever would—or could." She shook her head. "Only weak men use their strength against women, and your son definitely isn't weak. He's all bluster." Then she frowned. "And I'm no one's daughter."

Well, that was telling. More than she realized, Reynard guessed. He smiled warmly. "But I have always wanted to say the word. I have always wished for a daughter."

"You have only sons?"

"Four," he confirmed, nodding. "Lakeland men are destined to only have sons."

Reynard watched Jane's good hand slide to her stomach, his claim apparently making her wonder about the child she hoped to be carrying. And she appeared pleased with the idea of having a son, if the small upward curve of her lips was any indication. Lord, she'd really blush if she knew he was aware of that possibility. "You are tired. Why don't you go have a rest, and I'll come get you in a couple of hours and escort you to dinner," he suggested, standing up and reaching for her good hand.

"Thank you, but I should eat in my room."

"No. You are well enough to sit with us tonight. We have some guests from Europe; a businessman has brought his daughter to visit in hopes of catching the eye of the new king of Shelkova," he explained, looking for some reaction—which he certainly got. Jane Abbot exposed her thoughts in a telling, ferocious scowl.

"I . . . I don't think I should be there," she hedged, patting her tangled hair with her good hand. "I would be out of place. Mark will want to give a good impression to this businessman. And his daughter," she tacked on in a mutter. "I should eat in my room like I've been doing."

"Nonsense," he shot back, realizing everything Markov had told him about Jane's self-esteem was sadly true. "I'll sit beside you," he cajoled. "We can watch the proceedings from the foot of the table and whisper behind our hands."

"You would sit at the foot of the table? But you're still king."

"Who in two weeks will be a mere man again, Jane, so why not take advantage of my position now to sit wherever I please?"

"We would be a long way from Mark and his . . . guests?"

"Yes."

"I did see something rather pretty in my wardrobe. Do you suppose I should wear it?"

"That is why the clothes are there. Mark told me yours . . . blew up."

Her smile widened. "Trust me, it wasn't a great loss. I was planning on buying new clothes for my new life, anyway."

"New life?"

"I mean for when I got a new job down on the Maine coast, which was where I was heading when I met your son."

"I see," Reynard murmured, indeed seeing a lot. Mark had told him of his suspicion that Jane was running from something. It would have to be something big to make her leave her woods. "Then dress in the pretty clothes after you rest, and I will be at your door in two hours," he said, leading her out into the hall.

"Ah, can you tell me how to get to my room? I'm liable to end up in the kitchens."

"Wait here," Reynard told her, going back in the library and coming out with a book. "This is a history of the palace. You'll find several maps in it," he informed her, tucking the book under her good arm and then placing his hand at her back. "Come. I will show you the way today, so you won't end up in the kitchens, as Cook is liable to toss you a dishcloth and put you to work. Not that you look the part," he quickly added when he saw her frown and realized he'd just insulted the woman by telling her she looked like a dishwasher. Lord, the poor girl's ego was fragile, if even existent. "Cook would put me to work if I dared venture in. And don't ever try to steal any tarts, or you'll find yourself missing some fingers."

Still looking skeptical, Jane stopped and turned to him. "You shouldn't be walking the stairs, should you? You've been ill. Just tell me the way and I'll be fine."

"I most certainly can and will take you to your room. I'm supposed to exercise," he quickly added, feeling his neck heat to a dull red. "But thank you for your concern."

And that was that, the retired king decided. Now he had to go find Irina and tell her the new seating arrangements for dinner tonight, as he wanted a good seat for the fireworks.

Chapter Ten

❖ · ❖

Jane's bedroom door opened and a woman who definitely wasn't staff walked in. "I've brought you a dress, Miss Abbot," the fiftyish woman said. "And shoes. We dress for dinner," she continued, her gaze settling on Jane's old boots peeking out from beneath her slacks. "And I brought some stockings."

"I see."

The woman's hair was neatly tucked into an intricate bun at the back of her head, and she wasn't any taller than Jane, her figure trim and her eyes blue and intense. She didn't look like a Lakeland, although she spoke with an air of authority, her mannerism and very aura suggesting a person sit up and listen to what she was saying. But having grown up with more than one formidable nun looking over her shoulder, Jane had learned a few tricks to pluck the thorns from such a woman's mien.

Jane turned her smile to full power. "I'm Jane Abbot," she said, offering her hand.

"Aunt Irina," the woman said, seemingly startled as she held out her hand holding the shoes. Irina flushed, setting the shoes on the floor and the dress on the bed. "You have to hurry. His Highness will be arriving soon to escort you to dinner," she instructed as she walked over and opened the wardrobe.

"It's very nice of you to bring me the dress," Jane said, still smiling warmly. "But I'm afraid I can't wear it. Or the shoes."

"Can't?" Irina asked, obviously surprised by the calmly given refusal. "But you must. You can't wear pants to dinner. It's not done."

"Then I will have to miss dinner," Jane said, still smiling and still calm.

"But you must," Irina repeated, her voice rising. "Reynard said you would." Her eyes suddenly narrowed. "You are American, so it is understandable you don't realize the honor you've been given."

Jane's smile began to falter. "I realize the honor," she softly told the instructing woman. "But if you don't wish Reynard to be embarrassed, then I'll either wear pants or not go at all."

"You mean 'His Majesty,' don't you?" Irina corrected.

"Whatever," Jane shot back, her smile completely gone. "Whatever you want to call the man, I'm not going to dinner wearing a dress. Look," she said on a sigh. "I wear a brace on my right leg that reaches from my knee to my heel. I don't wear dresses because it's not a pretty brace, and I can't wear those shoes because they won't fit over it."

The woman slowly nodded as her gaze traveled to Jane's right foot. "Oh. I see. Well, then, we'll just have to . . ." Irina walked to the chair by the window and sat down, absently staring at Jane's leg. But her mind was obviously somewhere else—in some closet, likely. So Jane sat on the bed and patiently waited.

"I have a pair of shoes that would be fashionable," Irina offered, still vacantly looking at Jane. "They would go better with those slacks." She sighed. "But you will be the first woman since Katrina to come to the table wearing pants." Her eyes turned distant. "Reynard's wife. My sister. She died five years ago."

"I'm sorry. I would have liked to meet Mark's mother."

"You mean 'His Highness'?" Irina corrected.

Jane waved her hand in the air. "Whatever."

Irina looked directly at Jane, a small smile tugging at the corner of her mouth. "Kat would have liked you, I believe. But enough. We've got to get you dressed for dinner," she went on, standing up and pulling on a long, embroidered ribbon of cloth.

"Is that a bellpull?" Jane asked excitedly. She already knew the answer, since one of the maids had told her how to get their attention, but Jane was determined to win over this woman. Aunt Irina would be much better as a friend than an enemy. "A real one? There's a bell ringing someplace in this building right now?"

"Yes. Of course," Irina said absently as she returned to the wardrobe and rummaged through the clothes. Jane had seen the dresses in it days ago, but had pushed them to the side. Irina pulled them out and placed them on the bed with the dress she'd brought, then fondly patted the garments. "These were Katrina's clothes," she said, to herself more than to Jane.

"Really? I'm borrowing a queen's clothes?" Jane asked, disconcerted. "But surely there are some others I could use. I don't wish to borrow from your sister."

Irina gave her a small smile. "She died a year and a half before Shelkova reemerged, so she was never a queen. And before you even arrived, Reynard asked me to put some of her clothes in here for you, since Markov told him you had none."

"Oh," was all Jane could say, feeling a flush climb into her cheeks. "I . . . All mine were destroyed." She made a face. "And I wasn't given much notice that I'd be taking a trip."

Someone knocked on the door and Irina answered it, spoke in Shelkovan to a maid, then came and sat down beside Jane on the bed, sighing again. "It's not going to matter, anyway. Whatever you wear is going to clash with that awful sling. You need it?"

"If I don't use it, the weight and movement of my arm pulls on my shoulder."

Cocking her head, Irina studied her arm, then suddenly got up and went to the wardrobe again. Getting on her knees, she rummaged in the lower drawers and came up with a large, beautiful scarf. Beaming now, she returned and carefully undid Jane's sling.

"Your blouse is cream-colored, and this scarf would look nice over it, don't you think?"

Jane didn't think anything, never having paid much attention to fashion. Wool pants came in gray and green, that was it. Flannel shirts and fleece were colorful, but more practical than fashionable.

"And the colors go nicely with your eyes," Irina continued, holding up the scarf and trying to arrange it into a sling.

"My eyes?" Jane repeated, never having thought much about them, either. They were just a plain gray—as plain as the rest of her.

"You have beautiful, expressive eyes, Miss Abbot, such a light, warm pewter."

Her eyes were pewter? Starting to like this woman, Jane smiled in appreciation. "Please, can you call me Jane?"

"Certainly," Irina agreed with a warm, returning smile. "And I am known in this house as Aunt Irina. To everybody, it seems," she said with a sigh.

"Irina's a pretty name. Would you mind terribly if I left off the 'Aunt'?" Jane asked, realizing the woman would like to be thought of as just herself.

"I'd like that," Irina returned. "I came to the Lakelands just before Katrina's passing and ended up staying when Reynard asked me to. He said this family needed a woman to counter all the . . . the . . ."

"Male arrogance?"

Irina giggled. "Yes, they can be a little high-handed, can they not? But they are good men. Even Alexi. And since we have moved to the palace, I've seen to the running of things. I don't know what I will do after Markov marries," she said softly, more to herself than to Jane.

"I'm sure his wife would value your help," Jane assured

her, placing her good hand on Irina's arm. "And I'm sure you two will become great friends. You could probably use the female companionship right about now, I would bet."

Giving her a startled look, Irina stopped fiddling with the scarf. "You would not mind my staying?"

Jane snorted. "If I had to be a queen, I'd latch on to your friendship with both hands. I can't imagine a worse fate. A good friend will be a saving grace for his wife. Truthfully, I pity the poor woman."

The strangest look came into Irina's eyes just then, and not one Jane could read for the life of her. Then a grin slowly tugged at the corner of the woman's mouth again before she gently turned Jane around and resumed tying the scarf. She wasn't sure, but she thought Irina murmured something about pitying *her*.

Confidence carried her down the hall on the arm of an almost-former king less than thirty minutes later. Well, she was confident she'd cleaned up well this time. Irina had magic fingers when it came to working with unruly hair, and Jane had stared in awe when she'd looked in the mirror after Irina had finished fussing with her.

Familiar, startled, *pewter* eyes had stared back at her.

The clothes brought about most of the difference; the silk, the brightly colored shawl posing as a sling, dressy shoes, and shapely slacks. Jane had never seen herself dressed up before. And her hair? It waved down her back in shining coils of lively curls dangling from a gorgeous clip she was afraid contained real diamonds—which made her carry her head high and most carefully, and, unbeknownst to her, regally. She smiled at her escort with lips softly painted a blushing pink by Irina's hand. The lips were complemented by slightly rouged cheeks and discreetly shadow-brushed eyes that emphasized their sparkle of *pewter*, making her feel confident.

Jane was actually quite familiar with the feeling. She had mountains of confidence when she was walking her woods back home. She never hesitated or questioned herself, but simply listened to instincts gained from growing up surrounded by nature and many, many hours of aloneness. A person not only had to be confident but comfortable with themselves if all they had was themselves to rely on. In Maine, in her woods, Jane was comfortable with her lot in life.

She was not comfortable sitting at a table in a palace with an almost-king who'd taken her to bed, or that king's father, or three devilish princes. But Jane was confident she'd survive, and even live to laugh at this one day.

The clothes helped. The makeup helped. Reynard's warm, encouraging smile, which he graced her with as they walked arm and arm, helped.

"Your lips are smiling, Jane," Reynard said as he led her through the maze of halls, "but your eyes are not. Which worries me. I realize you may be nervous, but I think your eyes are darkened with distress more than fear. Or maybe anger? So now I am the one who is nervous."

"Oh no. Please don't worry, Your Majesty. I promise not to embarrass you." She shot him a frown. "Somebody else, though, I wouldn't mind embarrassing."

"Not Markov," Reynard said on a groan, stopping at

the top of the stairs and turning her to look at him. "What has he done now?"

She laughed at his expression. "Not your son. To tell you the truth, I haven't even seen Mark today." She suddenly snorted. "He did leave me a note, though." And then she gasped. "Your note! Oh, how could I have forgotten? Thank you for the flowers and lovely note, Your Majesty. Both were beautiful." She rolled her eyes. "Your son could take lessons from you in letter writing."

Reynard sighed. "But I have not achieved my purpose, apparently. You're not calling me Reynard. Am I going to have to call you Miss Abbot to make my point?"

"I'm not calling you Reynard in front of people."

"Why not? It's my name."

He was sounding perturbed, Jane decided. "I don't wish to be thought of as impolite; as a backwoods American with no respect for you." She placed her hand on his arm. "If I promise to call you Reynard in private, will you allow me my manners in public? I'll let you call me daughter when you want," she offered, giving him a cajoling smile.

His laughter startled her, echoing down to the foyer below. Carefully, mindful of her injury, the almost-ex-king wrapped her up in a hug, his lingering chuckles vibrating her entire body. "Miss Jane Abbot, I will give you this boon. And I certainly *will* call you daughter. With or without your permission," he added, his eyes sparkling mischievously.

"Careful. You're sounding like a king."

He barked in laughter again and kissed her on the

forehead before releasing her. "I apologize, daughter. It is in the genes, I'm afraid."

"Which you have obviously passed on to each and every one of your sons."

He rolled his eyes at her and started them down the stairs. "Now, come. Tell my why you were frowning so ferociously when you opened your door to me earlier. And who it is that you wish to put in their place."

Jane looked at him from the corner of her eye, her good hand tucked in his arm for support as they carefully made their way down the steps. "Well, I remembered you mentioned something about your having a European businessman visiting right now, and I think he might be the man I saw from my bedroom window just before you came to get me, since he was dressed rather formally. He was down in the courtyard with a woman and a young man who also looked to be dressed for dinner. His children, maybe?"

"Yes. He brought both his son and daughter with him."

"Well, the three of them seemed to be having a heated discussion. Or rather, the two men were heated. The daughter just looked . . . cowed, I guess I would say."

"And?"

"And the father struck his daughter," Jane whispered tightly. "Right on the face. I doubt the poor girl will be at dinner tonight. She'll probably be in her room with ice on her cheek."

Reynard said nothing as they gained the foyer, then stopped once more and turned to her, a small, sad smile on his face. "I would expect as much from Oswald. I believe he rules his employees with an equally heavy hand." He silently stared at her again, then asked very softly, "And so you are an avenging angel tonight?"

Jane shook her head. "I won't make a scene. I won't even open my mouth. It just made me mad. Like I said before, weak men use their fists, and I have no respect for those who do."

"And neither do I," Reynard agreed. "And I wouldn't dream of asking you to keep your opinions to yourself. You have my approval to say anything you wish to Oswald."

"I won't make a scene," Jane repeated. "But if he talks to me, I shall . . . snub him? Is that acceptable?"

Reynard laughed again. "It's going to take more than that. Oswald will merely assume you're worried about his daughter winning the race."

"What race?"

"Why, to the altar, my dear Jane. Oswald will think you're jealous and being spiteful because you want Markov to marry *you*, not his daughter."

It was Jane's turn to laugh. "Then maybe I'd better wait until after dinner to give him my opinions. So there won't be any misunderstanding."

"Not alone. Is that understood?" Reynard said rather firmly.

Jane sobered. "I'm not afraid of him."

He started walking again. "No. And that's the problem," he muttered.

They finally made it to the dining room and it was Jane's turn to halt their progress. She stopped just inside the door, stared at the room full of people, then pinched her escort on the arm. "There are over twenty people here," she hissed. "I thought it was just your family and

this businessman and his daughter." She took a determined step back. "I'm not staying. I'll eat in my room,"
she said, shooting daggers at him. "You set me up."

"I did not. This is a normal dinner," Reynard calmly
countered, tugging on her good arm. He finally just grabbed
her elbow, towed her into the room, and led her to the foot
of the table. "We must entertain ambassadors and our own
countrymen regularly. It comes with the job," he whispered,
pulling out her chair with one hand while still holding her
securely with the other. "And you will embarrass me if you
run off now," he added, grinning at her glare that told him
she knew just how low he was hitting.

"Do you happen to know, Your Highness, how to sleep
with one eye open?" Jane asked sweetly, sitting down.

Reynard Lakeland boomed with laughter again, leaning down and kissing her forehead right in front of the
twenty people all staring at them.

Jane wondered how embarrassed he'd be if she crawled
under the table.

"Pants! She's wearing pants," Alexi blurted out, smiling devilishly. "No one has worn pants to dinner since
Mother."

Jane looked halfway down the table and glared at him
through her reddening face. "I believe, Your Highness,"
she told the rascal prince, lifting her chin, "that it's impolite to mention a woman's dress, inappropriate or not,
unless it's to compliment her."

Alexi looked momentarily startled, then gave her an
unrepentant grin. "My apologies, angel. I am duly chastised," he said, bowing formally.

Jane wanted to run up and kick him in that bent-over

position. Instead she smiled sweetly, making sure she didn't look at anyone else at the table. She could tell only the Lakelands were laughing.

"I'm not your angel," she muttered. What in heaven was she doing here, making an ex-king sit at the foot of the table beside her and reprimanding royalty like Mother Superior?

"No, you are not. You are merely a woman who likes to fly out windows," the cad growled, obviously having heard her. Which meant everyone else probably had, too. Alexi suddenly gave her a whimsical smile. "But if I throw myself into the sea, will you fly to my rescue and give me the kiss of life?"

"No, I believe I would give you a rock."

Shocked silence and then laughter erupted around the table. Jane placed her napkin on her lap while smiling down at her plate for putting the now-frowning prince in his place. No matter that she'd embarrassed herself, Reynard, and probably Mark in the process. But she made the mistake of glancing at Mark, sitting at the opposite end of the table, causing her smile to vanish.

"I believe it's also bad manners to point out bad manners, is it not, Miss Abbot?" Mark asked, his eyes gleaming with amusement.

Jane lifted her chin. "I believe you're right, Your Highness. I, too, am duly chastised," she agreed, widening her smile. "And good day to you," she tacked on to cover her blush.

"Good day, Miss Abbot. I'm sorry to have missed you earlier. You went for a walk, I gather. After, that is, escaping my brothers. Feeling back to your old self?"

"Oh yes. I've discovered the less time I spend with you, the healthier I feel."

Several gasps followed that salvo. Mark merely looked at his father and arched a brow.

She probably shouldn't have spoken that way, especially in front of these strangers, but she refused to let any of these Lakelands make her feel inferior, especially Mark. And the sooner he realized that, the better. Still, Jane politely stayed mute after that embarrassing opening and concentrated on enjoying the wonderful food and committing everything to memory. Because really—when was she ever going to sit at such an elegant table again?

Well, she remained mute until the businessman made some stupid remark about women in his family being meek and seldom heard from as he darted a glance in Jane's direction.

Jane set her fork down.

Reynard did, too. Then he gave her a wink and addressed his son's guest. "Just today, a very smart angel told me that only weak men rule by domination. I believe this angel is right," he softly added, disgust apparent in his voice.

Oswald glanced at Jane then back at Reynard. "This angel was a woman, I gather?"

Jane raised her chin and decided to speak for herself. "I was told I would get to meet your daughter this evening," she said, making a point of looking at the empty chair beside him. "Was she not feeling well?" She narrowed her eyes at the red-faced man. "And I agree that any man who strikes a woman is a coward," she said softly. "I wonder if he'd be so quick to strike someone equal to him in strength?"

Jane continued glaring at the now obviously angry businessman through the long, stunned silence, not even looking to see if Mark was equally angry at her for speaking so bluntly in front of his guests. It was Oswald's son who broke the tension when he jumped up from his chair.

"Are you calling us cowards?"

Feeling secure sitting at a table full of Lakeland men, Jane simply nodded.

"In our family you would be beaten for your insolence," the young man snarled, ignoring his father tugging on his arm.

"You could try," she whispered, giving him a nasty smile.

Jane suspected the young man was sorely tempted to do just that. But his father forcibly tugged him into his seat when Mark slowly started to rise from his chair. The father, however, was no more willing to let the insult pass than his son and glared at the again-seated prince.

"Who is this woman that you let her speak so freely at your dinner table?"

"My fiancée," Mark said softly but quite distinctly.

Jane certainly heard him. And so did every single person in the room. She would have gasped if she could have found her voice. And Reynard Lakeland, bless the unholy Majesty, was suddenly squeezing her hand—which she took as a sign she wasn't supposed to dispute the host in front of his guests.

Well, by heaven, she intended to dispute him later.

Fiancée. Hah! She'd dig ditches before she'd marry Markov Lakeland. Jane tried without success to pull her hand free from Reynard's grasp.

"Your fiancée?" Oswald sputtered, his eyes bugged out as he gaped at Mark.

Mark nodded.

"But . . . but I thought . . ."

"Shelkova has no desire—or need—to align itself with a manufacturing dynasty, Mr. Oswald," Mark quietly told him, "as we are quite capable of turning our timber into finished product ourselves. And I happen to agree with the lady's opinion of brutes."

Looking ready to explode, Oswald pushed back his chair and stood, roughly grabbed his also-angry son, and left—his exit leaving a silence so complete the bubbles could be heard rising in the champagne flutes sitting in front of all the stunned guests.

Sergei clapped Mark on the shoulder, stood up and walked to the foot of the table, then leaned down and kissed Jane on her mortified cheek. "Welcome to the Lakeland tribe, sister," he whispered. "I can't wait to see what you have in store for us in the future."

Jane managed to shake off her shock enough to give him a good glare. He simply chuckled and kissed her again before returning to his seat.

Alexi picked up his champagne and waved it at the people at the table. "A toast, then, to my brother's wisdom," he said. "And his choice of a bride."

Finally coming out of their own shock, all the guests grabbed their glasses and raised them in salute, then drained them to the bottom.

Jane still hadn't gotten her hand back. Reynard was holding it hostage, apparently afraid she'd throw her champagne at his smugly smiling son. Wow; it would appear His Majesty had come to know her quite well in a very short time.

Chapter Eleven

✦ ⋯ ✦

"A re you insane?" Jane shouted at Mark as he negligently leaned against the mantel in the library, a drink in his hand and a satisfied smile on his face.

"No, I don't believe so," he answered calmly. "But then, I did suffer a blow to the head a couple of weeks ago." He sighed, pushing himself away from the hearth. "And I haven't been the same since." He smiled tightly. "I've been seeing angels, even in my sleep."

Jane tried to cross her arms, found her sling was in the way of doing so effectively, and contented herself with placing her free hand on her hip. She glared at Mark, then turned her glare on the four other Lakeland men, all of whom were calmly sipping drinks. She'd been offered one, too; an after-the-meal-from-purgatory drink, but had refused on the chance she might be pregnant. Not that she needed it anyway, as she was more than ready for battle.

She turned her attention to Mark again. "I am not marrying you."

"Yes, you are." Mark moved to stand by the glass doors leading onto the terrace, his back to her. "In two weeks." He turned at her gasp. "The day of my coronation. I will be crowned king of Shelkova, we will be married, and then I shall crown you *queen* of Shelkova."

Jane lifted her hand and let it fall back against her thigh. "Do I look like a queen to you?"

"Yes."

Her mouth opened but nothing came out. She took a deep breath and gathered her thoughts, then suddenly smiled. "Even your father knows I'm nobody."

"What!" Reynard shouted.

She looked at him and then at Mark. "Your father had me sit at the foot of the table, because he knew that's where I belonged."

Alexi, Dmitri, and Sergei broke into laughter. Reynard gaped in shock.

Mark nodded agreement. "He did know. You sat at the second most honorable place, Jane; the hostess's seat. It is where my mother would have sat had she lived to see the reinstatement of the Lakelands to this house. The queen's seat."

Jane felt her own jaw slacken and snapped it shut. And then she sighed. "You don't know who I am," she whispered. "You don't know *what* I am."

"And what is that, daughter?" Reynard asked.

She turned to him. "I'm an orphan with less of a

pedigree than the horses in your stables. I don't even have a real name."

"Jane Abbot sounds real to me," Mark said, drawing her attention as he stepped toward her. "And you are standing before us now; therefore you must be somebody. You're alive and breathing the same air we are."

She dropped her gaze from the intensity in his. "My full name is Jane Doe Abbot." She looked at the obviously confused men sitting around the room. "In America, when a person is found and nobody knows who they are, they're given the name Jane or John Doe. And Abbot is the name of the town where I was left on a hospital's steps."

A thoughtful silence greeted that revelation. Until Mark started cursing—in both English and Shelkovan—about the evils of unfeeling social workers. He was soon joined by four disgruntled Lakeland men.

Jane squared her shoulders and glared at the five of them. "Stop looking at me with pity. I have a good life in Maine. And I'm going back there and getting myself a baby, and then I'm going to keep on walking the next time a plane falls out of the sky."

Reynard stood up. "Jane," he said thickly, going to her. "No place is it written that you must have a . . . pedigree to be a queen. All you need to be is the woman my son wants to marry. And that, Jane Doe Abbot, is good enough. Your history made you the person you are today; the courageous, charming, beautiful, compassionate, intelligent, mischievous angel that I want for a daughter in a very bad way."

Try as she might, Jane couldn't keep a grin from tugging at the corner of her mouth. "All that?" she whispered to the golden eyes gleaming at her. "No more? Not troublesome, foolish, impertinent, opinionated, and stubborn?"

"Mischievous covered most of those, I think."

"It's settled, then," Mark interjected, walking over and grabbing her right hand, then dragging her toward the doors leading outside.

"It is not settled," she hissed, pulling free. "I'm not marrying you. You're a rat."

"Ah, yes. I seem to remember being likened to a rat after our first night on the *Katrina*."

"You crawled into my bed." She poked him in the chest. "You took advantage of my being sick and confused and tired," she continued, gathering steam and poking him again. "Didn't you, *just Mark*?" She tucked her right arm under her trussed-up left arm, her toe tapping the floor. "What do you have to say for yourself?"

"That I can't wait to do it again?" he asked back, crossing his own arms over his chest and spreading his feet in a challenging stance. "And that I intend to do it again very soon?" He bent down at her gasp and looked her directly in the eyes. "You gave yourself to me, Jane Doe Abbot. And you were a virgin. Now you're mine."

She took a step back, feeling her face heat up as she glanced at the other Lakelands to find them all grinning, all nodding agreement.

"I'm twenty-seven years old," she whispered tightly, glaring at Mark and lifting her chin. "I'm not . . . I'm . . . I was *not* a virgin."

* * *

Completely stunned, Mark could only stare at her. She was actually lying to him about her virginity! He would have laughed had he not realized she was serious. "I was there, Jane, and I distinctly remember taking your innocence."

"No, either you were mistaken or it grew back."

Mark halted his glass halfway to his mouth. "Excuse me?"

A chorus of chuckles rose from the couch, and Jane spun around and stepped toward them, her eyes sparking and her hand reaching for her empty glass on a nearby table. Mark threw his own drink first, hitting the wall behind his brothers and making them instantly sober.

Jane stopped in mid-throw and blinked at the mess he'd made.

Mark gave his brothers a look that sent them scrambling to their feet and out of the room. Reynard regally followed, his shoulders shaking.

"Virginity, Jane, does not grow back."

Obviously knowing her outrageous claim wasn't going to work, the woman apparently decided to change tactics. "Do you think you're the first man to ever want to have sex with me?"

Mark suddenly understood and instantly relaxed. "What I think is that I'm the first man *you* wanted to have sex with." He grinned. "And I hope that, like me, you're looking forward to doing it again—also very soon."

"Don't hold your breath," she snapped, apparently back to being angry. "I merely decided it was time I found out what all the men who asked me to be their mistress claimed I was missing."

Mark's amusement just as suddenly vanished. "*All* the men?" He stiffened. "How recently? Is that why you were running off to the coast?"

"That's not important. What's important is that you don't have to marry me just because we had sex. Even though *you* crawled into my bed, I take full responsibility for my own actions that night."

"Does that not contradict what your nuns taught you?" Mark drawled, walking over and fixing himself another drink. It was either that or throttle the woman.

"What nuns?"

"Those dear sisters in the orphanage who so lovingly named you."

"They were good to me! And the hospital staff are the ones who called me baby Jane Doe. I didn't actually go to Saint Xavier's until I was a month old, because of my ankle."

"And did the nuns not tell you what happens to people who lie?"

"They told me what happens to people who swear," she countered.

Lord, as long as he lived he would thank the Lord for dropping him into this woman's lap. "And were you ever tempted to become any man's mistress, Jane?"

She avoided looking at him by glaring down at her toes instead, and mumbled something unintelligible.

"Excuse me?"

"I said that's none of your business."

"I see." And he did. Jane was embarrassed to be caught a virgin at the ancient age of twenty-seven. He sighed dramatically. "Too bad," he said, turning to her in time to catch her worrying her lower lip. "Because I prefer an experienced bride in my bed."

She lifted her chin. "Then I hope you find one."

"Why not you?"

"Because I don't belong here," she said, now sounding exasperated as she waved a hand to encompass the palace.

Mark closed his eyes to gather his patience. They'd come full circle and were back to *belonging*. He was beginning to hate that word. "Jane," he said, his eyes still closed.

"I'm going home tomorrow."

That certainly opened them.

"I shouldn't stay here any longer," she whispered. "I won't go back to the mountains," she quickly assured him. "Or even to Bar Harbor. I'll head south to Portland or something. Those men will never find me, assuming they're still around. It has been eleven days, after all." She gave him an encouraging smile. "And I really am good at taking care of myself."

"And if you're pregnant?" he asked, trying to think quickly.

"Then I'll write and let you know what I had, a boy or a girl. I . . . I won't ask for anything from you, Mark."

"Would you give me until the coronation in two weeks?" He forced himself to smile. "At least stay and watch me become king."

She had to think about that, apparently. Mark turned to the window, but instead of looking out, he studied her reflection in the glass. And then he very nearly fell to his knees at the look of yearning on Jane's face as she stared at his back. "Just two weeks," he got out hoarsely, still facing the window.

"O-okay," she whispered, her shoulders slumping as she slowly walked out of the room.

Mark opened the door and stepped onto the terrace. He walked to the stone rail and looked out over the sea, then lifted his arm and threw his drink for the second time that night.

Chapter Twelve

—✦——✦—

Mark flopped back on the small patch of sand at the base of the cliff and rubbed the sockets of his eyes until they burned, then ran his hands repeatedly through his hair until it hurt, and then slowly beat his head in the sand in rhythm to the throbbing pulse causing his headache. Three days; the woman had given her word to stay a mere three days ago, and Mark figured he'd aged two decades. At this rate he wouldn't live long enough to wear the crown, much less get married.

She was going to kill him first.

It was as if Jane Abbot had folded her angel wings and packed them away that night in the library. The next morning a mischief-making little witch with Jane's beautiful, shining gray eyes had been sitting beside him at breakfast;

not from the foot of the table and not halfway down. Beside him. All warm and smiling and confident. A woman on an adventure who'd decided she was safe now. A woman on a two-week vacation to a foreign country.

In truth, she was the Jane Abbot who had pulled him from the lake, fired her gun at his assassins, then threatened to throw him back into the water. That woman had returned with a vengeance, apparently determined not to miss a thing.

The confident set of her shoulders all through breakfast should have warned him. Her questions to his brothers and father about Shelkova should have warned him. That sparkle in her eyes should have warned him.

But he'd simply been too besotted to care.

Mark worried his father was in danger of having a real stroke. If he hadn't just walked out of breakfast and gone about his duties, he would have noticed when Jane had walked out of the palace to explore the city of Previa— alone. Sighing, rubbing his temple to relieve the persistent pressure, Mark pictured the last three days in his mind . . .

First had been the panic when Aunt Irina had come to him around ten that first morning after searching the palace high and low and asked if he knew where Jane was. Hell, she told him she'd even dared venture into the kitchens looking for Jane. Irina's alarm had in turn alarmed *him*, since his aunt rarely panicked. Mark had calmed her, promised to find Jane, then gone on his own search.

He'd finally ended up at the gates. "What in hell do you mean, she left two hours ago? You just let her walk out of here *alone*?" he'd shouted at the sentries.

They'd paled and shaken their heads, and then offered him those heads on a platter.

Mark had walked back into the palace and gone in search of his brothers.

Sergei, Dmitri, and Alexi had returned home four hours later, their shoulders slumped and their tongues wagging with amazing tales of a foreign woman who had been seen everywhere in the city but was nowhere to be found. Mark had just picked up the phone to call out the army when he'd spotted his future bride calmly strolling in through the gates, leading the sorriest-looking horse he'd ever seen.

He'd met her at the stables . . .

"Jane."

"Oh, there you are, Mark. Come see. Look what I've brought you."

Mark looked at *her*, wondering why she wasn't dead from his glare. But she was still standing, still smiling, and still patting the pathetic excuse of a horse.

"Isn't he beautiful?"

Mark forced himself to look away from the blissfully unaware Jane to the . . . horse. His eyes focused and widened in horror. The beast was thirty years old if it was a day. It was obviously a work horse. Maybe. Once. When it was still alive. Right now it looked like it was barely breathing. Its eyes were closed and its head was hanging down to its knees. The poor horse's back was so swayed it was a wonder it didn't snap beneath its own weight.

"Jane. That horse isn't beautiful, it's pathetic," he whispered.

She slapped her hands over the horse's ears and glared

at Mark as if he'd just run up and hit the poor beast. The poor beast didn't even flinch. Maybe it *was* dead.

"What a terrible thing to say," she scolded, her chin tilting in what he recognized as her stubborn mode. "He is too beautiful," she went on, moving her hand lovingly over the horse's neck. "He's just old. And tired." She suddenly beamed a brilliant smile. "I bought him."

For the life of him, Mark couldn't think of a thing to say. She sounded so proud of herself. And expectant; like she expected him to praise her.

"May I ask what you bought him with?"

Her chin instantly lowered along with her eyes. "I signed a voucher for him. The guy who sold him to me will be coming here tomorrow to get his money from . . . you."

"How much money?"

She cocked her head. "I'm not sure." She named a figure and Mark merely closed his eyes again. "But you can take the money from my backpack—there's seventy-five dollars in there—and exchange it for Shelkovan money."

"Jane," he said calmly, "you just paid the equivalent of nine hundred American dollars."

"Oh."

He crossed his arms over his chest. "So how do you intend to pay for this . . . ah, horse?"

She frowned. She bit her lip. And she pondered. Suddenly she smiled. "I'll get a job."

Mark dropped his arms and stepped toward her. "You will not." He suddenly grinned. "Besides, where would you work?"

"I saw all sorts of neat little shops in town. I'll get a job at one of them."

His grin just as quickly vanished. "You can't. Or have you forgotten the men who tried to kill me?"

"You brought me here claiming I'd be safe, and now you're saying I won't?"

"Only in the *palace*," he growled, trying to rein in his temper. "Not traipsing the streets of Previa *alone*." He suddenly grinned. "And how can you work if you don't speak Shelkovan?"

She shrugged. "A dishwasher wouldn't have to speak at all. And I'll find a restaurant that's close by."

"You only have the use of one hand."

She shrugged again, turning back and crooning to her new, expensive pet. "I'll be able to take off the sling in another day or two."

Mark reached out and grabbed her good arm. "You will not wash dishes," he said, leading her from the barn and waving to a gawking stableman to tend the horse.

"Wait!"

He stopped and looked down at her.

"Tell the man the horse's name is Arthur. Tell him to take good care of him. He's hungry and his feet need trimming."

"Arthur?"

"I named him after King Arthur of the Round Table. Don't you think he looks like a majestic warhorse that would have carried such a noble knight?"

"I think," Mark had muttered as he walked back in the stables, "that if King Arthur rode such a horse, it's no wonder there's no trace of his kingdom today."

Mark rubbed his aching temple again and opened his eyes to the star-filled night, remembering the battle of wills that had followed the scene in the stables. For the last two days Arthur had been eating his ancient head off and Jane Abbot was anything but contrite.

She'd simply sat through a long, frustrating evening of five Lakelands trying to drill it into her head that she couldn't go roaming around town alone. And she couldn't drag home pathetic creatures. Jane had smiled and nodded, said she was sorry for worrying them, then simply gone to bed.

The next morning she hadn't even appeared at breakfast. It was learned, some two hours later, that she'd left the palace grounds and gone in search of a job.

She'd taken a young maid with her.

For translation, Jane had told Mark when he'd found her trying to bargain with the proprietor of a small inn, conning the poor, besotted fellow out of a job. She'd not ventured out alone, she'd pointed out, pointing to the poor maid quietly sitting in the corner of the inn's kitchen. At that imbecilic excuse, Mark had dragged her home and up to her room, where he threatened to lock her if she stepped foot off the grounds again.

Growls and threats, apparently, weren't enough to deter her. The next morning Mark learned from Alexi that Jane was gone again. This time she'd cajoled one of the gardeners into joining her.

"The gardener?" Mark had whispered so he wouldn't shout.

Alexi nodded. "She's assuming because he's male that you would approve, is my guess."

"Which gardener did she take?" Mark asked, closing his eyes and praying for patience.

"Duncan."

Mark didn't shout; he bellowed. "He's nearly eighty years old!"

Alexi shrugged. "He's also as soft as butter when it comes to pretty women. Don't glower, brother. Sergei, Dmitri, and I will go bring her back," he offered with a resigned sigh. "They can't have gotten far. Duncan is as slow as cold molasses running uphill in winter. We'll find them."

But all they'd found was Duncan at the gates, out of breath and frantic, wringing his hands and nearly in tears. There had been a street scuffle involving something to do with several women—of questionable morals—being kicked out of their apartments, and the police had been called. Jane, it seemed, had waded into the foray and started yelling at the authorities. In English, Duncan told them as he trembled with worry. The last the old man saw of Jane was when the police were lifting her into the back of their van. He'd tried to intervene, but had been knocked down by the mob that had gathered.

Mark listened from the front steps of the palace, until he let out a roar loud enough to make the guards at the front gates flinch. And then he took off, on foot, for the police station, which was a good five blocks away. Sergei, Dmitri, and Alexi followed, their mouths slackened and their eyes full of worry. It had been years since any of them had seen Mark in a blazing rage. All three brothers were thankful, on Jane's behalf, that he'd chosen to walk, figuring it might buy the angel enough time for her rescuer to calm down enough not to throttle her.

Which Mark was seriously contemplating doing to her

for blatantly disobeying him. If she'd been looking for work again, he would definitely throttle her. If she'd been looking for adventure, well, by God, she'd found it, hadn't she. And if she'd been looking to test his patience, she'd finally found his limit.

What he did, however, was go weak in the knees when he saw her.

She was a bedraggled mess, sitting forlornly in the corner of a cell, several women crammed together on an opposite wall, all of them bickering in Shelkovan. Jane's shirtsleeve was torn, her hair was back in knots, and one cheek was smudged with dirt. Her knees were muddy and she was cradling her tender arm to her chest, her sling nowhere to be seen.

At Mark's roar, silence fell in the overcrowded jail and several police officers scurried back, bumping into the confining walls. Mark swung around and pointed at one of them. Sweat broke out on the poor fellow's forehead as he listened to a scorching tirade from his future king. With shaking hands, the man finally fumbled his keys free and unlocked the cell.

Mark stood in the opened door of Jane's prison and counted to ten, breathing as deeply and as slowly as he could. He didn't say a word; he didn't dare. He simply walked in the cell and carefully led an also-silent Jane out to one of the policeman's cars. Sergei drove. Alexi and Dmitri elected to walk home. After, they promised Mark, they looked into the inciting incident that had caused their angel's halo to slip a bit.

The ride back to the palace was silent. The trip to

Jane's room was silent. And in silence, Mark had left her in the care of Aunt Irina.

Now being reasonable men, tonight Mark, his father, and his three brothers had ganged up on Jane again and tried to explain to her that the Lakelands had enemies. That a maid or an aging gardener couldn't help if those enemies found her.

"Then give me my handgun," she'd countered.

Two Lakeland men had choked on their drinks, Sergei had gotten up and walked out of the room, and Reynard had clutched his chest. Mark had simply snorted. "You can't go running around the city with a .357 Magnum in your pocket."

"But I have to work. I owe you eight hundred and twenty-five dollars for Arthur."

"I will pay for Arthur," Mark had gritted. "Consider him a wedding present."

She hadn't liked his mentioning the wedding. That much had been evident in her scowl. Jane had simply gotten up and followed Sergei out of the room.

All of which was why Mark was hiding down on the beach—what little of it there was before the tide came back in. Shelkova was not known for its beaches. It was known for its rugged coast, fine timber, and hardy people. Soon, Mark was afraid, it would be known for its outrageous queen.

He'd paid for Arthur when the man had come to the palace today looking more pathetic than his horse, which is why Mark had paid him the full amount.

And he'd gotten to the bottom of the police confronta-

tion in the streets. Three aging prostitutes had been
evicted from their home by a landlord who wanted to
bring in younger tenants. Mark had threatened to have
the landlord evicted. The women were back in their apartments and now had jobs at parliament. They weren't very
high-level jobs, but would give the women a satisfying
living. And they were perfect jobs, Mark had cynically
decided, figuring the women would probably be running
into plenty of their old *acquaintances* at work.

Maybe he should take the nine hundred dollars for
Arthur out of Jane's cute little hide. And a little extra for
the trouble and worry she'd caused him over the riot he
didn't doubt she'd started. Now there was a thought. Maybe
he'd just sneak up to her room tonight and get his due, at
the same time restating his claim. And maybe he'd also give
her the baby she wanted so badly. After all, what woman
would be so cruel as to separate a man from his child?
Surely he could talk a pregnant Jane into marrying him.

Maybe.

She was such an independent creature, headstrong and
stubborn. She refused to need anyone by hiding behind
the facade of being nobody. Mark suspected that when
those men had asked Jane to be their mistress, not their
wife, she'd been deeply wounded.

And when he'd backed down four nights ago in the
library, asking her only to stay until his coronation, he'd
wounded her again by not fighting for her hand in marriage. Maybe he shouldn't have capitulated so quickly.
But in truth, he hadn't conceded defeat; he'd merely
wanted to buy enough time to *talk* her into marriage.

Only it was going to take more than words to bring the lady around, apparently. More like a little trickery and a lot of patience.

Then again, a good dose of passion probably couldn't hurt, either.

Chapter Thirteen

‑◆‑ ⋯ ‑◆‑

For the fourth night in a row, Jane was crying herself to sleep. During the day she was usually okay, the adventure of seeing a new country and people keeping her occupied. It was only at night, alone, in the dark, that the yearnings came. And the tears.

Disgusted with her self-pity, her shoulder throbbing and her heart breaking, Jane rolled over and buried her face in her pillow. Darn, what a mess she'd made of things these last three days. Mark still hadn't spoken to her about finding her in jail, or about getting in a fight over some women who were down on their luck. Jane knew what they did for a living. She may have been brought up in the woods, but she wasn't ignorant. She was, however, very pleased with Mark. Irina had told her, in whispers, what he'd done for the women.

Which was another reason why she'd gone and fallen in love with the infuriating man. If that wasn't bad enough, she'd fallen hard for his family, too. Even Alexi, the rascal. But especially Reynard, who was fast becoming the father she'd always wanted.

They were so concerned about her. Their endless lectures gave her that idea. They actually seemed worried about her safety. She would laugh if she could quit crying. Imagine, five men worried about her. Nobody had worried about her safety since before she was twelve years old. That was when she'd gone to live with the Johnsons. Being old people and never having had children of their own, they'd simply treated her as an adult. For the first time in her life, Jane had been free of restraints—especially the rules that had been necessary for the nuns to control the number of children in their care. Living with the Johnsons, she'd been able to run wild in the woods surrounding her new home and not only explore nature, but herself; who she was and who she could *be*. And by the age of sixteen, Jane had arrived at the independent and admittedly self-contained person she was today.

Mark had ruined all that; first by literally falling into her life, then by turning out to be the first man she'd ever really been attracted to, and then by being attracted to her in return.

And sometime when she hadn't been looking, the rat had firmly entrenched himself in her heart.

It was unacceptable. She had no business falling in love with a king, much less expecting him to ever love her back. She didn't belong sleeping in this beautiful bed, being fawned over by staff, any more than she belonged sitting at a table full of important, worldly people. Looking back, Jane figured she should have let Mark drown two weeks ago instead of pulling him from that plane. It certainly would have saved her from getting her heart broken.

Darn, what a mess.

Jane was just about to sink into another deep sob of self-pity when she heard the noise. It sounded like a snarl of outrage followed by male snickering. And it seemed to be coming from the hall. Jane instantly stopped crying and held her breath to listen.

Voices carried then, of men right outside her door having a heated discussion in whispers. Unable to stop herself, Jane crawled out of bed, tiptoed to the door, and listened.

"Get out of here, Sergei."

"Now, Markov, you don't really want to go in there."

Jane heard Mark growl.

"Think, brother. You're going to ruin your chances with the lady."

"I'm going to improve them," Mark ground out. Jane fought back a grin, picturing him scowling. "I'm going to start clipping some angel wings," he continued. "Now move."

Sergei must have shaken his head. And he must have grinned. Because the next thing she heard was the door rattling with the impact of poor Sergei being shoved against it.

"Shhh!"

"Hell, if the woman's not awake now, she will be in two minutes. I need to talk with her," Mark said, sounding really close to the door, his nose probably only inches away from his brother's face.

"Talk?" Sergei barked, sounding incredulous.

"Our interfering father set you here as sentry, didn't he?"

Sergei, the fool, must have nodded. And probably grinned again. Jane now had her ear pressed up against the door and was nearly knocked to the floor when the man was slammed against it again.

"Dammit, Markov, cut it out! I'm trying to help you."

"Then leave!"

Jane opened the door.

Two men fell into the room. Sergei grunted when he hit the floor, and grunted again when Mark landed on top of him. Both men muttered something when Jane started laughing.

Then she simply walked out of the room and down the hall, ignoring their calls to come back echoing after her. She also ignored the trudging of feet that began to follow.

"Where are you going?" Mark asked from behind her.

"To get a cup of hot cocoa," she said, not breaking stride.

She had to stop, though, when he caught hold of her good arm and turned her around. His eyes were narrowed, his hair was mussed, and he had flecks of sand caught in the crinkled corners of his scowl.

Darn, she loved him.

"I'll have someone bring you chocolate. You can't go into the kitchens."

"I'm not going to let you wake people up just to make me a cup of cocoa. That's rude. Besides, I've been going to the kitchens every night for the last week."

His eyes widened. "Holy shit."

Jane frowned at him. "You shouldn't swear."

His eyes narrowed again at her chastisement. Suddenly he smiled. "I'll come with you, then. I've never seen the kitchens."

"What?" she asked incredulously, which caused Sergei to laugh. Jane looked at him and then at Mark again, only to grow more incredulous. "You guys really are afraid of Cook?"

Both towering giants nodded. Then Mark started dragging her back to her room.

"I want my cocoa," she persisted, trying to plant her feet.

"After you get on a robe and slippers. And your sling," Mark ordered, still tugging.

Jane gave a small gasp, realizing she was standing in the hall in her nightgown. She lifted her left arm higher, cradling it over her bosom, and meekly followed. Heavens, she was parading around the palace half dressed!

Once in her room, which suddenly shrank with the presence of the two men (Sergei had pushed the door open when Mark had tried to slam it in his face), Jane hurried to find her robe. Mark snatched it from her and carefully worked it over her sore arm and around to her good shoulder, then picked up her sling and carefully fitted it to her arm.

Sergei got down and tried to dress her feet. Jane quickly grabbed the slippers and threw them on the bed. "I have on thick socks. I don't need slippers," she told him through a blush, not wanting him anywhere near her deformed ankle. He frowned at her actions, but finally stood up and stepped away.

Jane was suddenly amused. They were acting like big brothers. Well, Sergei was. The look in Mark's eyes as he knotted the sling around her neck, his face close to hers, was anything but brotherly.

"You've really been going into the kitchen and making yourself cocoa?" Sergei asked in awe, shoving Mark out of the way and grabbing her good arm to tuck it in the crook of his. He started leading her back out to the hall. "And Cook hasn't caught you?"

"Of course she did," Jane told him, hiding her smile as Mark trailed behind them muttering something in Shelkovan. She really was going to have to learn the language.

"What did she do?" Sergei asked.

"She sat down and had a cup of cocoa with me. She even dug out some marshmallows to put in it, just like Sister Roberta used to do."

"Sister Roberta?" Mark asked, now walking beside her, having possessively slipped a hand under her hair and around her neck.

"She was the Mother Superior of Saint Xavier's," Jane explained. "She used to catch me in the kitchen making cocoa, and would just sigh, wipe the sleep from her eyes, and join me."

"This is a habit, then?"

Jane tried shrugging. "I guess so."

"What does Cook look like?" Sergei asked in a near whisper as he leaned closer, which made Mark gently tug Jane nearer to him.

Jane stopped walking. "You're kidding, right? Are you saying you've never even met the woman who cooks your meals?"

Both men shrugged and started her walking again. Taking them by surprise, Jane pulled free and darted toward what looked like a blank wall and opened a secret door.

"That's the staff's passage," Mark told her.

"But it leads straight to the kitchens," she countered, feeling for the switch and flooding the stairs with light. "This is quicker."

"You shouldn't be using the servants' stairs," Mark said.

Jane turned to him. "Why not?"

He gave her an exasperated look. "Because these narrow hallways travel like spiderwebs all over the palace. You'll get lost."

"I have a map."

He arched a brow. "I thought you didn't care for confined areas."

"Oh, put a sock in it, Ace." Jane started down the stairs. "And don't remind me. I'm training myself."

"Training yourself to what?" Sergei asked, thoroughly confused.

She stopped again and looked at him. "To tolerate closed spaces."

"Why?"

"Because I don't like them."

The prince obviously still didn't understand, and Jane decided to leave him confused. Because she sure as heck wasn't going to admit to spending five panicked hours locked in a closet by another orphan when she was six. Mark was back to staring at her with that funny gleam in his eyes, so she turned around, grabbed the banister, and started down the stairs again.

They eventually entered the kitchen, and it was a

comical sight to see: two grown men—one an almost-king, the other a prince—looking around like frightened children expecting Cook to come running in brandishing a knife and threatening their imperial lives. Carefully containing her smile, Jane made for the large walk-in cooler and found the milk. She poured some in a pan, put it on the monstrous range to heat, then went to the pantry to get the chocolate.

S he's limping more than usual," Sergei whispered to Mark. "Is her foot paining her? We should have carried her."

Mark smiled at his concerned brother. "She would have punched you in the nose, had you tried. She isn't wearing her brace."

"She has a brace?"

Mark nodded, watching his angel limp into the pantry, her robe trailing in billows around her, her hair a tangle of knots. He didn't doubt that Jane had charmed Cook into joining her for these late-night visits, as what person alive, man or woman, could resist such a beautifully disheveled wood-sprite?

"She's beautiful, isn't she?" Sergei commented, his thoughts obviously running along the same vein. "And she's courageous and compassionate, if that little scene in the streets is any indication. But she's also shy and unsure. I'm trying to figure her out, and I can't."

Mark crossed his arms, leaned back against the counter, and grinned at his brother. "And you never will. Nor will I. Jane is . . . Jane."

"She's an orphan."

"Not anymore."

Sergei nodded agreement. "But you're going to have to curb her willfulness."

Mark shook his head. "I doubt that's possible."

"You'll never get her to the altar unless you do."

"I'll get her there. She may be bound and gagged, but she'll be there."

Sergei raised a brow.

"I was pursuing that very end tonight when I found you blocking my path," Mark growled. "Tell Father to stay out of it."

"He can't. None of us can."

"Why the hell not?"

"Dad's also fallen in love with her. We all have. Her happiness is as important to us as yours is."

Mark snorted.

"You can't force her."

"I can't seem to reason with her, either," Mark said on a weary sigh. "It's like hitting my head against a stone wall. She gives herself no importance. How am I supposed to counter that?"

"By making her part of this family. Part of this country." Sergei ran a hand through his hair. "She's an intelligent woman. And she's caring. So make her care about *us*."

Mark stilled, then suddenly straightened away from the counter. "Go wake Dmitri and Alexi and bring them to Father's room."

"What do you intend?" Sergei asked, looking skeptical.

"You're right. Jane is intelligent and caring. Maybe it's time we all stop trying to order her around and explain why we're so concerned for her safety. And maybe we can get her to start worrying about *our* safety."

"How?"

"If Jane understands the threat against this family, maybe she'll become just as determined as we are to help Shelkova break into the world market. And maybe once that little temper of hers is directed at something besides me, I can sneak up when she's not looking and have her wed before she knows it."

Muttering and shaking his head and looking skeptical, Sergei went off to wake his family for a midnight conference.

"Include Aunt Irina," Mark called after him.

Sergei's muttering increased in color and volume.

Jane came out of the pantry, her good arm laden with cocoa, marshmallows, and cookies. She stopped when she saw Mark taking down another pan and pouring more milk into it.

"Are you expecting company?"

Mark turned and caught his breath. God, she was gorgeous.

And looking quite kissable at the moment.

He was also alone with her, Sergei never realizing he'd been successfully routed from his role as chaperone.

Now, to kiss an angel. Mark took Jane's burden, ignoring her frown at not getting an answer, and quickly picked her up and plopped her down on the counter. Before she could finish her squeak, he'd settled between her knees and captured her face in his hands. "Tell me why you were crying earlier."

"Crying?" she asked breathlessly, her eyes wary.

He ran his thumbs under her chin, lifting it. "When you opened your door tonight, your eyes were red and swollen. Tell me," he added when she tried to pull away.

"I'm homesick," she lied, the set of her jaw daring him to challenge her.

He shook his head. "That's possible, I suppose, but not likely." Mark settled deeper between her thighs while reaching down with one hand, clasping her bottom to pull her against him, and stifling a grin when her eyes widened in alarm. "I'm going to kiss you again, Jane Doe Abbot," he whispered.

She tried to shake her head, her good hand going to his chest to push him away. It was a futile attempt, she soon discovered, as Mark wasn't about to be deterred, unsure when he'd get her alone again. He covered her lips with his, stifling the squeak that opened her mouth.

Lord, this woman truly was an angel sent to tempt him. She tasted sweet and innocent and vulnerable; her independent nature not liking to be vulnerable to him, Mark guessed when he felt her resistance.

But he persisted by carefully wrapping her up in his arms and slanting his lips across hers to tease her now-retreating tongue. Such a shy woman, if a little bewildered by his passionate attack. She held herself stiff in his arms, a wary sprite. And then she suddenly relaxed, gave a little moan, and wrapped her good arm around his waist and hugged him back. Her tongue stopped retreating and began a cautious exploration of its own, and she began making little mewling whimpers while trying to gather him closer by wiggling her bottom and wrapping her legs around him.

The shriek startled them both. Mark stopped Jane from falling and pushed her face against his raggedly breathing chest, then turned his head to find Cook—huge, disheveled, gloriously angry—charging into the kitchen like a screaming banshee. She stopped before his ferocious glare, instantly changed direction, and headed for the stove. Spewing a litany of Shelkovan curses that did him proud, the woman shut off the burners and began dumping scorched milk down the sink.

Mark watched the rising steam and felt much like that milk himself. Damn, if he hadn't just been set on fire by an angel.

One who was struggling against him in earnest now. Mark leaned away only enough to look down, and saw her face was blistering red as she peeked around his shoulder and watched Cook slam the pot back down on the stove, still cursing the air blue.

Jane shyly looked up at him.

He kissed her again, then pressed her face back to his chest. Feeling the scorch of her cheeks through his shirt, he strung off a list of orders to Cook in Shelkovan, only able to hope the woman could hear him above her caterwauling over the fine mess they'd made of her stove. This was why, he remembered, they didn't venture into the kitchen. It was Cook's sacred domain, with only cowed kitchen staff—and disheveled wood-sprites, apparently—allowed.

Deciding he'd been cursed enough, Mark swept Jane off the counter and headed for the door. He looked down to see her looking back over his shoulder, her eyes still wide and her blush still bright. They were halfway up the stairs before she found her voice.

"Put me down."

As soon as he reached the top, Mark did as she instructed. And he kissed her again before she could start to bluster. But it wasn't going to work this time; she was onto him now.

"Stop doing that," she snapped the moment he stopped.

"No."

"I'm warning you, Ace. I know how to protect myself from unwanted advances."

He grinned. "Then you must have wanted mine back in the kitchen. I'm still alive."

She tried to push him down the stairs. Mark laughed and started leading her in the direction of his father's bedroom. But soon he sobered. "Tell me why you were crying tonight."

"Where are we going?"

"Were you crying because your shoulder pains you?"

"My room's the other way."

"Or did we hurt your feelings with our lecture tonight?"

She gave an unladylike snort at that suggestion.

"Were you crying because you're hopelessly in love with me and you don't know what to do about it?" he asked.

He felt her stiffen, which made her stumble and nearly fall. Mark kept walking, stifling his grin. Silent tears alone in her room and sweet little whimpers when he kissed her; hell yes, the lady was falling in love with him.

And she didn't like it one little bit, apparently.

"This is your family's wing. Why are we here?" she asked, sounding alarmed.

"For a family meeting."

"I want to go back to my room. I'm not family."

"You will be," he countered, throwing open the door

of his father's bedroom. Everyone was there already, including a sleep-tousled Aunt Irina. And everyone was smiling except Sergei—who was looking at Jane's kiss-swollen mouth.

Sergei jumped up and swept a startled Jane into his arms, his snapping gaze never leaving Mark as he set her on the bed beside their father. Reynard immediately wrapped an arm around Jane and turned his own disgruntled glare on Mark.

The poor woman was looking bewildered again and sought out Aunt Irina—who only shrugged and rolled her eyes.

"Now, as much as I like these family gatherings, Markov, it's almost one in the morning," Reynard reminded him. "Care to tell me why you've all descended on my room?"

"I want all of us to explain to Jane why she has to have protection. What the threat is to our family and to Shelkova."

"You're her biggest threat," Alexi sleepily piped up from the foot of the bed.

Mark tried to scowl at him, but it was wasted. Alexi had his eyes closed. Dmitri, his hair standing on end and his shirt buttoned crookedly, walked around the bed and sat beside Jane, sandwiching her between him and their father. So Mark turned his scowl on Dmitri, but the younger brother simply grinned and took hold of Jane's good hand.

She let him keep it. But her blush was back as she stared at her small hand inside of Dmitri's. Mark shoved Alexi over, taking his place at Jane's feet, which she quickly pulled up beneath herself and covered with her robe.

"This couldn't wait until morning?" Irina asked, smiling at the picture before her.

Mark patted a place beside him, beckoning her over. The woman didn't hesitate, but soon made a place for herself. Sergei, not about to be left out, gave Alexi another push and crammed himself onto the bed.

Thank God it was a big bed fit for a king. This was not the first time they'd all gathered this way, but it was obviously beyond Jane's comprehension. Her eyes were incredulous as she looked around at the seven people crammed together like a comfortable, contented family of sardines.

"No, it can't wait till tomorrow, as we're all scattered to the winds during the day. And," Mark added in a growl, "Jane is usually nowhere to be found."

She lifted her chin.

"So," he continued, "I want us all to explain why I landed in a lake in Jane's forest, why she's stuck here with us now, and why she can't go traipsing around Previa alone."

"I agree," Reynard said, patting Jane's thigh, careful not to bump his shoulder into hers. "It's time she understood. Then she will not take our concern so lightly?" he finished, smiling at her remorseful blush. "So begin, Markov."

Mark frowned. Where to begin?

"Before Shelkova gained back its sovereignty," he started, his attention on Jane, "we were merely a state of the USSR known mostly for our forests. An outside consortium of investors was in the process of closing a deal for our timber at the time of the breakup. But when we gained our independence back, the people of Shelkova, under the guidance of my father, halted the deal. Had we continued with it, we in effect would have been giving away our most valuable resource, as our timber is what will make Shelkova an economically strong country."

Mark paused, watching Jane to see if she was following. She nodded for him to continue, her cute little brow now furrowed.

"These investors were not happy. They still aren't. They became angered not with Shelkova, but with us personally. They hold my father responsible for foiling their scheme, as he was the voice of reason to a scared people trying to become a viable nation. The money they were willing to pay us was considerable, and we certainly needed it, but even when they upped their offer, it was still only a quarter of what our timber is worth. And they intend to bring in outside workers to cut the forests. First my father, and now I, have refused their deal."

"And so they tried to kill you?" Jane asked in a barely audible whisper, her blush having vanished.

"Well . . . yes. But they did not want my death to be linked to them in any way. My plane crashing was the second attempt on my life while I was in America."

Any remaining blood drained from her face, and her eyes became huge metal discs of anguish as she sucked in a ragged breath.

"Jane," he said gruffly, reaching out and grasping her left foot, which was peeking from beneath her robe, and giving it a gentle squeeze. "I'm not trying to scare you. I am alive and well, thanks to you."

Reynard leaned over and kissed her hair. "And your breath of life, daughter," he added.

Mark tugged on her foot. "I'm only trying to explain our concerns. Our enemies are watching and waiting for us to make a mistake they can take advantage of." He looked at his father, then at his brothers, and then at Irina. Finally, he looked back at Jane. "We appear to be relatively safe in our own country, since there have been no attempts to harm any of us on Shelkovan soil. So far, at least, we've been vulnerable only when we leave, as the odds of making our deaths look like an accident outside the country are better."

"So you're all safe if you just stay home?" she asked, her eyes still huge and worried.

"So it has seemed to date, although we still take precautions whenever any of us leave the palace grounds. We can't count on the consortium assuming that if the king of Shelkova were to be assassinated in his own country, there would be such anger that it would never gain the land it seeks." Mark shrugged. "But if that king, or his heir apparent, dies overseas under vague circumstances, it will be easier for them to cry anger along with our people. They would act just as outraged, saying they're willing to step in and help a struggling country during its loss."

"But there are five of you," she pointed out. "They can't kill you all. If they had succeeded with you, they must have realized your father and brothers would have continued the fight."

Mark had no trouble stifling his smile, because even though Jane was becoming outraged on their behalf, as he'd hoped, it was a hollow victory. She was sincerely scared for them. That hadn't been his goal; he'd simply wanted her to care. And understand. "They would take advantage of having the wind knocked out of us and act quickly to cement their position before we were through mourning our loss."

"Do you know who the guys in this consortium are?" she asked, her face getting red again, only this time with anger. "Do you actually know their names?"

Mark nodded. Oh yeah, his avenging angel was emerging.

"Then kill them first."

Aunt Irina gasped. Reynard sputtered. Sergei barked in laughter, and Alexi finally opened his eyes. Dmitri merely rolled off the bed to kneel on the floor and gape at Jane.

And Mark let his grin finally escape. "Sister Roberta would have you in church for a year, on your knees, saying penance for even thinking such things."

She lifted her chin and tried to wiggle off the bed, but failed when Reynard stopped her.

"You can't just sit around waiting for it to happen," she railed at the lot of them.

"We're not."

"So what are you doing?"

"Along with the small army and navy we acquired during the breakup, we were lucky enough to obtain a few good intelligence officers. They're looking into the matter for us."

"And meanwhile?"

"Meanwhile, you will consider yourself one of us," Mark said rather forcefully. "You're not a prisoner here, Jane," he continued, softening his voice. "You may explore Shelkova and enjoy yourself, but with *trained* bodyguards."

She looked stunned. She turned her head, apparently looking for Reynard's opinion. He nodded his agreement, his features leaving no opening for arguments.

She looked back at Mark. "Then I actually am a prisoner, because I'm not about to let somebody place himself in the line of danger to protect me."

Mark instantly took Dmitri's place right beside her, so he could get his face really close to hers. "You will have protection, and you will let the men do their jobs."

"Why can't I just go home?"

"You *are* home," he growled. "As long as I breathe, you will be living here with me."

Her eyes narrowed. "We'll see," she muttered through gritted teeth.

A timid knock sounded at the door. And while Mark and Jane continued trying to stare each other down, Alexi crawled off the bed and went to the door. Two hastily dressed servants came in bearing huge trays of hot cocoa and warm, sweet-smelling rolls.

With an unexpected and rather ferocious shove, Jane pushed Mark off the bed, causing him to land on the floor with a grunt-inducing thud. Still glaring while somehow managing to smile smugly, Jane crawled off the bed, stepped over Mark, and went to meet the startled staff.

Mark grinned at his father, who was leaning over and grinning back at him, as they all heard Jane profusely thanking the servants and feverishly apologizing for having them pulled from their own warm beds.

Chapter Fourteen

❖ ⋯ ❖

Y ou have impeccable manners, Jane," Irina commented
as the two women served the cocoa to the late-night
gathering that didn't seem to want to break up. All the
men were happily re-ensconced on the bed, and Reynard,
using some of that old Lakeland charm, was blatantly trying to cajole Jane back onto the bed with them.

"You can thank Sister Roberta and Emily Post that I
have any manners at all," Jane responded to Irina.

"Who is Sister Roberta?" Alexi asked, apparently wide
awake now and greedily wolfing down Cook's sweet rolls.

"She was the Mother Superior of Saint Xavier's." At
his quizzical look, Jane continued. "That's where I grew
up. Saint Xavier's is an orphanage."

"Come sit with me, daughter, and tell us about your
home," Reynard tried again, this time capturing her hand

before she could escape. With only a slight tug, and much rattling of cocoa cups, the bed dipped and Jane was once again settled beside him.

Brushing her hair from her face, she finally seemed resigned to the inquiry. Mark thought about again routing Dmitri, who had resumed his place beside her, but decided to remain at Jane's feet so he could better see her face.

"And who is Emily Post?" Dmitri asked.

"Emily Post is the author of a book on manners," Jane explained. She smiled whimsically. "From the time I could sit in someone's lap, there were two books that were constantly read to me—the Bible and Emily Post. And when I was old enough to read myself, I was required to read both books from cover to cover at least once a year."

"Good Lord," Sergei groaned on a shudder. "Rather dry reading on either count, weren't they, for a child?"

Jane arched a very queenly-looking brow over the rim of her cocoa cup. "But quick by the third or fourth time. Heck, I could recite from either one of them, even today."

"Were you allowed to read other books?" Alexi asked.

"Oh, sure. Sister Patricia used to read *The Little Engine That Could* to me all the time. She started right about the time I was learning to walk."

"How many children were at this Saint Xavier's?" Aunt Irina asked.

"Oh, anywhere between six and eight of us at any one time."

Jane looked at all their sympathetic faces and immediately puffed up indignantly. "I had a wonderful life at the Home. The sisters were good to me. And as I got older, I was important to them. I helped them with the younger children."

Mark couldn't contain his grin. Yes, she had fond memories of her youth, where she had been important and needed. "And later, when you left Saint Xavier's," he asked, "were you still important to someone?"

"When I was twelve, I went to live with the Johnsons," she explained, frowning at his choice of words. "They owned a set of sporting camps just north of Pine Creek. They were getting old, and they needed my help. Especially Ann. She taught me to cook for the sports."

"Sports?" Sergei quizzed.

"That's what we call the people who come to fish and hunt."

"Ah. And this is where you learned to use a gun?" Reynard asked, a gleam in his eye.

"Well, yes," Jane hedged, squirming uncomfortably at his reminder of her foolishness. "Mr. Johnson— Hank—taught me to hunt and fish."

"And Mr. Johnson is the man who gave you your shotgun?" Mark asked.

She frowned at him again. "Yes."

"It's a quality weapon."

"The Johnsons liked me," she countered, her chin rising.

"I can understand why," Mark countered back.

"How long did you stay with them?" Reynard asked, drawing her attention again.

"Until I was nineteen. Hank died in a boating accident on Pine Lake and Ann went to live with her sister in

Georgia. I worked for the people who bought their sporting camps for a while, then got a job managing another set of camps farther north."

"This is where you met Silas?" Mark asked.

Jane nodded and broke into a smile. "Yeah. Silas was the handyman there."

"Until you talked him into buying Twelve Mile Camp."

"Something like that," she agreed, her smile broadening.

"Mark called Silas a damn Yankee," Alexi tattled. "What does that mean?"

"It means," Jane answered, her eyes lighting with mischief, "that Silas got the better part of your brother."

"And most of my cash," Mark added.

"We have sporting camps," Alexi piped up. "In the north."

"Really?" Jane said in surprise. "Do many people come to Shelkova to hunt and fish?"

"Both," he answered. "We have caribou and some elk for hunting. But the fishing; now that's grand," Alexi finished dreamily.

Mark rolled his eyes. They were in for it now. Alexi had a passion for fishing. And if they weren't careful, Jane was liable to sneak off with the man one of these days, and disappear into the north woods and not come out until they were both laden with trout. As it was, the bedridden group found themselves having to listen to another one of Alexi's famous fishing tales.

So they dutifully listened until Mark noticed Jane was beginning to nod off, her empty cocoa cup slipping quietly from her fingers. He gave Alexi a poke in the leg to shut him up. Everyone looked at Mark, then followed his eyes to Jane, and everyone smiled.

Mark scowled at the lot of them. "I'm taking her back to her room. Alone."

Everyone shook their heads.

Mark got off the bed. "Yes, I am."

"Just leave her here," Reynard suggested. "She's comfortable."

"She won't be in the morning when she wakes up. She'll be embarrassed."

"Then Alexi will accompany you to her room."

"No, he won't," Mark growled. "Butt out. Let me court the lady."

Reynard snorted—quietly. "I trust your *courting* as much as I trust your intentions."

"I promise to drop her in bed and leave," Mark grudgingly offered.

"Tomorrow we'll move her to this wing," Reynard added, obviously not believing him.

"She won't come. I put her in the room she has to give her some space."

"More likely so you could get her alone," Sergei said with a snort.

"She will come," Reynard said, ignoring the brothers' banter. "You forget the stories, Mark. Your mother was just as reluctant. But I charmed my way around Katrina, and I shall charm my way around Jane." Reynard sighed. "Too bad you didn't inherit that gift from me."

Not wanting to wake their angel, Mark's three brothers snickered in agreement. Reynard turned to Aunt Irina.

"Prepare the room next to yours, Irina. Jane can stay there, and you can keep a watchful eye on her," he added meaningfully.

Irina wholeheartedly agreed, giving Mark a mischievous wink. And Mark winked back. Oh, he had enough charm to get his aunt to look the other way when he wanted.

Bending down to finally pick Jane up, Mark must have startled her awake. Because the next thing he knew a sharp fist caught him in the chin at the same time as a fierce pain shot up his thigh far too close to his groin for comfort.

Male laughter and a distressed shriek followed him to the floor, and Mark looked up to see a wide-eyed Jane blinking down at him. She quickly scrambled off the bed while trying to apologize, but her ankle gave out and she ended up on top of him instead.

The laughter continued.

What he could see of her face through her knotted hair was bright red. "Your ankle is sore," he whispered, wrapping his arms around her and holding her on his lap. "Let me carry you to your room."

She mumbled something incoherent into his shirt that Mark took as permission. So once again he picked her up and easily gained his feet, and Jane buried her face in his neck as he carried her from the room—that is, after giving Sergei a warning glare not to follow.

"Your ankle is tired?" he asked once they were in the hall.

"Yes. I'm sorry I hit you," she said, still not looking at him. "You startled me."

His long strides quickly carried them down the hall as he thought about that. Finally, he took an educated guess.

"You've been startled from sleep before," he said, not as a question.

"Yes."

"Recently?"

"A-about a month or so ago," she softly confessed.

"About the time you decided to move to the coast." Again, it wasn't a question.

"Yeah, about then."

"Possibly by someone looking for a . . . mistress?"

"Something like that."

She still wasn't looking at him. And Mark pretty well knew why. This was not an easy admission for her, and to be truthful, he was surprised she was making it at all. He finally reached her room and carefully set her on the bed, going down on his knees in front of her and holding her hips with his hands.

"That man was a fool, Jane," he said thickly, ducking his head and trying to see her eyes. "Only a fool would settle for you as a mistress. Only a fool would not put a ring on your finger and give you his name. Only a fool, angel, would not hold you tightly forever."

Her eyes finally met his. And oh, the sadness he saw there. And the yearning.

"Only a fool would marry me," she softly contradicted.

"I've been called that once or twice in my life." He cocked his head. "My mother, I think, was the last to dare."

Jane hesitantly smiled, still sadly, and gently brought her hand up to his jaw. "Let me go home."

"You're already here, Jane," he whispered. "This is your home now, and will be the home of our children." He gave her hips a soft squeeze. "It's not by a lake and it doesn't have a picket fence, but it has a family of your very own. And it has an ocean out back and uncles and a grandfather for our babies. Stay here with me, Jane. Make Shelkova your home."

"But why me?" she asked, tears in her eyes as her thumb stroked his jaw again.

"Because *I* need you. Because you're important to *me*. Because if you leave, you'll take a good part of my heart with you."

Her hand stilled. And the threatening tears finally spilled free as she suddenly threw herself against him and wrapped her good arm around his neck, nearly choking him. "Oh, I wish I could believe that," she softly cried into his shoulder. "I really wish!"

"You'll believe, angel," he vowed, hugging her as tightly as he dared. "Eventually. Now, come. Let me put you to bed. And let me see what I can do to help your ankle."

As he expected, that last offer got her to release him. It also got her tears dried and her scowl back. "My ankle's just fine."

"And sore. You shouldn't have run around the palace without your brace."

Her chin lifted. "I don't need the brace to walk."

"Your limp is more pronounced without it," he pointed out, deciding to challenge her. It was time she got over being shy about her scars and learned to trust him.

Hell, it was time she started *believing*.

"The brace is just for support because my ankle is weak. That's all."

"And now it is sore," he repeated. "Tell me what you do to relieve the pain after putting in a hard day."

She tried raising her chin higher, but Mark grabbed it so he could look her right in the eye. "I'm not leaving until this is settled. And Jane?"

"Yes."

"I'm bigger and stronger and more stubborn than you."

She suddenly smiled. "Then what were you doing on the floor of your father's room?"

"Contemplating ways of getting even," he drawled, bobbing his brows and standing up. "Does heat help? Would a hot towel ease the ache?"

"Okay," she ungraciously conceded. "Get me a hot towel and then leave."

Mark went to her bathroom and turned the hot water tap and pulled a thick bath towel off the rack, his thoughts turning inward as he held the towel in the water. When he'd told her she would take a good part of his heart with her if she left, he'd declared not just his intentions, but his love, hadn't he?

Had she even *heard* him?

Wringing the towel more forcibly than necessary, Mark returned to Jane, unable to stifle the foolish grin he knew he was wearing. She didn't grin back. In fact, the love of his life was scowling at him and holding out her hand for the towel. Mark took that hand and used it to push her back on the bed.

But she sprang right back up when he moved toward her feet. "I'll do that."

He gently forced her back down, then loomed over her. "No, Jane. I will. Don't panic. I'm going to place the towels over your sock, so the heat won't scorch your skin. Relax, angel."

She stayed down this time, but her lips were pursed.

He guessed she was silently reciting more nun-approved curses at him. Still grinning like the besotted fool he was, Mark carefully laid the towel over her right ankle.

"You're going to get the bed all wet. This is embarrassing."

"This is part of believing, Jane."

Satisfied the towel was secure, Mark gently pushed her over and stretched out beside her.

She squeaked.

He grabbed the hand trying to push him away and anchored it against his chest. Then he took his other arm and tucked it under her head. Then, still holding her hand, he moved his arm to her waist and pulled her up against his hip. Then he sighed and closed his eyes.

"You can't stay here," she said huskily.

"It'll be dawn in an hour," he pointed out, not opening his eyes as he wiggled closer. "I'll just settle here for a little while. Don't worry, witch, I won't take advantage of you." He opened one eye. "If you want a baby, you're going to have to marry me first."

Mark wasn't sure, but he thought she was close to cursing for real. "One minute I'm a witch and the next I'm an angel. Can't you decide what to call me?" she asked instead.

"On our golden anniversary, Jane, I'll tell you which one you are." He sighed and snuggled closer. "Hopefully I'll have it figured out by then."

Holy smokes. He intended to sleep here.

Jane didn't know what to make of that.

Or what to make of what he'd said earlier.

Or what to make of the fact that he'd just wrapped her ugly ankle in a towel.

What if the morning maid or the nurse or somebody came in? Mark had actually gone to sleep. Right beside her. In his father's house!

Darn. Jane thought about pushing him off the bed, but feeling his warmth, hearing his breath so steady and unguarded, and loving him, made the task impossible. She didn't want to kick him out; she wanted to snuggle closer.

Had he really said she'd take part of his heart if she left? A good part of it?

And that she should believe?

Believe in what? Herself? Him? Love?

Jane lay in the dark beside Mark and thought again of Sister Patricia reading her *The Little Engine That Could* so many times that she knew it by heart. Crippled, in pain after each operation and wanting to give up, she had clung to that story with the hope of a child wanting so much to be normal. To walk. To be like the other children.

She still owned a well-read, battered copy of that book. Or she had until those men had blown up her car. And right now she'd like to read it again; to look at the pictures; to see the expression on the little engine as it struggled up an impossible hill. And she wanted to see its expression when it had topped that hill and started down the other side.

She needed that little engine's determination now to believe she could overcome insurmountable odds and become not merely a queen, but a wife to the man she loved, a mother to their children, and a daughter to a retired king who desperately wanted one.

Either the Lakeland men were blind to who she was,

or she was the blind one. Maybe she wasn't nobody after all. They simply accepted her—limp, non-pedigree, and temper. They seemed sincere. All of them, including Aunt Irina. And especially Mark. He kept kissing her.

And now he'd fallen asleep in her bed.

Jane scooted closer and finally did the same.

Chapter Fifteen

✦━━✦

Jane. Jane, wake up."

She tried, she really did. Irina's voice was soft and cajoling and inviting, but Jane felt like she'd just gotten to sleep.

"We're leaving in an hour. You've just enough time for a quick shower and lunch."

"Leaving?" Jane croaked, finally getting her eyes opened enough to see Irina backlit by the late-morning sun. She became aware of others moving in the room.

"We're stopping at the hospital first, and then we're going shopping."

"Shopping?" Jane echoed, realizing she sounded like a sleepy parrot.

"We'll have fun, yes? Spending Markov's money?"

"I'm not spending his money."

The woman's smile broadened. "He says he owes you a new wardrobe."

That's right, he did, since *his* enemies had blown up her car. "You're going with me?"

"Yes, if you don't mind. I know all the nice little shops in the city. And," Irina added, a twinkle in her eyes, "I speak Shelkovan."

Jane groaned. Not speaking the language had gotten her thrown in jail. "I'd love for you to come with me." She finally sat up. "It's been forever since I went shopping with a friend."

"Thank you for calling me your friend."

"Oh, Irina. You're only the second female friend I've ever had," she whispered, scrambling out of bed. Jane hesitated. "Maybe I'm being presumptuous. You may just be helping me for Mark."

Irina planted her hands on her hips. "I would do many things for Markov, but never pretend friendship for him." She took Jane's hand. "I want to be your friend. I've been alone in this male household since Katrina died."

Jane practically threw herself at Irina and wrapped both arms around the older woman and hugged her. "Yes," she whispered, her eyes misting. "Oh yes. Thank you."

Irina leaned away, her own eyes misted. "No. Thank you. Now come. Let's go fortify ourselves for the enjoyable task of spending Markov's money. It's a rare occasion when that one opens his purse."

"Really?" Jane asked, headed for the shower. "He was practically throwing the contents of his wallet at Silas."

"Which says how worried he was about you," Irina called after her.

Jane thought about that while she showered. Thinking back, Mark *had* seemed frantic about her illness. Heck, he'd bought her enough M&M's and Pepsi to feed a school. All of which she'd managed to clean up on the painful jet ride to Shelkova.

Maybe he did care.

It wasn't until she emerged from the bath that Jane realized there were two other women in the room. They were packing all the things she'd been using. "What are they doing?" she asked Irina, who was laying out clothes for her to wear.

"You're moving."

"I am? Where?"

"To our wing of the palace."

"Why? What's wrong with this room?"

"What if I told you we need to clean this wing?" Irina offered, not turning, but clasping the slacks she was holding to her chest.

"I'd say you're prevaricating."

"Then how about it being easier for the staff if we're all in one place?"

"I'd say you're reaching with that one."

Irina turned to face her. "Then I would say Reynard simply wishes it."

"A decree?"

"Close enough."

Jane gasped, covering her blushing cheeks with both hands. "Oh no! He found out Mark spent last night here."

Irina laughed. "That rascal. He said he was just going to escort you to your room."

"He did."

"Hmmm . . ." Irina suddenly frowned. "He didn't . . . pester you, did he?"

"If I say yes, would it get him thrown in the dungeon?"

Irina laughed again. "Doubtful. Reynard would have a mutiny of the staff if he did. No, about the only thing Markov would get is a scorching lecture on proprieties."

"He only stayed a little while. And he didn't pester me."

"Too bad," Irina returned with a wink. "Markov is a handsome man. And very sought after by many women."

"He's a prince who's about to be a king."

"He can't help that."

"He wouldn't want to if he could."

"What's wrong with being a king? Aren't you being a bit prejudiced?"

Jane gasped. "I am not."

"You think because you're an orphan he couldn't want you. But you don't want him because he's a king." Irina turned back to her task. "Sounds like prejudice to me."

"But it's not only my being an orphan," Jane tried to explain, moving around the bed to face her. "I have a terrible limp."

Irina picked up a blouse and shrugged. "We all have flaws."

"And I don't know anything about being married to a king, much less anything about being a *queen*. Heck, I never even went to college."

Irina looked at her. "Yet you obviously have a brain. Learn to be a queen."

"But I'm nobody!"

Irina sighed and sat down on the bed, closing her eyes.

"Jane," she said quietly, "when you pulled Mark from his sunken plane, he wasn't anybody, either. He wasn't a prince or a son or a nephew. He was nobody to you." Irina looked at her. "But you risked your life to save his. And you kept on saving him by leading him out of the woods and getting him to his meeting on the coast. He was only a man named Mark, but still you helped him. You also fell in love with him, didn't you?"

Jane bit her lip, completely unaware her eyes answered for her.

"Even if he were nobody special, your love would have made him the most important person in the world to you. Think about that," Irina finished softly, getting up and walking out.

And think Jane did, all through dressing and lunch. Which was why she was surprised to find herself sitting in the backseat of a huge car full of Lakelands less than an hour later.

"Are you all going shopping with us?" she asked Mark.

"I am," he answered. "Sergei and Alexi are only riding with us as far as the hospital."

"Hospital?"

Mark frowned. "Did Irina not tell you we're stopping there first?"

"Yes, but she didn't say why."

Mark sighed. "To have your shoulder checked."

"My shoulder feels just fine. I don't need to have it checked."

"You have stitches," he explained, sounding exasperated, if a little annoyed. He waved a hand in front of her face. "Where have you been for the last hour?"

"Mentally going over maps in my head, trying to remember where the dungeons are."

Only Irina laughed at that one. But she kept the secret to herself, despite the questioning looks she got from the three men.

When they stopped in front of the hospital, Jane noticed the car that had been following them. As Sergei and Alexi exited to the sidewalk and two men got out of the other car and started down the sidewalk behind them, she grew alarmed. "Someone's following them," she told Mark.

He turned and looked. "Their bodyguards," he explained, leading her to the hospital door. "We have a couple ourselves," he added, nodding toward the two men following them.

"I don't feel like going shopping after."

"Jane, don't. There's no reason for you to be afraid."

She blinked at him. "I'm not afraid. I just don't want to go."

"And there's no reason for you to worry about the men. It's their job, and they're trained very well to do it. They can take care of themselves as well as us. Let them."

"I don't like it."

"You'll get used to it."

"No, I won't."

"Yes, you will."

She was about to give him a scathing comeback when she spotted Dr. Daveed, and wiggled free and all but ran up to the man.

"Dr. Daveed! Hello!"

"Hello to you, Miss Abbot," he returned, bowing formally.

"Oh, stop that. You used to call me Jane. How's everyone on the *Katrina*? How's Dorjan?"

"The envy of his shipmates," he said, laughing. He stopped suddenly, turned, and bowed formally to Mark and then Irina. "Your Highness. My lady."

"Daveed," Mark answered, smiling at Jane's surprised look. It was as if she kept forgetting they were royalty. Which was fine with him, as the more often she forgot, the less guarded she was. "We've come to have you check your work."

"How come you're not on the *Katrina*?" Jane blurted out.

"I've been transferred here, to the city of Previa."

"Oh. Did you ask to be transferred?"

"No," he admitted with a smile. "I was . . . offered the position."

Jane shot a frown in Mark's direction.

"Which he quickly accepted," Mark added. "As he wanted to come home."

She took Dr. Daveed's arm and started down the hall. "Then let's get to it, Doc. I've got lots of shopping to do," she said loudly enough for Mark to hear.

"You're healing well, Miss Abbot," Daveed decided ten minutes later as he carefully removed her stitches.

"Because of your good work."

"And the special care you've received?" he added.

"Maybe."

"Miss Abbot. Jane. I . . . I would talk to you candidly, if I could," Daveed said softly, still standing behind her, still working on her shoulder.

"Sure."

"It's about your ankle."

She turned just enough to see his face. "Did Mark put you up to this?"

"His Highness? No. This is my own forwardness. While you were on the *Katrina*, I took the liberty of looking at your ankle."

Heavens, the poor man sounded like he was confessing a cardinal sin.

"I realize I was supposed to be treating your shoulder, not your ankle, and I'm sorry for invading your privacy."

"But?" she urged, smiling now.

"But I was curious. I've been a military doctor for thirty years," he explained, "and have seen every injury a body could have. Your ankle was crushed, no?"

For all of his remorse for invading her privacy, Jane could tell Daveed wasn't merely curious but sincerely interested. "Yes. Nobody knows how it happened. I was discovered with the injury, only a few days old."

That startled him. "Discovered?"

"I was left on the hospital's doorstep."

"Oh. I see. So you were just an infant when you were injured. You've had operations."

"Three."

"And now you wear a brace." He smiled a little. "A rather battered brace."

"This one is six years old."

"Can I ask if it pains you to walk?"

"Only when I've overdone it a bit. Then my ankle just gets lame."

"But when you walk, you're not limping because of pain?"

"No."

"Do you know why you limp?"

She frowned at him. "Because my ankle's deformed."

He shook his head, making Jane wonder if the man had been tipping a bottle of vodka. She gave him an exasperated look. "It's not deformed?"

"Yes, it is, but that's not why you limp."

"Maybe I limp because I like to," she shot back, getting annoyed. "Or maybe I want everyone to feel sorry for me."

"Or maybe your right leg is slightly shorter than your left," he said, not the least bit intimidated.

"Shorter!"

He walked around to face her, took her right foot in his hand and pulled off her shoe, then pulled off her brace. And then her sock. Jane instinctively tried to tug her foot away, but he held fast and tickled the bottom of her toes, so surprising her that she stopped tugging. "Now look," he began, lifting her leg. "There is a lack of muscle around your ankle, thus you need the brace for support. But the bone itself is what was crushed. When it healed, and with ensuing operations, this leg ended up shorter than your other one. Do you understand?"

"I guess so," she agreed, leaning over and peering down at her ankle. It looked like its same old ugly self to her. She'd never thought it could be shorter.

Lovely. Just what she needed—something else wrong with her.

"Would you like for me to take precise measurements to see how much shorter it is?"

"Why?" she asked, trying to tug her foot back again.

"So we can make up the difference."

"What? You mean to make my legs the same length by jacking up my shoe?"

"Something like that," he agreed with a nod. "Only I don't think the difference is so great that you would need an obviously thicker shoe. I could fashion you a new brace to not only fit under your arch, but under your entire foot."

"But then my boots won't fit."

"I would make the sole out of neoprene, which would be supple for when you walked. You'd only have to pull the bottom lining out of any shoe you wished to wear and it should fit fine." He held up her old brace and examined it. "And this," he continued, tapping the metal hinge, "would be made of hard nylon and pivot easier. And I don't think it would have to come all the way up to your knee," he added, setting down her old brace and lifting her foot again. He touched her leg just above her ankle. "The bone and muscle is fine from here up. I can make you a lighter, less cumbersome brace."

"Really?" Jane whispered, staring at her right foot. She looked up at Dr. Daveed. "Okay, then measure it." His face turned red again, making Jane smile. "Let me guess. You already did on the *Katrina*."

His face darkening more, he nodded.

"And?"

"And there could be a problem."

"Now what?"

"Well, you've been walking this way for how many years?"

"I'm twenty-seven. So?"

"The muscles in your legs, hips, and back are used to

your having one leg shorter than the other. Your entire body structure has grown accustomed to this. If I elevate your foot to the proper height, those muscles are going to protest."

"So, let them. Will this stop my limping?" she asked hopefully, anticipating the answer.

"No."

"Then why are you telling me any of this?" she snapped, wanting to throttle the man.

He tickled her toes again, his face amused. "You will always limp, Jane, because your ankle will never flex properly. But I can make your limp much less pronounced. And your ankle will not tire so quickly."

"Really?"

"Really."

Jane pondered that possibility. "Um, how much would this new brace cost?"

Her question seemed to startle him. "I have no idea."

"You're going to have to give me a price, or at least a fairly close estimate, before I agree. I, ah, I'm a little strapped for cash right now, and I don't know when or even *how* to access my savings account from here."

He looked even more startled, but then suddenly grinned. "How about if I simply add the cost of the brace to your gunshot surgery and subsequent care? I doubt the naval accounting clerks even read the bills I submit."

"Works for me," Jane suddenly decided, figuring saving Shelkova's prince from drowning was worth the cost of one measly brace. "But this is just between us, okay? I'll let you make me a new brace, but only if you keep it a secret. Agreed?"

He didn't look happy about her little caveat, but finally

nodded. "It's going to be painful at first," he cautioned, "as you discover muscles you didn't know you had in some fairly odd places."

"But I'll limp less?" she clarified, ignoring the threat of pain.

"Not noticeably at first. I would like to introduce your muscles to the new height gradually."

"Why not tell my muscles this is the way it's going to be from now on and just get it over with? There might be more initial pain, but it won't last as long."

He grinned at her thinking. "Twenty-seven years is a long time to instill stubbornness."

"Are you talking about my muscles or me?" she asked, her eyes narrowed in warning.

Daveed shrugged. "Both, by my guess." His face reddened again as he walked to a small table and pulled a towel off it, picked up a small plastic brace, and came back to her. "I . . . ah, I made this up for you," he admitted. "Just in case." He gently settled the brace over her foot, then carefully turned her leg back and forth while studying the fit. He worked the hinge several times and checked to see if the brace allowed any lateral movement. Apparently satisfied, he looked at her and smiled. "Start out using this new brace only a few hours each day and gradually work your way up to all day," he murmured, putting on her sock and then her boot.

Jane didn't want to hit him anymore, she wanted to kiss him. So she did, throwing her arms around him and laughing and crying at the same time. "Thank you," she whispered in his ear. "You can invade my privacy anytime you want."

He covered his embarrassment with a cough. "Well, that's good. Because I'm about to invade it again. Are you pregnant, Jane?"

Well, darn; talk about riding an emotional roller coaster. She was back to wanting to hit him. "I don't know."

"It's still early yet. It would only be about two weeks since you could . . . you were . . ." He covered his mouth with his hand and coughed again.

Jane did the same.

"Yes. Well. When will I know for sure?" she asked in a squeak.

"Another week, perhaps. Unless you begin . . . unless you have your . . ." He gave a heavy sigh and shook his head. "I'm a military doctor, Jane, not a baby doctor."

She patted his arm. "But I bet you still know more about this stuff than I do," she said with a laugh. "I was brought up by nuns."

Daveed laughed with her. Soon, he sobered. "If you suspect you're pregnant, I want your promise you will tell me."

"I will."

"You may be carrying the next heir to the throne," he reminded her.

And if Reynard hadn't been fibbing when he'd told her Lakelands only fathered male children, she could be pregnant with a Shelkovan prince!

Shopping with Irina turned out to be a novel experience. It was nothing like her shopping trips to L.L.Bean in Freeport with Katy, when they usually came back with food and books and camping gadgets. In fact, Jane was pretty sure she'd just purchased more clothes today than she had over the course of her entire life.

To begin with, Mark had escorted them into the first shop, given Irina orders to outfit Jane completely even as he'd given Jane a good frown, and then left them. But not alone. No, there were two men conspicuously stationed by the door, both looking big and rugged and mean, which Jane guessed they had to be if they were bodyguards. One never took his eyes off the street and the other one never took his eyes off the two women in his charge.

"We should start from the inside and work out, I guess," Irina suggested, holding up a satiny bra and panty set.

Jane grabbed the garments. "Good heavens, I can't wear something like this."

"Not naughty enough for you?" Irina drawled, taking the garments back.

"Not very serviceable," Jane countered, going to a rack of simple, white, rugged-looking bras. "And stop waving that around. Mutt and Jeff will see."

"Mutt and Jeff?" Irina repeated, giggling now.

"Those two men Mark left with us. And what's wrong with this?" Jane asked, holding up (out of sight of the men) a white bra.

"I bet your Sister Roberta has one just like it," Irina whispered out of the side of her mouth. She grabbed the bra and gave the straps a good snap. "Serviceable, but not very pretty."

"No one's going to see it."

"You don't think your husband will? You're going to get dressed in the closet?"

"I'm certainly not going to get dressed in front of my husband." Jane suddenly gasped, her eyes nearly crossing. "I'm not going to *have* a husband."

Irina merely raised a brow.

And the shopping excursion went downhill from there. Mark rejoined them an hour later, and Jane was thankful she'd already talked Irina into letting her get some jeans, which were safely tucked in the trunk of the car thanks to Mutt. Or Jeff.

At Mark's insistence and with Irina's guidance, Jane tried on and bought not only comfortable slacks and blouses, but several evening dresses that came to the floor. She couldn't even use her brace as an excuse, the dresses were so long. At the next shop Irina was able to find her a pair of low-heeled shoes to go with the dresses that would fit over her new brace. The silk stockings Irina insisted she buy, however, were alarming. Never having worn pantyhose, Jane held up a pair—out of sight of Mark—and asked how she was expected to fit into them, since she was pretty sure they wouldn't fit a three-year-old. Irina assured her they stretched.

But it was the last shop that finally made Jane balk. "I don't wear jewelry."

"You need it to go with your evening wear," Irina argued.

"We're supposed to be replacing my blown-up wardrobe, not buying gowns and silk stockings and jewelry."

"You can't wear wool pants and flannel shirts to a ball," Mark interjected.

"I'm not Cinderella."

Mark bent at the waist, getting really close to her face.

"No, you're not. You're Jane Doe Abbot, and you're going to dance with me at my coronation ball."

"Da— Did you say dance?"

Mark nodded. And then he gave her a quick kiss on the lips. When he pulled back, his smile was more nasty than nice. "And at our wedding."

She couldn't even think of anything to say, since she was beginning to believe—and fear—there really was going to be a wedding. "Then I want something simple," she said, trying to ignore the sudden gleam in his eyes as she turned to the counter.

The jeweler, bless his Shelkovan heart, couldn't be more excited to have royalty in his shop. His chest was puffed out like a drumming partridge and his brow was sweating. But the poor man's face fell when Jane passed over his diamonds and chose a simple gold locket in the shape of a fir tree. "I like this," she offered, holding it up for Mark to see.

And she did, as it reminded her of the Lakeland stationery.

"My people are going to think I'm miserly if all my bride wears is a simple locket."

"You're pushing, Your Highness," Jane said sweetly.

"If I push hard enough, will you fall into my arms?"

"I'll probably step to the side and let you fall on your face."

"Witch."

And on and on it went, until Jane finally made it back to the palace and up to her new room in the family wing. It took Mutt and Jeff four trips to bring in all her purchases, and she was both thrilled and ashamed. She was

so excited to own such beautiful, colorful clothes, and so
guilty of the sin of gluttony. She loved each and every
piece, even the beautiful evening gowns. But she especially loved the frilly, not-so-serviceable underwear.

Sister Roberta would have her doing penance for a
month. And then she'd make her give all the clothes back.
Jane was darn glad she was twenty-seven instead of seven,
and that Sister Roberta was half a world away.

The nun was retired now, but Jane kept in touch with
her. She wrote regularly and drove to Bangor to visit her
each summer and at Christmas. And instead of raising
children, Sister Roberta now spent her time taking walks
along the Penobscot River and reading late into the night.
And she always told Jane during her visits that she was
her most favorite orphan of all.

Jane had stopped believing that venial lie twelve years
ago, but loved Sister Roberta for still attempting to make
her feel special.

Just like Mark was always trying to do.

And that was just it. All the Lakelands were making
her feel special by the simple act of treating her as though
she were no different from themselves. They each sought
her out at various times and talked with her as if she were
an old friend. They hauled her into midnight meetings,
cramming her onto their patriarch's bed as if she were
one of them. And each of the men had taken their turn
scolding her, as if she were a real sister or daughter—just
like Katy MacBain's family did to Katy. Heck, even Irina
had spoken plainly about Jane belonging if she wanted
to. They weren't trying to make her feel important or
special, but like one of them.

The worry was they were succeeding.

Jane felt comfortable here, and darn it, she wanted to stay.

I f I were to tell you I'm going to marry Mark in six days," Jane whispered the moment Katy said hello, "would you come be my maid of honor?"

There was a long, stark silence. "Are you pregnant?" Katy asked softly.

"I don't know."

"Do you love him?"

Jane sucked in a deep breath. "Yes," she more exhaled than said.

"And is he in love with you?"

"I don't . . . I'm not . . . Does it really matter?"

Another silence. "I'm pretty sure it does, Jane." And then a sigh. "Did he happen to mention the word 'love' when he asked you to marry him?"

"Um . . . he never actually asked. He just announced to a room full of people at dinner one night that I was his fiancée. I didn't tell you when I called a couple of days later because I figured Mark had only said it to stop some businessman from throwing his daughter at him. But since then, everyone—including Mark—has been acting like we really are engaged."

"I don't care if you do love him," Katy said, still softly. "You can't marry the man just to save him from a scheming businessman. Are you sure you're not mistaking lust for love?" There was an equally soft snort. "Not that you have a whole lot of experience with either one."

"If how much my heart aches when I even think about a future without Mark is any indication, I'm definitely more than in lust with him. I don't want to leave after the coronation," Jane admitted, closing her eyes against the pain merely saying it out loud elicited. "I want . . . His father and brothers and aunt treat me like I'm *family*."

"But you wouldn't be marrying his father and brothers and aunt," Katy gently countered. "You'd be marrying a man who might only be in lust with you."

"When I called you last week, you told me Robbie and Jack Stone gave Mark their blessing."

"To keep you *safe*." Another heavy sigh came over the line. "If you don't even know if you're pregnant, then what's the rush?"

"Maybe so Mark will know I'm marrying him because I love him and not because I have to? And I'll know he's marrying me because he *wants* to and not out of obligation?"

Katy hesitated, then said, "I realize that sounds perfectly sensible, but it makes more sense to know he loves you *before* you make that kind of commitment."

"Wouldn't marrying me for no good reason mean he must love me?"

"Then why hasn't he *said* it?"

Jane suddenly smiled. "I guess you'll have to come to Shelkova and *ask* him," she returned, mimicking her friend's exasperation. "You're only volunteering on the ambulance, and that mountain climbing and rescue school in Colorado doesn't start for a couple of months, so come talk some sense into me *in person*. But you need to get here before Mark's coronation," she rushed on over Katy's sputtering, "because the wedding is taking place the same day. And," she added gruffly, turning serious, "I can't imagine getting married without the closest thing I have to a sister standing beside me."

"Dammit, Jane," Katy whispered. "I'm not going to let you make me cry."

"Then come."

"I . . . I can't," she said thickly. "I had to pass up a trip to Quebec just a few days ago when I discovered my passport was expired."

"Mark can get you in Shelkova without one," Jane drawled. Oh, yeah, she was definitely winning this one.

"But *Uncle Sam* won't let me back in America when I try to come home. And besides," she rushed on in a growl—Jane assumed to cover up a sob—"I'm committed to covering for a full-time paramedic who's out on maternity leave for the next six weeks. Oh, honey, I'm sorry," Katy added when Jane went silent. "You know I'd give my right arm to be there with you."

"I know. And . . . and I understand."

"How about if I promise to be there when you have the baby?"

"If there even is one."

That got her a weak laugh. "If there isn't one now, there will be soon. And you know why? Because I'm not sending that *box of condoms*," she finished in a shout over the blare of an alarm. *"Gotta go, kiddo. Duty calls. I love you!"*

Chapter Sixteen

◆ ⋯ ◆

Mark was sitting in the chair that for the last three years he'd teasingly called his father's throne, which was on the verge of becoming his. He was leaning back with his feet propped on the desk, quietly sipping a glass of Jack Daniel's whiskey. He'd discovered the stuff on his sojourn to America and promptly had five cases of it shipped home. At the moment, however, he was worried five weren't going to meet his immediate needs.

It was bad enough the whole palace was in an uproar over the coming ceremonies with carpenters and caterers and people running in every direction, but he also had a security staff on the verge of a nervous breakdown over all the strangers in the house. Yet here he was only three days shy of his coronation—and hopefully his wedding—dealing with familial complaints.

And again, Jane was the topic of discussion.

"I found her in my library, sitting in my chair, smoking one of my cigars," Reynard said. "Smoking! A cigar, for God's sake!"

Mark set his drink on the desk and scrubbed at his face with both hands, then looked at his father. "When?"

"This afternoon."

"At around three? The time you usually hole up in your library?"

"Well, yes. You have to do something, Markov. We can't have a cigar-smoking queen!"

Mark picked up his drink again to hide his grin at the picture of a cigar-smoking angel.

"And yesterday," Sergei said in turn, "I found her behind the barns teaching half the house staff how to play something called horseshoes. She was filthier than any of them and waving her hands like a madwoman trying to explain the game."

"Did you try this game?" Mark asked before taking another sip of whiskey. "Is it fun?"

"That's not the point. She can't go around wallowing in the dirt and yelling her head off like a fishwife."

"I see."

"And every morning she goes to visit those women who caused her to be thrown in jail," Dmitri spoke up, pacing to the front of the desk. "Some of them are still practicing their old . . . profession."

"Does she go alone?"

"No. She has her bodyguards trailing behind her. But that's not the point. The future queen of Shelkova can't be associating with prostitutes."

"I see."

"And Markov," Aunt Irina added softly, "all she wants to wear are her jeans and boots. Our staff dresses better than she does."

Mark smiled at his aunt and took another sip of whiskey.

"Do something," Reynard ordered. "If you can't control her, then—"

"Let me get this straight," Mark said quietly, cutting him off. "After saying just last week that she was a breath of fresh air, you're now asking me to make Jane stop being Jane?"

His face darkening with his scowl, Reynard strode to Mark's stock of whiskey. "Her antics may be endearing to *us*, but our people might not feel the same way about their *queen*. We're only asking that you persuade her to be more . . . circumspect."

Mark set his feet on the floor, set down his drink and stood up, then placed his hands on the desk, palms flat, and looked at Alexi. "Any complaints about my future bride?"

Alexi shrugged. "She takes that old horse for a walk each day down Main Street."

Mark slowly looked from one family member to the next, all of them staring back with righteous indignation mixed with the hope he would fix their future queen. He shook his head. "You haven't realized, have you?" he asked, a grin tugging at the corner of his mouth.

"Realized what?"

"We're being tested. And from the sound of things, we're failing."

"What in the hell do you mean, tested?" Sergei asked.

"Jane's been acting outrageous on purpose to see if we

truly accept her." He straightened and crossed his arms over his chest. "And from what I'm hearing, we don't."

"Bullshit," Dmitri snarled.

Mark shook his head again. "Tell me, have any of you tried to curb her behavior?"

"I've lectured her repeatedly about going into that part of the city," Dmitri said.

"And I'm guilty of scolding her for smoking cigars," Reynard confessed, frowning sadly and shaking his own head. "And so I failed, didn't I?"

"Well, we'll know tonight," Mark told him.

"We will? How?" Alexi asked, suddenly looking hopeful again.

"I'm going to ask Jane to marry me."

"You've already done that," Dmitri said.

"No, I haven't. I've told Jane I'm going to marry her, but I've never asked."

"Really?" Aunt Irina said in surprise. She stood up and started shaking her head like the rest of them. "Oh, Markov, every woman dreams of receiving a proper proposal. You must ask."

"I realize that, Aunt. I may have momentarily forgotten that truth, but hopefully I've come to my senses in time."

Reynard sat down with a loud sigh of relief. Dmitri and Alexi did the same. Aunt Irina shot Mark a wink and then left.

Sergei, however, continued staring at him, his eyes narrowed in suspicion. "And once she's your wife, she'll settle down?"

"No," Mark drawled. "I imagine she'll test us all the way to our graves."

Sergei groaned and headed to the bar. He didn't pour American whiskey, but good Shelkovan vodka. "You've apparently also forgotten how to tell the difference between an angel and a witch," he muttered just before lifting the glass to his grinning mouth.

Mark lifted his own glass in salute. "It doesn't matter what she is, so long as she's mine."

Walk with me."

"I . . . ah . . . I can't."

"Why not?"

"I just can't."

"I've been watching you this week. Been enjoying yourself?"

"I don't know what you mean."

"Come down to the ocean with me."

"It's cold out."

"Then take me to the kitchen and make me cocoa."

"Cook said she'll cut off your fingers if she catches you in her kitchen again."

"Cook doesn't speak English, Jane."

"She doesn't need to. She gets her point across."

"While watching your antics this week, I've noticed you walking like an old woman."

Silence.

"You're in pain now."

"It's nothing."

Mark tucked a finger under her chin and raised her gaze to his. "Tell me."

"You'll think I'm vain. That's a sin, you know."

"What I think?"

"No, vanity."

"Sister Roberta's teachings?"

"The Bible says so."

"What vanity causes you such pain?"

"My limp. I'm wearing a new brace in my shoe to make my legs the same length. Dr. Daveed gave it to me."

"How does this new brace make walking painful? And why wear it if it does?"

"Daveed said I have to retrain my muscles." She scrunched up her nose. "And they're protesting."

Mark smiled, finally understanding—some of it, anyway. "So how is a new brace vain?"

"It's supposed to make my limp less pronounced."

"Ah. And this is important to you?"

"Of course."

"I see."

And he did see—probably better than Jane did. She may have been acting outrageous all week, even while trying to lessen her limp to make herself more acceptable.

"I could carry you to the kitchens."

"You still couldn't go inside."

"I'm not afraid of Cook."

"Yes, you are. I've figured you out, Markov Lakeland. You're all bluster."

"You think so? And do you think I'll be blustering when I vow my love to you in three days in front of God, my family, and my people?"

Silence again.

Mark took her hand and led her over to the library chair he'd found her reading in a few minutes before.

She'd jumped up when he'd entered, looking as guilty as sin and just as tempting. She probably thought he was here to scold her after Reynard tattled on her for smoking. Mark knew she'd timed his father's arrival in the library down to the minute.

She was dressed in jeans like she had been all week, her hair escaping its bonds and her cheeks pink with guilt and the glow of the fire she'd set in the hearth.

And he loved her.

Mark eased her down in the chair, then knelt in front of her. Pleased she no longer needed her sling, he took both her hands in his and smiled into questioning eyes now level with his own. "I didn't fail your test, angel."

Those deep pewter eyes went from questioning to innocent. "What test?"

"There is nothing you can do that is outrageous enough to make me stop loving you, Jane."

"Oh, Mark."

He let go of her hand to reach in his back pocket and pulled out a small fir bough. He held it up to show her the small, simply set diamond ring dangling from it on a silver ribbon. And then he smiled when he saw that innocence turn to worry. "I wish to ask you, Jane Doe Abbot, to be my wife."

"Mark," she repeated on a whisper.

"You can wear jeans to our wedding if you wish, instead of the dress Irina is having made for you. You can invite your friends from jail to the ceremony, and come to me riding Arthur. And you can teach our children how to shoot a gun and curse like a nun. But Jane?"

"Y-yes?"

"The only thing you may never do is leave me. Please marry me in three days and make me the most important man in your life."

"Are you sure? How can you be sure?"

"I've never been more sure of anything. I love you, Jane."

"Can . . . can I think about it?"

Mark inwardly frowned while outwardly smiling. "I've given you since that night on the *Katrina* to get used to the idea. And I haven't slept a peaceful night since."

Jane, it seemed, had no qualms with outwardly frowning. But when she looked down at the ring dangling from the fir bough, her eyes misted again. She started to reach for it, but stopped and looked up at him. "You . . . you believe?"

"In us. I believe in us, Jane. Marry me."

She reached out again with shaking hands and untied the ribbon, then carefully placed the ring in his waiting hand. Shaking almost as much as she was, Mark slowly slid the ring onto her finger, then raised her hand to his lips. "Thank you, Jane. I promise you this is right for us. Together we will make it right."

"You know, I . . . I actually believe you."

He stood up and brought her with him, then carefully pulled her into his arms and hugged her. "You'll give me the words back? Soon?" he asked, kissing the top of her head. "I love you, Jane."

She buried her nose in his shirt and mumbled something to his chest.

Mark touched her chin and lifted her gaze to his. "Again."

"I love you."

He nodded, then pressed her face back to his chest to hide his grin.

Ah, thank the good Lord, but he'd just captured an angel.

A nd a shy angel she was the next morning at breakfast. Jane was still walking like an old woman, but her face shone with the realization that love had come to her with simple acceptance. And her own love was radiating back at her new family in the form of a blush.

"I . . . I've accepted Mark's proposal," she told them. "And agreed to be his wife."

The table erupted, everyone jumping up and pouncing on the startled woman with hugs and kisses of welcome. Reynard couldn't seem to stop squeezing her, calling her daughter over and over again. They were all careful of her shoulder, but Mark finally had to rescue the poor overwhelmed woman. It took him three tugs to get her away from Reynard in order to return Jane to her chair, but the almost ex-king let go only to steal Alexi's seat on the other side of her.

"We're sorry, you know," Reynard whispered to her.

"What for?" she asked in both surprise and confusion.

"You can smoke all the cigars you want. I promise not to scold."

Jane's flush turned crimson.

"And you look nice in jeans," Sergei offered from across the table.

Jane looked down at her plate.

"And I've been thinking," Dmitri broke in, "that maybe we should pay more attention to all Shelkovans. Even—or rather, especially—your women friends." He gave her a sheepish look. "We are guilty of forgetting some of our people. It took your eyes to make us see them."

Jane peeked at Mark and then quickly went back to studying her breakfast.

"Will you teach me to play horseshoes?" Alexi asked.

"Yes."

"Can I see your ring?" Aunt Irina softly petitioned, leaning forward.

Jane held her hand out over the table to oohs and aahs and compliments from everyone but Sergei.

He just lifted a brow at Mark. "Rather tightfisted in the jewelry department, aren't you?" he drawled, nodding toward the simple ring.

"Oh, no! It's perfect," Jane said before he could answer. "I love it."

"That's just a promise token," Mark added. He shot Sergei a wink. "Wait until you see the wedding band."

Jane pulled back her hand and looked at him. "What does that mean?"

"You'll love your band, Jane. I promise."

Mark let her know the topic was closed by resuming his breakfast, stifling a grin when his soon-to-be wife stabbed at her own food. The rest of the day was lost in preparing for the coronation and wedding. Mark was busy greeting and entertaining foreign dignitaries already starting to arrive for the ceremonies, and the palace was bursting at the seams by mid-afternoon.

Jane and Irina, he'd learned, had escaped the confusion by going to visit a nearby orphanage Irina had told Jane about. When Mark had looked out the window, it had been to see two women and two bodyguards departing, the four of them laden with gifts. The poor trunk had barely closed and the bumper had nearly been touching the ground as they'd driven through the gates, and Mark was quite pleased at his future wife's interest in her new country and people.

His pleasure, however, lasted only until six that night, when Jane burst through the door of his office with enough force to slam it against the wall. Either not seeing or not caring about the group of men with him—all of whom stood up at her entrance—Jane stormed up to Mark and slammed her fist down on his desk.

"I won't have it!"

"What won't you have?"

"I won't have *anybody* getting hurt because of me!"

"Who almost got hurt?" he asked, straightening in his chair.

"Petri. My bodyguard."

"Calm down, Jane," he whispered, finally rising and reaching for her.

She stepped away. "I will not calm down, dammit! There was a series of three loud pops just as Irina and I came out of the orphanage, and Petri threw himself on top of me to protect me from only God knew what."

Mark became alarmed that Jane was cursing for real, which meant she was more than just a little angry. "What was the noise?" he asked, looking at the man who'd rushed in after her.

"It was nothing," Jane answered for him. "A car back-firing. That's not the point!"

"What is the point, then?" he asked, inwardly relaxing.

"If that had been a bullet, Petri could be dead. Or hurt. Trying to protect me!"

"That's his job," Mark said, also no longer caring about their audience. He could only focus on Jane right now and his own escalating anger. "That's what bodyguards *do*."

"I won't have it, I tell you."

"Yes, you will," he snapped, walking around the desk to her. "It's either that or sit in your room, all safe and sound, forever."

"Do you know Petri's married? And that he's got two little kids?"

Mark closed his eyes and counted to ten. It didn't help. He knew exactly where this conversation was going, and he didn't like it. "No, I wasn't aware of that," he softly confessed. He opened his eyes, only to sigh when her glare intensified. "I know you don't want anyone's death on your conscience, but *none* of us have a choice in the matter."

"I don't like it," she whispered, her own eyes suddenly filling with tears. "I couldn't stand it if he got hurt. What makes my life more important than his?"

"That's not a fair question to ask me, angel. Your life is the most important thing in the world to me. And I imagine Petri is the most important thing in his wife's world. But that's not what this is about."

"It's not about anything else."

"He chose his profession, Jane. Nobody coerced him into guarding your life. And he's well trained. Basically, it boils down to it being no one's decision but his and his wife's." Mark waved the man in question to come closer. "Petri, please tell Miss Abbot how long and hard you've worked to get the position you have."

Petri looked at his mistress. "I have trained for three years, and was finally promoted to guarding the royal family six months ago," he told her in heavily accented English.

"But does your wife know *exactly* what you do?"

Petri nodded and smiled. "My Ileana is proud. She say it is safer than common soldier. And I am near home most time."

Some of the bluster went out of Jane at his obvious pride. Mark led her back around the desk with him, sat down, and settled her on his lap. He nodded to Petri and bid him farewell in Shelkovan, then lifted her chin to look at him. "He's right, you know. Being a bodyguard is actually safer than being a soldier. And Jane, soldiers have been dying since the dawn of man, protecting their loved ones." He softly rubbed her arm. "No occupation is safe. Our fishermen risk their lives every day so people they don't know may eat. And some of them die at sea. Our lumberjacks face untold dangers in the forest, but go to work anyway. Petri and the other guards are doing the jobs they've chosen. Let them."

"I couldn't stand it if he got hurt."

"I couldn't stand it if you did," he softly countered. "So we will all be careful. I assure you Petri is. He's trained to see a threat before it arrives. The sudden sound took him by surprise and he reacted instinctively to protect you." Mark then swept her hair back on her bent head to see her face. "What of Aunt Irina?"

"She didn't take it very well, either, and was shaking all the way home. The other man had grabbed her and actually carried her back into the orphanage."

"Then I should give both of them raises, should I not? They are good men."

"I don't think this is going to work, Mark," she whispered to his chest. "I don't know if I can live like this."

"We will make it work," he said, giving her a gentle squeeze. "But understand that because you've spent twenty-seven years taking care of yourself, it will take time to get used to letting others taking care of you."

She pulled in a deep breath and looked up, appearing hopeful. "You're sure?"

Mark cocked his head. "Did you not risk your own life to save mine in Maine? Couldn't you have drowned in the lake or been killed by my assassins? And after, when you led me to safety, what were your thoughts? How did saving me make you feel?"

"I didn't think or feel anything about it," she admitted. "I knew you were in the plane, so I just went in after you. And it was only natural to help you after."

"And you didn't even know me. So imagine how I want to take care of you, especially knowing how much I love you."

"I . . . I guess I understand," she said, looking away— only to suddenly stiffen and look back at him, her eyes widened in horror. "There are a bunch of people in here," she whispered. "I've been carrying on in front of strangers."

"Then I guess I should introduce you."

Jane suddenly looked as though she wanted to punch him, but apparently was too busy blushing in mortification. She was also eyeing the underneath of his desk.

Mark set her on her feet and stood up, keeping a possessive arm around her. "Gentlemen, I would like to introduce you to the woman who has agreed to marry me in two days, Miss Jane Abbot of Maine." Keeping a possessive arm around her—more to keep her from bolting for the door than for support—Mark led her to the still-standing men. "Jane, this is Randall Creighton, the American Ambassador to Shelkova. The embassy is just now under construction."

"Mr. Creighton," Jane responded, her blush kicking up a notch.

"And this is Richard Sholms, an old school friend of mine from Oxford."

"Mr. Sholms."

"I'm enchanted, Miss Abbot. And Mark is lucky," he returned, taking her hand and kissing the back of it.

"And lastly, this is Peter Banks. He's from England, and very interested in buying finished lumber from us. He, too, is an old school friend."

"Mr. Banks."

"Hello, Miss Abbot. I must say, I wasn't sure they made a woman brave enough to beard this lion," he said, also taking her hand but not kissing it.

Mark took pity on Jane, who he knew was fighting to remain calm. "Why don't you go check on Aunt Irina," he suggested as he started walking her to the door. "You'll see our guests again at dinner tonight." He left the office with her and closed the door to shield them from the onlookers, looked up and down the hall at the dozens of people running in different directions, and decided he didn't care. He kissed his fiancée until she started kissing him back, and continued kissing her until he heard her whimper.

"Just two more long nights and we won't have to stop," he promised, kissing her swollen lips again when they opened slightly in shock. "Can you wait that long?"

"Y—" She had to clear her throat. "Yes," she finally got out, staring at his mouth.

Mark used her chin to lift her gaze to his. "And Jane?"

"Yes."

"I won't be the only one shouting this time."

He left her standing in the hall after firing that shot, his last glimpse before he closed his office door being Jane's eyes nearly crossed and her cheeks a hot, passionate pink.

Chapter Seventeen

✦ — ✦

Jane came instantly awake just as a large hand closed over her mouth. The decision not to panic didn't come easy as she felt a large, masculine weight dip the bed. But most alarming was the realization there was more than one man in the room.

"Don't scream," a masculine voice whispered in her ear. "You'll wake the others."

That wouldn't be a bad thing, Jane decided.

"Get up and get dressed. Quietly," he ordered, the voice beginning to sound familiar to her. "But you must hurry. Is five minutes enough?"

Enough for what? A light suddenly came on and Jane blinked up at the man whose hand was still covering her mouth to find herself eye-to-golden-eye with a rascal prince. "Mhmlexi!"

He made the mistake of winking at her. "Ow! Don't bite, you witch!" he hissed, quickly drawing back his hand.

"Alexi. What are you doing? You scared the daylights out of me."

"It's not daylight yet," he countered, giving her a frown as he rubbed his palm on his belly. "But the sun will be up by the time we get there. Now hurry."

"Get where?" she asked, sitting up and brushing her hair from her face.

"We're stealing you," he told her instead of answering, "to go hunting."

"We?"

"Sergei and me. We're sneaking out and taking you with us. Ever hunt snow grouse?"

Jane turned to Sergei, standing at the foot of the bed—looking much like she imagined the devil would look—holding three shotguns cradled in his arms. Slung over his shoulder were two packs. Jane recognized her gun and her long-lost backpack.

She looked at Alexi and smiled. "No, I haven't. Are snow grouse tasty?"

"Delicious. If you're lucky enough to get one in your oven. They're elusive creatures."

Jane eyed both brothers again. "Why the secrecy?"

Sergei shrugged his free shoulder. "We thought it would be easier to escape this madhouse while everyone was sleeping."

"Sounds like a plan to me," she agreed. "Now leave and I'll get dressed. Five minutes."

It took her nine, but the men were patiently waiting in the hall when she came out of her room. Jane followed them down the stairs and out the front door to find two huge four-wheel-drive trucks waiting, with dark-tinted windows and three men standing between them. She recognized Petri, who smiled at her as he moved forward to open a door in the first truck.

She smiled back, but instead of getting in she turned and gave Alexi an incredulous look. "It's going to take two big trucks to carry home all our grouse?"

"No, little witch," Sergei answered before Alexi could answer. "It's going to take these trucks to escape Markov, if we don't get going." He turned serious. "I forgot your wounded shoulder. Will you be able to hunt?"

"I'd have to be dead not to be able to hunt. I hold my gun against my right shoulder, anyway." She grinned at him. "Lucky for me, Dorjan didn't choose to hit that one."

Sergei's eyes darkened with his frown.

"Ah . . . Why aren't we stealing Mark to go with us?" she asked. "He could probably use a little escape himself."

"This is our day to spend with our new sister," Alexi said on a chuckle, all but lifting her into the backseat of the truck. "After the wedding, he'll have you all to himself."

Wow, he'd called her *sister*. It hit Jane then that she was about to get an entire family—a rowdy, bossy *family*, consisting of an aunt, a father, three big brothers, and a husband. Wow.

Petri drove the truck that she and Sergei and Alexi were riding in, the other two men following in the other truck. Within minutes they were out of the city and heading north into the forested land of Shelkova.

"Oh, it's gorgeous!" she exclaimed, looking out her window at the passing countryside.

"I'm glad you like your new home," Alexi said. He was sitting in the back with Jane, but was looking at her instead of out the window. "You can understand now why we are so adamant to keep this land for our people. Today we'll be hunting a tract of forest that was cut about two years ago, but you'll notice plenty of old growth still standing. Clear-cutting would be more efficient, but we prefer to leave the best of each species of tree to reseed."

Jane nodded that she understood. "And zonal cutting is better for the wildlife," she added. "And new growth springs up quickly. Maine didn't have much of a deer and moose population until harvesting began back in the seventeenth century and opened up the woods."

"Which is why we're holding firm again the consortium, as they're known for coming in and raping the land, then simply going in search of another country to exploit."

"That won't happen here," Sergei growled from the front seat. "Not as long as there's a Lakeland on watch."

Jane nodded again, having no problem believing him. "But is it true what Mark said? Can you really stop these men?" she finished asking in a whisper.

"We'll stop them." Sergei turned in his seat to see her. "Maybe not by killing them as you suggested, but the law we're about to pass should be just as effective when it becomes illegal to sell any lands to outsiders—only lumber and finished products like furniture."

"And that will stop the threat against you?"

"Against *us*, Jane. And yes, it will, as the consortium won't be able to operate in Shelkova—with or without Lakelands in power."

"When will the law take effect?"

"It's complicated," Sergei said. "Although most of the forest is government-owned, there are many other large and small landowners we must consider in order to be fair to everyone. Parliament is debating those very details right now." He shrugged, facing forward again. "The law should be in effect in another few months."

Happy to hear that news, Jane went back to looking out her window. They made one stop before they began their day of hunting. The two trucks pulled into a homestead that was full of clutter, children, and lots of dogs running around.

Jane was immediately enchanted.

She didn't even wait for Petri to open her door, but bounded outside and made for two small children having a party with no fewer than eight jumping, yelping puppies. She threw herself right into the center of them, sitting down in the dirt and suddenly getting swamped by clumsy legs and lolling tongues. "Oh, heavens! What happy little beasts you are," she laughed, trying to protect her face. Not that she cared. Within seconds her hair was in tangles from being tugged on and chewed by the young dogs. The two children stood off to the side, their eyes widened in either awe or confusion.

Jane made a grab for one of the puppies and pulled it away from her face so she could smile at the children. "Come," she beckoned, waving them over and then patting the ground beside her. The little girl, looking about four years old, shyly moved closer. Jane laughed as one of the puppies grabbed the girl's coat and pulled her down onto Jane's lap, and she immediately protected the girl's face from a tongue washing.

Guessing the children didn't speak English, Jane contented herself with starting a tug of war with the puppies, carefully wrapping an arm around the girl and encouraging her to help win the small war. Soon the boy joined them, not about to be left out.

Sergei stood beside Alexi and watched their new sister make a complete ass of herself over two children and the boisterous litter of puppies.

"Have you figured her out yet?" Alexi asked his brother.

"Not yet," Sergei said, shaking his head and grinning. "And you know what? Neither has Markov. He believes he has, but she's going to keep surprising him for years to come. I'm afraid getting her to agree to marry him was nothing short of opening Pandora's box."

"I like her."

"So do I. She's genuine."

"She's also perfect for Shelkova, and exactly what we need for a queen."

"And for a sister. Have you noticed how happy the household is? Dad looks and acts ten years younger. He's like . . ."

"Like before mother died," Alexi finished softly. "We've all missed her, but Dad was especially hit hard by the hole she left in his life. Even the challenge of rebuilding a country wasn't enough to reignite that spark, which is why he's turning it over to Markov."

Sergei chuckled. "Poor Jane. She's been fawning over Dad since she got here, telling him not to overdo it and to rest. She's always trying to get him to rest."

"She's going to explode when she finds out the lie we've all been perpetuating."

"Dad can't help it. He's enjoying her concern too much. It's been five years since he's had such babying from a woman. Aunt Irina's been great, but she knows Dad too well to fall for his sympathy attempts."

Sergei turned and held out his hand to the man approaching them. The poor fellow's eyes kept darting from the two brothers to the crazy woman sitting on the ground playing with his children.

"Yearman."

"Your Highness."

Sergei slapped the man on the back. "Today, Yearman, it is Sergei and Alexi. No 'Highnesses.'"

The man nodded agreement, his eyes darting back to the woman in the dirt, one daughter and four puppies on top of her. Between the yelping and giggling and shrieks, the din was near deafening. Sergei noticed an uncomfortable Petri standing nearby, looking ready to jump in should one of the young canines turn assassin.

"I'd like for you to meet your future queen, Yearman," Sergei offered, starting the stunned man on his way toward Jane.

Alexi finally had to haul Jane out of the chaos and then dust her off. He tried to pat down her hair, but it was a hopeless task.

"Jane. This is Yearman, the owner of the dogs and children. He's coming hunting with us," Sergei explained to the disheveled woman. His grin broadened as Yearman hastily pulled off his hat and bowed to Jane.

"Your . . . Highness," Yearman stammered, turning a dull red.

Jane first looked bewildered by the title, and then

startled. But she suddenly smiled and reached for Year-man's hand. "Hello, Yearman. And my name is Jane. I like your household."

"Th-thank you."

"You've got some beautiful dogs. And children."

Yearman beamed, although Sergei didn't know if it was the dogs or the kids he was more proud of.

"They good hunters," the man said, puffing up his chest.

It was the dogs, apparently.

"I have two come with us today," Yearman went on. "They find you many grouse."

"Oh! It's been years since I've hunted with dogs."

"Then let's go," Alexi chimed in as he brushed away two puppies that had just discovered the tassels on his boots.

Jane turned to say good-bye to the kids and puppies, intending, apparently, to wade back into the group. But Sergei latched on to her and pulled her back to the truck. Yearman and his two dogs got into the second truck, which took over the lead as they left the homestead.

Sergei, who was now sitting in the back, with Alexi in front, watched with amusement as Jane wiggled excitedly and asked question after question about grouse hunting in Shelkova, about Yearman, and about his dogs. Alexi did most of the answering, as he was the more avid hunter in the family. Or he had been, until Jane Abbot had arrived.

It turned out to be a day Sergei would not soon forget. And neither would Alexi, judging by the scowl he wore all the way back to Yearman's house. Jane and that infamous shotgun of hers had taken two grouse to every one of theirs.

At first his new sister had complained they wouldn't get any birds, considering seven people and two dogs would be tramping around in the woods making enough noise to scare the whales clear out at sea. But the bodyguards kept their distance and the dogs lived up to Yearman's bragging. Alexi was soon disgusted and Jane was soon gloating, not the least bit shy about rubbing her success in Alexi's face.

Now they were all tired, Jane especially, Sergei feared. Their walk back to the trucks had her limping considerably, and Sergei was ashamed that he'd forgotten her bad ankle.

It was because she made them forget. Once a person got to know Jane, they stopped seeing her limp. All they saw was her vitality, her enjoyment of life, and her impish smile. Those gunmetal eyes would light up at the least provocation and dance with merriment.

No, a person didn't see her limp at all.

As soon as they arrived back at Yearman's house, Jane was back out of the truck, sore or not, and back in the middle of the puppies. It was as he was standing there, as mesmerized as the rest of the men, that inspiration struck. Sergei turned and smiled at Yearman, then pulled him aside to have a little talk.

"He should have accepted my gun," Jane complained thirty minutes later, back in the truck that was headed home. "It was the least he could have taken. I know it's not a fancy gun, but it's serviceable."

A snort came from the backseat. "Are you kidding?" Alexi said. "Yearman's going to *triple* the price of his puppies now. Between the prestige of having his dogs living with the royal family and what he'll get for his pups, you just made him a rich— Ow!"

Sergei grinned. Wisely having claimed the front seat again, he'd left Alexi to cope with Jane's two new *bois-terous* puppies—one of which was apparently fond of fingers.

He couldn't wait for Mark to see what his bride was dragging home this time.

F irst there was a bellow, then a curse (in Shelkovan), and then her name was *roared*.

Jane walked into Mark's office, not even trying to hide her smile, and went over and pulled one of the puppies out from beneath the desk, only to laugh when it brought Mark's pant leg with it.

"Dammit, Jane, these animals are going to be the death of me. That little monster just latched on to my ankle, and it won't let go," Mark said, forcibly prying the puppy's jaws apart.

Once free, he stood up and glared at Jane and her puppy, who was now happily ensconced in her arms and trying to lick her face. She did stop laughing, but couldn't seem to quit smiling. And the puppy was anything but contrite. It went after him again, this time leaping out of her arms and going for his face. Mark caught the animal in midair and firmly set it on the floor, then pushed the puppy's bottom down. "Sit!" he barked.

The puppy lunged, and Jane broke into laughter again. And out of nowhere, the other puppy joined them, yelping crazily at the new game.

"No! Down! Bad dog. Bad dogs!"

They didn't listen. That is, until Mark gave a deep, warning growl that sounded like a huge male wolf readying to pounce. Both puppies were so surprised, they immediately sat down.

Mark nodded.

And then he closed his eyes. "This better not be another test," he whispered. He looked at her. "Because if it is, then you're the one who's going to fail."

"I don't know what you mean."

"If you're trying to see what kind of father I'll be, then pay attention."

Mark hunched down in front of the two canines and stared at each of them. When one started to rise, he sat it firmly back on its bum and told it no. When the puppy stayed, Mark gave it a pat and a word of praise. The other puppy was jealous and whined but didn't move. Mark praised it next. Then he looked up at Jane. "I will be a father who is obeyed and have peace in my home. Now, these two brats are going to learn some manners. And since you're such an authority on manners, Miss Abbot, I expect you to teach them."

"But I've never had a dog before."

"Well, thanks to my brothers, you now have two. Teach them to behave, or they'll be living in the barn."

"That's not fair. They're just babies. If they move to the barn, then so will I."

Mark stood up and stepped close and spoke softly. "No, as of tomorrow night, you will be moved into my bed."

She knew that. She just didn't like to be reminded about it. Especially when Mark got that unholy gleam in his eye. That same gleam he'd been watching her with all week. The one he got just before he kissed her.

And heavens, could the man kiss.

Kissing was good. At least Mark seemed to like it as much as she did. But that's what worried her. Tomorrow they were getting married, and tomorrow night she was sleeping in his bed. They'd kiss again, she knew. But they'd also do what they'd done on the *Katrina*, and what Mark had done was suddenly shout and stop.

What if he did that again? What if, again, he didn't like it?

Jane dropped her gaze to the maddeningly obedient puppies, whose eyes were only for Mark, their dripping canine tongues hanging out of their mouths and drooling all over the rug, looking pathetically hopeful of pleasing their new master.

Did she ever look at Mark that way?

Jane was afraid she did. More than once this week she'd actually had to pinch herself to stop from staring at him, unable to believe such a beautiful man wanted to marry her.

And as much as it pained her to admit, she really had been testing him this past week. Heck, she'd been testing them all. And Mark still wanted to marry her, Reynard still wanted her for a daughter, and Irina still wanted to be her friend. Sergei, Dmitri, and Alexi still lectured her, but Jane could only smile at the memory of those lectures lately.

"Now what in hell are you smiling at?"

She immediately wiped the smile off her face, carefully schooled her features so she didn't resemble the two puppies still patiently sitting on the floor, and frowned. "What was it you were saying?"

He growled again.

Both puppies cocked their heads and whined.

Jane's smile escaped for the second time. "Oh, yeah, I remember now. You want me to train my dogs. Any suggestions?"

"Buy a book," he snapped, looking down at the puppies and scowling. "What are their names, anyway?" he asked, trying to look unaffected by their worshipful gazes.

"I can't decide, so I think I'll run a contest."

"What kind of contest?" he asked warily.

"I'll get the schoolkids of Shelkova to name them," she explained. "Kids have great imaginations. We'll give them a prize."

"A prize," he repeated, that golden gleam back in his eyes. "What kind of prize?"

"How about a ride in one of your fighter jets?"

He shook his head. "Their parents would have fits."

"How about dinner here at the palace?"

He nodded, that gleam intensifying. "Know what I'd ask for a prize?"

"What?" she whispered, a little wary herself.

"A kiss from an angel," he said softly, moving around the worshipful pups and over to her, his eyes now alight with mischief. "A long, passionate, promising kiss."

"Wh-what kind of promise?"

"A promise of things to come. Tomorrow night, to be exact. Kiss me, Jane, and give me your promise of passion."

She snapped her eyes to his chest. "I . . . I don't know how to promise passion," she told his shirt buttons. "You're the only man I've ever even *wanted* to be intimate with, so I'm not really sure I know how." She leaned closer as she rose on her tiptoes and stopped just short of kissing him. "You . . . you'll teach me? How to please you?"

"Oh, yes, angel." He wrapped his arms around her waist, then straightened and brought her with him. "We'll teach each other."

Chapter Eighteen

❖⸺❖

It was the night of the Coronation Ball—which they were having before the event, since Czar Markov Lakeland and his new queen would be otherwise . . . occupied the following night. Jane was in her room with Irina and a small army of maids. The entire room smelled of wildflowers and the scent of the ocean coming in through the open windows. It was mid-autumn in Shelkova, but the weather had turned out beautifully for the occasion.

And right now Jane needed the fresh air.

"Do stop squirming, Jane. I can't get your hair done if you don't sit still," Irina softly scolded. She looked at Jane in the mirror. "You needn't be nervous. You look beautiful, and you'll do well tonight."

"I don't dance."

Irina winked at her reflection. "You did just fine during practice."

"I stepped on Alexi's feet."

"Then you can step on Markov's."

"What if someone else asks me to dance?"

Irina smiled. "Then lift your nose in the air and regally tell them no."

"I couldn't do that."

"Sure you can. You're the queen."

"Not yet."

"Soon enough."

Jane sighed. "I'm not going to make a good queen."

"And just what makes a good queen?" Irina asked, lifting one perfectly arched eyebrow.

"Someone who knows how to dance with ambassadors, how to converse about worldly things, and who doesn't have shaking knees at just the thought of tonight."

"There is no such woman," Irina said. "I've attended many of these functions since the Lakelands took the throne, and my knees still weaken at the prospect."

Jane turned on her seat to face her in person. "You're nervous? But why?"

"Because I step on toes, too."

"No!" Jane exclaimed in mock horror.

Irina pushed her back around. "And I have embarrassed myself in conversation more times than I care to remember."

"I can't picture that," Jane said, frowning at her in the mirror. "You're always so calm."

A knock on the door forestalled Irina's answer. One

of the maids looked at her in question, and Irina nodded at the woman to open it.

"Jane Abbot. What sort of calamity have you gotten yourself into this time?" a stern, well-remembered voice boomed from the doorway.

"Sister Roberta!"

The nun glided into the room, her long black habit billowing around her as she headed to Jane, who was now standing. The nun placed her hands on her hips and stood in silence, using the time to give her former charge a thorough inspection from her toes to her nose. She suddenly smiled and opened her arms.

Jane ran into them. "Oh, Sister."

"My, my, child. How you do clean up."

"Sister."

"But then, having dealt with and now finally meeting Markov Lakeland, I can understand why you made the effort."

"Oh, Sister."

She couldn't say anything other than that. All she could do was hug the nun, her nose buried in an aging, loving bosom. Sister Roberta hugged her back, rocking Jane as she used to do half a world away and nearly two decades ago.

Sister Roberta finally pulled back and looked at her again. And then she sighed. "You still haven't tamed that hair."

Jane pulled some tresses over her shoulder and clutched them protectively, knowing what was coming next.

"Why don't you just cut it?" Sister Roberta asked.

"Because then it sticks straight out," Jane reminded

her. "Remember the one time you tried. I looked like a poodle for over a year."

The nun rolled her eyes. "I remember. Sister Patricia brought it to my attention often enough while we waited for it to grow back."

"What are you doing here, Sister?"

"Your man invited me—and I'm being generous calling it that. He basically hunted me down, told me who he was, and said he was sending a plane and some men to fetch me." Sister Roberta gave Jane a dignified sniff. "He didn't even ask if I wished to come. He just told me to be ready."

Jane looked at Irina, only to gasp. "Oh, my manners. Sister Roberta, this is Irina, Mark's aunt. Irina, if you haven't guessed, this is Sister Roberta."

"I'm so pleased to finally meet you, Sister Roberta. Jane's told us all about you and her time at Saint Xavier's."

"Yes. Well. I assume she left out the better parts."

"I would say, Sister, that's probably the biggest reason Markov brought you here. He will tell us he wanted you to be here for Jane's wedding, but I suspect his ultimate motive was to get you to explain his new wife to him."

"Explain what?" Jane asked, alarmed.

"Why, your charm, dear," Irina responded innocently.

Sister Roberta sniffed again. "Charm, indeed." She walked over to a chair and slowly sat down. "I declare, I feel like I've been on a plane for three days. You would think that I'd be tired of sitting, but God's truth, I'm just tired."

"Oh, Sister. I'm sorry," Jane apologized, instantly contrite at seeing the aging woman heave a weary sigh.

"That's fine, dear. I just need to get my bearings." She looked at Jane with awe. "We flew right over the North Pole. Imagine, me flying over the North Pole. I've never even left New England before, and here I am on the other side of the world."

"I bet some tea and sweets will gain you back some energy," Irina quickly offered, calling to one of the maids and giving her instructions in Shelkovan before guiding Jane back to her seat in front of the mirror. "Now, let's do wonders with your beautiful hair, and then I can go get ready."

"Good luck," both Jane and Sister Roberta piped up together.

But within minutes, Irina had worked her magic again and Jane's hair had been lifted up in intricate curls on top of her head, exposing her long neck and dainty ears.

"You're going to have to get your ears pierced," Irina commented as Jane turned her head back and forth, awed at what she was seeing.

"Wow. I don't even look like me."

"Katrina didn't have pierced ears," Irina continued, smiling at Jane's expression. "I'm sure Reynard would like for you to borrow some of her earrings. I'll send a message to him."

"Oh, no. I couldn't."

"You can't go to the ball with naked ears."

"And why not?"

"You're a queen."

"Not yet."

"Soon enough. Now, don't argue."

Jane sighed and looked over at Sister Roberta to see

the poor nun had her mouth hanging open. "A queen?" the old woman whispered.

"Well. Yes. It would seem so," Jane murmured. "Just what did Mark tell you, anyway? In order to get you to come."

Sister Roberta gathered her wits. "He told me he was Markov Lakeland, king of Shelkova, and that he intended to make an honest woman of you. I guess I didn't put two and two together to come up with your being a . . . a queen."

Jane turned red, both from embarrassment and from anger at Mark for implying to Sister Roberta they *needed* to get married. But as Jane tried to figure out how to explain that "honest woman" part, the maid returned with a huge tray of tea and fancy pastries and set it on the table next to Sister Roberta.

Irina pulled up another chair and motioned Jane over. "I'll go get ready and leave you to renew your friendship," she explained as she urged Jane to sit down. "Reynard said he will come escort you down tonight. And you, too, Sister, if you're up to it."

"I would like to see this ball," the nun admitted. "Maybe I'll stay just a short while."

"Then drink your tea and refresh yourself. Your room is just across the hall, and you can relax for a bit before you go down." Irina's eyes twinkled. "The real fun doesn't begin for another three hours. It is mostly formalities and receiving lines at first. I can send one of the men to get you then?"

"Alexi," Jane suggested, her own eyes twinkling.

"That will be fine," Sister Roberta agreed. "Who is Alexi?"

"Markov's brother. A rascal, Sister," Irina offered in way of explanation as she headed for the door. "Just tug the bellpull when you wish to go to your room," she called back over her shoulder. "And welcome to Shelkova," she told the nun just before she closed the door, taking all of the maids with her.

Sister Roberta looked at Jane. "There's really a bell-pull? Like in the old movies?"

Jane nodded and began pouring the tea. "Thank you for coming to my wedding," she whispered to her old friend. "It means a lot to me, Sister. I've dreamed of being able to talk with you more than once these past few weeks."

"I was able to get a very sketchy picture of how you came to be here from the men who escorted me. Now," the nun said with a sigh, leaning back in her chair and taking a sip of her tea. "I would like to hear *your* version of the story."

Jane sighed and then started at the beginning, at the lake in Maine, and ended with her preparing to attend the coronation ball that night, and the coronation and her wedding tomorrow. She spared nothing of her foolishness; not about getting shot in the shoulder, not about getting thrown in jail, and not even about smoking Reynard's cigars. She did, however, omit the little incident on the *Katrina*.

By the time the telling was done, Sister Roberta could only stare and shake her head, her cup of now-cold tea forgotten on her lap.

"You rode in a submarine, an aircraft carrier, and a military jet?" Sister asked softly. And then she frowned. "And you tried to shoot a prince?"

"The gun wasn't loaded," Jane reminded her.

But the nun just kept shaking her head. "And you got thrown in jail. With . . . with . . ."

"They were being evicted," Jane explained again. She raised her chin. "And Mark has seen to it that they now have nice jobs," she said proudly.

"And you are about to become a queen," Sister Roberta said, still with awe but also with pride. "You're going to make a wonderful queen, you know. If you stop acting like a little heathen," the nun tacked on, sounding like the Sister Roberta she remembered.

"So I've been told," Jane responded with a weary sigh.

"You don't think so?"

"I always thought queens were important people."

"No one is more important than anyone else in God's eyes."

"Um . . . they're not Catholic, you know."

"The Lakelands?"

Jane nodded.

"I guessed as much. I may live in the woods, but I read. They are Russian Orthodox?"

Jane nodded again.

"Is this a problem for you, child?"

"No. You raised me Catholic, but you also taught me about all religions. You . . . you don't mind that I'm not marrying a Catholic?"

"Are they good people?"

"Oh, yes," Jane answered honestly. "Even Alexi."

"I can't wait to meet this rascal prince."

"Why are you wearing your old habit? You'd begun

wearing the less strict habits years ago, and I thought you switched to regular clothes when you retired."

Sister Roberta gave another airy sniff. "I dug this out of the closet just as soon as I finished talking to that man of yours. I decided I needed the . . . clout that goes with it," the old nun explained with a little puffed-up importance of her own.

Jane stood with a chuckle and refilled her tea. "Oh, yes, Sister. I've seen more than one man back away all but genuflecting when you're trying to make a point wearing your uniform of God. Remember Silas?"

"That man," Sister spat with fond disgust. "He came with you to Saint Xavier's one day reeking of whiskey and needing a bath."

"He still needs a bath," Jane said, scrunching up her nose. "But he no longer smells of whiskey."

"Which is why you're going to make a fine queen. You care. Now, are you pregnant?"

Jane nearly spilled the tea she'd been about to take a sip of all over her dress. As it was, she dropped the cup on the floor. "Pregnant?" she squeaked, feeling her cheeks fill with fire.

Sister Roberta nodded, her eyes silently saying Jane better be truthful.

"I . . . ah . . ." Jane lowered her eyes. "It's possible," she confessed, watching the tea slowly seep into the beautiful, ancient, and probably priceless rug.

"Look at me, child."

Jane lifted her gaze.

"Do you love him?"

"Yes."

The old nun suddenly smiled. "That's good. A wife should love her husband."

Jane frowned. "Aren't you going to ask if he loves me back?"

Sister Roberta gave a wave of dismissal, then awkwardly pushed herself up from her chair. "Oh, the man loves you, all right."

"How do you know that?" Jane asked, disgruntled.

Sister's eyes widened in mock horror. "Only a man blindly in love would ever call you an *angel*," she said, as if stating the obvious. "Now show me to my room, so I can rest up before I have to meet Alexi the rascal."

"Maybe it's him I should warn," Jane muttered under her breath, taking Sister's arm and leading her to the door.

You've been crying again," Mark said quietly as they glided—thanks to his strong arms and stalwart toes—across the ballroom floor.

The room was nearly the size of a football field and had once been the throne room. Hell, there was still a throne sitting at the far end, raised up on a dais and looking imperial and intimidating. The room was also near to overflowing with people, all of them turned out in formal attire, all of them diplomats and businessmen who'd come to pay court on the new king.

And his new nearly-queen.

"Answer me," he demanded, squeezing her waist. "Why have you been crying?"

"Your father gave me these earrings."

Mark danced them over to the nearest wall and

stopped, then smiled when she finally looked at him, only to sigh when he noticed her tearing up again. "You're killing me, angel. Why would that make you cry?"

"He *gave* them to me. To keep forever. They were his wife's," she explained as she reached up and fingered one of the earrings. "He gave me your mother's diamond earrings."

Mark sighed again.

"He told me they were from Katrina and him. And then he kissed me and hugged me and called me *daughter*. And then he . . . he cried."

Mark drew her wet face down to his chest. "Ah, baby. What am I going to do with you?" he whispered to her hair.

He didn't really want an answer, so he ignored her mumbling into his shirt, reached into his pocket and pulled out a handkerchief, then carefully dabbed her eyes.

"I—I was afraid he was going to have a real stroke," she said between sniffles. "He looked so sad and happy at the same time that I started crying with him."

Mark instantly picked up on the one thing that would dry her sentimental tears. "What do you mean, a real stroke?"

It worked. She blew her nose, frowned up at him, then rolled her eyes. "I know a man on the make for attention when I see one. Your father shamelessly let me believe he has been gravely ill." Her dry eyes narrowed. "Come to think of it, you've all been letting me believe he was sick."

Mark knew better than to answer that accusation. "When did you find out?"

"Not long after I arrived. One day I saw him walking his horse away from the house, then saw him gallop that same horse down a wooded path. He didn't ride like a man recovering from near death."

"Then why have you allowed him to keep up his charade?"

"Because he's enjoying it so much," she said, sounding exasperated.

"And all the hours you spend with him taking therapeutic walks? And all the times you've scolded him to rest? You were just playing along?"

"No. The orders to rest were to tease him. He always turned a dull red whenever I worried so long and loud about his illness."

Not caring where they were or who was watching, Mark kissed her right on her surprised lips. And then he hugged her again and closed his eyes, turning enough to shield her when everyone suddenly stopped dancing and started clapping. He shot a smile over his shoulder, then swept Jane out onto the balcony before she started crying again—this time with embarrassment.

"I hope Sister Roberta didn't see that," she muttered into his soggy shirt—just before she hit him. "Don't you dare do that again."

"You like my kisses," he said, kissing her again, this time on her forehead. "Admit it."

"Not in front of half the world."

"Nor your Sister Roberta."

"And thank you," she snapped.

"For?" he asked with a chuckle.

"For bringing her here." She suddenly looked worried. "You . . . you won't believe everything she tells you, will you?"

"Believe her? Jane, the woman's a nun. Of course I'll believe her." He arched a brow to keep from grinning. "What will she tell me?"

She ignored the question. "Although she's a nun, Sister sometimes . . . embellishes things. And she's old. Her memory's probably faulty."

"So the woman's going to tell me colorful stories of your childhood?"

"I was a good kid. Most of the time," she muttered, looking back at the ballroom.

Looking to escape, Mark guessed. Although he knew she was uncomfortable in a room crowded with strangers, she was apparently more uncomfortable with the subject at hand.

"I love you, Jane Abbot."

Damn. She looked ready to cry again. The poor woman was on an emotional pendulum tonight, wavering between nervousness, excitement, and the realization she was loved—not only by him but also by his family. And tomorrow she would be loved by an entire nation needing the joy of a new, angelic queen.

"I love you, too," she mumbled, looking out onto the city of Previa, only to suddenly pull away and run to the rail. She leaned out to see what the commotion was about on one of the streets near the palace. "What's going on?"

Mark narrowed his eyes until he was able to discern what was happening. And then he silently cursed and led Jane toward the ballroom. "It's nothing. Just some revelers."

"No, it's not," she said, pulling out of his grasp and

running back to the rail. "It's a mob. And there's a woman screaming."

"Jane. Come inside. I will send someone to go see what is happening."

"I can already see!" she snapped, pulling her arm free again. "Some man is assaulting a woman, and everyone's just watching. They're urging him on! Mark, we've got to stop it," she cried, turning and heading for the stairs.

"No, you may not go out there, Jane!"

She whirled in his arms when he caught her. "You're not going to stop it?"

"It is a personal matter. That man is her husband."

"I don't care who he is. Oh my God, Mark, look. He's tying her to a post!"

"Jane. Stop struggling. I will send someone to stop it if you wish."

"If I wish!" she shouted, enraged. "That woman's being assaulted and . . . and humiliated. Why?" she cried.

Still holding her arms, Mark shrugged. "My guess is she's most likely an adulteress. Now calm down and I will explain."

"No. Do something!"

"Jane, for centuries men have made examples of their unfaithful wives this way."

"That doesn't make it right."

"No," he growled, pulling her against him. "It doesn't. And we will change it, Jane. Together, *you and I* will change it. But you can't halt generations of a practice in a matter of one night. I will stop this one incident from going any further, but for now, that's all I can do."

"What about the man?"

"The husband?"

"No, the man she was unfaithful with. What's his humiliation?"

Mark winced. "There is none. The husband will leave his wife tied to the post until someone—usually family—frees her, and she'll not be allowed back in her husband's home. If her lover wishes to come forward and claim her, he may."

"That's not fair."

"No, but it is the way things are. Or have been," Mark assured her, leaning away enough to give her an encouraging smile. "We will change it, okay? Together."

"Yes. We'll shift things so the *lover* is the one tied to the post. He should be stripped naked, flogged, then tied to that post for a week."

"My, what a bloodthirsty angel you are sometimes."

"Even God used a heavy hand once or twice in history," she said, the anger still glowing in her eyes. "Now come on. Let's go stop it."

"Not you. You are to stay right here."

Her chin rose. "I thought I was supposed to be a queen or something."

"You are," Mark said, nodding slightly.

"Then I might as well begin as I intend to go on. I'm going down there and marching right up to that woman, and if her husband tries to stop me, he'll hear a thing or two from me. And I'm bringing her back to the palace."

Mark didn't want to smile, because he wanted to stay looking angry enough to get her to obey him. And he didn't want to remind her that the husband probably wouldn't understand what she was saying, anyway. So he simply started dragging her toward the ballroom.

She planted her feet. Mark picked her up and carried her inside, right up to the huge throne at the end of the room. Conversations ceased as they passed, and silence descended as he gained the dais and deposited Jane on the throne. He leaned over her when she tried to rise, and put his nose nearly touching hers. "If you move from this chair, if your feet so much as touch the floor while I'm gone, I will sit myself on this throne and put you over my knee right in front of everyone, including Sister Roberta. Understand?"

Eyes wide, she nodded.

Mark nodded back and walked down the dais, pushing his way through the staring crowd. He found Sergei, Alexi, and Dmitri and motioned them to follow.

"Mark!" came an angel's bellow, making him look back to see Jane standing on the seat of the throne—her feet definitely not touching the floor. "You bring her back here! Do *you* understand?" she shouted. "Take her to Cook!"

Hiding his grin, he bowed to the almost-queen of Shelkova standing on his throne shouting orders at him like a tyrant.

The ball went well, don't you think?" Reynard asked as he stood beside Mark on the balcony overlooking the now-quiet city of Previa.

"If you don't count your new daughter bellowing like a fishwife," Mark agreed, taking another sip of his much-needed American whiskey.

Reynard shrugged. "She didn't exactly look like an

angel, did she, standing up on that throne and yelling." He smiled at Mark. "But she forgot to be nervous."

"Especially when she went to the kitchen later and found that poor woman still crying. I thought she was going to ask for one of her guns and hunt down the husband."

"I would have helped," Reynard admitted sadly. "This practice has to stop."

"Oh, it will. And not by a gradual reeducation, but by the wrath of our queen."

"Yes. Jane will stop it. And the people will do so just to please her. She's going to be an involved queen, isn't she?"

"And a very important one."

"Do you think she'll ever realize how important?"

"Probably not." Mark took a sip of his drink only to stop in mid-swallow. He brought his glass down and watched the dark figure moving through the shadows, headed for the gates, then nudged his father and used his drink to point at what he was watching. "Although she's already beginning her duties," Mark told the old man.

"That's Jane? Where's she going?"

"To begin our people's reeducation."

"She can't leave the grounds. Not alone," Reynard said in alarm.

"She's not alone. Seeing the expression on her face when I walked her to her room earlier, I set Petri on quiet guard. He's not to deter her, just keep her safe."

"But where is she going at this late hour?"

"Watch."

And watch they did. Jane was carrying something heavy as she quietly limped past the guards, who were intent on keeping people out, not in. Jane then marched up the sidewalk, every step fairly shouting her anger. And finally both men watched her take out that anger on the now abandoned post in the town square. If they listened carefully, they could hear every biting chop of the axe as it slowly, painstakingly destroyed the offensive relic of the past.

It took her well over twenty minutes to cut through the aged, hardened wood, but with a final shove and angry shout, the post toppled to the ground with an anticlimactic thud. Her shoulders slumped, Jane made her way back to the palace, startling the guards at the gate. After a little discussion and lots of bowing, Jane reentered the palace, and Reynard and Mark watched Petri talk briefly with the guards and then follow her inside.

"Yes, a damn fine queen," Reynard said, slapping Mark on the shoulder. He chuckled. "But you're going to have to station some guards facing *in*."

"Beginning tomorrow night the woman will be in my bed where I can keep an eye on her. Don't worry, old man, I can handle one slip of an angel."

"An angel who appears quite capable of handling you," Reynard got out as a parting shot, just before he walked into the throne room.

Mark looked up at the sky studded with blinking diamonds. All angels of God, he decided. And he was glad one in particular had been sent to Earth, to the woods of Maine, for him to find, and love, and give the gift of importance.

Chapter Nineteen

✦ · · ✦

She had very nearly missed her wedding.

Jane stood in front of the tall window and looked out at the moonlit northern Pacific churning against the rocky cliffs below her new home. The first home she could actually call her own. Simple wedding vows had given it to her. And those same vows had given her a husband and made her a queen by the mere act of conferment.

It had been a trying day.

And it wasn't over.

First she'd overslept this morning, due to the fact that she hadn't gotten to bed until nearly dawn. And when she had finally roused, it had been to a throbbing shoulder protesting her nighttime journey into the city. Swinging an axe had been no easy feat, and she'd paid the price by not being able to lift her left arm this morning.

Then, once she'd come fully awake and was able to quit groaning in agony, Jane had spent half an hour hunched over the toilet, groaning some more. When she'd finally straightened and looked in the mirror, she'd almost fainted at her reflection. Her hair had been standing on end, her eyes had been teary, and her skin had looked green. It had taken a whole pot of tea and three toasts to settle her stomach.

And so had gone the rest of the day in a haze of nerves. As soon as she'd said "I do," in what Jane hoped had sounded like passable Shelkovan (Irina had taught her the words), Mark had all but slapped a dainty tiara onto her head and said something even more important-sounding—also in Shelkovan. Then he'd given her a long, satisfied, possessive look and turned her to face all the people in attendance. Jane had barely made it back down the aisle before she'd been sick again. And teary again. And hot and sweaty and as cold as a clam all at the same time—again.

That second bout of nausea may have had something to do with nerves. Or it may have been the fact that Mark had carried her out to the top step of the beautiful, onion-domed church and had held her in his arms in front of a cheering crowd of Shelkovans.

Or it may have been another bout of morning sickness.

She was pregnant. Just this morning, after swearing Petri to secrecy, she'd taken a little trip in to see Dr. Daveed.

And yup, she was about as pregnant as a girl could get.

And tonight—her wedding night—she really should consider telling her husband.

But at the moment she couldn't even manage a smile, having turned from the window to face her new bedroom. Mark's bedroom. Their bedroom, now.

The one he was standing in, naked but for a towel wrapped around his waist. His hair was damp and curling slightly at the neck, his face was once again clean-shaven, and he was back to giving her that butterfly-inducing smile of his.

That smile of anticipation.

That smile of promise.

She really should smile back, if only to let him know she loved him.

Jane fingered her new wedding band instead.

It was an outrageously wide band, solid gold, with inlaid fir and pine trees made of what Jane worried were real emeralds. It probably cost a kingdom. Not that she would have to worry about ever losing it, since the darn thing was darn tight.

Mark had forced it onto her finger with a satisfied grunt, then winked at her. Sister Roberta, standing beside Jane as her witness, had actually sighed with what had sounded like relief. Alexi, Mark's witness, had groaned and shaken his head, mumbling loud enough for everyone to hear, "God deliver us, we've just acquired an angel." Sister Roberta had stopped smiling at that, and leaned forward and given Alexi a good glare and a sniff.

Mark had laughed out loud. And in a voice even more carrying than Alexi's, had said, "Ah, but an angel with the kiss of life." And then he'd swooped down and kissed her life-giving lips right there at the altar, in front of God, the Shelkovan priest, and the Catholic priest Sister Roberta had somehow found to co-officiate.

Nobody had dared contradict the nun when she'd stated the wedding would be blessed by a man of her church, as Sister Roberta had been wearing her own uniform of God at the time.

"Are you going to stand sentry at that window all night?"

"No."

Mark cocked his head. "What are you thinking?"

"That the band I gave you today is rather plain. And loose," she tacked on.

"And perfect. I love it. Just as I love its giver."

"Aunt Irina said as much when she took me shopping for it. And I know not all men wear rings."

"I like that you wanted me to wear one."

"I just wish I had a real wedding present to give you."

He cocked his head again and studied her, a small grin on his lips and that twinkle still in his eyes. Jane was glad he was keeping his distance—as if he were afraid she'd bolt out the window if he came too close.

She wondered if she would.

"You feel you come to me with nothing," he said, not asking but stating. "With only the clothes on your back."

"Yes. And an old shotgun."

"And if I tell you giving yourself to me, in love, is gift enough, will you believe me?"

Okay, she finally believed he might actually love her, although she still didn't understand why. But she wanted to give him a proper wedding gift. Something special.

She suddenly smiled. Oh, but she did have something for him; the perfect gift for a king.

Jane finally approached her husband, which she knew he was waiting for her to do, and pressed her right hand over his heart to feel it beating strong and steady. "I just realized I do have a gift for you. Something every king wants."

"And what is that, angel?" he whispered thickly.

"An heir."

There was suddenly no chest under her hand, as it had disappeared, along with her husband. She looked down to see him sitting on the edge of the bed. A bed even larger than Reynard's; one that could fit a whole new generation of rascal princes . . . and just maybe a princess or two.

"You're pregnant?" he whispered, staring up at her.

She nodded.

"You know for certain?"

She nodded again.

Mark spread his knees, wrapped his arms around her waist, and pressed his forehead to her belly. "A baby," he whispered in awe. "A son. You're giving me a son."

"Or daughter," Jane whispered back, running her fingers through his hair. "I just might break tradition, Markov Lakeland, and give you a princess."

"That is fine," he said, lifting his head to look at her.

The twinkle was gone, replaced by . . . something else. Jane didn't want to hope that was moisture in his eyes, didn't want to believe she'd been able to bring this huge, strong, noble man to tears, that only she was able to give him something so special.

Before she could hope for any more, Mark pulled her down on the bed by simply lying back and taking her with him. He still held her tight, his arms still around her waist, and Jane found herself in the very interesting position of lying across his chest, staring down at him.

She smiled again. "So what do you think about that, Mr. Your Majesty? How about I give you a daughter? She'll have golden eyes like her daddy, and hopefully hair like her daddy, and she'll have my keen sight for shooting and my sweet disposition."

The body she was lounging on began to rumble, then shake, then nearly threw her off but for her husband's arms still tight around her. "He'll have my eyes, your hair, and hopefully not an ounce of your disposition, witch."

"We'll teach her to camp in the woods, swim in your cold lakes, and fly a plane. No, a jet. We'll teach her to fly a fighter jet off the *Katrina*."

"He'll be taught diplomacy, compassion, and the law. He'll learn to ride horses and shoot a gun, and he'll learn how to fight for what he wants."

"She'll be taught manners. And how to dance. And she'll be taught how to cook."

"Our son will be taught to look after his younger brothers."

"Our daughter will be taught to look after her younger sisters."

"My father will have a real stroke."

"He deserves it. And he deserves a granddaughter."

"You're daughter enough for the old man. Granddaughters, if they're at all like their mother, will surely kill him."

"I love you, Mark."

"And I love my little Maine angel. Now kiss your husband and let us start this marriage."

M ark's new bride was suddenly shy again. And worried. Oh, what a worrier she was. But now, at least, he understood her easily sprung tears and swinging emotions.

She was pregnant.

As Dr. Daveed had told her on the *Katrina*, if a child was meant to be born, it would.

This babe may not arrive as timely as Reynard would wish, but it was fitting that Jane had conceived on their odyssey home together; during their discovery of each other and the blossoming of their love that had flourished despite the fact that they had both tried to deny it.

Mark rolled over, placing Jane beneath him. He looked down into her huge, worried eyes and smiled. Then he started kissing her face, slowly working his way to her lips. He didn't stay there long, though, but continued his journey of gentling her, raining small, warm attention over her neck and shoulders. He had to pull the gown she was wearing to the side, but she didn't seem to notice. Her hands were hovering over his shoulders until they finally landed. And then they squeezed him tightly as Mark found a sweet little sensitive spot on her collarbone.

"I'm going to do it properly this time," he crooned in promise between kisses. "I'm going to go slow, and I'm going to drive you mad with want for me. And Jane?"

"Yes?" she breathed on a whisper.

"Don't be afraid to shout."

His words came back to haunt him more than once that night. Their wedding bed became their own private world of exploration and fascination and, ultimately, satisfaction. As promised, Mark went slow, educating Jane to his body and also her own; teaching her to glory in their senses. And after a long, intimate, gentle assault, he was able to get her to shout with fulfillment, not once, but twice, before his own shout overtook her echoes.

Wondrous, dazed eyes looked back at him. "Wow."

It was an arrogant grin he gave her.

"I understand now," she whispered breathlessly. "About that night on the *Katrina*. You did like it."

His grin broadened at her blush. He nodded, still not able to find his voice.

"That didn't hurt our baby, did it?" she asked, suddenly all worried again.

"No," Mark said with loving tenderness. "Each time we make love while you're carrying, it will let our child know how much its parents love each other. Each time, it will make our baby more secure in its new life."

"Her new life."

Mark groaned and rolled off. "Let's not start that again. We'll wait eight months and see what we get."

"Yes, we'll see," Jane agreed, a mischievous, utterly feminine smile breaking free. She cuddled up to him, trying to stifle a very unfeminine yawn.

Mark hugged her tightly. "Sleep, Jane. You've had a very hard day," he ordered, pulling the blankets up over them.

Mark settled down to also sleep, laying one of his legs

over hers to pull her more firmly against him. That was when he felt his foot touch not skin, but wool.

The woman was wearing socks. On her wedding night. He almost burst into laughter, despite the fact that he probably had no energy left.

Damn, but he hadn't known angels wore socks to bed.

Chapter Twenty

❖┄❖

"What do you mean you don't have a job for me? I thought I was supposed to be the queen. I thought that meant I'd go to work every day, just like you."

Mark stood up and walked from behind his desk, then leaned against the front of it. He crossed his ankles and then crossed his arms over his chest while he studied his disgruntled wife. Despite her frown, she still looked enough like an angel to make him smile.

She was dressed very . . . queenly this morning. She was wearing her new slacks and a silk blouse. The colors were earthy; brown and a deep forest green that made her eyes look dark and deeply seductive. Her contrary hair was acting very un-queenly, though. It refused to be tamed, trying to escape the confines she'd given it, rebellious against the constraining knot she'd tried to fashion at the nape of her neck.

She'd marched into his office this morning looking for work—queen work.

"You don't have a specific job. You're more of a . . . a figurehead. An example."

Her frown turned to a scowl. "Then what am I supposed to do all day?"

"You are supposed to simply be my wife," he said, scowling back, deciding to tease her a little. After all, wasn't it a husband's privilege to make consuming, passionate love to his wife by night and tease her by day? "You're supposed to grow my son healthy and strong, run my house, and be at my beck and call."

That did it. She took a step toward him. "Beck and call?" she whispered, her eyes darkening to nearly black.

He nodded.

She exploded. She threw herself at him, a tiny growl coming from her throat.

Mark straightened and caught her. He wrapped his arms around her, still mindful of her injury, and soundly kissed her before she could start hurling nun-curses at him.

Within thirty seconds she stilled. Within sixty she was kissing him back. And within two minutes the growl had turned to tiny mewls.

Lord, Lord, he was a contented man today.

But he reluctantly pulled back, having to steady her. "I'm just teasing, Jane. I know you want to be useful, but it's going to take time. There really isn't an actual, everyday job for you, other than running the household. Not yet."

"But that's Irina's job," she reminded him, looking disappointed and thoroughly kissed.

"She only did it because there was no real mistress here. Now that we're married, this is your home. You make the rules concerning it. You'll work out the menus with Cook, take charge of the staff, and entertain guests. Things like that."

"But then what will Irina do?"

Mark shrugged, still holding her within his arms. "She could help. Teach you."

"No."

"No?"

"I'm not going to take that away from her. She needs to still be important here."

Ah. Yes. Jane would see things from that point of view. She would see Irina's need. And he could only love his wife all the more for her insight. "Well, then, I don't know what to tell you. Things will eventually arise that will need your attention as queen." He kissed her quickly on the nose. "I'm sure our people will be coming to you with petitions soon enough. Now that they know there is a woman's influence in a seat of power, I'm sure you'll be swamped with causes before you know it."

More prophetic words were never spoken.

Only his impatient, impetuous, impossible wife hadn't exactly waited for the petitions to come, but had gone looking for them. Mark could only shake his head at his father. They were both in Mark's office, and both quite ready to throttle the new queen of Shelkova. It hadn't been three months since the wedding, and Jane had been able to manufacture enough trouble to try the patience of a saint—and five Lakeland men.

She was . . . settling in.

And the people of Shelkova loved her.

"She had them paint all the cells a bright color and buy new mattresses for the cots at the city jail," Reynard told Mark, sounding more awed than disgruntled. "And the police commissioner is scrambling to recruit more women officers. And Markov, there are known prostitutes coming to the palace for afternoon tea," Reynard whispered, his silly grin saying he was more proud than appalled.

"That's nothing," Mark countered. "Everywhere I walk, if I'm not tripping over those two damn puppies, I'm tripping over children. She's bringing the kids here from the orphanage several days a week."

Reynard's grin widened. "She's rewarding them, she says, for doing well in school."

"She's spoiling them rotten, you mean. I swear, if I have to sit down to another meal of idolized gawking from those urchins, I'm going to . . ."

Reynard laughed. "You love them as much as we all do."

"Yes, as does my wife. I'm worried she'll try to adopt them all."

"No. She's found good homes for six of them already."

Mark closed his eyes. "Yes. And thank God Sister Roberta has finally gone home."

"I liked the old nun."

"I did, too. But she was rather straight-talking at times."

"But that's not our problem right now, is it; the children or Sister Roberta or afternoon teas? Our problem is Jane's latest bee in her bonnet."

Mark leaned back in his chair. "It's an old bee. She wants me to decree it illegal for the men of Shelkova to publicly denounce their wives."

"It's time."

"But it's also a very dictatorial move. I don't want to blatantly tell our people they can no longer do something they've been doing for centuries. That will make me a dictator. Our people deserve better."

"Have you explained this to Jane?"

Mark gave his father a crooked smile. "She told me the women are also our people. She wants to give them a stronger voice in parliament while we're at it."

"It's time for that, too."

"By decree."

"There will be riots in the streets."

"And my wife will be leading them kicking and screaming all the way to parliament," Mark said on a sigh. "The women of Shelkova are no more prepared for change than the men."

"They're going to have to mature to the modern age, Mark, if we are to compete in this modern world."

"And Jane thinks a good kick in the butt will mature them just fine," Mark agreed, nodding his head.

"Maybe she's right."

"And she has the nerve to call me pompous. In less than three months, I've created a monster."

"No. You've created a queen. You've given Jane an importance that she now believes in. And she's trying desperately to use that importance for the good of everyone."

"And I'm going to have to give her bodyguard a raise. Petri is being dragged from one end of this city to the other. He hasn't complained, but have you seen him lately? He's losing weight."

"And your wife is gaining it."

Mark suddenly frowned. "Yes." And then he grinned. "Her pregnancy is showing."

"I'm glad you two decided to tell us that last night," Reynard snapped. "Including the fact that she's *four* months along."

Mark's grinned broadened. "We wanted to enjoy the anticipation for a while. Don't be upset. Jane has promised to give you a granddaughter."

The old man's eyes lit up. "Wouldn't that be something; the first girl-child in this family in generations." He suddenly stood up. "So let's see to it that my granddaughter is born healthy. Curb your wife, Markov. Slow her down. And make her happy. Give the people your decree that women will now be first-class citizens. Give them the vote."

Mark stood up with a groan and walked his father to the door. But Reynard stopped and turned before he opened it, love, tenderness, and fatherly pride shining in his eyes as Mark was caught in a firm, back-slapping embrace. "I'm glad for you," Reynard softly told his son. "And for Jane. I hope this child is the first of many."

"It will be," Mark quietly promised, hugging him back. "And don't worry. Both Jane and I will pull our people forward, by their teeth if need be. In two days I'll make my speech outlining their future." He pulled back, giving his father a wry grin. "It will be an interesting future, will it not?"

"Most interesting," Reynard agreed, walking out the door. "Most interesting."

Mark was dressed in formal attire, his hair newly barbered and his boots polished to brilliance. His speech was tucked in his jacket pocket, despite the fact that all the words were dancing around in his head like fairy dust.

And he was late.

And again—and as usual—he couldn't find his wife.

"Petri. What are you doing standing out here?" Mark asked, relieved to find the man outside the kitchen, since wherever Petri was, Jane was bound to be near.

"I'm waiting, Your Majesty."

"Where's your mistress?"

"In with Cook."

Mark had to smile as Petri darted worried looks at the kitchen door. "You should probably go in and get her. She's going to be late."

"I know, Your Majesty. But she said she wouldn't be long."

"Chicken," Mark whispered just before he threw open the kitchen door and walked past the very smart bodyguard. Petri may be ready to step in front of a bullet for his mistress, but the man wasn't quite ready to face Cook for her.

Mark found his wife—dressed in a very beautiful,

very elegant gown, her hair wisped away from her face in graceful curls—sitting on a stool at the counter, her back to him and her fingers dipped into a bowl of what looked like frosting.

He stopped and enjoyed the sight. Jane Lakeland had become a sugar hound in her pregnancy. More than one night he'd accompanied her down to the kitchens to steal sweets from the pantry. And Cook, Mark suspected, always had a stash waiting for just that reason. His wife was going to rival the whales at sea before she finally gave birth in five months.

"We're late, wife," he whispered just as he leaned down to nuzzle her shoulder. "And since this is all your idea, the least you could do is show up."

Jane spun around on her stool with a gasp, the hand she'd been eating with grabbing at his shoulder to steady herself. She glared up at him, but it wasn't much of an intimidating glare, what with the frosting covering her lips and chin and nose. Mark decided he was growing rather fond of sugar himself, so he kissed her sweet lips.

She dropped the bowl on the floor and grabbed both of his shoulders.

He kept kissing her.

She started to kiss him back.

Cook started screaming again, and Mark decided it was time to retreat—with his wife.

"Come on, angel. You're going to get me killed," he said with a chuckle, pulling her after him to the safety of the hall. They nearly ran into Petri, who was standing in awe and listening to the tirade still echoing out after them.

"You made me make a mess in the kitchen," Jane

scolded, busily brushing her hands together, then licking at her fingers, trying to clean them. "You deserve to be yelled at."

Mark decided to ignore her scolding as he walked to the second car of the small motorcade parked at the front of the palace. His father and brothers and aunt Irina were already in their cars, patiently waiting. Jane waved to them just before Mark helped her into theirs. Once they were finally on their way to parliament for him to give his speech, he turned to his wife.

"Are you sure you don't want to say something today, Jane? The people should hear your endorsement of this plan. It would maybe help them . . . swallow it a little easier."

"They wouldn't understand me. I don't speak the language, remember?"

"But you're learning," Mark reminded her with no little pride at how Jane had thrown herself into Shelkovan language lessons. And despite the fact that she all but slaughtered his native tongue, and despite the fact that she constantly complained the alphabet was weird, Mark was proud of her. Everyone else was just surprisingly patient.

"Then couldn't you at least stand beside me and nod and smile? Even that would help."

"I couldn't stand up there in front of everyone and the television camera," she whispered, her sticky hand self-consciously going to her hair. She took her other hand and patted his sleeve. "You'll do just fine. And even if every man in parliament is glowering, just remember that every woman at home, watching television, will be smiling."

Mark had to grin at her sincere, confident, encouraging

look. Jane Doe Abbot from the woods of Maine not only had the gift to make him feel important but ten feet tall and possessing shoulders of steel—which he would need to push his people forward in the coming years.

His speech today was about his vision for Shelkova; for its people and lands and its place in this world. It was also a lecture on humanity. And definitely a decree.

It had been coauthored by his wife.

And it was going to hit their people like a size twelve boot right in the butt.

But for all of his planning, and all of Jane's reluctance to be a visual part of things, Mark should have realized that if his wife was involved, things usually went from organized chaos to disasters in the blink of an eye. They walked into parliament arm and arm to the standing cheers of all the members—likely because none of them knew what he was going to say today.

He pulled his wife up to the podium with him despite her tugging, then stood before the still-standing, still-cheering crowd and the cameras that were going to broadcast his speech live to all of Shelkova. The light on the camera was on, and Mark knew his countrymen—and women—were watching. Those without televisions in their homes were probably gathered in community centers and pubs and churches. Nearly the entire population of the city of Previa was standing outside, in the streets, listening to loudspeakers.

"Smile," Mark whispered to his nervous, stricken wife.

She glared up at him. "I'm going to get you for this," she whispered through smiling, gritted teeth.

"You have my permission to try," he whispered back, his smile sincere.

Hers disappeared.

Mark wrapped an arm around her and waved for parliament to quiet down. And then he spoke into the microphone and told his country they were going to be getting a new prince or princess in five months. Parliament rose with a roar this time, which was all but drowned out by the roar of excitement coming from the streets.

"What did you tell them?" Jane shouted, pressing herself against him in near horror.

"I told them that in five months Shelkova will have a new baby to fawn over."

She relaxed and smiled again, only to suddenly stiffen. "Five months?" she squeaked. "You didn't say five months!"

He nodded.

"But we've only been married three! Mark! Your people can count!"

She was back to looking horrified. He kissed her, on the cheek this time, and hugged her closer. "I'm fairly certain they would have been counting five months from now anyway, Jane. Let them get used to the idea."

"You're a rat."

"But you love this rat. Now be a good little wife and go sit down. I have king work to do. Did you bring your shotgun?" he asked, releasing her as the cheering finally began settling down.

"No. Why?" she asked, looking confused.

Mark shrugged. "I thought it might come in handy when we try to escape the angry mob I'm about to create."

"Mark," she said, sounding exasperated, her hands on her hips. She was no longer embarrassed, anyway. "You're doing the right thing. And everyone will realize it . . . soon."

"I'm going to say it was all your idea. Right at the end of my speech, in Shelkovan, I am going to tell them all to blame you."

She gave him a thoroughly un-intimidated smile. "And look like a weak, henpecked husband? I don't think so, Your Majesty."

"Go away," he growled. "And let me get to work."

She started to. Really, she did. She took a step back and started to turn, but suddenly his wife gasped, and her eyes widened in horror. Mark stiffened and looked around for some threat, only to flinch when Jane ran up to him, her cheeks bright red again, and frantically started swiping at his shoulders. He looked down, wondering if he was on fire the way she was beating at him. But what he saw was his pregnant queen industriously trying to wipe away the powdered sugar imprints of her hands.

On both shoulders.

As if a sticky-fingered wife had been kissing him silly.

And every swipe, every worried and loving rub, was being televised to the nation and probably the world. It wouldn't be his speech that made cable news tonight, Mark guessed with a confident smile. It would be Jane Lakeland performing an act that would be understood by every woman on the planet who had ever had a husband. Hell, he wouldn't be surprised if she wetted her finger and straightened his hair next.

Good God. There was nothing his little angel could

have done to endear her to his people more than that simple wifely act.

It was a private Lakeland dinner that night; no guests, no children from the orphanage, no one but family. Everyone was dressed in casual attire again. Jane was actually in yoga pants. Mark guessed her new clothes were becoming a little tight in the waist, and that Petri was going to be supervising another shopping expedition in the near future.

"I can't believe the silence today," Alexi said, voicing what was on everyone's mind. "You could have heard a pin drop in parliament when you finished your speech."

"And in the streets," Sergei added. "Every last person was stunned."

Mark grinned through his worry. "I did come down a little hard on them," he admitted. "But I've had enough of parliament's bickering over this land issue."

"You gave them one week to produce a law for you to sign," Dmitri whispered in awe.

"I'm not sure that's what stunned everybody," Irina offered. "I think it had to do with your words on family traditions."

"I think it had to do with everything," Sergei argued. "My God, man, you sounded like a scolding father. You boxed their ears in."

"He laid down the law," Alexi added, nodding agreement. "Telling them to look not at themselves, but at their children. That the next generation of Shelkova will be—how did you put it? World-wise. That our concentration of funds will be going to our schools."

"And then you told them the women are going to vote," Alexi said. "Half of parliament nearly choked on that one. A few of those men are going to lose their seats to women."

"I like when you dared to decree that the posts in all town squares were to be taken down. That certainly took guts," Sergei said with brotherly pride.

"I imagine the woman will happily see to that little chore," Reynard added.

Mark glanced at his silent wife, who was very busy eating her dinner instead of adding anything to this discussion. "What did you think of my speech, Jane?" he asked.

She finally looked up, and he had his answer.

"I think you did a wonderful thing today," she said, her eyes bright with her own pride in him. "And I think the people will agree with you . . . eventually. They're probably all sitting at their own dinner tables, like us, and discussing the same things we are. I think husbands are looking at their wives a little differently tonight. And parents are looking at their children differently, too." She turned to the rest of the table. "In their hearts they know that Mark is right, that it's time for change. Since they gained their independence, they've been standing at a fork in the road, and Mark just pushed them along in the right direction today. Now that they know which way to walk, they'll walk forward."

Reynard reached out and patted her hand. "Yes, daughter. They will walk with you and Markov now. What was done today was right. And timely."

"We're going to have to be on guard more than ever," Mark told the table in general.

"You think the people will rebel?" Alexi asked in surprise.

"No. We needn't fear anything like that. But I pushed the issue of the land rights, and in one week the consortium will have no hope of acquiring our timber." Mark looked at Jane. "Are you satisfied now, Your Queen Majesty?"

"Me? I—I don't know what you mean."

"I've kicked our people in the butt, just like you wanted."

"I think you may have embellished the speech we wrote together," she muttered. "I don't remember it being that long or that . . . heated."

Mark sighed. "Jane. I had just had my jacket brushed like a little child. And I thought you were going to slick my hair and wipe my nose. I had to gain back my manhood by sounding forceful. Otherwise all that would have been remembered was your wifely concern."

Jane promptly went back to eating her dinner, industriously trying to ignore the chuckles surrounding her. Heavens! She couldn't believe she'd really done that. In front of the world, no less. But geesh, Mark had been standing up there all proud and kingly with handprints on his jacket. Everyone would know how they'd gotten there. She'd been so horrified that she'd run up and started wiping them off, just like he said, as if he were a child.

Well, she wasn't showing her face in public for a year.

And she wasn't going to even *look* at sugar again as long as she lived.

They finally made it up to the sanctuary of their bedroom after watching the nightly news, and watching her—in vivid color—wipe her husband's jacket again, this time in front of the entire world. Sister Roberta was probably laughing her head off back home right now.

Jane was still cringing inside as she undressed for bed. She could hear the shower running in the adjoining bathroom and remembered her husband's petition that she come in and scrub his back. It had become a frequent request lately, but one she certainly enjoyed doing. Showering with him was a novel experience, and usually a prelude to a long, tender night of lovemaking. But now her belly was bumping out. Jane stood naked in front of her mirror and studied herself. Yes, she was definitely showing. And every so often lately, when she least expected it, her insides would start to flutter with the gentle stirring of her growing child.

She was having a baby.

She was going to be a mother to a young person who would need her.

Just as much as her husband did. Jane finally believed Mark needed her just as much as she needed him—which she needed like air to breathe. And the three of them, all tucked together lovingly in bed each night, reconfirmed that one single truth.

Sometime in the past three months, Jane realized, she'd stopped being an orphan and started being a wife, a mother, a daughter, a sister, a niece, and even an example for the women of her new homeland. And if she didn't start getting the language right, she was going to start cursing like Cook.

"The water's getting cold!" her impatient husband called from the shower.

Jane smiled and patted her protruding belly. "Come on, baby, let's go clean up your daddy," she whispered, kicking her brace out of the way with her naked right foot. "Our king is calling." She didn't hesitate at the door of the shower, but pushed it back and entered the steamy room, blinking and then staring at the sight before her.

Dear God in heaven, she loved this man. And she would never get used to the idea that he was hers, and that she could look and touch and kiss and adore him to her heart's content. Mark was built like Atlas himself, possessing an inner strength that would always amaze her. Jane boldly moved up to him and lovingly began running her hands over his chest, marveling at the way his muscles instantly contracted at her touch. She wiped away the soap, pushing him back under the spray and soaking herself, then began to kiss him all over, wherever she could reach. His hands came up to hold her.

She stopped him, shaking her head and pushing them back to his side. "No," she whispered. "Let me love you tonight, Mark. Let me touch you."

Chapter Twenty-one

—◆—◆—

"We promise, Petri. Just one more store and then we'll go home," Jane assured her patient bodyguard with a sheepish smile, realizing she'd said that same thing two stores ago.

"We only need to pick up a few more items," Irina added. "This is our last stop."

They were shopping for maternity clothes. Jane was nearly five months pregnant and couldn't fasten any of her pants any longer. Irina was showing her some of the smaller, quaint little shops in the less traveled part of the city, and Petri, bless his soul, was stoically following, despite his obviously increasing unease.

They entered the last shop only to be greeted by an excited, downright flustered woman who couldn't believe she was being patronized by her queen. Irina did the talking, explaining what they wanted, and Jane went about browsing.

She was a little overwhelmed by it all; the maternity clothes and all the baby things. She picked up a tiny gown that looked like it fit a doll, and stared at it with amazement. A baby. She was really going to have a baby.

She'd actually asked Mark's permission to come out today. Not because she was a meek wife, but because she didn't want to worry him. She could tell the entire household was on edge this week, what with the land bill pending. But Mark had smiled at her belly and told her to go. Petri, ever vigilant, had brought along reinforcements. There were two guards and a driver; all armed, all alert.

But despite his precautions, disaster struck—swiftly and from the back of the store.

The back door crashed in, the proprietor screamed, and Petri lunged for Jane. He never made it. He was shot several times as he came toward her, his gun drawn and his cold eyes pinned on the threat behind her. Jane scrambled out of the way to give him a clear shot, but he was down in a pool of blood before she got out her own scream.

More gunfire erupted as the other bodyguards charged through the front door only to also fall in a hail of gunfire. By this time Irina was in the clutches of one of their attackers, and Jane was scurrying backward, throwing anything she could get her hands on at the two men approaching her.

The chaos was over within two minutes.

Just like that, grief had come and terror reigned as Irina and Jane were bound, gagged, and shoved into the trunk of a waiting car in the back alley. Within another minute they were speeding through the streets of Previa, locked in dark, confining, swaying blackness.

Jane could hear Irina's sobs mingled with her own over the rev of the engine and throb of the tires. It took willpower for Jane not to throw up and choke in her gag. She could only huddle close to Irina and cry silent tears at the slaughter she'd just witnessed; at the defeat of a good man she'd come to care deeply about. Her only salvation was an equally silent prayer that Petri was not dead, merely wounded. And with the prayers of her childhood, Jane asked God for this hope—at the same time asking that she and Irina be delivered back to the family she loved. And she prayed for Mark to be given strength, for the noble man not to lose his wife and child as a result of trying to save his people.

"Jane," Irina choked. "Can you pull off your gag?"

They'd shackled her hands in front of her, then bound them with a rope around her waist. But she was finally able to work the gag down her cheek and to her chin, able to breathe in huge gulps for the first time since the terror had begun. "I—I've got it," she gasped back.

"Oh, my God! Petri. He's dead," Irina sobbed, burying her face against Jane's shoulder. "And the others. I don't know what happened to them."

"No!" Jane hissed. "He always wore a special vest. He may just be wounded," she said, rubbing her cheek against Irina. "We have to believe that."

"Where do you suppose they are taking us?"

"I don't know," she whispered, closing her eyes on another wave of dizziness. The motion of the black hole they were in was making her sick. Despite the freedom of her mouth, she still couldn't take in enough air. And what she did take in was becoming stale and stifling. "We need to try to relax," Jane told her friend. "And concentrate. Can you tell anything about the road we're on?"

"No. But it's smooth. And we seem to be going fast. It must be a good road. They must be taking us out of the city."

"But in which direction?"

That was a good question. She and Irina huddled together for what seemed like hours in their dark cocoon, until the car suddenly slowed and turned onto a bumpy, jarring road. Another hour and Jane and Irina, bruised and sick from fumes and fear, nearly fainted with relief when the car finally stopped. But their terror was not over. They were unceremoniously dragged from the trunk and pushed toward a large, decaying building. They didn't need to blink to adjust their eyes, as it was now dark. The only light in the eerily silent, dense forest came from the building.

There were three men in all that had brought them here, each carrying guns and just as silent as their surroundings. They were all large, hard-featured men.

And they didn't look like Shelkovans.

Barely able to walk after the cramped ride in the trunk, Jane tripped twice going up the stairs. She was harshly grabbed by her weak shoulder, which was just beginning to feel normal, and a pain shot through her, causing her to cry out. She was roughly jerked forward, which caused her to almost fall again, which caused the man holding her arm to jerk her upright. Jane thought she was finally going to throw up from the pain.

They were ushered into a large, dirty room and brought

to stand in front of a man Jane instantly recognized. She'd met him at Mark's coronation ball, and the next day at her wedding feast. He was from someplace in South America, if she remembered correctly, and had been all smiles and good wishes to Mark and her. She wondered if Mark's intelligence officers had known they were inviting the enemy to the ceremonies.

"Well, Your Majesty," the ugly little man crooned, walking toward her, "how nice of you to visit."

Jane thought about spitting in his ugly face, but one of the men still held her bad arm and she didn't think she could stand another wrenching. "The pleasure is mine, Señor Guavas," she said, nodding regally.

Her manner disarmed him, but only momentarily. His grin turned nasty. "So, you remember me, eh? And your little trip here has not daunted you, I see." He grabbed her neck in a bruising choke hold and jerked her close to his face. "We will see how impudent you are when you leave here. If you leave," he hissed, pushing her back at the man still holding her arm. "Take them upstairs and lock them in," he ordered, just before he reached for her neck and snapped the chain holding the fir tree Mark had bought her on their first shopping trip.

Irina and Jane were shoved up two flights of rickety stairs and pushed into a dark, dusty room. Jane could see an old metal bed with a sagging mattress and two boarded-up windows before the door was shut, throwing them into darkness.

"Don't panic," she whispered when she heard Irina's broken sob. Groping, shuffling, she was able to approach and nudge her gently. "Come on. You've got to help me untie my hands."

"We are bound with handcuffs," Irina choked back.

"But untie the rope at my waist. Then I will do the same for you. We'll feel better."

"I can't see."

"There's a little moonlight coming through that broken board in the window. Let's move over there." With more shuffling and hitting of shins on boxes strewn throughout the room, they made their way to the window, and Jane turned Irina and went to work on her knots first. Once she had her free, Irina did the same for her. "Let's see if we can loosen some of these boards."

"We're up two flights," Irina reminded her.

"I just want some light," Jane muttered, tugging one of the boards.

They had to try several before they managed to work one free. It was too high overhead to see out of, but it did let in enough moonlight to see the room more clearly. It showed that there was an old kerosene lamp on the nightstand. And, amazingly, some matches. Awkwardly, because of the handcuffs, Jane was finally able to light the lamp and breathe easier again. Irina carefully sat down on the bed and looked around.

"Pigs wouldn't stay here," Jane offered, also looking around.

"Are you afraid of spiders or mice?" Irina asked softly, as if afraid to disturb any of the critters.

"No." Jane sat on the bed beside her. "I'm only afraid of the dark."

"Then how did you stand it? I was near to screaming with hysterics in that trunk."

"I recited passages from the Bible," Jane told her. "And from Emily Post."

Irina gave a little giggle that quickly turned into a sob. "What are we going to do?"

"We're going to wait. Mark will come get us."

"He doesn't know where we are. Neither do we. How can you be so calm?"

Jane's handcuffs rattled as she patted Irina's knee. "Because I'm going to load my shotgun with rock salt and hunt him down if he doesn't." She sobered. "He'll come. He has to. He loves me."

Irina found a weak smile. "So sure you are," she whispered.

"Darn right. He needs me."

Irina closed her eyes and swayed slightly. "I am so tired. And thirsty."

Both women looked around, but saw no food or water. They did find a dented, chipped chamber pot, and Jane walked over and rattled it with her toe. "I say we fill this up and throw it at the first man to walk through that door."

"Do . . . do we dare ask for some water?"

"I dare," Jane said, walking to the door and rattling the knob. It was locked, as she'd expected, so she began pounding on it. When that brought no results, Jane picked up the board she'd broken and started banging on the door.

It finally, suddenly opened.

She took a step back, dropping the board, and meekly asked for some water. The door was slammed shut in her face. But ten minutes later, a battered, dented bucket was brought in by one of the men. Another man brought in another bucket with what Jane guessed was supper. A third man stood sentry, a gun pointed at the two dangerous prisoners.

Jane stuck out her tongue at the closed door. "Did they think we were going to overpower them?" she asked as she awkwardly picked up the bucket of water. "The least they could have done was give us a cup," she muttered, setting the bucket on the nightstand. Peering down in it, she made a face. "Do you think it's drinkable?"

"I don't care," Irina said, lugging over the other bucket and setting it on the bed, then looking inside. "I'm willing to drink mud. Oh, look. A cup," she cried, like a child at Christmas.

"You go first," Jane told her, rummaging around in the food bucket. She pulled out a plastic bag. "Oh, boy. Bread and water. How quaint."

"But better than nothing," Irina said, drinking greedily, spilling the water down her chin.

Not having anything else to do, they both ate three slices of bread and drank some of the water. And then they politely each turned their backs while the other awkwardly, almost comically, tried to use the chamber pot. And then they all but fell on the bed and into a restless sleep.

Bright sunlight came through the broken window the next morning to find Jane and Irina huddled together and shivering. Blinking, looking up at the window, Jane nudged Irina awake. "Good heavens. It snowed last night."

Irina followed her line of sight. "It did," she said in disbelief. "We must be inland and possibly even in the mountains to be seeing snow, as the ocean current brings more temperate weather to the coast by the end of February."

"Well, now we know where we are."

Irina snorted. "Fat lot of good it does us."

Jane sighed. They could be five miles from home and it wouldn't do them much good. There were three pit bulls guarding their prison, all of them with guns and all looking ready to use them. The day held no surprises and no less worry. They were kept locked in the room, the only light they dared allow coming from the broken window. The oil in the lamp was getting low, and Jane wanted to keep it for the darkness.

They explored their little prison, looking in all the boxes. What they found were ancient, mildew-covered books on logging and forestry and wildlife. There were no tools, nothing metal whatsoever to use to pry more boards off the windows. And so the women spent their time talking about their childhoods, reading, and worrying.

Jane learned, much to her surprise, that Irina had been married for twelve years to a wonderful man she still mourned and had no desire to replace. No one, Irina told Jane, could compare to George Spanes, an American from Alaska who had stolen her heart one warm summer eve when he'd come to her father's home on the coast of Shelkova to buy fish from their village. George had died six years ago in a plane crash on one of his buying trips. Irina had returned home to Shelkova, and then she'd come to live with the Lakelands when Katrina had suddenly taken ill.

Jane's heart went out to the woman. Smiling sadly,

Irina said she'd loved and lost, and was glad for the time she'd had with her husband. The only true tragedy was that they hadn't been blessed with children. Markov, Sergei, Dmitri, and Alexi had become her sons.

Their bucket of water was refilled, they were given more bread, and, in a repeat of the previous night, both women cuddled together on the squeaky, rickety bed and went to sleep praying for deliverance from their prison. It was sometime in the middle of the night that Jane stirred to a faint sound. Shadows moved at one of the windows. She nudged Irina awake, and both women waited in suspense for what they hoped was a rescue.

What they got were two men peering in at them through the quietly sawed boards. Jane didn't know whether to run up and embrace the fools or push them off the ladder. They were fierce-looking men, what she could see of them in the faint moonlight. As quiet as mice but looking like lions, they climbed through the window and approached the bed.

Although she supposed elite soldiers on a covert mission might disguise themselves as . . . stone-age cavemen, Jane got a sinking feeling that her and Irina's predicament was about to go from bad to worse when a large calloused hand covered her mouth and she found herself looking into the most ghostly eyes she'd ever seen. Jane began to struggle when that hand was suddenly replaced by a rag and she was once again grabbed by the shoulders.

She'd had enough.

She lashed out at this newest threat by kicking violently, catching him in the thigh and gaining a satisfying grunt. Her satisfaction lasted only a second before she was wrapped in a heavy, smelly rug that she feared was actually an animal skin. And then she was tossed none too gently over a hard, muscled shoulder—making her quickly twist to protect her protruding belly.

From the sounds of things, Irina was experiencing the same rough handling.

Jane was mad now, but she didn't outright panic until she discovered the man intended to lower her out the window into the waiting arms of more men. She instantly stilled, scared they would drop her. It was a harrowing experience to be lowered two stories while relying on the strength of unknown men.

From the sounds of things, Irina was making the same journey.

Once on the ground, Jane was stood on her feet, still handcuffed, gagged, and blinded by the rug. The rug was suddenly removed just before she was tossed up onto a tall horse, into the waiting arms of the man who'd originally crawled in the window and stolen her.

And so their new odyssey began. Irina was mounted on another horse, being held tight against the broad chest of her own fur-clad abductor. Jane was barely able to see Irina's look of panic as they galloped past, along with no fewer than five others mounted on horses. Jane turned to peek around the broad shoulder of her rescuer and spotted two more men and horses before she was rudely jerked around to face front again. She pinched the arm around her middle, but was only able to get it to rise above her baby to beneath her breasts before it squeezed her tightly.

It was at that moment Jane decided to fear for her life. Not from the man behind her, but from the horse. It was a monstrous beast, tall and powerful feeling, galloping at breakneck speed over the frozen, snow-covered ground through the dense forest, seemingly oblivious to the branches getting in its way—sort of like an equine tank. With her still-handcuffed hands, Jane held its mane and closed her eyes. When that only made her dizzy, she tried to stare through the night and guess the horse's next move.

She was suddenly thankful for the man holding her so tightly. She leaned into his chest, which seemed more than adequate to hold her up as his free arm reached out to shield her from the oncoming branches slapping against them in a blur. But she soon started worrying again—if one hand was around her waist and one was blocking the branches, then who was steering the darn horse?

They kept up the grueling pace for half an hour and then slowed to a walk. The man holding her—whom she still hadn't dared look up at—suddenly reached between them and unbuttoned his coat. He let go of her long enough to wrap her closer against his warm chest, only to stiffen when his hand returned to her waist. He splayed his fingers to cup her belly, then growled something unintelligible—not at all sounding like the Shelkovan she was familiar with, but still recognizable to Jane as a curse—and so she pinched his arm to get him to raise it again.

He merely laughed and pulled his hand away, then finally wrapped her up in his coat and urged the horse into a less harried lope. Indignant at being manhandled yet thankful for the warmth, and growing more tired by the minute, Jane endured the dark journey for what seemed like another full hour.

The sun eventually rose, and with it came the sight of a village nestled into the crux of a valley cut by a swiftly flowing river. She sagged in relief against the man, although she still couldn't bring herself to turn and look at him. But she intended to tell Mark about her and Irina's rough handling the moment this harrowing mission was over.

Geesh, would a simple "You're safe now" have been too much to ask?

The returning rescuers were met at the center of the village by more men, several chickens, at least a dozen goats, and countless barking dogs. Jane looked around for signs of Mark, but when she didn't see anything that looked even remotely military—say, a helicopter waiting to whisk them back to civilization—she then tried to decide what disturbed her about the place. There weren't any utility poles, which meant there was no electricity or landline phones, but she did see that some of the crudely built cabins had small solar panels attached to their roofs. Were the panels for recharging cell phones, maybe? Hopefully?

She also noticed several ATVs—some looking older than she was—and two very shiny, definitely new and fast-looking snowmobiles parked next to a rather large barn. So why hadn't the men used the snowmobiles to rescue her and Irina?

Well, unless they'd felt the machines were too noisy.

So okay, then; their rescuers were at least from this century despite using horses for transportation. Yeah, she supposed it might have been more expedient to send a couple of elite soldiers to the area and have them enlist the men of a local village to help rescue her and Irina, and Mark was probably right now racing to them in a fast helicopter. But that still didn't explain what was bugging her about this place, as if something . . . important was missing.

Jane's attention was drawn to Irina being handed down to the outstretched hands of grinning men all trying to grab at her at once. The man who'd been carrying Irina growled low in his throat and shook his fist at them. And poor Irina, looking frazzled and dazed and scared, was frantically trying to climb back up on the horse.

The man holding Jane suddenly shouted, nearly unseating her. The men on the ground instantly stilled, and reluctantly backed off with disgruntled muttering. Her rescuer just as suddenly dismounted, making Jane realize she was up on the monster alone. But she had a death grip on the tangled mane and managed not to fall.

But she nearly did just that when the guy turned and Jane got her first good look at him.

Nope; this definitely didn't feel like a covert rescue mission, and those animal skins definitely weren't a disguise. The large hands reaching up to her were calloused and strong, the broad chest she'd leaned against stretched the suede shirt under his open jacket to the point it was in danger of bursting, and the guy's hair was a striking jet black that reached well past his shoulders. From behind he'd looked like an old mountain man from the historical west, but not from the front. No, the clean-shaven jaw, smooth brow, and prominent cheekbones surrounding keen, alert, ice-blue eyes belonged to a man of thirty or thirty-five hard-lived years.

He said something and beckoned with his hands.

Jane clung to the horse and shook her head.

His face grew harsh and he said something again, his fingers beckoning.

She didn't exactly like sitting on top of a scary horse, but the giant made it the lesser of two evils.

Ignoring the laughter coming from the villagers, the guy reached up and simply pulled her off the horse, only to have to prop her on his shoulder halfway down in order to untangle her fingers from the mane—only to have to hold her up when he set Jane on her feet and her legs buckled.

The man, whom she decided to name Conan—he certainly looked like a barbarian—let out a heavy sigh and swept her up in his arms and strode past the staring men. He carried her into one of the crude cabins, having to duck to make the door, and deposited her on a high bed covered in colorful wool blankets.

Irina was carried in and deposited beside her.

Irina looked at Jane with wide, bewildered eyes, and Jane noticed the woman's blouse was torn at the shoulder, her hair was more tangled than the horse's mane, and she was shivering from both cold and fright and looked ready to drop. "What is happening to us?" Irina asked the moment the men left.

"I'm starting to worry that instead of being rescued," Jane whispered, "we may have been kidnapped again."

Chapter Twenty-two

✦ ⋯ ✦

It suddenly dawned on Jane that not only had they just been abandoned in a room full of tools, but they were mobile. "Come on. Help me look for a weapon," she told Irina, getting off the bed. "A knife or something."

"You don't think to use a knife on that . . . that man," Irina said, even as she got up and began limping around the room.

"Did you hurt yourself?" Jane asked, forgetting her search to go to her friend.

"No. My legs are asleep," the woman confessed, groaning as she took another step.

"Mine, too. And yes, if Conan tries to paw me again, I'm going to do violence," Jane muttered, walking to the counter next to a rusty, heat-radiating cookstove.

"He pawed you?"

Jane turned to see Irina's cheeks were no longer pale, her handcuffed hands clutching her dirty jacket closed at the throat. Jane nodded. "He squeezed my belly."

"Oh, the man I rode with kept his arm tucked uncomfortably close to my breasts. There was no need for him to keep his arm that high. I got so mad I wanted to slap him!"

"Then find your own knife. If he tries to grope you or anything, stab him with it."

"Oh, Lord. I wouldn't dare. He's too intimidating."

"Well, these men don't scare me," Jane boldly lied, resuming her search for a knife.

"This place is a mess," Irina observed, awkwardly pushing around cans and foodstuffs on the counter. "And can you smell that? Something has spoiled."

"That's it!"

"What!" Irina cried on a gasp, spinning toward her.

"Women. There aren't any women here. That's what's missing."

Irina snorted and went back to searching. "That explains all the men shoving each other out of the way trying to be the one to help me off the horse," she muttered, only to suddenly smile. "Here are some knives. Quickly, take this one and hide it."

Jane limped over, thankful her brace was holding up better than the rest of her was, and took the knife. She lifted her pant leg and tucked the small weapon inside her brace, then quickly smoothed down the material again. "I saw solar panels on some of the cabins, including this one," Jane said, looking around the cluttered room. "I'm hoping they're for charging cell phones."

"There can't possibly be cell phone towers this far out." Irina straightened from hiding her own knife in her knee-high sock and also looked around. "Maybe they have a satellite phone or a ham radio."

"Did you recognize what language they—" Jane stilled at the sound of voices growing louder just outside, and both women rushed back to the bed and sat down again.

The door burst open and men began spilling inside. Or rather, they tried to bulldoze over one another to gain entrance. Within seconds the small cabin was full of smelly, hairy, staring men. Carrying a large, plier-like tool, Conan elbowed his way through the men pointing and snickering like children and strode directly up to the bed. Jane and Irina tried scooting back, but Conan grabbed Jane's knee to stop her retreat, then tugged her hands forward and indicated with gestures that she hold them out.

Getting the drift of things, Jane held out her hands as the blue-eyed giant carefully pinched the handcuffs with what she realized was a bolt cutter, breaking them free from one wrist and then the other. She immediately began rubbing her bruised wrists as Irina held up her own hands and received the same freedom.

Both women smiled and nodded their thanks.

Conan did not smile back.

Instead he grabbed Jane's chin and lifted her face to expose her bruised neck where the pit bull had grabbed her two days ago. She managed not to flinch, but couldn't stifle a wince when Conan ran his thumb over the bruise and then took her hands and examined her wrists. And then Irina's. And then he turned to say something to the older man beside him, who was also examining Irina's wrists.

Jane decided to call that one Grizzly Adams because of all the fur he wore. His knee-high boots were made of leather and his coat had a fur-lined hood, but the man had a beard of graying whiskers that would shame Rip Van Winkle. He was older than Conan and not quite as big, and his eyes were so dark they looked nearly black.

At least Irina's rescuer could smile—at Irina, anyway. And he said something and patted her knee. Irina glared at him and jerked her knee away.

The entire cabin broke into laughter.

Conan and Grizzly turned and walked away from the women, and Conan began stirring some foul-smelling concoction simmering in a huge cast-iron pot. Grizzly went to a cupboard and took out some bread and plates and utensils, and Jane and Irina held their breaths, hoping the knives wouldn't be missed.

Four men, Conan and Grizzly Adams included, sat down at the equally messy table and started eating. The remaining men stayed standing, crammed into the cabin like sardines, and simply continued to look at the attraction on the bed. Irina and Jane frowned at each other. The food may have smelled peculiar, but it was still food, and they were starved.

They were also being ignored again, the stares notwithstanding.

Conan suddenly turned on his stool and beckoned them.

Jane decided she had more sense than pride, regardless of how rude their hosts were acting, and instantly got up and made for the table. But she'd only taken four steps when Conan stood up, frowning as he stared down at her feet. Jane stopped walking.

He grabbed her left shoulder just as she stepped back, his fingers closing over her long-suffering wound. Jane shrieked and slapped his hand away. The man swept her up into his arms and dropped her back on the bed, but gently this time.

More laughing ensued.

Jane panicked when the giant reached for her right foot and drew it toward him, his other hand going to the lace on her shoe. She clawed at him, all the time tugging her foot back. "You leave me alone, you overgrown barbarian," she hissed, drawing an arm back to punch him when he wouldn't stop, only to halt in mid-swing at his piercing blue glare of warning. He quickly removed her shoe despite Jane's final attempt to pull free, then turned her foot back and forth to study the brace she wore. He pushed up her pant leg to see more of the brace, and Jane gasped again and tried to slap her pants back down, afraid he'd discover her knife.

When all that got her was another icy glare, she planted both feet on his chest and shoved with all her might, making Conan stumble back and land on the floor hard enough to shake the cabin. Wasting no time savoring her victory, and ignoring the raucous guffaws and whistles, Jane scrambled to the other side of the bed and pulled the knife out of her brace, then held it up threateningly.

Grizzly stopped Irina from following by wrapping his arm around her waist and lifting her off the floor, then letting her dangle forgotten as he watched the show.

His thighs stretching his tight buckskin pants and his muscles flexing beneath his shirt, Conan stood up and planted his hands on his hips. Jane saw the corner of his mouth twitch—only she didn't know if the man was holding in a growl or a smile—as he slowly pulled his own knife from a sheath on his belt. The thing looked like a machete next to her puny kitchen knife, and if she could have worked up some spit, she would have swallowed. As it was, all she could do was stare back with the realization she was in big, sharp, outsized trouble. He spoke to her in his guttural language, then beckoned for her to give up her knife. His voice had turned as deep as his chest was wide, and his eyes had softened to an almost lazy patience.

Jane darted a frantic look at Irina, and her friend closed her eyes in defeat and nodded. Jane let out a shuddering breath and closed her own eyes and tossed the knife on the blanket. She didn't hear the man coming, but was once again lifted up and set back down on the bed. This time she didn't protest, but simply closed her eyes again against her welling tears as he unsnapped the fasteners on her brace and pulled it off. Then he pulled off her sock.

Hating the man staring at her deformed ankle, Jane remained silent. And she didn't even flinch when she suddenly felt his hands leave her foot and go to the buttons on her blouse. He undid three of them and pulled her blouse to the side, exposing her left shoulder, then leaned her forward and examined her back. Jane opened her eyes in time to see his own eyes widen at the sight of her puckered scar, obviously knowing he was looking at a bullet wound, judging from his disbelief. He silently—and gently—pulled her blouse back into place, and Jane kept her gaze on his large, surprisingly deft hands while he buttoned it back up. And then she heard him sigh, which was quite audible in the now-silent cabin. And then he spoke.

Jane looked up to find him pointing at her while saying something to all the men as he gestured at her shoulder, then her foot, and finally in the direction of her belly—clearly listing all her flaws.

The prize they'd captured, apparently, wasn't turning out to be much of a prize.

"You think I'm full of flaws," she hissed. "But I'll have you know I'm the queen of Shelkova," she said, gaining back some of her spirit. She'd be darned if she was going to let this barbarian look at her with pity. She held up her left hand. "I'm married to Markov Lakeland," she said, jutting her wedding ring in his face. "And he loves me, flaws and all. And he's going to come get us, and then you and your other barbarian buddies are going to be in big trouble for stealing us."

His mouth twitched again.

Jane poked him in the chest.

He grabbed her hand, his face back to being hard, and held it up to study the ring while fingering the emerald trees.

Jane jerked free. "You try to steal it and I'll skin you alive with your own knife."

He finally broke into a wide grin, followed by a belly-rumbling laugh as he picked her up and strode to the table, where he deposited her on a stool with little ceremony.

Jane nodded regally, quite pleased with herself for putting the oaf in his place.

Neither she nor Irina knew what they'd eaten for lunch, and neither one of them dared to guess. But as soon as it was over, Conan and Grizzly shooed all the men out of the cabin and then told Jane and Irina to rest, using their hands to get the meaning across. The women gratefully complied, but not until after Grizzly had pulled Irina into his arms and given her a big bear of a hug. The poor woman had been so taken off guard that she barely got out a gasp before it was over. Irina had looked so outraged and Grizzly had looked . . . smitten.

Now they were lying on the bed, warm and full and comfortable for the first time in two days. They still didn't know where in heck they were or who in heck had them, but they were safe—at least for the moment. "Do you recognize the language?" Jane asked Irina as they both rested but couldn't sleep.

"No. But even in this day and age, there are still many tribes of nomads that use the northern lands of Shelkova. They travel by the seasons all the way from easternmost Russia, through here, and even into your Alaska."

"You think these men are one of those tribes?"

Irina shrugged against her pillow. "It's likely."

"How are we going to get home? Mark is never going to find us now."

Irina looked at her. "When you told your Conan," she said, giggling at the name, "that you were married to Markov Lakeland, the man holding me suddenly stiffened. I'm sure he recognized the name, even if he didn't know what you were saying."

"You think so? Conan didn't even flicker a lash."

"If they know who we are, they will have to return us. They're free to travel the borders by the mere fact they bother no one. If they were to keep us and then be discovered, it could prove disastrous for them. They have to know that."

"I hope so. I can't sleep. I know I should be dead tired, but I can't sleep."

"Me, neither." Irina lifted her head and glanced around the cabin. "Maybe we can gain some grace with them if we tidy up a bit in here. It would take our minds off our worries."

"Sounds like a plan to me. By actually cleaning the place, we can disguise the fact that we rifled through their belongings looking for a phone or radio. And maybe we can cook supper. Do you have any idea what we ate?"

Irina visibly shuddered. "Some kind of stew, but I'll not speculate on what kind of meat."

"It wasn't so bad," Jane offered, getting up from the bed and going to the table. She looked down at the mess and shook her head. "These men are starving for women," she observed aloud.

"I have no sympathy for the lechers," Irina said, going to the counter. "I swear if that man hugs me again I'm going to kick him. And did you see the way all the men have been looking at us? Several of them touched my hair, and one actually smelled it."

"They're just lonely. I wonder what happened to their women. If they're a tribe, they should have women. And there are no children."

"I'd say the smart ladies packed up and left, taking their children with them."

"They must have been watching the building where Señor Guavas brought us and decided it was a chance to get some women," Jane finished in a whisper. "Um, do you think they intend to . . . to . . . ?"

Irina stilled and gave Jane a worried look. And then she shuddered again. They finished cleaning in silence after that, until they were finally tired enough to lie back down and go to sleep.

There was another skirmish that night, and again Jane and Irina lost the battle. Grizzly Adams forcibly carried Irina out of the cabin as soon as they were done eating the meal of still-unidentified meat the women had made. Irina had pulled out her knife in desperation, only to be quickly disarmed by her laughing captor. Jane had screeched and clawed and fought like a she-devil for them not to be separated, but strength had prevailed.

And now she was alone with Conan.

And there was only one bed.

Darn.

But she was flawed. Conan had looked her over like a horse at auction and found her wanting, so maybe he was simply stuck babysitting her tonight while Grizzly tried to have his lonely, wicked way with Irina.

Poor Irina. Her eyes had been riddled with fear when she'd looked at Jane from the shoulder of her own personal demon. Jane had fought her own barbarian for ten minutes trying to go after her, but Conan had simply let her tire herself out. Now she was sitting at the once-again messy table, and she'd be darned if she was going to clean it again.

She jumped when silent feet suddenly appeared before her, and she looked up to see Conan holding a hairbrush out to her. Jane touched her hair, only to inwardly wince at the mess she felt. Guessing she looked like a barbarian herself, she reached for the brush.

He pulled it back, making her look up at him. "Lakeland," he said, pointing to her. "Gunnar," he said, pointing to himself.

Gunnar? This guy's name was *Gunnar*? That sounded much too civilized for the giant Neanderthal. "Jane Lakeland," she said, pointing to herself.

"Jane Lakeland," he repeated. "Shelkova."

"Yes."

"Gunnar Wolf."

Well, that fit. The man looked like a wolf, what with his long mane of black hair, piercing arctic eyes, and fur vest. He must have seen the gleam in her eye, for he tucked the brush in his belt and walked to a cupboard, pulled out a pencil and scrap of paper, came back to the table and wrote something, then handed the paper to Jane.

The print was boldly written and neat to near exactness. Which surprised her, as she hadn't thought these uncouth men would even own pencil and paper, much less know how to use them. Gunnar Wolfe. With an *E*.

"Gunnar Wolfe," she repeated, waving the paper at him. "With the *E* or not, you're still a barbarian," she said with a smile, confident he didn't know what she was calling him.

"Jane Lakeland," he repeated, smiling back and shoving the pencil at her.

He wanted her to write her name. Jane complied, holding it up for him to see once she'd finished. But not until she'd printed the word *barbarian* beside his name. He frowned at the paper, then raised his brow and looked at her, the corner of his mouth twitching ever so slightly.

Just for a second, she worried he knew what she had written, but then relaxed. If he couldn't understand English, he sure as heck couldn't read it.

He took her left hand and fingered her wedding band. "Markov Lakeland," he said, looking from the band to her. Jane nodded. He then leaned down and touched her belly. "Markov Lakeland?" he repeated, this time in question.

Disconcerted, Jane nodded and pushed his hand away. "Yes. Markov Lakeland's baby. And he's going to come get me and his baby, and you, Gunnar Wolfe, had better be ready to grovel."

She sighed when his mouth twitched again, then took the brush he handed her. The man hadn't seemed the least bit intimidated by the threat of her husband—likely because he didn't understand a word she had said. While she painfully worked at getting the knots out of her hair, she tried to ignore the fact that her . . . babysitter began stripping off his clothes, slowly revealing his true size and strength.

And as each item came off, his size didn't diminish one bit.

As comfortable as a nun in a convent, Gunnar Wolfe stripped until only his buckskin pants remained, exposing a torso of solid, rippling muscle that made Jane's mouth go dry.

The man was huge. His sun-darkened skin was smooth and taut, his chest covered with a full pelt of hair that tapered down to his . . . his . . . She tried to swallow, only to get her tongue caught on the roof of her mouth. Holy smokes. Jane realized she'd stopped brushing her hair and shook herself out of her stupor, turning crimson with the realization she was a married woman and had no business ogling a . . . a . . .

She frantically looked around the cabin, hoping to discover that another bed had popped up when she hadn't been looking. Nothing. Only some old furs thrown in the corner.

Well, by heaven, she'd sleep on the furs. She'd pull them near the woodstove and sleep there. Or maybe outside. Yeah, she was suddenly hot enough that outside sounded mighty appealing right now.

"Jane Lakeland," the barbarian said from the bed, his hand beckoning.

She stood up and went to the furs. "I'll sleep on these," she said, dragging the furs over to the stove. "You take the bed. It is yours, after all. I'll be fine on these furs."

Living up to his barbaric name, the man simply shrugged and closed his eyes. Jane plopped down on the lumpy pallet she'd made with a sigh of relief, closed her own eyes, and finally fell asleep praying that the Lakeland name would also protect Irina tonight.

Chapter Twenty-three

✦⋯✦

J ane woke to the sound of Irina coming into the cabin on the run. She slammed the door shut and all but threw herself at Jane, who had bolted upright to discover she was lying on the bed—thankfully alone.

"Jane. Jane, are you okay?" Irina cried, leaning away to run her worried eyes over her.

"I'm fine," Jane said, hugging her back. "And you, Irina. How are you?" she whispered, pulling away to look directly at her. "Did he hurt you last night?"

Irina flushed a deep red and lowered her gaze. "No. He . . . he didn't hurt me."

"Thank heavens," Jane said on a sigh, hugging her again. "I was so afraid for you."

"Me? But I would have been fine, no matter what."

Irina scowled. "It is you I worried about all night. You and your . . . your Conan!"

"His name is Gunnar."

"He told you his name? My Grizzly Bear is Anatol," Irina said, flushing again.

"Anatol? And it's Grizzly Adams, not Grizzly Bear."

Irina shrugged. "Either way, at least he was enough of a gentleman to sleep on the floor and give me the bed," she said, picking something off Jane's blankets. "Nor did he . . . touch me."

Jane laughed softly. "A civilized barbarian."

"He even gave me one of his shirts to change into," Irina continued, looking embarrassed and confused. "You . . . you were not touched?"

"Nope." Jane snorted. "But unlike Anatol, Gunnar is no gentleman and made me sleep on the floor," she told her, conveniently forgetting that she'd refused the bed when he'd offered. Or that he must have picked her up and put her on the bed before he'd left this morning.

Probably because he didn't want Irina to know he was a jerk.

"It's the Lakeland name," Irina said. "That's why they haven't bothered us . . . that way. All evening Anatol kept calling me Irina Lakeland. I didn't dispute him. I think the name somehow intimidated him."

"You mean inhibited him," Jane drawled, relieved her friend was okay.

"That, too," Irina added. "But why separate us if they didn't intend to do anything?"

"I believe your Grizzly—I mean your Anatol—likes you and wanted to get you alone."

"Well," Irina breathed on a sigh, "I am glad it's over."

"Until tonight," Jane reminded her.

"We've got to get away from here. Wait; you must have snowmobiles in Maine and know how to drive them. Maybe you could nonchalantly wander over to one of the snowmobiles as I wander toward the woods, and you could steal the machine and pick me up, and we could drive off before anyone realized what we were doing. It would be even better if you could do something to disable the other snowmobile first so they couldn't follow us."

"And drive off in which direction? We don't even know where we are. And personally, I prefer a bed of furs to sleeping in a snowbank."

"Then what are we to do?" Irina whispered. "We can't just take up housekeeping here."

"We wait," Jane said. "I bet within an hour of finding out who we were last night, Anatol and Gunnar sent someone to contact Mark. Depending on how far the guy had to go to find a phone, I'm sure it's just a matter of time before Mark comes to get us." Because they sure as heck hadn't found a phone or radio when they'd cleaned yesterday—unless they'd been in the large, *locked* trunk at the foot of the bed.

Irina pushed her slightly graying hair off her face with a sigh. "I hope he comes soon."

"Afraid to start liking your Grizzly Bear?"

Irina blushed again. "He is rather strong for a man of his age."

"Oh—ho. You *do* think he's cute."

"Cute?" Irina choked. "How would I know with all that hair on his face!"

"Ask him to shave."

Irina gaped at her, then suddenly smiled. "You think he would, if I asked?"

Jane nodded, suppressing a smile of her own at the mischievous gleam in Irina's eye.

"Maybe I will then, just to goad the man." Irina nodded. "Yes, I'll let him know he'd gain my favor if he shaved. How long do you suppose he's been growing that mane? I think I'll get him to cut his hair while I'm at it."

"Irina Spanes, shame on you! We're going to be gone from here in a matter of days, and that poor man will have to live nearly naked for years before he can grow that beard again." Jane cocked her head at the smiling woman. "I've never seen this side of you."

Irina looked repentant—but only a little. "I was not always the paragon of virtue I am today," she confessed. "At one time I was considered a little wild."

"I bet that was when you were married to George."

Irina merely smiled again.

"Then it's men. They bring out the imp in you. I say go for it. Make a fool of the man."

Irina sobered. "But what if he makes a fool of me?"

"How could he do that?"

"I could come to . . . like Anatol," Irina softly explained, looking away. "I already find him attractive, and that hasn't happened to me in eighteen years. Since I met George, no man has ever captured my eye."

"Until now?" Jane asked, touching her arm.

Irina looked at her with sadness. "Isn't it foolish? We are kidnapped and dragged to the end of the Earth, and I am smitten by a grizzly bear. And at my age."

They fell silent after that little disclosure and began their morning chores. But no sooner had they gotten the dishes done when Jane took a sniff of herself and wrinkled her nose. "I stink," she announced.

Irina laughed as she turned from making the bed. "So do I."

"Shouldn't you be making Anatol's bed?" Jane asked.

"I already did," the woman said on a cough, turning away and busily fluffing the pillows.

Jane stared at her back. "I bet you cleaned his cabin, too, didn't you?"

"Maybe," Irina muttered, *beating* the pillows.

"If you're not careful, you won't want to be rescued."

"I had to find something to do this morning."

"How long have you been up?"

"Three hours."

"Then why didn't you come wake me?"

"Anatol said I couldn't."

Jane eyed her again. "And just how did he do that? He doesn't speak Shelkovan."

Irina finally looked at her. "He told me with a good glare just before he left the cabin. Your Conan isn't the only one who can intimidate with just a look."

"He's not my Conan."

"He is until we leave here. And judging by the looks we've been getting from all the other men, you'd better stick to your barbarian's side. I don't think the others are quite as . . . civilized."

Jane went to lift a bucket of water to put on to heat.

"Don't lift that," Irina scolded, coming over and grabbing the bucket. "You're pregnant."

"That doesn't make me helpless."

"You have to be careful, though. You're carrying a prince."

"Well, I'm not going to treat him like a prince and spoil him rotten."

Irina laughed as she nudged Jane out of the way and poured the water into a pan on the stove. Heavens, the woman was becoming a domestic wonder. Jane gave up and decided to look for something to wear while she washed out her clothes. She eyed the trunk at the foot of the bed for several seconds, but didn't think she'd be able to pick the lock. So she kept looking until she found a nook on the back wall that had some clothes hanging on pegs. She gave them a sniff and decided they smelled better than she did, and threw them on the bed. "I'm taking a bath, then I'm washing my clothes. If you stand lookout for me, I'll do the same for you."

"Deal," Irina agreed.

Jane guessed she was a comical sight an hour later, dressed in baggy pants she'd had to roll up several times and a shirt she'd had to wrap around herself twice and tie with a piece of twine she'd found. She was standing sentry outside the cabin while Irina took a sponge bath and washed her own clothes, having found some other things for her to wear while they dried.

Jane had come outside to a surprisingly warm day, and hung her wet clothes over a rope running from the cabin to a tree, making her realize somebody did laundry around here . . . sometimes. Now she was guarding the door and glaring at all the men who had gathered and were rudely staring back at her.

Realizing they'd probably started congregating during Irina's shift as sentry, Jane was about to start throwing rocks at them if they didn't stop edging closer. Several dogs had already gotten brave enough to sniff her legs, but she'd shooed them away so the men wouldn't think they could do the same.

Conan and Grizzly were nowhere in sight.

And so went the day. And the next day. Irina and Jane were left pretty much alone while the sun was up, the staring men the only exception. And by night, Irina was hauled off to Anatol's cabin and Jane slept on the pile of furs next to Gunnar's stove.

Although by the third night, Irina had stopped protesting the separation.

And after having lived as Mark's wife for only three months, Jane could see where Irina probably missed the company of a man who was smitten with her. Especially after having had the privilege for twelve years and then not having it for the last six. No, Jane was in fact silently hoping Irina found happiness with Anatol, even if only for a little while.

It was on their fourth afternoon here, as both women were outdoors enjoying the warm sun, that they heard the helicopter. They blinked at each other to make sure they weren't hallucinating, then gave an excited whoop and started running to the open land down by the river where the men were already gathering. Gunnar caught up with Jane and pulled her to an abrupt stop just as

Anatol did the same to Irina. Jane tried to kick free, but Gunnar gave a deep growl and lifted her off her feet, all the time giving her a good scolding in his native tongue.

Both men carried them away from the river, and Jane and Irina began protesting in earnest at the sound of the chopper getting closer. Gunnar suddenly set Jane down in the middle of the village, manacled her wrist in his beefy paw, then glared at her hard enough to solidify antifreeze.

Jane stopped struggling. Not because of his threat, but because she heard the helicopter landing. Gunnar pushed her to his side and planted his feet, put both of his hands on his hips while retaining a firm grip on her wrist, and stoically waited for his guests. Jane leaned back enough to look behind him and see Anatol holding Irina the same way beside them.

As soon as she spotted Mark striding up the hill, his piercing golden eyes locked on her face, Jane cried out and tried to run to him—only to be rudely, abruptly stopped and pulled back to Gunnar's side. With the patience of a child in need of the bathroom, she stood glaring up at the barbarian; not that Gunnar noticed, since he was looking at Mark. Jane could see that every muscle in her captor's body was tensed and ready to move.

She turned back to watch the three men approaching, forcing herself to remember to breathe as she soaked in the sight of Mark. Despite his aggressive stride, he looked tired, gaunt, and as tense as Gunnar as he stopped ten feet away, with Sergei and Dmitri—looking just as haggard and equally ready for battle—halting slightly behind him.

Mark slid his gaze from Gunnar to her, his eyes suddenly softening. "Hello, wife," he whispered, his voice easily carrying through the starkly quiet air.

"Hello."

"Are you okay?"

"I am now."

"Are you ready to come home?"

She nodded, too choked up to answer.

Mark moved his once-again piercing eyes to her captor. "I've come to take my wife home, Gunnar."

Gunnar relaxed but for the hand holding hers. "Are you sure you want her, Markov?"

Jane nearly fell over from her gasp. Gunnar Wolfe had asked that question in perfect, barely accented *English*. She swung her free arm and hit him square on the chest, at the same time moving to face him. "You jerk! You speak English!"

He nodded without even looking down and raised a brow at Mark, totally dismissing her. "Are you sure you want her back?" he repeated, negligently rubbing his chest where she'd smacked him. "She's got a bit of a temper."

Jane spun to Mark, nearly falling when Gunnar wouldn't let go of her wrist. "Did you bring my shotgun?" she asked softly so she wouldn't scream.

Mark shook his head, a slight grin tugging the corner of his mouth.

"My handgun?"

He shook his head again.

Jane eyed the helicopter. "Any machine guns in the chopper?"

Mark crossed his arms over his chest, his amusement

finally reaching his eyes. "And just what do you want a gun for, angel?"

She ignored Gunnar's snort. "To shoot me a barbarian." She turned to Gunnar again. "Right between the eyes. Just see if I don't, you jerk!" she finished, tugging on her arm.

The jerk merely pushed her to his side and looked back at Mark. "It's good to see you again, my friend. Ruling a nation agrees with you?"

That grin blossomed, washing more haggard lines from Mark's face as he nodded. "Once I get my household back in order." He just as quickly sobered. "May I ask how you got your hands on my wife?"

"I stole her from the men who stole her from you," Gunnar offered in explanation. "Anatol seems to have lost his women, and when we saw these two, we decided to steal them."

"Like a thief in the night!" Jane interjected, not about to let go of her anger and wanting Mark to be angry, too. Heaven help her, they were conversing like old friends.

"What happened to Anatol's women?" Mark asked.

Gunnar shrugged. "While the men were gone to their hunting grounds two years ago, another tribe raided the village and took the women and children. Anatol eventually tracked them down, but by then the women had already integrated into their new tribe." Gunnar glanced toward the silent Anatol, then back at Mark. "So they only brought their older sons home."

Jane snorted and leaned back to arch a brow at a smirking Irina upon hearing they'd been right about the women leaving their men. And who could blame them?

"So they've decided to steal replacements?" Mark asked, obviously fighting a grin.

Gunnar shrugged again. "They took a vote."

"But you do intend to return my wife."

"Only if you're sure you want her. Is she that important to you?"

M ark nearly dropped to his knees when he saw the shadow of worry suddenly cloud Jane's eyes, unable to believe his brave, pregnant little wife still doubted her value. He slid his gaze back to Gunnar. "She's more important to me than the air I breathe, and I would give up my kingdom for her. And if you don't soon let her go, I'm going to break your arm," he softly added, the lethal edge in his voice more for Jane's benefit than for Gunnar's.

Gunnar simply opened his fingers and released her. She bolted for him and Mark caught her with a groan, lifting her off her feet and burying his face in her hair as he took his first full breath in six days. He looked at Gunnar and nodded, his eyes saying *thank you* the only way a man at the end of his rope could.

Gunnar merely nodded back.

"Well, I'm not letting this one go!" Anatol boomed into the reunion. "She's got no man, so I'm keeping her."

Irina gasped.

Mark grinned. Gunnar's surrogate uncle looked damn serious. And Irina looked damned stunned. Mark was equally stunned; only not at Anatol's announcement, but that Aunt Irina wasn't struggling or rushing to dispute his claim.

"You can't keep her, old man," Sergei shouted from behind Mark. "She belongs to us."

"She's only your aunt."

"No matter. You can't just keep her."

"I can," he growled back, tightening his grip on his prize.

Mark continued looking for signs of protest from Irina. Even Jane had lifted her head, but surprisingly wasn't rushing to Irina's defense. Mark would love to have been a bird perched in a village tree these past few days. "Irina?" he asked softly, pressing Jane's head back to his chest. He didn't want his aunt influenced right now, which she would be if he didn't curb his wife. But instead of fighting him, Jane appeared to be holding her breath.

"Irina?" Mark repeated.

"I . . . I don't know," she whispered, her eyes darting to a clean-shaven, obviously newly barbered Anatol. Mark always remembered the man as having a bushy beard and hair down past his shoulders, which in itself told him Anatol was serious.

"Do you think you would know in the morning?" Mark offered, looking at Gunnar and receiving his nod of agreement.

"May—maybe."

"Then we will stay until morning."

Jane tilted her head up. "Mark, you got anything . . . sweet to eat?"

Her request dispelling the last knot of worry strangling his heart, Mark reached in his jacket pocket and pulled out a bag of M&M's. With a small squeal of delight and the greed of a starving woman, she grabbed the candy and ripped it open, suddenly oblivious to the village, the men, and Irina's plight.

Mark led his ecstatically munching and groaning wife away from the crowd and into the woods, accepting the pelt of fur Gunnar handed to him along with a nod toward the path running along a ridge following the river. Mark walked in that direction while simply savoring the feel of Jane against his side, until he found a ledge overlooking the river that the sun had melted clean. He tossed down the fur and urged Jane down on it, then knelt facing her. He palmed her cheeks, using his thumbs to wipe away her persistent tears as she looked into his eyes with such hunger that Mark was humbled.

"I love you," he said just before he kissed them. He slowly pulled back. "God, how I've missed you, angel."

"Oh, Mark. I was so afraid I'd never see you again and that you'd have to go on without me," she said, kissing his jaw and chin and mouth and leaving a tasty trail of chocolate from her lips. "I love you, too."

"So you believe, then."

"Believe what?" she mumbled, trying to unbutton his shirt.

He had to capture her hands and then lift her chin to look at him. "That you're the most important person in the world to me. Thank you."

She looked momentarily startled, then smiled. "You're welcome," she said succinctly, going back to work on his buttons.

Mark chuckled as he tried to think of a way to slow her down. Not that he intended to leave this rock without loving her thoroughly. But he wanted—needed—to savor this. "Have you been taking good care of my son?" he asked thickly just as her hands slipped inside his now-open shirt.

"Yes. Our daughter's fine, Mark. Now shut up," she muttered as her lips followed her fingers down the front of his chest toward his belt buckle—apparently on a mission as desperate as his own.

So with a groan of resignation, Mark resigned himself to his wife's impatient attack.

And damn if he didn't help.

G ood heavens, the stars are bright from here," his wife marveled aloud half an hour later as she cuddled up to him, both of them naked but for the fur blanket.

"Yes. We're past the Arctic Circle."

"That's why the days seemed so much shorter."

"You've gotten a view of our country this last week, haven't you?" Mark said, also staring up at the stars as he patiently waited for her to ask.

"Yes."

And still he waited as several minutes of worried silence passed.

"O-okay. I'm ready now. Tell me about Petri," she finally said, turning into him and burying her face in his neck.

Mark knew this would be the hardest thing for her to hear, even though it was also the best news he had to give her. "Petri's body armor stopped what would have been a mortal wound, but he also took a bullet to his leg and one in the arm. He's going to be fine, Jane, and is right now recuperating under the care of Dr. Daveed." Mark tilted her head back to look at him. "But two men died that day, Jane—one of the other bodyguards and one of your assailants.

"Oh, God," she cried, letting her tears flow again. "That poor man. His poor family."

"He had no wife and children, not that it makes his death any less tragic. All of Shelkova was his family, and we've already given him a hero's burial. Cry for him, sweetheart, but also honor him by knowing he was doing something he believed in, which was protecting his country's freedom by protecting his queen. Fredrick chose to protect you so you could help lead his homeland into the twenty-first century. Allow him the privilege to die for what he believed in."

"But it's hard. I . . . I understand, but it's hard."

"Shh. I know, baby. It's hard for me, too. But nowhere near as hard, had I lost you. I love you, Jane. And I will continue to protect you as best I can."

"Petri really will be okay?"

"He'll be home being pampered by his wife and distracted by his children in about two weeks. He won't be able to work for a few months, but he will heal." Mark wiped an escaping tear and gave her a crooked smile. "He's had to be sedated all week, as he kept threatening to go out and hunt you down himself."

"Thank God," she breathed in relief, closing her eyes and snuggling against him. "It was the man from the coronation ball, Señor Guavas," she said sleepily. "He stole Irina and me."

"I know. Gunnar told us where to find Guavas, and the

bastard is now in custody. Most of the consortium had given up hope, but Guavas persisted and will rot in prison for his crimes."

Jane's head snapped up with a frown. "When did Gunnar contact you?"

"The morning he took you from Guavas."

"Then why didn't you come get us that morning?" she asked, sounding disgruntled. "You left us in the hands of that barbarian for *three days*."

Mark caught her hand just before it could pinch his stomach. "Gunnar may have told us where to find Guavas, but he neglected to tell us where to find you. His last words to me were, 'Come find me, my friend, and claim your prize.' It took us that long to locate the village."

She straightened higher. "Why would he do that?"

"As payback," Mark drawled, "for having him thrown in jail a couple of years ago."

"The despicable jerk probably deserved it. I really am going to shoot him, you know. He . . . he . . . All the time he understood English and knew what I was saying!"

"And what were you saying, witch?" Mark asked with a laugh, catching her hand again and this time holding on to it. "Been calling the man names?"

"You would do worse than call him names if he made *you* sleep on the floor. While you're five months pregnant, I might add."

"Did he touch you? Jane," Mark said on a sigh when she didn't answer. "I'm not going to shoot the man. He did rescue you from Guavas. I just want to know if I'm going to have to break any of his bones."

She finally looked up, wondering if maybe she'd just

found a way to pay back Gunnar for tricking her. "Is . . . is he a really good friend?"

"He may have been. What did he do?"

She shrugged. "He's been without a woman for over two years, Mark."

"Well, that says it all," he snapped, sitting up. "Get dressed."

"Why?"

"I have to go get the machine gun from the helicopter."

Okay, maybe that hadn't been such a good idea. "No, he didn't . . . We didn't . . . Mark!" she said on a laugh, catching hold of his arm before he could rise. "I'm just miffed that Anatol gave up his bed to Irina, but Gunnar made me sleep on a pile of furs by the stove. Other than that, he was a perfect gentleman."

"Now you are defending him?" he asked, incredulous.

"Hell, no. Dammit, Mark, leave it alone!"

He stopped dressing at the realization Jane was cursing for real. Which meant she was either worried for Gunnar or for *him*. "Do you think me a weakling?" he snapped. "Gunnar Wolfe may be slightly heavier, but I've taken him before and can take him again—even if only to teach the bastard how to treat a pregnant woman."

"Oh, put a sock in it, Ace. You can't go beating up the man who saved your wife and aunt." She came up to her knees and laid a hand on his arm, the emeralds of her wedding band twinkling in the moonlight. "And I'm not worried about you in a fight. You're my hero, Mark."

Well, damn. He threw down his shirt, slid inside the fur, and pulled Jane against him with a sigh. "You, angel, are dangerous," he muttered just before he kissed her again.

It was a full hour before they came up for air this time.

"Tell me how you met Gunnar," Jane whispered, her head resting in the crux of his shoulder as they once again watched the stars make the night sky seem alive.

"It's a long story," Mark warned.

"I'm not going anywhere."

"Well," he began, pulling up the fur until only their heads were exposed to the chilling night air. "I met Gunnar before the breakup of the USSR, when I was a fighter pilot on the *Katrina*. Only then the carrier was named the *Casmir*."

Chapter Twenty-four

❖┄❖

Jane's head popped up. "You really were a fighter pilot?"

Mark pressed her back to his shoulder. "Remember, the Lakelands were just another family at the time. Are you going to listen without interrupting?"

Mark grinned when he felt her frown against his shoulder. "We were at sea in the Pacific when news came to us the USSR was falling," he continued quietly. "Most of the crewmen, including the captain, were from the area now known as Shelkova. That was a blessing, it turned out. It was also the longest week of my life. Until this week," he growled, kissing the top of her head. "For three days the entire crew monitored the events in Moscow, all of us anxious about our future. But on the fourth day my father called the ship and asked to speak to me. He told me he intended to lead our people in a subtle revolt to gain our independence, certain that it was then or never."

"And he did," Jane whispered, only to snap her mouth shut when he gave her a squeeze.

"I wanted to go home and join him," Mark said, the memory making him smile. "But Reynard can be a crafty old fox when need be, and he told me to stay with the *Casmir* and be patient, that he would call back in a few days."

"Did he?"

"Yes. That was when he asked me to approach the captain, whom he knew personally, and have a little talk with him. You see, for all of our timberland, Shelkova also has thousands of miles of coastline, and Dad wanted the *Casmir* to help keep our new nation safe."

"Wow. And the captain just went along?"

"No," Mark said with a chuckle. "He put it to a vote."

"A vote?"

Mark sighed. "Yes, Jane, a vote. Did you listen to stories with this much enthusiasm when you lived at Saint Xavier's?"

"Oh, yes. Sister Patricia said I was always such an interested child."

"And a test of her patience," he muttered.

"Well, how did the vote go?"

"You rode on the *Katrina*, didn't you?"

"And then what happened?"

"Shelkovans being the greater number of crewmen was why my father wasn't worried. But there were still many others against it, especially after the good captain announced Reynard had just been named king." He snorted. "And that one of their shipmates was now a prince."

Mark paused, expecting her to pipe up again, but when only silence answered him, he grinned up at the stars and continued. "I had to be on my toes for a few days and was given a private room. Actually, I was given the captain's quarters," he whispered with remembered embarrassment. "I protested, but the captain feared for my safety, and so I finally agreed."

Mark waited again, expecting her to ask why he'd thought to agree. He sighed when she remained mute, and decided he'd be an old man before he figured her out.

"And so we sailed the *Casmir* to Shelkova and were met by a cheering, boisterous crowd of families and well-wishers. Reynard told any crewmen not from Shelkova that they could return to their homes if they wished, then promptly rechristened the carrier the *Katrina* and declared her the flagship of our navy. Within two days the *Previa* sailed into port, only then it was named *Red Dolphin*. Dad rechristened her after our new capital city."

Jane's head finally popped back up. "Did he know the captain of the *Previa*?"

"No."

"Then how did he get her?"

"The destroyer he'd . . . acquired helped."

Her eyes widened. "Just like that?"

"Just like that. The people didn't make Dad their king on a whim, Jane. Reynard wanted a navy, so he stole one before anyone realized what was happening." He waved a hand in the air. "Besides, Russia still had plenty of warships; what were a few missing boats?"

And to this day, Mark still marveled at how Reynard had managed to build a nation without one shot being fired. Oh, yes. His father was a wily old fox.

"Wow," was all his wife could say to that. She stretched her shapely legs down the length of his. "But that still doesn't explain how you met Gunnar," she said on a stifled yawn.

Mark frowned at her, but her eyes were closed. "We . . . ah, ran over him."

Her head suddenly popped up again. "What do you mean, you ran over him?"

"At sea. The *Katrina*, then the *Casmir*, ran over his boat." Mark scowled. "It was his fault for carrying full sails in a fog with no running lights. We didn't see him and he didn't answer our horn, so we . . . ran over him."

"Good heavens," she said, no longer looking sleepy. "What happened then?"

"We fished him out of the sea." Mark grinned. "Gunnar came out of the water swinging, and my face got in the way of his fist."

"I would have hit you, too, if you'd just run over me."

"I wasn't driving the ship. Besides, it was his fault. He had no business being that far out at sea so unprepared."

"Why was he, then?"

"He was running."

"From what?" Jane asked, looking confused. "A herd of dolphins?"

"They're called pods, angel. And no, I believe the threat to Gunnar was human. He's actually a mercenary by trade," Mark explained. "And from what I gathered, something . . . unpleasant had happened on his last mission and he was trying to get to Anatol's village. Anatol isn't really his uncle, as Gunnar is actually . . . well, last I knew he had four different passports claiming he was born in four different countries." He pressed Jane back down and kissed the top of her head with another chuckle. "Hell, I doubt Gunnar Wolfe is even his real name. But I do know that even if his degrees from Oxford *and* Harvard are fake, his intelligence certainly isn't. The guy is what you would call a modern Renaissance man; he's fluent in several languages, can hold his own in conversation on any number of subjects, and probably knows more about the art of war than most past or present-day generals."

Mark felt her stiffen. "I called him a barbarian," she whispered. "To his face."

"Which may be the real reason," Mark drawled, "he refused to tell me where you were when he called to tell me he had you." He gave her a squeeze when she started to protest. "Do you want to hear this story or not?"

"Did Gunnar ever tell you what he was running from?"

"No. And I didn't ask. Not after he saved my life."

"Saved your life?" she said, her gasp lifting her head again. "When?"

"Two days after we ran him over. I kept him in my quarters, as I didn't trust him."

"And he saved your life," she repeated, snuggling into his shoulder again. "I'll have to thank him, I guess. But how did he save you?"

"There was a small mutiny on board the *Casmir*, and about a dozen men tried to take me hostage in order to take control of the ship. And although still half-drowned and weakened by hunger, Gunnar fought like an ancient

Viking berserker." Mark sighed. "Which is possible, I suppose, since I'm pretty sure one of those passports is from Iceland."

"That explains those gorgeous ice-blue eyes," she said dreamily.

Mark gave her another squeeze. "*Gold* eyes are more appealing."

"If you say so," she said, patting his chest. "And so he saved your life and you've been friends ever since."

"No. We've been occasional enemies over the ensuing years. Gunnar is a highly specialized mercenary, which means his services don't come cheap."

"What are his services?" she asked without looking up.

"Terrorism."

"He's a *terrorist*?"

"No, he hunts them. And he's been known to use the vacant coast of Shelkova to lure them into a trap. That's when we were on opposing sides. I locked him up and threatened to throw away the key, friendship or not, if he continued this practice."

"Well, I would think so. We don't want terrorists lurking around our coast." Jane yawned and went back to staring up at the stars. "You know what Gunnar needs?"

All he knew was that whatever Jane thought Gunnar needed, it was going to cause trouble. Then again, maybe the rogue deserved some angel-inspired trouble.

"He needs a wife."

Mark groaned. It was worse than he thought. And Jane sounded rather confident of her diagnosis. And very enthusiastic. "Who do you hate enough to pair with Gunnar?"

"Oh, he's not that bad. Not really."

"You called him a barbarian. To his face," he reminded her.

"I think he's just lonely. It can't be much fun living in a village of all men."

"Don't worry, he only visits when he needs to recharge. He's still accepting jobs, last I heard. And I'm sure he . . . plies the sheets when he gets a chance. Besides, the man's rich enough to buy a harem," Mark muttered, throwing back the fur and rising, only to look down at his naked, wide-eyed wife.

"He is?" she squeaked, apparently too intrigued to be modest. "Oh, that's perfect."

"Perfect for what?" he asked as he tossed clothes at her.

"For Katy. Because if Gunnar has a little money stashed away, he can settle down and not take any more jobs."

Mark nearly fell as he tried to slip into his pants. "A little money? Jane, do you know what a country will pay to get rid of a terrorist group operating within its borders? Gunnar Wolfe is probably a multimillionaire. I told you, he's highly specialized, he works alone, and he delivers. And for that he costs the moon. And who is Katy?"

"You remember my mentioning Katy MacBain, my friend from Maine."

Mark stopped hopping into his pants again. "You said you had no female friends."

"Katy and I went to school together when I lived at Saint Xavier's," she explained as she sorted through her own clothes. "And we ended up together again in high school because the foster family I went to live with was in the same school district. Katy couldn't come to my wedding because her passport was expired, but she promised to come for the birth."

"What does any of that have to do with Gunnar and the conversation we were just having?" Mark stilled with his pants halfway up his thighs and gave her an incredulous look. "Please tell me you don't intend to fix your friend up with Gunnar."

"Well, why not? If Katy can't handle him, no woman can. She has lots of experience staying one step ahead of huge, contrary, old-fashioned men."

Mark closed his eyes. "This is crazy. You will not play matchmaker to a mercenary and some poor friend of yours."

"It was just a thought," Jane murmured, glaring down at her shirt as she tried to find a buttonhole. "And it fits perfectly with an idea I started thinking about while watching all the men in the village these last few days. They aimlessly walk around like lost children looking so dejected and lonely that I thought—"

Mark held up his hand. "Stop; I don't want to know what you're plotting. I don't even know how we got on the subject of Gunnar's love life," he whispered as he finally buckled his pants before his ass froze solid and fell off.

"You don't like that idea? Well how about this one, Your Majesty? I'm going to invite Anatol to bring his men to Previa. And if he says yes, I'm going to invite all the single women from jail and any who are living on the streets to a social at the palace, and see if they might be interested in starting a new life up here with these lonely men."

"Jane."

"After, that is, I teach the men some manners," she muttered, going down on her knees and searching for her socks and brace.

"Jane."

All he got for answer was a gasp. "Oh no, my brace rolled off the ledge and fell in the river!" she cried, crawling to the edge and peering down.

Mark made a dive for her and pulled her back. "Jane. You want to follow it into the water? Leave it. Dr. Daveed can make you a new one."

"Oh, Dr. Daveed. Does he know you found us and that we're okay?"

"He knows of Gunnar's call four days ago. But I'm sure Dad will tell him and Petri that you and Irina are safe, as Sergei would have called him by now."

"I haven't even asked about Reynard. How . . . how did he take what happened?"

Mark just shook his head. "He will be fine once he sees you. Now come on; I'll carry you back to the village."

"Are you sure you have enough strength left, Atlas?" she whispered, her eyes laughing as she threw herself at him. "You're not too . . . worn out?"

"I think I can manage," he growled, sweeping her up into his arms.

The journey back was silent, although whenever Mark looked down it was to see Jane smiling. But what really worried him was that instead of looking happy and sated and well-loved, that smile looked more crafty than angelic.

Oh, yeah; Anatol and his womenless tribe of nomads were in for a world of trouble, as it appeared his wife had just found another cause deserving of her queenly . . . importance.

You're sure, Irina?" Jane whispered to her friend the next morning.

"If Anatol wants me, he's going to have to come to Previa and court me properly."

"He'll come," Jane assured her.

"But maybe only because of your offer to find all of them women," Irina speculated sadly. "He didn't say anything about us this morning when I told him I was leaving with you."

"He's got a man's pride, Irina. Did you expect him to beg you to stay?"

"No," she admitted. "But I have my pride, too. I will not be stolen like some object and then ordered around like a witless child."

"Well, for what it's worth, I think you're doing the right thing," Jane said as she glanced at the scowling Anatol standing by his cabin. "He'll come get you. And he'll spend the time until then getting his priorities straight. And hopefully also straightening out his men's."

Irina snorted, apparently not holding any hope for that likelihood. And then she smiled again. "I can't believe the ruckus you caused at breakfast, telling Anatol that you knew a few women you thought would love to come live here. The men shook the trees with their cheers."

"I hope they understood the rest of what I said. No woman is going to live with them unless they clean themselves up and start acting like gentlemen."

"Anatol told me they're already planning to fix up the village and make it more permanent, hoping to impress the women with the pictures Gunnar is going to email to us," Irina confided in a whisper.

Because, apparently, Gunnar had a huge satellite dish hidden up on some ridge, which gave him Internet access when he was . . . recharging with his nomadic buddies between jobs.

"Do you really believe your little scheme will work?" Irina asked. "Because Jane, some of those women are . . . they're . . ."

"Only down on their luck," Jane finished for her. "Do you think that as little girls they decided they wanted to grow up to be prostitutes? They each have a story, and each story is sad. They're really good women and will make fine wives."

Irina sighed. "I know. I'm not judging them. But the men might."

"Oh, no they won't. They'll treat them like queens or answer to me."

"And you, little queen, will answer to me," Mark said from right behind her. "And your king says it's time to go home. I want to get out of here before these men realize you intend for them all to become henpecked husbands."

"They deserve it," she answered in a huff as she carefully made her way to the waiting chopper without her brace, holding Mark's arm and waving at all the staring men.

Gunnar lifted her into the helicopter, his eyes taking on a gleam just before he kissed her—quite loudly—right on the lips.

"Oh," she gasped, her cheeks feeling hot enough to poach eggs.

"I will come to Previa with Anatol," he told her, his eyes narrowing in suspicion, "and meet your friend Katy MacBain. Make sure she's there in three months."

Jane wanted to glare at his arrogance, but couldn't seem to narrow her own eyes enough to accomplish the feat, apparently still shocked by his kiss. He was still a barbarian—although she didn't doubt Katy could handle him. Heck, Katy could probably teach him a thing or two about women in general and first-generation Scottish highland lasses in particular.

Jane suddenly gasped when she noticed the bruise beginning to darken Gunnar's cheek and making the eye above it swell, now that she looked closely. And he winced slightly as he straightened. "What happened to you?" she asked, reaching up to touch his cheek.

He stepped back before she made contact, his mouth turning down instead of answering as he glanced past her at Mark.

Jane also looked at Mark, who was sitting beside her, and gasped again. "What happened to you?"

When his only answer was a rather possessive grin, Jane puffed up indignantly. "I am quite capable of exacting my own revenge, Markov Lakeland." She smiled at Gunnar, now standing up on the ridge overlooking the river. "Oh yeah, Katy is just what Gunnar needs."

Jane turned and looked into the fierce golden eyes of her husband, and her heart swelled with love just as she felt the strong, distinct flutter of their child move inside

her. She threw herself against his broad, solid chest and
wrapped her arms around him. "Take your queen and
princess home, Your Majesty," she said over the sound of
the chopper starting, just before she kissed him with all
the confidence of a woman he'd give up his kingdom for.

Epilogue

❖ ⋯ ❖

J ane decided she really didn't need this right now.

Her beautiful, regal home had turned into a mad-house. Anatol had brought his entire tribe to Previa; a total of twenty-three men ranging from seventeen to seventy years old, all bright-eyed and bushy-tailed and poking their noses inside every room they walked past on the off chance their future wife was hiding in one.

Much to Jane's surprise, nearly forty women had answered the ad she'd placed in the local paper, all of them seemingly just as eager to find husbands. She only hoped they were still eager after the . . . social she and Irina had planned for tonight. Because although the nomads had cleaned up remarkably well—Jane figured every bird living within five miles of their village had nests lined with more human hair than grass—it was obvious none of them had read any of the books on manners she'd sent them. Heck, she'd even included three illustrated books aimed at children, having learned from training her puppies that even small victories were signs of hope.

Anatol, the love-struck grizzly bear, was so busy courting Irina that he wasn't controlling his men. And Irina, the love-struck imp, was apparently too busy leading him in circles to notice the chaos. Such as when one of the men had boldly walked into the kitchen and taken an instant liking to Cook, and was now walking around with a bandaged hand. Rumor had it he'd tried to steal a kiss, but when all that had gotten him was a scorching lecture, he'd apparently picked up Cook and tried to carry her away. Jane guessed it had been a rather rugged man— who was either very dumb or very desperate.

Petri was back at work guarding her; which, considering she was two weeks from her due date, consisted of shooting warning glares at the invading army of nomads on the chance one of them might try to steal her again.

Gunnar was here as promised, but Katy MacBain was not. Having missed the wedding, Katy had promised to come for the birth, assuring Jane she'd have her passport renewed by then and conveniently be between jobs.

Only instead of arriving the week before, Katy had called to say she was sorry for having to renege on their deal, then quickly launched into what had sounded more like a prepared speech than an apology. She'd said that just like Jane had been smart enough to follow her heart straight into the arms of Markov Lakeland, she simply couldn't walk away from the amazing, once-in-a-lifetime opportunity she'd been given. Not that she'd fully explained what that opportunity was, only that it had popped up at the remote rescue school she'd attended in Colorado—which was supposed to have ended weeks before Jane's due date. And no, Katy had said, her breaking her promise didn't involve a man, but it definitely involved her little addiction to pushing her mental and physical limits. And as an added bonus, this particular adventure meant she'd still be out of cell phone reach and away from her overprotective father and brothers another two whole weeks.

Jane often wondered how such polar opposites—an orphan who craved a family and a girl with more family than she knew what to do with—had ever become such bosom buddies.

For the last week, however, she'd only wondered what secret her friend was hiding. Because the Katy MacBain she knew and loved was never vague about anything. Heck, she was often bluntly honest to a fault. But the longer Jane had listened to the lame apology and half answers, the more certain she'd become that instead of rushing headlong into a once-in-a-lifetime opportunity, Katy was in fact running from something.

The one-sided conversation had ended almost as abruptly as it had begun by Katy promising that she'd call the moment she got settled in her new job serving the good people of Spellbound Falls, Maine, as a full-time paramedic on the newly formed rescue squad, which she was supposed to start on June first.

So while her friend was smack in the middle of some sort of personal crisis, instead of being there for Katy, Jane was barely able to waddle around on her bum ankle from having gained too many pregnancy pounds. Nor was she able to do more than smile and nod at the man pacing in front of her, seeing how she was smack in the middle of a contraction.

Well, or else her baby had really bad hiccups.

Not that Gunnar knew she was in labor. In fact, nobody knew, since she'd only figured out what was going on half an hour ago. But instead of running—okay, waddling—to Mark in a flat-out panic, she was in the library, sitting by the fireless hearth, dealing with Gunnar Wolfe—with an *E*.

"Tell me exactly what she said," he demanded.

Jane guessed she'd piqued his interest more than she'd realized when she'd mentioned some of her and Katy's more memorable childhood antics in her emails to Gunnar over the past four months, and he'd obviously been looking forward to meeting her friend in person. At least, that's what he'd politely told her when he'd arrived an hour ago.

Jane hadn't seen anything resembling politeness in his eyes at the time, though, but rather anticipation and what she'd immediately recognized as . . . lust.

At the moment, however, those fathomless blue eyes were unreadable.

"She said she was sorry, but that she can't come to Shelkova right now."

"Why?"

"She was rather vague as to why," Jane muttered. "Something about a once-in-a-lifetime opportunity suddenly dropping in her lap."

"She sounds like a selfish, flighty woman to me." He set his hands on his hips as he stood over her. "Or is she a frightened mouse? Did she know I was coming here to meet her?"

"Um . . . sort of," Jane prevaricated. "I didn't name you specifically; I just said Mark had a friend I thought she might like to meet."

Gunnar Wolfe bent at the waist to bring his face level with hers. "You have not been honest with either of us, have you?"

Jane frantically shook her head, hoping to disguise another contraction—this one still short but definitely sharper than the last one. "Everything I told you about Katy is true, including the fact that she'd be here if she could."

"Then why isn't she? Tell me," he said quietly, straightening and walking to the window, where he then stood looking out and silently waiting.

Jane took advantage of his back being turned to rub her belly and pull in a deep breath, then slowly released it in an attempt to relax her muscles. And then she sighed, deciding she couldn't dance around the truth and birth a baby at the same time—assuming she *was* in labor, seeing how she wasn't due for *two more weeks*.

"Okay, look," she said on another sigh. "I've never known Katy to break a promise—not to me or anyone or even to herself. So my guess as to why she's not here is that I think something happened in Colorado that—oh, darn it," she growled in frustration. "Best case is Katy got injured during the mountain climbing part of the rescue school she was attending, and she doesn't want to sit through another lecture from her father and brothers about the risks she's always taking."

"And the worst case?" he asked softly, still looking out the window.

"I'm afraid something may have . . . frightened her, which she definitely wouldn't want her family to know." Jane shrugged when he turned to face her. "And I'm worried it must be something really bad for Katy to break her promise to me."

"What do you mean, frightened her? Like what?"

"I *don't know* what. Mostly because I can't imagine Katy being afraid of anything. Unless it had something to do with . . . ah, with a . . ."

"A man," Gunnar finished. "You think a man may have hurt her?"

Jane dropped her gaze to her belly and shook her head. "I can't imagine that, either." She looked up. "I sent you a copy of the picture Katy sent me; she's taller and more athletic than most men, and her father and brothers started teaching her how to defend herself before she even started walking."

"Maybe the hurt wasn't physical," Gunnar countered thickly. "Maybe she met someone in Colorado and he broke her heart."

Jane nonchalantly rubbed her belly to sooth another mild contraction. "A broken heart wouldn't stop Katy from being at the birth of her best friend's baby. She couldn't make my wedding because it all happened too fast and she was covering another paramedic's maternity leave until the rescue school started." Jane shook her head again on a sad smile. "And she'd only been in Colorado a month when she called to say she couldn't come, and that's not enough time to get her heart broken."

He arched a brow, a small grin tugging at his mouth. "This from a woman who married a man she'd known a sum total of three weeks." He just as quickly sobered. "What about her family? Have you called to tell them you're worried about your friend?"

Jane snorted. "Not if I want to *keep* Katy as my friend. Or did you not get the part about her being from an old-fashioned Scottish *clan* in my emails? The woman's twenty-eight years old, and the job in Spellbound Falls will be the first time her mailing address won't be the same as her parents'." Jane waved at nothing. "The only reason Katy went to live in Bangor while she studied to be a paramedic was to get out from under the watchful eye of her overprotective family, so she could date a guy longer than a week before he got scared off. And then the job she's starting June first is a concession to her father, because she has several male cousins living in Spellbound Falls." Jane suddenly smiled. "They're MacKeages, not MacBains, and Katy's pretty sure they're all too busy keeping their own love lives in order to worry about hers."

Up went Gunnar's brow again. "Have you considered maybe your friend has poor taste in men, if they're so easily scared off by a little male posturing?"

That made her laugh. "There's nothing *little* about any of the MacBains or MacKeages. Well, except Katy's mom, who makes *me* look like an Amazon." She just as suddenly scowled. "But if Katy doesn't call me by June second to say she's safe and sound at her new job in Spellbound Falls, I *am* calling her family. Well, her mother," she finished in a whisper, closing her eyes when her belly tightened under her hands.

Okay, that definitely had been a contraction. She opened her eyes on a gasp when Gunnar suddenly picked her up. "What are you doing? Put me down," she said when he started for the door. "You want Petri to shoot you?"

"You want to have your baby here in the library?"

"You know I'm in labor? And you just stood there asking me questions about Katy?"

That made him grin. "It's hard for a woman to withhold information when she's otherwise occupied," he drawled, giving the library door a kick.

It opened on Petri's glaring face.

"Where's Markov?" Gunnar asked.

Jane remained quiet in Gunnar's arms as he followed Petri through the palace to Mark's office, and wondered if it might be okay to start panicking now. Four men Jane recognized as parliament members immediately stood up when Gunnar strode into Mark's office and over to the desk, then plopped Jane into Mark's arms when he also shot to his feet.

"Take your wife to the hospital, Markov. She's having your baby," was all Gunnar said before he leaned over and kissed her cheek, then straightened and looked at Mark. "Have fun, my friend," he said with a nod. "I'll see you in a couple of months."

"You're leaving?" Mark asked in surprise, following him to the door with Jane still in his arms. "Now? But you just got here."

"A pressing matter has come up," Gunnar said, not looking back.

"A job?" Mark asked, still following, still holding Jane. Gunnar stopped and turned back. "Not in my usual line of work," he said dryly. "This matter is personal." He moved his dancing blue gaze to Jane and grinned. "Would you happen to know Maine's requirements for paramedic certification? Never mind," he said when she gasped, giving Mark another nod before heading for the door again. "I just remembered I have firefighting credentials kicking around somewhere that should work," he continued with a negligent wave over his shoulder as he disappeared down the hall.

Mark looked at Jane, totally confused—until she clutched her belly. "You're having the baby. *Now.*" He stepped into the hall and frantically looked around. "Petri, get the car!" he shouted, despite the fact that Petri was standing five feet away. "And tell somebody where we've gone."

Jane patted Mark's cheek, his panic suddenly calming hers. "The contractions are weak and still far apart."

"You weren't supposed to have *any* for two weeks," he snapped. He closed his eyes on a deep breath. "Can you not do anything the easy way?"

"What, and only have boring stories to tell our children?" she asked, wrapping both her arms around his neck and kissing him.

"Markov! This one isn't even out yet and you're trying to make another one!" Alexi shouted, running into the hallway to catch them kissing, only to slide to a stop when Jane suddenly clutched her belly on a small moan. Her brother-in-law turned the color of snow and took off down the hall. "Father! Dmitri! Sergei! Irina! God help us, the angels are multiplying!"

LETTER FROM LAKEWATCH

❖ ·· ❖

Dear Readers,

For those of you who have been following my stories
from the beginning, I hope you enjoyed the little surprise I snuck into this book. Yes, I know this was supposed to be a straight contemporary romance (no matter
its over-the-top premise), but I simply couldn't resist
having Jane Abbot's best friend be the daughter of one
of my time-traveling highlanders.

For those of you new to my writing . . . well, let me
explain. You see, the lion's share of my books have a
touch of the magic in them (okay, maybe more than a
touch), and throughout our journey together I've been
asking my readers to believe that the magic is real. Yes,
that's right; *the* magic, which implies there's only one.
And from what I've gleaned from my ethereal characters, it's what powers the world.

They tell me the magic is there in the first breath we
take and in our last, in those rays of sun hitting our face
and the stars we gaze up at in awe every night. It keeps
our hearts beating, shines from the eyes of a newborn,
and pushes all those tender little sprouts out of the

ground. It fuels our hopes and dreams and desires, and kindly picks us up, dusts us off, and nudges us to keep going when we're about to give up.

Sometimes the magic's so subtle it's impossible to hear, like hair growing, a smile from a stranger, or inspiration dawning. Other times it speaks to us directly in the crunch of an apple, the haunting call of a loon, or an unsolicited "I love you." And sometimes when we're too caught up in our everyday dramas to be paying attention, it jolts us out of ourselves with the force of a sudden and unpredicted thunderstorm sweeping down the lake. But maybe the coolest thing about the magic is that it goes about its business creating big and small miracles whether or not we believe it even exists. (And in case you're wondering, my ethereal buddies assure me it is *always* benevolent, even or especially when life throws us a curve.)

Some of my characters are pretty powerful magic-makers who can manipulate time and matter in order to go about their own business of protecting mankind from the lesser gods—and also just as often from ourselves.

But even mighty wizards are looking for happily-ever-afters. Remember the saying that the bigger they are, the harder they fall? Well, boy, do my magical men fall hard—usually for a no-nonsense woman merely focused on getting her own life in order. Only I don't want you to think the magic is exclusive to my books featuring larger-than-life heroes, because, trust me, without the help of a good miracle or two, my mere mortal men might not get the girl, either.

Which brings us back to the little surprise I snuck into this book . . .

What if I were to tell you that for years I've been looking for a way to . . . marry my contemporary and magical stories into one body of work? I mean, really, Maine is only so big; how could my characters *not* bump into each other? My mountain loggers live in the general vicinity of Pine Creek, and Midnight Bay is on the Down East coast not very far from Puffin Harbor and Keelstone Cove. Bangor and Portland and Ellsworth are often referenced, a lot of my characters shop at L.L.Bean, and tourism is a statewide industry.

So let's just go ahead and consider *From Kiss to Queen* the ceremonial book in which I married all my series together by the simple act of making Jane Abbot and Katy MacBain best friends. Because in doing so, I am now free to bring Gunnar Wolfe, a very contemporary hero, to Spellbound Falls—where, I might point out, the magic is *rarely* subtle.

Until then, you keep reading and believing.

And don't worry, I promise to keep writing!

Janet

Turn the page for a preview of
the next Spellbound Falls romance from
Janet Chapman

CALL IT MAGIC

Available soon from Jove

Katy MacBain sat on a bench in front of Spellbound Falls' new state-of-the-art safety building, sipping the worst cup of coffee to ever cross her lips, and tried to decide how she felt about this sudden turn of events. Because even with her parents' blessing, she was no longer sure if moving to this magical little wilderness town would still be the best decision she'd ever made, or if it had just become the biggest mistake of her life. The empowerment of going after and actually getting a position on what was being referred to as the most advanced fire and rescue squad in the state had certainly helped pull her through these last three weeks, only she'd just learned the team she was so proud to be part of was going through its own personal crisis.

What on earth had made the jovial, grandfatherly chief

who'd hired her four months ago suddenly up and quit what had to have been his dream job? Family reasons, the teenage intern had said when Katy had found him out back washing mud off an impressively large rescue truck. The four firefighters were taking showers, he'd informed her, having returned dirtier than their vehicle after spending most of last night reaching a party of backcountry hikers—one of whom was being transported to a hospital sixty miles away with a busted ankle.

Katy had headed back inside to the kid's muttered speculation as to what their remote access ambulance was going to look like when it returned, and she'd spent several minutes roaming through the likewise impressively large station before finding the kitchen. She'd hunted down a mug, filled it with the questionable remains of the coffeepot, and come outside in hopes that the bright June sun would help banish the chill of this morning's news.

Damn. She'd really liked Chief Gilmore. His keen hazel eyes had been filled with warm, patient humor as Katy had spent her entire interview in a nervous sweat trying to persuade him to take a chance on her, despite knowing she was the least experienced applicant competing for the final slot on the team he was pulling together. Heck, all the international news channels had carried the story of Chief Gilmore's search for the bravest and best firefighters and paramedics to man Spellbound Falls' innovative, multifaceted squad, subsequently drawing in applicants from all over the world.

Katy figured she must have been temporarily insane to even apply.

Or else Chief Gilmore had been for actually hiring her.

All of which had her worrying how the new chief would feel about inheriting a medic who possessed a sum total of three years of mostly volunteer experience. Would she be dismissed before even seeing her first paycheck, or would she be given the chance to—

"Must be nice."

Katy squinted into the sun at the elderly gentleman standing on the sidewalk in front of the station. "Excuse me?"

"I was just saying how nice it must be," he repeated, gesturing in her direction, "to have hard-earned tax dollars paying you probably double what anyone around here makes just to sit in the sun drinking coffee in front of a ridiculously overpriced fire station."

"Be grateful she's here," a deep male voice softly growled from behind her, "instead of out on some road trying to keep your wife or granddaughter from bleeding to death while we're cutting them out of what's left of their car."

Katy spun on the bench, only to gape at the tall, broad-shouldered man standing in the open bay doorway, his ice-blue gaze locked on the complainer. Despite not seeing a badge, she immediately recognized he was a firefighter rather than a medic; although he wore a dark blue T-shirt identical to hers, his matching station pants didn't have cargo pockets to get in the way of quickly slipping into bunker gear.

"That was rather aggressive," Katy said, even as she fought the urge to jump up and flee right along with the duly chastised gentleman scurrying off down the sidewalk toward town.

The firefighter turned those piercing eyes on her and shrugged. "When people stop making stupid comments, I'll stop correcting them. And speaking of not smart, lose the badge," he added, nodding at the ID card she had clipped on her light jacket.

"Excuse me?"

"Our jobs are dangerous enough without pinning a target on our chests. Pissed-off people having a bad day often start shooting at anyone who looks like a lawman."

Katy turned back around on the bench to watch the fleeing complainer disappear into the Bottomless Mercantile and Trading Post, and willed her heart to stop racing. Holy hell, were all the firefighters on the squad as imposing as this one? Even though she was used to being around large athletic men—considering there wasn't a male in her family under six-foot-three—Katy had a feeling that even a solid wall of her overprotective brothers and cousins wouldn't rattle this guy. "Thanks for the advice," she said in what she hoped was an even voice, "but I think I'll wait for the new chief to tell me to lose the badge."

"He just did."

Katy shot to her feet and turned to face him in time to see his eyes flare briefly as they traveled up the length of her before coming to rest on hers. "You're the new chief?"

He stepped forward and held out his hand. "Gunnar Wolfe—with an *E*," he said, using his other hand to tap the name *Wolfe* printed on his shirt. He dropped his unshaken hand when she didn't move and reached inside his pocket. He pulled out a flat leather case, held it up and studied it, then turned it facing her and nodded. "Yup, the badge they gave me at the council meeting last night definitely says I'm chief of Spellbound Falls Fire and Rescue—at least for the next three months." A sudden grin crinkled the corners of those insanely blue eyes. "And although my expertise runs more toward fire and rescue, I think you should know that I intend to be hands-on in all departments."

Crap, a bossy boss. "What do you mean by 'hands on'?"

"I mean that instead of spending all my time doing paperwork and placating three crews of cocky firefighters and medics, I intend to fight fires and rescue idiots off mountains in the pouring rain like I originally signed up for."

"If you didn't want to be chief, then why didn't you just say no?"

"Because I definitely didn't sign up to take orders from the next guy in line."

Katy refrained from asking who that was—partly because she didn't want to get involved in office politics her first day on the job, but mostly because she preferred to form her own opinion of any coworker she might have to trust with her life. "Does that mean you intend to go on a lot of the ambulance runs?"

His grin returned at her obvious alarm. "Don't worry, MacBain; I'm fairly certain Gilmore didn't hire you just to pretty up the station. So my deal is you stay out of burning buildings and I'll stay out of your bus." He held out his hand again. "Welcome to the team."

Double crap. Not only was this guy about as grandfatherly as she was, he appeared to be persistent. Katy grabbed his decidedly large, calloused hand for a quick firm shake, only to find herself trapped when he refused to let go.

"You're one of four females, Katy," he said, his tone matching the sudden seriousness in his eyes, "on an exclusive squad mostly made up of arrogant, overconfident men who don't have the words 'back off' in either their professional or personal vocabularies. Anyone gives you any grief, I expect to be the first and *only* person to hear about it." He just as suddenly grinned. "And by anyone, I'm including your female teammates. Although," he drawled, his gaze traveling down the length of her then back to her eyes—which were only a few inches shy of being level with his—"I'm guessing you can handle anything the women might send your way."

"I can also handle the men," she said, giving a small tug on her hand.

His grip remained firm and his grin vanished again. "But you're not going to let it reach the point of having to handle anything, are you? Your first verbal cue that trouble is brewing, I want you running straight to me instead of those three burly cousins of yours who kindly introduced themselves to all us firefighters last week."

Oh yeah; did she know her family or what? "Did you give this same warning to the other three women?"

He spun on his heel with a rumbling chuckle, a full two seconds passing before Katy realized her hand was being held by nothing but air. "Go feather your little home away from home with whatever lucky charms and inspirational posters you brought, then meet me at your bus in half an hour," he said as he strode away. He stopped inside the open bay door, gestured toward the far end of the station, and shot her a grin. "That would be the smaller black and yellow truck with *ambulance* written backwards on the hood."

Several more seconds went by before she realized she was staring at nothing, and Katy released the breath she'd been holding. Although Gunnar Wolfe—with an *E*— could probably give cocky lessons to the men temporarily under his command, she really couldn't take offense at his trying to head off something she now knew could in fact become a major problem.

And just like that, without really understanding why, Katy decided everything was going to be okay. She also decided—again without understanding why—that she could trust Chief Wolfe. At least professionally, such as when it came to his holding the other end of a rope she might be dangling from halfway down some cliff, or trusting his judgment that it was okay to crawl inside a wrecked vehicle to reach a patient.

But outside of work, such as going to the Bottom's Up with the rest of the crew for beers after a particularly bad day? Katy unpinned her ID with a snort, stuffed it in her pocket, and headed inside. No, if she ever did find herself in a bar again, she wasn't even ordering water.

But then she suddenly smiled at the realization that she appeared to still have a job.

Standing in the private bathroom tucked behind the chief's office, Gunnar stopped wiping the water he'd splashed on his face and scowled at himself in the mirror. He rarely got caught off guard these days, and only years of surviving by the skin of his teeth had saved him from not reacting when Katy MacBain had stood up and turned to face him. He'd known she was beautiful; hell, the photos he'd found of her on the Internet were partly responsible for drawing him here. But no picture, nothing he'd read about her, or any of the childhood tales Jane Lakeland had unapologetically used to pique his interest could have prepared him for the flesh-and-blood woman. Even knowing Katy was six-foot-one, he'd still been stunned to find himself barely having to look down to see the vibrancy in her startled gray eyes.

No, not gray; those long-lashed, sexy-as-hell eyes were the deep silver of an Icelandic fogbank backlit by the sun. And when she'd spun to him in surprise, the whip of that single long braid of mahogany hair as thick as his wrist had sent him even further back in his youth, to when he would sit on a bluff overlooking the wind-whipped northern Atlantic and dream of escaping his island home on an ancient Viking war boat in a bid to conquer the world.

She hadn't wanted to shake his hand, even though he had enough notches on his bedpost to know he didn't turn women off. And having met her three cousins—en masse—he figured Miss MacBain should be comfortable around large men. Hell, her chosen profession practically guaranteed she'd be surrounded by firefighters dwarfed only by their egos.

No, he was more inclined to believe her reluctance had to do with the last three weeks of her life that he couldn't account for. He'd managed to track down the rescue school she'd trained at in Colorado, only to learn that no one had heard from Katy since graduation. She had surprised everyone, though, one of the interns had told him, by getting falling-down drunk when they'd gone to a local bar on the last night to celebrate, since they'd only seen her have an occasional glass of wine during the course. The head instructor had personally helped her into the van taking several other students to a motel near the Denver airport, making sure a couple of the women promised to see that Katy was safely tucked into bed. The kid had shrugged and said he assumed she'd flown home the next morning like she'd planned.

Only instead of using the rest of the round-trip ticket she'd purchased five weeks earlier, Miss MacBain had simply vanished.

It was then that what had started out as a potentially sensual distraction inspired by Jane Lakeland—queen of the fairly new country of Shelkova on the Bering Sea across from Alaska, and Katy's best friend since childhood—had suddenly turned into a personal mission to track down the missing, promise-breaking woman.

Jane had still named her and Markov's little bundle of joy after her BFF. Gunnar suddenly grinned at the mirror, figuring Princess Katherine Maine Lakeland—the first female born to a Lakeland male in twelve generations—was already ruling the palace, if not also firmly entrenched in the hearts of every last Shelkovan. Hell, when he'd called last week to make sure Jane was keeping *her* promise not to tell Katy the guy she'd hoped to fix her up with was headed to Maine to meet her, Markov had said his countrymen were still partying in the streets.

So the question wasn't only why had Katy broken her promise to be at the birth of her best friend's very first child, but why had she gone into hiding?

He'd drawn that conclusion after spending three days in Colorado—along with several hundred palm-greasing dollars—learning exactly nothing. Which was as disturbing as it was vexing, considering he really made his living hunting down people who didn't want to be found.

He'd at least been able to leave Denver fairly certain that Katy hadn't been kidnapped or murdered, thanks to a now somewhat wealthier motel clerk who had suddenly recalled seeing the woman in the photo Gunnar had showed him getting into a rental pickup truck she'd had delivered three days after she'd checked in. He hadn't been on duty the night she'd arrived, but the record showed she'd asked not to be disturbed for the next week—a small notation beside it mentioning sanitizing the room because the night clerk had been told she had a bad cold.

Told by one of the female babysitters who knew she was only drunk?

Finally resigned to the fact that he was only digging up more questions instead of getting answers, Gunnar had hopped in his jet and continued on to Spellbound Falls, Maine, to establish himself as just another one of the firefighters two full weeks before Katy MacBain was supposed to start her new job as a paramedic.

He'd swear it had been the longest two weeks of his life waiting for her to show up, with him not taking a decent breath until the computer hacker he'd had keeping watch finally texted him the night before last with the news that Katy MacBain's cell phone was pinging loud and clear in Boise, Idaho. Which meant instead of pointing that rental truck east two weeks ago, the woman had headed *away* from Maine. More texts had come in throughout yesterday stating the phone signal kept going off only to start up again in another city, his tech guru also discovering that Miss MacBain was making her way to Maine by buying tickets—*finally* using her credit card—on standby, resulting in a zigzagging series of flights heading east.

Gunnar had known down to the minute when Katy had landed in Bangor, but he didn't dare celebrate until she'd checked into the campground south of Spellbound Falls last night at nine thirty—which was about the same time the skies had opened up and the station alarm had gone off for an injured hiker some fifteen, almost straight-up miles away on a nearby mountain. It had also been a mere three hours after he'd walked out of the town council meeting carrying a badge that said he was the new—interim—fire chief.

Suddenly realizing the guy in the mirror was glaring, Gunnar shot him a derisive grin, unable to blame the poor bastard for being in a foul mood. He'd not only run an entire gauntlet of emotions over the last two weeks—from frustration to anger to relief then back to anger—he'd nearly dropped to his knees at the sight of Katy MacBain finally standing in front of him looking beautiful and vital and seemingly fully recovered from whatever in hell had sent her on that three-week side trip to Idaho.

So okay, then; he guessed it was time to get out there and see if this harebrained little fantasy would net him a Maine wilderness angel of his very own, or if he was going to spend the rest of his life rotting in a palace dungeon for throttling a busybody, matchmaking queen.

From *New York Times* Bestselling Author
Janet Chapman

The Highlander Next Door

A Spellbound Falls Romance

Legend has it love is carried on the rising mists of Spellbound Falls, and not even time-traveling highlanders are immune to its magic...

Birch Callahan has seen the trouble men can cause. After witnessing her mother's four marriages, Birch now runs a women's shelter and doesn't want a man in her life. But there's something about her neighbor, Niall MacKeage. Birch can't figure out how the cop can be so big and gruff and yet so insightful and compassionate—and sexy. Or how she's falling for a man who acts like someone from the twelfth century.

Niall knows that Birch is attracted to him, even if she seems to distrust all men. Yet he also knows she has a secret—something that drives her to place herself in harm's way for the women of her shelter. Niall would gladly rush to Birch's side to protect her from harm, but with their secrets standing between them, he'll have to reveal his own truth if he wants to keep her...

janetchapman.com
facebook.com/LoveAlwaysBooks
penguin.com

M1677T0515

*Falling under the spell of love can
be the biggest risk of all . . .*

From *New York Times* Bestselling Author
JANET CHAPMAN

THE SPELLBOUND FALLS NOVELS

Spellbound Falls
Charmed by His Love
Courting Carolina
The Heart of a Hero
For the Love of Magic
The Highlander Next Door

Praise for Janet Chapman:

"Janet Chapman is a keeper."
—Linda Howard, *New York Times* bestselling author

"A perfect 10."   —Romance Reviews Today

"Readers will be enchanted with Chapman's love of
Maine in her latest romance, a story filled with wit and
tenderness."   —*Booklist*

janetchapman.com
facebook.com/LoveAlwaysBooks
penguin.com

M1195AS0913